Guilty Little Secrets

Connie Lane

Guilty Little Secrets

A DELL BOOK

GUILTY LITTLE SECRETS

Published by Bantam Dell
A Division of
Random House, Inc.
New York, New York

Dell® is a trademark of Random House, Inc., and
the colophon is a trademark of Random House, Inc.

ISBN: 0-7394-3315-6

Manufactured in the United States of America
Published simultaneously in Canada

*Every book has people who help it
(and its author) along the way.
My special thanks go to:*

Peggy for brainstorming and Goat Wine.

Mary for reading and listening.

*Anne for her expertise when it
comes to CPR.*

*David for the black candle and the
yellow candle.*

*Tom for explaining how undercover
operations work.*

*And all the Spanish speaking members
of the Schuff family.*

1

The only thing Rosie Malone hated more than a bad guy was a bad guy who couldn't tell time.

With a sigh that fell dead against the atomic heat of the Las Vegas afternoon, Rosie pushed up her sleeve and glanced at her watch. Two forty-five. If her informant didn't show up sometime soon, this just might be the shortest undercover operation in the history of the Bureau of Alcohol, Tobacco and Firearms. And a stain on Rosie's perfect service record. It would also be the biggest clandestine lemon since the Bay of Pigs if she waited around, was late for rehearsal, and got fired from her showgirl job before she ever had a chance to find out what was really going on at the Silver Swan.

One more look at her watch and her mind was made up. Rosie headed toward the three cement steps that led up to the landing outside the door to the Swan's receiving area. If she was quick, she could get to the theater just in time. If she was lucky, no one would notice she was late.

Then again, if luck had anything to do with the way things were going, she wouldn't be in a back alley in the first place. She also wouldn't be dressed like a clown.

She was already trying to work out the physics of getting her two-foot-long clown shoes on the one-foot-wide steps when she heard the sharp rap of high heels against the pavement. Rosie turned just in time to see a woman round the corner. For a moment, the sight of a brunette with long, long hair and a short, short skirt took her by surprise. Then again, Chuck had never been specific. When her boss called earlier that morning and told her an informant wanted to talk, Rosie had automatically pictured a man.

Looked like she was going to need to revise her thinking.

Looked like she wasn't the only one.

Six feet away, the woman stopped and squinted through the shadows over to where Rosie was waiting. "Nobody told me nothing about a clown," she said.

"No . . . well . . ." Rosie stepped forward, closing the distance between herself and the woman. "It's kind of a long story. Are you the one who called Chuck?"

"Yeah, that was me." The woman stepped back. "But that Chuck guy, he didn't say a clown. He said a special agent and I was expecting . . . you know . . ."

"You were expecting a guy in a navy-blue suit, a white shirt, and a striped tie. That's the FBI." Her attempt at humor was met with a blank stare, and Rosie got herself back on track with a shake of her head. Fuzzy bits of her red clown wig floated up into the air and stuck to her lips, and she blew them away. "Everybody expects the guy in the suit. They're usually surprised to see me even when I'm not dressed like this." Briefly, she glanced down at the yellow shoes and the blue-and-white-striped costume that looked like a cross between a jumpsuit and a Thanksgiving Day parade balloon.

For a woman whose most daring real-life outfit was a knee-length black skirt that she wore with a tailored gray jacket when she was feeling frisky, her costume was the ultimate irony. That and the fact that she had spent the better part of her twenty-eight years yearning to blend in with the masses of everyday, vanilla-ice-cream, middle-of-the-road people she saw everywhere but in her own family.

So much for listing her fourteen years of dance lessons on her employment application for the ATF.

Rosie reached inside the neckline of her costume and pulled out the ATF ID card and badge that dangled from a chain. "Rosie," she said by way of introduction, and tucked her credentials back inside her costume. She stuck out her hand. "And you're . . ."

The woman hesitated. "I'm Neeta." She didn't take Rosie's hand and Rosie got the message. She moved back a fraction of an inch, giving Neeta the room she so obviously needed.

Neeta reached into the tiny purse she had slung over one shoulder and pulled out a pack of unfiltered Camels and a hot-pink lighter. It wasn't until she propped a cigarette between lips the same color as her lighter that Rosie realized Neeta's hands were shaking. She lit the cigarette, pulled in a deep breath, and blew out a cloud of smoke. "I . . ." The alley had an entrance at either end, and Neeta took a good, long look at both of them. "I need to talk to someone."

"Then you've come to the right place." Rosie exhaled a tiny sigh of relief. So far, so good. Clown suit or no clown suit, Neeta was comfortable enough to admit that she had something to say. Now the trick was to get her to relax enough to say it.

"You from Vegas?" Rosie asked.

Neeta rolled eyes the color of the dome of Nevada sky above their heads. "Nobody who's from here calls it Vegas. It's *Las* Vegas. Always *Las* Vegas. You'd better remember that if you're trying to fit in. You are trying to fit in, aren't you?" Neeta looked Rosie up and down. "I mean, what are you supposed to be? Some kind of freaky magic act or something?"

"It's just a disguise," Rosie explained, poking one finger at the red plastic clown nose that in these temperatures was starting to slide off her face. "You know, so no one recognizes me. I thought it would be easier, for you and for me. Just in case someone sees us together."

Neeta jumped as if she'd touched a finger to an electrical line. "You're shitting me, right? Nobody better see us. I mean, if anybody comes along and recognizes me—"

"Don't worry. No one is going to see us. That's why Chuck decided this would be a good place to meet. Nobody's around."

Neeta took a long, shaky breath and tossed her cigarette on the ground. She stubbed it out with the toe of one stiletto. "You're right. I know. I shouldn't be so jumpy. It's just that . . . I don't know . . . I know this sounds crazy . . . I mean, I know it sounds really nuts . . . but I think . . ." She glanced around. "I think someone's been following me."

Rosie's heart plummeted right along with her hopes of wrapping up this case fast so she could get back to her life as she knew it: gray suits, tidy little San Francisco apartment, and all. Too often, people who called themselves informants were nothing more than eager beavers who thought they knew more than they actually did. Or bad guys who wanted to find out how much the Feds knew about what they were up to. Sometimes they were nutcases and sometimes they were lonely and just wanted to be part of the action.

Which was Neeta?

If she were pressed for her final answer, Rosie would have gone with the nutcase theory. "Followed, huh?" She tried to sound as if she hadn't just realized that she was probably wasting her time—and risking her showgirl status—on a wild goose chase with an informant who was more paranoid than she was informed. "Why would anyone want to follow you, Neeta?"

"I told you it sounds crazy." Neeta reached for another cigarette. It took her three flicks of her lighter to get it fired up and another few long seconds of inhaling and exhaling the nasty stuff before she started talking again. "It's a feeling.

You know? And this morning, there was a black SUV outside my apartment. I saw one there the other night, too. And a couple days before that. I don't know if it's the same one all the time but—"

"You see an SUV that might be the same SUV you saw before, so you call the ATF?" Her comment was a little too harsh and Rosie knew it. Chalk it up to the heat. Or the frustration of recognizing that she was getting nowhere fast. Not with Neeta. Not with her case. It might have had something to do with the sinking feeling in her stomach. Or the slow slide her plastic clown nose was making down her face. She slapped the red nose back in place and offered Neeta what she hoped looked enough like a smile of apology to pass muster.

"Not my job to editorialize," Rosie said. "Sorry. It's just that Chuck isn't exactly a forthcoming guy. He didn't explain. Neeta, why would anyone want to follow you? And what does it have to do with us?"

A tiny sob escaped Neeta's hot-pink lips. "It's complicated," she said. Whether Neeta's fears were justified or not, they were genuine enough to make her bony knees tremble and her pointy chin quiver.

Rosie's heart went out to the woman. "Maybe the best way to get it all sorted out is to start at the beginning. What do you say, Neeta? Want to try?"

Neeta sniffed and nodded.

"So . . . when did you first notice you were being followed?"

Neeta's forehead creased. Her fingers worked over the strand of beads she wore around her neck. "It wasn't right away. Not the first time I ran into him, anyway. And that was kind of like an accident, you know? I mean, I didn't even know he was in town. Last I heard, he was living in Denver with some woman who made sculptures out of beer cans. I figured he probably emptied all the cans she ever needed. It wasn't until he came over to my place and—"

"Hold on a minute!" Rosie held up one hand, stemming the tide of Neeta's story. "He who? Who are you talking about?"

Neeta let go a breath along with a mumbled curse when she realized her story had gotten away from her. "Who else?" she asked. "Gus."

"Gus?" This time Rosie was the one who felt as if she'd been plugged into an electrical outlet. A tingle of excitement scooted up her spine. Maybe Neeta wasn't so crazy after all. If she knew Gus . . .

Rosie reminded herself that she couldn't afford to blow this opportunity. She controlled her voice and her emotions. "Were you a friend of Gus Friel?"

"A friend? Hell, no!" Neeta laughed. It was a thready sound, more full of tension than amusement. "I'm . . . I was," she corrected herself, "Gus's sister."

Sister? In the mile-high stack of reports she'd read about the case, Rosie didn't recall seeing anything about Gus having a sister.

"Half sister, actually," Neeta said as if reading Rosie's mind. "Same mother. Different fathers."

Which explained why a search of Friels hadn't turned up Neeta.

"We didn't get along. But that doesn't mean I had anything to do with him getting killed." Neeta's face went pale beneath a coating of expertly applied blush, and Rosie knew she had to rush in before Neeta talked herself out of talking.

"It's all right to admit you didn't like Gus," she told Neeta. "Hey, I don't exactly see eye-to-eye with my family, either." It was the understatement of the century and hardly new when it came to the insight department, but Rosie was surprised she admitted it to a stranger. Before she could get trapped into analyzing herself, her motives, or the left-of-center free-for-all that was the Malone family, she set the thought aside and went on. "That doesn't mean I want to see any of them dead," she said, and unexpectedly, she found herself grinning. "Though there are times I wouldn't mind wringing a couple necks."

Neeta forgot her nervousness long enough to almost grin back.

At this stage of the game, *almost* was good enough. Rosie moved fast while she still had the advantage. "I'll bet you felt the same way," she said. "Like it was nice when Gus showed up. And nicer when he went home."

"Yeah." Neeta lifted one shoulder in a twitch of agreement. "Something like that. Only I hardly ever saw him. He told me . . ." She looked up at the sign next to the door to the receiving area. "He told me he had a job at the Silver Swan. Said it had something to do with the show. Which was a relief. I thought for sure he was going to hit me up for money."

Rosie nodded. "He was a sort of gofer who worked in the theater. You know, ran errands, helped with the sets, did some small repairs. Gus had only been at the Swan a couple months. Then he disappeared and the cops found—"

Rosie gulped down the words she'd nearly let escape. After two and a half years of working as a special agent with the ATF, she was used to the kind of mayhem she often saw out on the streets. Like law enforcement officers everywhere, she'd learned to deal. She'd cordoned off a little corner of her mind, and it was there she stored the memories she didn't dare bring out into the light of day. Which didn't mean they weren't sometimes disturbing. That sometimes when she got home at night and put away her forty-millimeter SigSauer and climbed out of her gray suit and into her fuzzy slippers and her comfy jammies, she wasn't haunted by the images of all she'd seen on her ten-hour watch.

A cop learned to build defenses, and one of those defenses was learning to talk about murder as if it were just another part of her job. That didn't mean it didn't hurt. It didn't mean the sight of dead bodies and the thought of wasted lives and the misery that crawled in the wake of every murder didn't bother her.

But referring to Gus as the *decomp the cops found out in Red Rock Canyon* was probably just a little too flip. Especially when that decomp was Neeta's half brother.

"The cops found him out in Red Rock Canyon," Rosie said, firmly ignoring the decomp part. "They identified him by the tattoo of a snake on his right forearm." Gus Friel's tattoo was another piece of the puzzle that had forced Rosie out of her San Francisco comfort zone and into the sequined and feather fantasy that was Sin City.

Three months before Gus was found melted by the desert sun and half-eaten by whatever creatures lived over in Red Rock Canyon to the west of the city, a fourteen-year-old named Jake was arrested for holding up a local convenience store. He wasn't the youngest armed robber any of them had ever seen. Sad but true. What was unusual about Jake's crime was the weapon he'd used to carry it out. His gun was a nine-millimeter 9A-91, a small-size assault rifle capable of shooting through a steel plate. It could be equipped with a silencer, optical night sights, and even an underbarrel grenade launcher. Chances were, Jake had no idea what kind of firepower he was packing, or that the 9A-91 was produced in Russia especially for the MVD, the Russian Ministry of Internal Affairs.

Which should have made it as scarce in these parts as subtlety, taste, and discretion.

Trouble was, it was the sixth 9A-91 the local cops had seen in the last year and a half. That was enough to clue them in to the fact that something was up. They called in the ATF.

Unfortunately, neither the local cops nor the Feds had much to go on. Nothing but Jake, the kid nabbed in the store robbery, who told them he bought his gun for a song from some guy named Gus. A guy with the tattoo of a snake on his forearm.

If they knew anything, the few friends Gus had weren't talking. Neither were his fellow employees. Which left the cops thinking that the Gus line of the investigation had died along with him.

But that was because none of them knew he had a half sister.

"So . . . Gus . . . he came to see you, huh?" Rosie toed her way back into the conversation. "Did he say anything about the gun he sold?"

Neeta tossed what was left of her cigarette on the ground. "Gun? I've got news for you. It wasn't *a* gun. Gus, he couldn't freakin' stop talking about guns. Plural. Guns, guns, guns. How he sold a couple of them and made some quick cash. Only when I asked where he got them in the first place, all he did was laugh." Neeta shook her head.

"Gus, he was like that. He liked to have secrets. Liked to pretend he was important because he knew something nobody else did. But somebody must have known. You know what I mean? Because somebody killed Gus. And those same people . . . they must think he told me something, because now they're following me." Neeta blinked back tears that suddenly threatened to overwhelm what was left of her composure. "I don't want them to do that to me. I don't want nobody to find me out in the desert with a bullet in the back of my head."

"Don't worry. There are ways we can protect you, Neeta. But you're going to have to help me out. Tell me everything. Share your secret and it's not a secret anymore. That's the only thing that's going to keep you safe."

"Safe. Yeah." Neeta pulled in a shaky breath. "Wish I felt safe."

"Once you tell me everything, you will be." Rosie dared to take a step closer. She was relieved when Neeta didn't retreat. "What do you know about the guns, Neeta?"

"I know—"

Whatever Neeta was going to say was as much of a mystery as why Rosie didn't hear the sound of a vehicle turning into the alley long before she did. Maybe she was too intent on listening to Neeta. Or just too hot inside the blimpy clown costume to be aware of much else besides the fact that she felt as if she were melting. Maybe the fuzzy red wig kept her from hearing as much as she should have. Whatever the reason, by the time Rosie heard the squeal of rubber against pavement, it was already too late.

She caught sight of the look of pure panic on Neeta's face and spun around just in time to see a too-wide-bodied black SUV squeeze its way into the too-narrow alley. It didn't take a rocket scientist to work out the physics. Alley. Truck. Two dazed and confused women. And no wiggle room.

Not a pretty picture. Especially when all Rosie could picture was how she and Neeta would look riding the front bumper.

"Neeta!" Rosie called out a warning, but it was no use. Terrified, Neeta stood rooted to the spot, staring at the truck that was getting closer by the second.

There was only one thing Rosie could do. She told herself to count to three. She got as far as one. Timing her move, holding her breath, and praying she wasn't about to make the biggest mistake of what was looking more and more like a too-short life, she launched herself off her feet and tackled Neeta, catapulting her toward the opening of the alley that led to Fremont Street.

She hit her right where she wanted to, somewhere between her shoulders and her waist, and sent Neeta flying. It might not have been the most graceful of moves, but it was enough to snap Neeta back to life. She took off running, out of the alley and into the street.

Rosie wasn't so lucky, and thanks to the clown shoes that weighted her down like anchors, not nearly as agile. She hit the pavement and bounced back up. By the time she got her balance, the SUV was closer than ever.

Nowhere to run. Nowhere to hide. At her back was the wall of the strip club next door and a few overflowing dumpsters. On her left, a row of garbage cans. Across from her was the back door of the Swan, the receiving dock, and those three cement steps that would take her to a landing just far enough off the ground to assure her safety.

"Desperate times, desperate measures," Rosie reminded herself and, before she could also remind herself that whoever had thought of the catchphrase probably hadn't meant to include certain death in the desperate measures category, she scrambled across the path of the oncoming truck.

2

SIN CITY STRIPPERS

The flaming neon-orange sign that screamed at Mack from the nearest window made him cringe but he kept his shoulders squared and his jaw steady. Just like he kept the feelings gnawing at his insides as under control as they were likely to get.

Outside the strip club, an overly made-up hostess in tiny black shorts and a pink tube top flashed a practiced, toothy smile at his companion. Mack pretended he didn't notice.

Not so easy to pretend when she swung her gaze around to Mack and gave his red-and-black silky shirt and his snug black slacks—and everything inside—a long, slow appraisal, a nod of approval, and a look that was nothing short of a come-and-get-it come-on.

He managed.

He'd better get used to Las Vegas in all its tasteless glory, he reminded himself, switching the duffel bag he was carrying from his right hand to his left. He was here for the duration.

Mack twitched his shoulders. As usual, he refused to let

anyone know what he was feeling. Instead, he decided it was safer—and smarter—to change the subject.

"You really need to get rid of that hat."

Mack glanced at the man walking along next to him. Lenny Underwood was short and wiry and from this angle, all Mack could see of him was a brown-and-orange plaid fedora with a white feather tucked into the hatband. "You get that at a thrift shop?" he asked.

"Careful, pal." Lenny raised a hand and gave the hat a loving tap. "Been in my family a long time."

"No kidding." Mack shook his head. He had known Lenny and his wife, Barbara, for a couple years and if there was one thing he'd learned about both of them, it was that they had what could charitably be called eclectic tastes. Barbara, fiftyish and round, favored flowing caftans and toe rings. Lenny, a couple of years older and set in his ways, was more conservative. If white patent leather shoes, brown polyester pants, and a white golf shirt (not to mention the fedora) could be called conservative.

"Hey, what's the matter?" Lenny stopped and glanced down at his outfit. "You don't think this makes me look like a bonafide gambler?"

In the short time they'd been in Vegas, Mack had come to realize the city was a microcosm of sorts. From the sublime to the ridiculous. With the emphasis on the ridiculous side. When they'd cruised the megaresorts on the Strip, he'd seen people wearing everything from designer jeans to cocktail dresses. Here in the downtown area, the crowd wasn't quite so latest-thing conscious.

"I've got to hand it to you, Lenny," Mack conceded, "you do fit right in. At least with the crowd I've seen around some of the nickel slots."

The joke was lost on Lenny. He pulled a cigar as thick as his thumb out of his shirt pocket and lit it. "That's the whole point," he said. "I've never been pretty, but I'm damn good at blending in. Did I ever tell you about the time I was in Cleveland and—"

Mack raised a hand, cutting him off. Lenny had told him about what happened in Cleveland, all right. Lenny had told everyone about what happened in Cleveland. The story was so old, they all knew it inside and out.

"Not in the mood for Cleveland stories," Mack admitted. "Just want to get this over with."

Lenny nodded. As if he understood. As if he could.

"Cheer up, kid." He thumped Mack on the arm at the same time he looked over the lay of the land. There was a cross street nearby that would take them around the block and to the front of the Silver Swan, and he walked past the strip club, headed that way. "We'll get this over with and get out of here fast. And someday . . ." Lenny smoothed a hand over his golf shirt. "Someday when you're older and wiser, you'll be the one wearing the polyester pants and the fedora and pretending you're just one of the good ol' boys."

It wasn't much of a consolation.

Of course, neither was the little *chica* who walked by handing out flyers advertising Mamie's House of Pleasure. She shoved one of the bright yellow papers into Mack's hands and gave him a wink.

"What do you say?" she asked.

"Sorry." Mack pushed the paper back at her. "I'm in town on business."

"I know." The girl giggled and headed over to a group of guys just coming out of a bar. "So am I."

"See, that's just what I mean." Watching her go, Lenny nodded. "That's why you'll go far. You're focused on business, Mack. You always have been." He took a puff on his cigar and let the smoke escape his mouth in a ring, and though he did it discreetly enough not to make it look like a big deal, Mack knew Lenny was sizing him up.

"You're not going to let this place get to you, are you?" Lenny asked.

Mack raised his chin. "Think I'd let that stop me?"

"Think I'd let you be here if I did?"

"You know I appreciate this opportunity, Lenny." Mack knew he didn't have to, but he said it anyway. The old warhorses deserved a certain amount of respect, and it was the job of the younger guys to show they realized it. "I might have put up a little fuss at first but—"

"A little fuss?" Lenny laughed. "If that full-blown snit you pulled on Dom was any indication, I'd say it was more than a little fuss."

"I've apologized. A hundred times over. Dom caught me by surprise."

"That's what he's supposed to do. Catch us by surprise. It's in his job description."

"Yeah, but . . ." Mack glanced around at the neon signs that would light the desert night once the sun went down, and at the gamblers just itching to lose their money. Here in the older part of town, the crowds weren't as upmarket as they were over on the Strip. This was hard-core Vegas. Local gamblers. Tourists looking for a thrill. Men out for a little lap-dance hanky-panky and women dressed in everything from souvenir T-shirts to outfits that shouldn't be seen outside the bedroom.

The new-and-improved Mack—the Mack who had worked long and hard to keep himself together and in charge—looked at the whole scene with the cool eye of a professional. Las Vegas was interesting, that was for sure. It was also tacky, distasteful, and a hothouse for breeding every one of the seven deadly sins talked about in the Bible, and a couple others the ol' Bible writers probably never even thought of.

But there was that other part of Mack—he didn't need to remind himself—and that was the real reason he'd tried like hell to change Dom Carlucci's mind. In his imagination, he'd pictured himself setting foot on Vegas soil and having the old Mack resurface.

That was the Mack who understood the appeal of Vegas in all its glory. Las Vegas was an out-of-this-world, out-of-body, out-of-the-ordinary experience. It was raw. It was real. It was all about walking on the edge.

And walking on the edge was what the old Mack was all about.

"I thought I was beyond all this." Lenny was a good enough sport to pretend he didn't realize Mack was talking to himself. "You are beyond it." Lenny pushed his fedora back on his head. "You've come a long way, Mack. Don't let yourself forget that."

As if he could.

"I told myself never again. Not in a thousand years. Not if hell froze over. Not if I was tied down and tortured with hot pokers."

"And then Dom—"

"The second Dom told me he had a special assignment that only I could do, I knew there was about to be a frost warning in hell."

Lenny laughed. "You're catching on. So what do you say?" He glanced across the street. "You ready?"

Was he?

Mack wasn't sure. What he was sure of was that he didn't need a babysitter with him when he found out.

With a look, he told Lenny to stay back and he headed toward the street that would take him around to the front of the Silver Swan. Just as he did, he heard the sound of tires squealing from the alley next to the casino. Metal grated on metal and Mack caught the distinctive sounds of garbage cans flying in all directions.

His reaction was pure instinct. Mack's muscles tensed and his head whipped around.

"Hey, kid." Lenny had a hand on his arm even before Mack had a chance to move. "Not our business."

"I know. Old habits die hard," he said, and he shrugged

out from under Lenny's hand and raced over to check things out.

At the mouth of the alley, a skinny woman with long brown hair careened around the corner and slammed into him.

While he fought to catch the breath that had been knocked out of him, Mack steadied the woman, one hand on her shoulder.

"Are you all right, ma'am?" he asked.

The woman didn't answer. She twisted out of his grip, glanced back over her shoulder, and took off running.

More interested than ever, Mack ducked into the alley. He was just in time to see a dark SUV headed in his direction at warp speed.

No question about it, the skinny woman with the brown hair had the right idea. She knew what do to, and so did Mack.

Get the hell out of the way. Fast.

He would have done it, too. If not for the fact that there was a clown standing—frozen—between himself and the truck. Not exactly something he'd expected to see, even in Vegas, and for one second, Mack was too surprised to move.

It was one second too long.

The truck was one second closer to turning the clown into blue-and-white-striped roadkill.

A flash of adrenaline shot through him. He debated whether he had time to get out the Smith & Wesson five-shot revolver inside his duffel bag.

His mind was made up for him when the clown took off at what was probably supposed to be a run but was more like a lope thanks to shoes the size of an airport runway. Running was crazy enough. Loping was way past crazy. Especially when loping meant heading directly across the path of the SUV.

Mack groaned and tossed aside his duffel bag. Just what he needed, a clown with a death wish.

The SUV moved a mile a second. So did Rosie's heartbeat. Somewhere in the back of her mind—the part that wasn't busy being filled with terror and the ATF SPECIAL AGENT KILLED IN FREAK ACCIDENT headline she imagined would accompany the less-than-flattering picture on her credentials for her obituary—Rosie knew what she was planning. If she could make it across the alley, she could hit the steps up to the loading dock. If she could make it to the steps, she could scramble up and get to the back door. If she could make it to the back door without getting squashed—

She never got that far.

No sooner had she started out than someone grabbed her from behind. Two muscular arms went around her and all the air *whooshed* out of her lungs. The same arms lifted her from her feet and swung her around once, twice. By the time her vision cleared, she was pointed right in the direction of the oncoming truck.

"Son of a . . ." Rosie squirmed and kicked. It wasn't any use. Her assailant wasn't about to give up. At least not easily.

Which she figured was only fair since she wasn't, either.

She managed to elbow the man in the ribs and was rewarded when he made a choked, *harrumph* sound. At the same time, she got one of her legs hooked around one of his. The strategy worked. She knocked the man off balance, and still hanging onto her, he tripped over his own feet and lurched toward the back wall of the strip club. There were a couple of Dumpsters there and luckily for Rosie, the guy staggered between them. Just as the SUV zipped by.

With the little bit of air she had left in her lungs, Rosie breathed a sigh of relief. She was home free. At least as far as the SUV was concerned.

Too bad she didn't have the luxury of congratulating herself. Even as she heard the truck peel rubber and head out of the alley and back onto the street, she knew her work wasn't done.

She took as deep a breath as she could and reminded herself that the federal government had spent a lot of its money teaching her how to take care of herself. There was no way she was going to let some two-bit street thug get the better of her. She was a highly skilled special agent.

It was time she started acting like one.

Her arms were pinned to her chest and Rosie punched them outward as she kicked back. She aimed for the guy's groin, but thanks to her clown shoes, she caught him in the thigh instead. She didn't inflict the kind of damage she'd hoped for, but she sent the right message. He loosened his hold and that was all she needed.

She hit the pavement, rolled on her side, and scrambled to her feet. Her instincts told her she should take a clue from Neeta and run like hell. Her training reminded her that she needed to take control and handle the situation with the cool head of a professional. Her emotions overruled them both.

Rosie gave in to the outrage that filled every inch of her. In one fluid movement, she spun and got off a textbook left hook. Right to her assailant's nose.

The man ducked and sidestepped out from between the Dumpsters. He darted around her, grabbed her left arm, and wrenched it behind her back.

Amateur move.

Rosie braced herself and grabbed hold of the man's left arm. She gathered her strength and flipped him over her back and onto the ground.

"Yes!" She took a step back just as she heard him slap against the pavement, and she would have punched a fist into the air if she didn't feel a hand clamp around one of her ankles. The man tightened his hold and yanked. Hard. So much for thinking of him as an amateur.

The pavement went out from under Rosie. The world spun. She managed to bunch her right hand into a fist and got her arm cocked, but before she had a chance to do anything else, she found herself with her nose to the man's nose. And her breasts to a chest that felt like the Rock of Gibraltar.

Rosie looked down into a face that could have belonged to one of the guys her friend Maureen called a Hunk of the Month.

He was a hunk, all right, and if Rosie had to choose, she'd pick one of those hot, sultry months. That would explain the skin the color of burnt sugar and the tiny spiderwork of lines around his eyes that made it look like he spent too much time out in the sun. It would explain the eyes, too. Ones that were a green she'd only seen in fireworks shows.

It was hard not to recognize a fantasy come to life.

It was also hard to forget that this guy had nearly tossed her beneath four steel-belted radials and a couple tons of metal.

"What the hell are you doing—?"

"Hold on there, *chica*." The man gave her cocked arm a wary look. "I was trying to save your life. You have an odd way of saying thank you."

"Thank you?" She lowered her arm, but she didn't relax her fist. She didn't stay where she was, either. There was something about being stretched out against a delicious, hard-bodied guy that struck her as being just this side of decadent. Even if they were stretched out together on the pavement in the middle of an alley.

Rosie sat up. Not the best plan, either. Nose to nose was one thing. Breasts to chest was another. Crotch of her clown costume to zipper of his tight, tight black pants was nothing short of insane.

Not that the guy was complaining. At the same time he glanced down to where their bodies met, one of his eyebrows slowly slid up. When he looked at Rosie again, a spark flashed in his eyes and in his smile.

"Or maybe . . ." His voice was suddenly heavy with a Texas accent thick enough to cut with a knife. "Maybe, ma'am, this *is* your way of saying thank you."

His smile was as disturbing as the tingles that shot through her when he rotated his hips, and eager to get away from both, Rosie rolled and sat down on the pavement. Knees up and arms draped over them, she did her best to still the wild thumping of her heart. At the same time, she tried to convince herself that all that thumping was because someone had just tried to kill her. And not because of anything this guy had done, was able to do, or might possibly do in the future.

Just so she wouldn't forget, she looked toward the street. The SUV was long gone. "Maybe this is my way of saying, What the hell is going on here?" She snapped her gaze back to where the man was lounging on the pavement, his hands behind his head. "Who are you?"

"Mack." In spite of the fact that his eyes were hooded and his posture told her he didn't have a care in the world, the man gave her a look thorough enough to make her squirm inside her blue-and-white balloon of a costume. "And you're. . .?"

"I'm pissed. That's what I am." Rosie returned him look for look. "What are you doing here?" she asked. "And why did you just try to kill me?"

"Kill you?" The accent disappeared under the hint of laughter in Mack's voice. Good thing he controlled it. It wasn't wise to laugh at a woman who'd just seen her entirely too brief life flash before her eyes. He propped himself up on his elbows. "In case you didn't notice," he told her, "I wasn't trying to kill you. I was trying to pull you out of the way of that truck. And if I hadn't—"

"If you hadn't . . ." Rosie didn't enjoy admitting she needed help. Not from anyone. Especially when it came to the staying-alive department. "If you hadn't," she insisted, tugging her wig into place, "I would have been just fine."

"Yeah." Mack allowed a sound to escape that was almost a snicker. "Provided your definition of fine includes being a hood ornament with about two hundred broken bones."

"Provided my definition of fine doesn't involve trying to get out of the way of an oncoming vehicle and then getting yanked right back into its path."

"Which was your fault." Mack sat up, toe-to-toe with Rosie's clown shoes. "If you would have just let me—"

"Let you what? Throw me in front of that truck?" Rosie fought to school the thread of too-close-for-comfort, too-soon-after-the-excitement, too-much-of-an-adrenaline-let-down panic that made her voice squeak over the words. "If I hadn't tripped you—"

"If you hadn't tripped me, we would have been just fine. What's wrong with you? Don't you recognize a genuine hero when you see one?" He touched a finger to the bridge of his nose and winced. "Instead of just letting me save you, you had to go and start acting like one of Charlie's Angels. Where'd you learn to fight like that, anyway?"

Rosie's jaw tightened and her shoulders went back. "I have brothers." She didn't bother to point out that while her answer was technically correct, it wasn't technically an answer. She had brothers, all right. Three of them. But fighting was as anathema to her brothers as good taste was in Las Vegas. Unless they were fighting to save the whales. Or the Antarctic ice shelves. Or whatever hell other cockamamie cause they happened to be worried about at the moment.

Not worth thinking about. Especially now when there were far more pressing things to worry about than whales and ice shelves and Hubert, Pete, and John. Rosie pulled herself to her feet and brushed off the seat of her costume.

Mack got up, too. He straightened his shirt against a chest that looked as if it had been chipped from marble and smoothed a hand over his slacks. In light of everything Neeta had said—and the fact that someone had just tried to kill her—Rosie told herself it was professional interest to give the guy a long, careful look. Was he carrying? She let her gaze wander from his highly polished black shoes to the button front of his pants. No way this guy could hide anything in slacks that tight. No way he could be carrying. At least not anything he wasn't supposed to be carrying.

Just the thought made Rosie's face fiery, and for the first time since she'd put it on, she was grateful for the costume. How many women had the luxury of hiding under a mile-wide red wig while they made fools of themselves ogling a complete stranger?

This complete stranger was a tad under six feet tall, just about the same height as Rosie was herself. He had line-backer shoulders and a slim waist, arms that were just this side of too muscular, and legs that were long and lean.

The whole package (minus the eighties-vintage red-and-black silky shirt) was great when it came to the nice-to-look-at department. And not so great when Rosie considered that in spite of his wanna-be hero tactics, Mack had nearly gotten himself—and her—killed. That on top of losing her informant—before she could inform about anything, even her last name and a number where she could be reached—was enough to take a sour mood and change it to downright grumpy.

It didn't help that the entire time she studied him, Mack didn't budge. Fists on his hips, chin up, his eyes dared her to look as much as she wanted, for as long as she liked.

It wasn't until she was done that he shook his head. "What will they think of next?" he asked. "A clown act in the alley? That is what you're doing out here, right? These folks in Vegas are one smart bunch."

Rosie shook herself away from the spell of his compelling green eyes. "It's *Las* Vegas," she muttered. "Always *Las* Vegas. And if you're looking for the casino, you took a wrong turn." When Mack went to pick up a black duffel bag lying near one of the Dumpsters, she clumped her way toward the steps. By the time she got there, he was standing with duffel bag in hand. Smack dab in her way.

"You should have gone right at the restaurant," she told him. "Not left. So if you'll just . . ." She gave him an impatient wave, urging him to move aside. Or move on. Or just plain move so that she could get around him.

He didn't. He gave Rosie the kind of scrutiny she'd just given him. His gaze touched the fuzzy red wig. It brushed the blue-and-white monstrosity of a costume. It drifted down to her shoes, then back up again.

"You lost your nose," he said.

"My—" Rosie slapped a hand to her face. Some time while she was busy staying alive, her nose had gone south. Way south. She looked around and saw it lying on the pavement. Before she could make a move to retrieve it, Mack stooped down and scooped it up. He tossed it up and down in one hand like a bright red ball.

"You never told me if you were the dinner show," he said.

"You never asked." Rosie made a grab for the nose and missed. She sighed her annoyance and tapped one gargantuan shoe against the pavement. "Look, this is great fun. Honest." It wasn't, but the way Rosie figured it, this guy didn't have to know that. Too much Las Vegas glitter and too many of the free drinks the Swan served to gamblers had apparently gone to his head. Drop-dead gorgeous or not, he was starting to wear on what was left of her nerves.

"I've got to get inside." She made the kind of ninety-degree turn that should have been second nature. In her clown shoes, the maneuver was nothing short of clumsy. She *thumped* her way around Mack and *clumped* sideways up the steps. "I'm late for rehearsal and—"

"Rehearsal? Great."

The enthusiasm in his voice stopped Rosie cold. She turned just in time to see him sprint the steps behind her.

"I got lost," he explained with a smile that was nothing short of disarming. "Looking for the theater."

3

"The theater?" Rosie gave Mack another quick once-over. She'd bet a week's salary (showgirl *and* ATF) that he wasn't a dancer. He was plenty good-looking enough to attract attention on stage and off, but he didn't have the lithe build of a dancer. Or the kind of fluid movements she'd learned to recognize long ago, the kind that helped her identify a fellow dancer in an instant.

Mack's every move was more raw than graceful. There was a certain kind of energy around him even when he was standing still, a certain sort of something that made the air hum and shiver, the way it did around a fire. Like every dancer she'd ever met, he was plenty comfortable with his body, but it had nothing to do with the elegance she always associated with dance.

This had more to do with power and animal attraction. Attributes that shouldn't have figured into the sudden heat that prickled through Rosie.

She reminded herself that she was supposed to be working and that—at least as far as she could remember—prickling heat and hunks with drop-'em-at-fifty-paces smiles didn't have anything to do with her case. "Stagehand?" she asked.

"Something like that." His smile settled to one corner of his mouth and he fell into step next to Rosie. "You been with the show long?"

She gave him a noncommittal shrug. "Long enough not to get lost on my way to the theater."

He acknowledged the hit with a tip of his head and opened the door to the receiving area. Once they were inside, he snapped the door closed behind him and followed her through the dingy hallway that led along the back of the warehouse and on toward the freight elevators.

"Aren't you going to thank me?" Mack asked. "You know, for saving your life?"

Rosie gave him a stiff smile. "Thank you."

"That wasn't exactly sincere."

"Neither was your little stab at heroics, you almost got us both killed."

"As opposed to you almost getting just yourself killed."

As much as she hated to fall into the there's-two-sides-to-every-story and you-have-to-walk-a-mile-in-the-other-person's-shoes psychobabble trap she grew up hearing morning, noon, and night, Rosie knew he was right. Mack had taken a risk. He'd tried to help. He'd succeeded in keeping her from ending up looking like one of those flattened fruit roll-ups her parents bought at their local health food store.

And how had she shown her gratitude?

There was an OUT OF ORDER sign on the freight elevator and at the same time Rosie grumbled her displeasure and headed toward the doors that would take them out of the back rooms and into the public areas of the Swan, she gave Mack a sidelong glance. The bridge of his nose was red and his eyes were still watery from the sting of her fist hitting him full force.

She swallowed down the funny, sick feeling in her stomach. "I'm sorry I punched you in the nose."

"That's a start." Mack grinned. The effort must have hurt, because his expression teetered on the edge of discomfort. "And the thank you part?"

However warm and fuzzy she was feeling, Rosie hated a guy who couldn't leave well enough alone. "Thank you," she uttered on the end of a sigh. "Thank you, thank you, thank you. Happy?"

"Getting happier. I might be positively giddy if you'd explain why that SUV was trying to run you over."

Ready to punch open the double doors that led into the casino, Rosie eyed Mack and reminded herself that it wasn't wise to trust a perfect stranger. Even if *perfect* was the operative word.

"You've got some imagination! What makes you think that guy wanted to kill me?" She didn't give Mack a chance to answer. She punched the door with her fist and the instant it opened, they were enveloped in the sounds of ringing slot machines, clattering dice, and buzzing voices. She propped one shoe against the door and stepped aside to let Mack by first. "Maybe he was just a really bad driver," she suggested, raising her voice to be heard over the drunk right outside the door who'd decided a rendition of Elvis's *Viva Las Vegas* was exactly what his fellow gamblers needed to make their day complete. "Maybe he was drunk like this guy. Or really lost. Or maybe the cops were after him."

"Maybe." His duffel bag in one hand, her red nose in his other, Mack walked past the aisleway that led toward row after row of slot machines. He didn't spare a look for the roulette tables or the blackjack dealers or the cocktail waitresses who wore phony smiles along with the feathery swan wings strapped to their backs. He glanced at Rosie out of the corner of his eye. "You always hang around out in the alley?" he asked.

"You always ask too many questions?"

"Yeah." The smile that broke through his expression was

even more dazzling in the close confines of the casino than it had been outside. "Always."

Rosie returned his smile with one that was just as wide and not nearly as genuine. "Just like you always steal other people's noses?"

He tossed the nose up and caught it neatly with one hand. "I don't know. Never had the opportunity to steal a nose before."

"I hope you're planning on giving it back."

He tipped his head, considering the request. "Have dinner with me one of these nights."

She wasn't about to let him know how much the invitation threw her for a loop. Or how, in spite of the fact that it was crazy—and she was anything but—she was tempted to say yes.

"You're a little quick on the uptake, aren't you?" She wasn't quite sure if she was reminding him or herself, but she figured it didn't matter. Looked like they both needed a little dose of reality. She stopped and waited for a group of senior citizens to troop by, paper cups of coins clasped in their arthritic hands. "You don't know who I am," she told Mack. "You don't know my name. You don't even know what I look like."

"Wrong. I do know who you are. A showgirl. And before you think I'm the new mind-reading act, you should know I've seen the poster." He tipped his head toward the front of the casino where a larger-than-life, garishly colored poster advertised the dinner show and promised the thrills and spills of the big top. At least for one of the production numbers. "And as far as your name . . ." He tossed her nose up and let it slap back down against his palm before he started walking again. "I'll find out your name. Never been known to fail when it comes to that."

"I'll bet." In spite of her shoes, Rosie kept pace with him. "And the looks part?"

"That's the easiest one of all. You're a showgirl and showgirls . . ." He let his gaze drift over the costume again and, as if he could picture everything that was covered by the yards of fabric, a slow smile tugged at one corner of his mouth. "I know showgirls, *chica,* and showgirls are long-legged, big-breasted, and gorgeous. Which makes me wonder why they're bothering with all those stripes."

Rosie led the way to a bank of elevators. Though most of them were reserved for guests, the one tucked into a corner between a men's room and a cigarette machine was the freight elevator Swan employees liked to call *Just in Case.* Just in case the freight elevator near the warehouse didn't work. Which it pretty much never did.

She jabbed at the call button and fluffed out the way-bigger-than-baggy legs of her costume. "Maybe I'm the ugly stepsister. You know, the only showgirl in the history of Las Vegas who's not the long-legged, big-breasted, gorgeous type."

"I don't think so." When the elevator came, he stepped in behind her and settled himself with his back to the side wall. He gave her a careful look. "Nice nose. Cocoa-colored eyes. Lips that are a little on the thin side. Hair . . ." He bent at the waist for a closer look. "Red?"

Automatically Rosie tucked a loose strand of hair up under her wig. "Red," she said. "And why is that a bad thing?"

"Oh, it's not a bad thing at all. I like redheads. They're feisty."

"Charming." She offered a smile. "Feisty. Like a puppy."

"I was thinking more like sunset or fire or—"

"A danger sign?"

"Really?" He didn't look convinced. "You? Dangerous? Is that why you were hiding out in the alley?"

He just wasn't going to let it go.

Rosie let out a sigh of surrender and allowed her shoulders to droop. "Busted," she said, and she pulled a pack of Virginia Slims out of her pocket, one she'd tucked there in case she needed an alibi. "The answer to the mystery," she said, waving the pack in front of him. "Now you know my dirtiest secret. I was in the alley for a smoke."

"Except . . ." His grin as much as said *gotcha*. "Smoking is allowed in the casino."

"Down in the casino, yes. But not backstage. Too many costumes. Too many props. Too much chance that someone will drop a match and the whole thing will go *poof*!"

The elevator bumped to a stop and as if to prove she knew what she was talking about, the doors opened on a hallway packed with props and pieces of scenery. Along the wall, costumes and feathered headdresses had been left on hooks where they could be easily reached between numbers. There was a flurry of excitement all around as a line of showgirls, all of them dressed in crazy clown stripes and fuzzy wigs, streamed passed.

Mack took one look at it all and grinned. "Lots of ugly stepsisters, huh?"

It was too good of an opportunity to pass up. "Or lots of long-legged, big-breasted, gorgeous showgirls." She tossed a look over her shoulder at him. "Think you can handle it?"

"Rosie! There you are!"

Before Mack had a chance to answer, Angela Andrews reached into the elevator and grabbed Rosie's arm, hauling her along with the rest of the clowns. "Good thing we haven't started yet." She wagged her head and her wig bounced. "Carpathian's here today and you know how nervous everyone gets while he's here. He's got an audition scheduled, so our rehearsal was pushed back. But the guy he's auditioning isn't here yet and—"

When Mack stepped out of the elevator, Angela caught sight of him and her mouth dropped open.

"You're not—"

"Mack." He stuck out his hand and as soon as Angela shook off the momentary paralysis caused by his thousand-watt smile, she shook it. "That's me," he said. "And this

Carpathian guy . . ." He darted a look toward the stage. "He's the owner of the casino, right? He's waiting?"

"Waiting is right, and he's not exactly the patient type." Apparently seeing that the benefits of hanging on to a handsome guy far outweighed those of leading Rosie to the stage, Angela grabbed hold of Mack's arm and pulled him into the crowd.

Rosie followed behind, feeling suddenly a little left out and a lot dissatisfied with the way the afternoon was going.

She got as far as the wings, but when Mack set down his duffel bag and stepped onto the stage along with Angela, she pulled back and waited to see what was going on.

"He got lost," Angela called out to Emery Carpathian, who was standing near the first row of dinner tables beyond the footlights. "Here he is, Mr. Carpathian. He got lost."

In the time she'd been with the Swan showgirl chorus, Rosie knew enough about Emery Carpathian to know that *got lost* wouldn't hold water as an excuse. Carpathian was a short, slight man with impeccable taste and a neatly trimmed moustache. He could be difficult and he was, more often than not—at least according to the girls who'd been with the show long enough to know—demanding. His exacting standards had made the Swan a Las Vegas favorite since long before Rosie was born. Trouble was, it was getting tougher for places like the Swan to compete with the new resorts up on the Strip. Which only made Carpathian more determined to make the Swan stand out in the crowd.

Apparently, waiting for whatever he was waiting for didn't live up to Carpathian's standards. He let go a sigh of annoyance that was nothing short of long-suffering. "All right," he grumbled. He waved toward Mack at the same time he shooed everyone else from the stage. "Let's get on with it. We'll run through the circus number after."

"After?" As soon as she walked off the stage, Rosie caught Angela's arm. "What's going on?" she asked. "He's not a dancer. You can't tell me that guy's here to audition for the chorus. There's no way."

"A dancer?" Angela laughed and ducked into the wings. She plunked down on the floor and patted the place beside her. "Sort of, but not exactly." When Rosie sat next to her, Angela pointed toward the stage. "That's the yummiest thing I've seen in a week of Sundays. Something tells me this is going to be good."

Before Rosie could ask what she was talking about, the stage lights went out. Someone cued the music—a song Rosie couldn't name but recognized from the Top 40 rock station some of the other girls listened to backstage. It started with a pulse-pounding drum solo that kicked into a searing guitar riff.

The spotlight hit Mack and he did a showy turn and aimed a drop-dead smile at his audience. He glanced over at Rosie, winked, and tossed her the red plastic nose.

Right before he started taking off his clothes.

Mack didn't have to think about what he was doing. Six years of stripping in public and he pretty much had the routine down pat.

He hooked a thumb through one of the belt loops on his slacks, did a little hip gyration that made the showgirl sitting closest to the stage gasp, and congratulated himself.

Even after his years away from stripping, he still had all the right moves.

Good thing, too. As much as he was tempted, he couldn't afford to blow this audition.

He popped the top button on his shirt and gave the girls who'd gathered around Emery Carpathian a smile guaranteed to knock their socks off. Or in this case, their clown shoes.

The old smile still worked its magic. A couple of them smiled back. One woman fanned her face with one hand. Another one tapped her hand against the table in time to the grinding beat of the music, her body swaying to the same rhythm that fueled each of Mack's steps.

And Mack breathed a little sigh of relief.

Stripping in front of a crowd of middle-aged ladies out for a night of laughs was one thing. Taking off his clothes at bachelorette parties where, more often than not, the guests had guzzled a few too many fruity drinks was something else. Doing it in front of a room full of professional dancers . . .

As much as he hated to admit it, just the thought had made him far more nervous than he'd ever felt when he worked the Studs Corral back in El Paso.

Mack slipped another button from its hole and watched as a couple of the women down front let their gazes roam over the strip of bare chest he exposed. They might be professionals, but one look at the unmitigated lust that flared in their eyes and he knew something else: He shouldn't have wasted his time worrying. These women weren't different from any others. He'd never met one yet who was oblivious to the sexy dance moves he'd taught himself in front of the mirror of the pay-by-the-week motel where he'd lived back in Texas.

Satisfied that he was clicking on all cylinders, Mack dance-stepped his way closer to the audience.

Grind to the beat. Smile. Toss a hot-as-hell look left. Then right.

The moves were second nature. Just one of the things in his life he'd tried to forget and knew he never would. Kind of like the promise he'd made to himself about never stripping again.

So much for promises, good intentions, and fresh starts. They didn't stand a chance. Not when it came to what Dom Carlucci wanted.

The plan was simplicity itself. Or at least that's what Dom and the others told Mack. They needed someone to infiltrate the Silver Swan, and the fact that Emery Carpathian was looking for a male stripper to add to the show was the perfect opportunity.

As soon as he realized what they were asking, Mack was tempted to disavow any knowledge of anything even remotely connected with his past. He knew better than to try. He'd never lied about his life. There was no point. They knew about the father who walked out on him long before he was born, about the mother who didn't want him. They knew about the foster homes that couldn't handle him and the educational system that pretty much gave up on him. They knew he'd skirted trouble with the law—but just barely—and they knew that he'd beaten the odds. He'd finished high school. He'd gone on to college.

They knew exactly how he'd worked his way through.

They hadn't forgotten.

Hell had frozen. The fat lady was singing. And like it or not, Mack was back to doing two-a-days at the gym and listening to music for the sole purpose of deciding which songs had the best beat for getting nearly naked.

Mack undid the last button on his shirt and pretended there was nothing he liked better than hearing the little purr that rose from the crowd of admiring women. He took a quick look around. There were clowns on his left. Clowns on his right. Clowns sitting out in the audience and clowns crowded in the wings, watching as he inched his shirt back to give them a better look at his chest.

Could one of them be hiding more than a pretty face and a body to die for behind the clown getup?

It was a daunting thought and now, like so many times since he'd hopped on his Harley Night Train and headed out of Seattle, his mind reeled at the possibilities. So many clowns. So little time.

Another quick scan of the audience and Mack located the clown named Rosie. Poor kid. She must be shaking in her clown shoes. What had happened with the crazy driver out in the alley was enough to unsettle anybody's composure.

He had to give her points for the whole stiff-upper-lip routine. As tough as it must have been, she managed to keep herself together. The least she deserved was a smile and a little extra attention.

His eyes still on Rosie, Mack danced his way closer. She was sitting on the floor in the wings, her knees drawn up to her chin, her arms wrapped around her legs, and she was easy to recognize. She was the only one not wearing a red plastic nose.

That's pretty much where the difference between Rosie and the other clowns ended.

Like the rest of them, Rosie was watching his every move, her eyes wide with interest, her cheeks just a little dusky.

Like the rest of them, she looked a little out of breath, a little stunned, a little taken aback that any guy would have the nerve—or was it just the ego?—to stand up in front of a crowd and peel away his clothes along with their inhibitions.

Like every other woman in the place, Rosie looked as if she couldn't wait to rip off the rest of his clothes and jump his bones.

The thought caught Mack off guard. Kind of like the out-of-left-field dinner invitation he'd dangled in front of Rosie back in the elevator. He didn't usually allow himself the luxury of thinking about any individual woman while he was performing, and he chalked the whole thing up to first-audition-in-a-long-time jitters.

He knew better than to fall into that trap.

When he missed a step, he covered instantly, the way he'd covered back in the days when stripping was his ticket off the streets. He gave Rosie—and the rest of the audience—a look that was pure sin, and unbuttoned his fly.

The trick worked. Like every other woman there, Rosie leaned forward, straining to get a look at the neon-yellow thong he was wearing underneath his black slacks. Was it his imagination, or was there something more than just hormone-induced interest in Rosie's eyes? She watched him like she could read every thought that was racing through his mind.

Ridiculous.

Mack tossed the thought aside at the same time he inched his slacks down to expose a bit of bare hip. He'd never met a woman yet who could plumb the depths of a mind that was—at least according to the guys he worked with, a free-clinic counselor back in El Paso, and the couple of women he'd tried to have honest relationships with over the years—a little off-kilter, even on his best day.

Reading his mind, huh? Mack slipped out of his shirt. Maybe all Rosie needed was a little distraction.

He twirled his shirt over his head and tossed it in her direction. She reached up and snagged it with one hand.

Maybe it wasn't such a crazy idea to take Rosie to dinner, he decided. She was as good a place as any to start. She might know the lay of the land, who was who around the theater, and who the players were. And weren't. It was worth a try.

She wouldn't be a pushover; he only needed to remember the velocity of her left hook to remember that. Then again, that wasn't surprising. If there was one thing Mack had learned in the thirty-two years he'd been on this earth, it was that nothing was easy. He would need to work his butt off—literally and figuratively—to find what he was looking for. He would need to do some digging and maybe even some sweet-talking. He would need to pour on the charm and turn on the sex appeal and ask all the right questions of all the right people.

It was the only way he could get this over with and get out of Vegas before the music took over his bloodstream like a drug and the excitement of walking on the wild side made him forget that there was more to life these days. More to Mack.

He kicked off his shoes. Sometime when he'd been thinking about her, he'd taken a couple steps in Rosie's direction and he gyrated nearer.

Though the casual observer wouldn't notice, Mack's slacks were specially made. They were tear-aways and tear away was exactly what he did. One leg at a time. He was left in something that reminded him of cutoff shorts, and he got rid of those, too.

Fortunately for his plan to infiltrate the Swan—not to mention for his ego—he still had a body that was better than average and the nerve to use it shamelessly. Fortunately for his plan to infiltrate the Swan—and for his ego—everything worked as planned. When the audience gave his yellow G-string and everything in it a hoot of approval, Mack smiled sleekly.

And Rosie?

He gave her one more look before he turned and danced the other way.

He would swear the toes of Rosie's clown shoes were curled.

Satisfied, Mack smiled. He was still smiling when the music ended, the audience cheered, and Emery Carpathian gave him the thumbs-up.

"¡Eso!" Still flushed with the excitement of the performance, Mack congratulated himself. Maybe the new Mack had more sense, more maturity, and a way better self-image, but for once, the old Mack had come in handy. Thanks to a few old tricks and a couple of new moves, he'd successfully wormed his way (or more precisely bumped and ground his way) onto the employee rolls at the Silver Swan.

He darted another look at Rosie. He was just in time to see her hop to her feet and head backstage. Before he had a chance to even think about following her, he was surrounded.

"That was terrific."

"Wonderful!"

"Sooo sexy."

He accepted the praise of the dancers who hurried on stage to welcome him to the show. He smiled at a couple of barefaced come-ons and made as much note as he could as to which clowns made them so he'd be able to use their interest to his best advantage. He forced himself to grin when more than one of the dancers looked him over at close range, even though more often than not, *close range* meant claustrophobic. He endured one slap on the behind and decided this assignment was either going to be heaven or the closest thing to *el infierno* he was ever going to live through.

No matter. It all boiled down to one thing. Less than one hour at the Swan and already he had met plenty of women who might provide him with information. Now all he had to do was use his contacts to his best advantage. And the only thing he had to worry about (besides stripping two times a night, six nights a week) was what each of them knew.

And who the hell had his guns.

4

It was probably politically incorrect for Rosie to begin her investigation with Tatiana Solvinesky. Just because the Swan's choreographer had, once upon a very long time before, danced with the Kirov Ballet back in the old Soviet Union, it did not necessarily follow that she knew anything about the source of the 9A-91s Gus Friel sold.

But it was better than nothing.

Rosie sidled into what was politely termed Tatiana's *office*, a battered metal desk strategically placed between a woman's rest room and the blue velvet curtain that served as the stage backdrop.

She'd picked the perfect time to go through Tatiana's things. There was no one around and it was no secret why. Mack was about to begin rehearsal and though he'd been at the Swan for only a week, it hadn't taken Rosie long to realize that when he was on stage, all other activity in the theater stopped. Showgirls who were supposed to be stretching were batting their eyes at Mack and yelling comments every bit as suggestive as his strip routine. Dancers who were supposed to be getting costumes fitted, producers who were supposed to be paying attention to business, and musicians who were supposed to be practicing were stationed in the wings and in the first few rows of seats, drooling over Mack's performance (not to mention his endowments).

It didn't take the Powers That Be long to catch on, and an announcement came out of Emery Carpathian's office: The staff was wasting time and from now on, Mack's rehearsals would be on a closed set. His first performance was scheduled in two weeks. If they wanted to watch, the dancers could buy tickets.

Carpathian should have known better. Showgirls (not to mention musicians and producers) weren't that easily discouraged. And they weren't about to miss an opportunity that had *chance of a lifetime* written all over it. Most of the girls had found a favorite Mack-watching spot. Some of them hung out with the lighting crew at the back of the theater. Others, braver than the rest, climbed up to the catwalk above the stage. A few less daring souls managed to watch Mack's gyrations from the wings.

All of which played into Rosie's plans just fine.

Quietly she slid open the top drawer of Tatiana's desk. There wasn't much in it besides a few pens, a file folder filled with notations about music and choreography, and a bottle of perfume. Rosie closed that drawer and went on to the next. She had no better luck there, or with the next drawer, and she'd just decided to give up when she heard the sound crew cue Mack's music.

She tensed and glanced at the curtain, a response that was so instinctive and so surprising she could barely believe it.

"Eleanor Roosevelt Malone," she grumbled to herself, "a nice, conservative federal agent does not—"

The music continued and over it, Rosie heard Tatiana call out instructions. "Shirt first, darling." Tatiana's accent was as thick as borscht. "A little at a time. There you go. Bit by bit."

Rosie shook away the images that automatically formed in her head.

Mack unbuttoning his shirt.

Inching it over his chest.

Tossing it away.

Unbuttoning his slacks.

Rosie's breath caught. "A nice, conservative, hard-working, dedicated federal agent does not get distracted." Her voice bumped over the words.

But even though she knew they were true—and before she even knew she was doing it—she hopped to her feet, looking for a gap in the curtain. She found a tiny hole and congratulated herself—it was the perfect outpost for watching Mack perform.

"You're being immature," she reminded herself. "Immature, irrational, and completely absurd."

Her words were a spin on the ones she'd heard from her family all the years she was growing up, the ones that warned her she'd never get anyplace worth getting to in life if she was always so mature it hurt and so rational that she couldn't lighten up, get down, and go with the flow. Then and now, she knew her straight-and-narrow view of the world was far superior to their let-it-all-hang-out philosophy.

Which didn't explain why she wasn't listening to her own advice.

Then again, just because she was a sensible, by-the-book, nose-to-the-grindstone federal agent didn't mean she was stupid. Or lacking a normal libido.

It would take a stronger woman than she was to pass on the opportunity of enjoying Mack's act.

The music stopped and out on stage, Tatiana stepped into the glow of Mack's spotlight. Her iron-gray hair pulled back in a severe bun, the bony angles of her body emphasized by her black leotard, she aimed a look as deadly as a heat-seeking missile all around the theater, just to let the gawkers know she realized they were there. As she shooed Mack back to center stage, she signaled the sound crew to cue his music again.

If the rigidity of Mack's jaw meant anything, he didn't think it was the best idea in the world. Then again, who could blame him? When it came to strippers, Rosie was hardly an expert, but she knew one thing for sure: Mack knew what he was doing and he did it right. Every single time. Why do another run-through when the first one was perfection?

Then again, she knew that wouldn't stop him. If there was one thing she'd learned about Mack in the last week (aside from the fact that he had a great body and could bust a move with the best of them), it was that he was more determined than any man she'd ever met. Tatiana wanted another run-through of the number? There wasn't one doubt in Rosie's mind that Mack would give it to her.

Hotter, sexier, faster, and harder than the last time.

Just as she expected, Mack got ready to start again, and Rosie found herself grinning.

The show wasn't over.

With the trained eye of a professional and the unmitigated lust of a healthy woman with healthy appetites, she watched Mack move around the stage, retrieving his red bandanna, his leather vest, and the pieces of his tear-away jeans that he wore for the biker boy stripper number. His biceps rippled and the stage lights helped define abs that made the six-pack description completely inadequate. As for his black leather G-string . . .

Rosie swallowed over the sudden dryness in her mouth.

She was being way too hormonal.

Not to mention unprofessional, out of line, and inappropriate.

Which didn't keep her from wondering when Mack was going to make good on that promise of taking her to dinner.

"What'cha doing?"

The question came from right behind Rosie and she cursed herself for not paying more attention to what was going on around her. She spun around and found Warren, the man who'd taken over Gus Friel's gofer job, standing just a couple of feet away.

Feeling suddenly and unaccountably guilty, she backed away from the curtain. "Just watching rehearsal," she told Warren. "You know, just watching—"

"That new Mack guy. Yeah." Warren nodded. He was a middle-sized, middle-aged man with brown hair and eyes. He always wore the same pair of tattered jeans and, as far as Rosie could tell, he had a wardrobe that consisted of exactly four T-shirts. Today's was the one that advertised one of the shows up on the Strip. Because he was mentally challenged and had the unsettling habit of walking into their dressing rooms without knocking, some of the girls were uneasy about having him around, but Rosie had found Warren to be good-natured, helpful, and pretty much harmless.

"All the girls like Mack," Warren said.

Looked like he was pretty insightful, too.

Not exactly something she wanted to discuss with Warren. Or anyone else. Even when Mack's music started up from out front, Rosie moved away from the curtain and into the hallway that skirted the back of the stage.

Warren followed along and although Rosie had noticed the gigantic plastic bowl of slightly wilted salad he was carrying and knew exactly where he was headed with it, she also knew how much he liked to talk.

"What are you doing today, Warren?" she asked.

He grinned. "Buffet," he said. "It's Monday and there's no show on Monday. But there is rehearsal. I set up a buffet in the greenroom for the dancers for after rehearsal. The dancers, they like salad. Are you going to eat salad, Rosie?"

"Only if you make it, Warren. You make the best salad in Las Vegas."

It was the same conversation they had every Monday, but Rosie didn't mind. She liked Warren, and besides, it didn't hurt to keep on the good side of a guy who pretty much had the run of the theater and who might see things the show-girls didn't.

When they got to the greenroom, she held the door for him and he set the salad bowl down on a folding table that was already covered with white plastic. When he did, the table tilted and Warren's expression clouded.

"The leg is loose. It's going to fall," he told Rosie, and though she didn't think the wobbly table leg would cause that much mayhem, she didn't argue. There was nothing Warren liked better than fixing things.

She took the salad bowl off the table and stepped out of his way, and Warren got his toolbox. Rosie had seen the box a dozen times before; it was his pride and joy, and Warren lugged it with him everywhere. But she'd never been near when he worked.

Which pretty much explained why, when he flipped the toolbox open and she saw the name *Gus* painted on the top of the inside cover in bright red letters, her heart thudded to a stop and her breath caught. Though she remembered reading in the police reports about the contents of Gus Friel's employee locker and his '94 Escort and the dingy apartment that he called home, there wasn't thing written about him owning a toolbox.

Which might mean something. Or nothing at all.

There was only one way to find out.

Afraid to say the wrong thing and spook him, Rosie took a careful step nearer. "That's a terrific toolbox, Warren. Wow, you've got everything in there that you could ever need."

"Yeah." He stooped down and moved aside the tablecloth so he could work on the metal table leg. "I've got a screw-driver and a hammer and pliers and—"

"Where'd you get the box, Warren?"

It was the wrong thing to say. Rosie knew that as soon as she saw Warren's hands still over the screw that held the table leg in place. She jumped in fast to try and redeem her-self before the situation got too out of hand.

"I mean, gosh, Warren . . ." She knelt down on the floor beside the box and took another look inside. "For a job like yours, you need tools, don't you? I'll bet Gus knew that. That's why he said you could have his toolbox if you ever got his job, right?"

"No." Warren sat back on his heels. His chin quivered and his shoulders drooped. "Gus, he never said nothing about the toolbox. Because he didn't know he was going to die. And after he did, that's when Greg told me I could have Gus's job if I had my own tools. I remembered, Rosie. I remembered that Gus kept his toolbox back there." With the screwdriver, he pointed over his shoulder. "In the room where the sets are painted. And I didn't tell nobody because I really wanted Gus's job and he wasn't using the tools anymore. And now I'm going to get in trouble because you know I stole them and—"

"Definitely not!" Rosie plunked down on the floor next to Warren. "This is definitely not stealing, Warren. It's using. And no one else was using them anyway. No one else even knew they were here. So you really did everyone a favor, didn't you? You found something no one else knew about and you're putting it to good use. It's like recycling. Only better." She put a hand on his shoulder. "I'm not going to tell anybody."

"Really?" Relief washed over Warren's face and his soft features pulled into a squishy smile "You're not gonna tell?"

"Nope." Rosie reassured him with a smile of her own. "Only . . . you wouldn't mind if I took a look inside the toolbox, would you, Warren?"

He laughed and gave her a good-natured little punch on the arm. "You're a girl! Girls don't like tools!"

"Most girls don't like tools. You're right. But I'm just sort of nosy. You know?"

"Like you're nosy when you hide behind the curtain and watch Mack dance?"

"Not exactly." Rosie reminded herself she needed to be

more discreet. "That's a whole different kind of nosy. This is more like . . . more like I just wonder what Gus carried around with him. Have you taken anything out of the box, Warren?"

He held up the screwdriver. "This."

"No, I mean, have you taken anything out? Thrown anything away? Cleaned up some of the stuff Gus had in here and replaced it with your own?"

Warren shook his head. "Everything's there, Rosie. Honest. I didn't want to touch too much. I never even looked much. It was Gus's toolbox and Gus, he's dead."

"That's right, Warren. So I don't think he'll mind if I take a peek in his toolbox, do you?" When he didn't disagree, she moved in for a closer look.

It was the simplest type of toolbox, metal, with a top that unlatched and flipped up. Inside was a metal tray that fit over a bottom compartment. There was nothing unusual at all about the contents of the top tray and, finished with it, Rosie lifted the tray to look beneath it.

"Two more screwdrivers," she said, carefully lifting out each item and setting it on the floor. "Long-tipped scissors. One pack of cigarettes. A nickel bag of pot . . ."

The horrified look on Warren's face told her it wasn't his. Convinced he shouldn't be found with it, she stuffed it into her own pocket so she could dispose of it later. She continued hunting through the toolbox. "Duct tape. Twine. A metal file. What's this?" At the bottom of the box, Rosie's fingers touched something plastic. She pulled out a snack-size Baggie and held it up to the light. Inside was a keychain.

"Is this yours, Warren?" she asked.

He shook his head. "Never touched it." He squinted at the keychain. "It's not pretty."

Rosie looked inside the bag. "Sure isn't," she agreed. As keychains went, it was pretty nondescript. It had a loop for keys on one end and a rough gray stone set into an oval of metal on the other end. "Doesn't look valuable, either."

Which made her wonder why it was tucked away in a Baggie and hidden at the bottom of a toolbox. And who had put it there.

"You can have it, Rosie."

Warren's offer surprised her and she looked up to find him watching her. "You're nice to me, Rosie, not like those other girls. And you're not going to tell. About the toolbox, I mean. If you want to keep the keychain, you can."

"That's sweet, Warren. Really." Rosie pulled herself to her feet. There were a couple of pieces of Saran Wrap stretched tight over the top of the salad bowl and she removed one piece and wrapped it around the plastic Baggie with the keychain inside. "I'll tell you what," she said. "I'll just borrow it for now. Just for a little while. And when I'm done with it, I'll give it back to you and you can keep it in the toolbox, right where Gus left it."

"OK." Warren stuck out his hand and they shook on the deal, and before he even had the table leg fixed, Rosie was headed to the door.

"Aren't you going to stay?" he called after her. "For salad?"

"Salad?" At the door, Rosie turned. "Not today," she told him. She glanced down at the keychain. "Today," she told him, "I have something else to do."

"Sixty-three dollars and forty-seven cents."

Everett Tancredi was a whole head taller than Mack. He had shoulders as wide as a U-Haul truck and a face that looked as if it had been molded out of Play-Doh by an artist with a warped sense of humor. His nose was too big and as crooked as the hairpin turns through the nearby mountains. His eyes were set too close together. His ears were too large, but that didn't stop Everett from keeping his hair buzzed military short. He had a penchant for wearing black pin-striped suits with dark shirts and monochromatic ties and the habit of sporting Ray-Bans anytime he was outside, day or night. When he was told (as he frequently was) that the outfit made him look like a wise guy, he always had the same reaction. A snort of disbelief.

If he knew that behind his back he was known as Everett the Enforcer, he never let on, though something told Mack the nickname would have rolled off Everett like water off a duck's back. Or maybe not. Maybe he would have looked on the moniker as the ultimate compliment.

Everett looked like a wise guy now as poked his Ray-Bans into the breast pocket of his suit coat and waited with Mack at the sporting goods counter of the local Wal-Mart. He waved a piece of paper under Mack's nose.

"Sixty-three dollars and forty-seven cents." Everett repeated the figure with as much gravity as if he were announcing the federal trade deficit. "You're over budget, Mack. By sixty-three dollars and—"

"Yeah, yeah. I know. Forty-seven cents." Mack was hearing it. He just didn't believe it. He scraped a hand through his hair and shook his head. It was late, and after rehearsing the biker number far more times than he thought was necessary, he was tired. Maybe he was in bed and dreaming?

Maybe not. The way he remembered it, the dreams he'd had for the last week (both daydreams and the nighttime variety) were all about a clown in a blue-and-white-striped costume who morphed in a heartbeat into a woman with cocoa-colored eyes.

Not the time or the place for thoughts like that, he reminded himself. Not when the Enforcer was breathing down his neck.

"Look . . ." Weighing what he wanted to say against what he knew he could get away with, Mack leaned against the counter, waiting for a teenage clerk with blotchy skin to get him the box of .38 cartridges he'd asked for. "Dom is going to have to understand that I've got expenses."

"Ain't Dom asking the questions."

"Then Lenny's going to need to realize that—"

"Ain't Lenny, either. It's me." As if that were all the authority he needed to back up his statement, Everett neatly folded the piece of paper and tucked it into his breast pocket along with his sunglasses. "You're paying how much for rent?"

"You know exactly how much I'm paying for rent." Mack shifted from foot to foot. He wasn't uncomfortable with Everett's questions. He wasn't even nervous. He was mad as hell.

Which was a good thing, he reminded himself. What was it his counselor back in El Paso had told him? It was all right to be angry? It was important to recognize the truth of his emotions? So far, so good. But just because he could give a name to the way he was feeling didn't mean he had to act on those feelings. He'd learned that back in El Paso, too.

"There are legitimate expenses at the beginning of every operation," Mack explained, and he congratulated himself. He managed to keep his voice level and his temper firmly under control. "Gas prices are up and you know I drove down from Seattle."

"Yeah." Everett nodded, and Mack swore he could see the older man's mind working over the numbers.

"Besides all that, I've had some other things I had to take care of," Mack told him. "I can't exactly go on stage dressed like this, can I?" He gestured toward his jeans and the Princeton T-shirt that had been given to him by a long-ago lover who'd thought she could turn a West Texas frog into an Ivy League prince. She'd found out how wrong she was— fast—but even when she left and took her Gucci bags and her Versace clothes and her sweet little yellow Mustang convertible with her, Mack had refused to get rid of the shirt. Just to remind himself of exactly where his roots weren't.

"I had extra expenses. I had to spend money on costumes and shoes and—"

"The kind of stuff you can rip off and throw into the

audience doesn't come right off the rack, huh?" There was a hint of a smile on Everett's face.

Mack chose to ignore it. He'd pretty much had his fill of getting razzed about this assignment. Not letting the razzers know how mad they made him was another useful skill he'd learned back in El Paso.

He set his jaw. "I tried to tell you that when you were setting up my budget. You wouldn't listen."

Everett pushed off from the counter and walked toward a display of fishing rods. When he got there, he spun around and came back at Mack. "I'm still not listening," he said. "Not my job to listen. It's my job to see that you stay within your budget. Make sure you make it up somewhere."

"Make it up? You mean, not spend sixty-three dollars and—"

"Forty-seven cents. Yeah, that's the ticket. Next month. You could cut down on food. Or gas. Or maybe not take so many of them showgirls out to dinner?"

Mack had been on the verge of acquiescing. He was willing to eat macaroni and cheese a couple of nights a week if it meant keeping the peace. What he wasn't willing to do was let Everett ride roughshod over him.

He found himself automatically adjusting his stance, but it wasn't until his hands curled into fists that he realized what he was doing. He forced himself to take a step back and a calming breath. He counted to ten in Spanish and when that didn't work, he tried it a second time. Slower and in English. It wasn't until after he was sure he was in control that he spoke.

"Taking those showgirls to dinner is what I'm here for, remember?" He pinned Everett with a look that was sharp enough to make even the Enforcer squirm. "I'm not out for laughs, in spite of what you and the rest of them think. How am I ever going to find out anything if I don't get people to talk? I'm not going to stand backstage and pepper them with questions as they dance their way off. We both know that wouldn't work."

Everett apparently thought better of whatever argument he might have made. Or maybe he saw that Mack's hands were still curled into fists. He held up one hand. "Agreed," he said. "But . . ." He reached into his back pocket and pulled out a stack of copies of credit card receipts. "Steak at New York-New York, lobster at Mandalay Bay, pasta de mer at Bellagio. These girls, they've got expensive tastes. They got any information to go along with it?"

"No information. Not yet." Mack hated to admit it. He hated to confess that though he'd wined and dined three of the showgirls from the Swan, he'd yet to find out anything helpful.

Almost as much as he hated to confess that even while he was out with each of those clowns, he was thinking about another clown.

Mack shook the thought away. Not so easy to get rid of the picture that flashed in his head. Like it did every time he ran into Rosie backstage, the realization hit him somewhere in the region of his stomach. Like a fist.

Rosie in her clown costume was as cute as a button. But she wore that costume for only one of the numbers in the show. The rest of the night, she was dressed just as he'd always pictured a showgirl would dress, and just as he'd always pictured, showgirl reality pretty much filled the bill of his showgirl fantasies.

Long-legged.

Big-breasted.

Gorgeous.

The first time he'd gotten live-and-in-person confirmation of his theory was the night of his audition. He'd hung around the theater in the hopes of finding out something useful and when he rounded a corner, he came face-to-face with a woman in sequins and feathers.

No. Mack corrected himself. Not just a woman. Even a

man like him, who didn't have an ounce of poetry in his veins or a whiff of it in his soul, knew the truth when it looked him in the eye.

This was a vision in sequins and feathers.

He recognized the nose and the brown eyes instantly. He'd been surprised by the rest of the package. It wasn't the long and leggy part that threw him for a loop. It wasn't even the tiny bikini-type costume Rosie was wearing, one that was cut high on her hips and so low in front that the deep vee neck had a piece of sheer fabric sewn into it. Just to keep everything where it was supposed to be and the patrons on the other side of the stage lights from getting more than their money's worth.

No, that wasn't what had surprised him. He'd expected the figure that was nothing short of to-die-for and the legs that were pure fantasy.

What he hadn't expected was hair the exact color of the sandstone out in Red Rock Canyon. Or the very unclownlike intelligence that shone in Rosie's eyes. He hadn't expected the subtle fragrance of raspberries that rose up around her, or the fact that she looked a little uncomfortable when he made no bones about looking her over and enjoying the sight.

He hadn't expected to react to her so fiercely, either, and Mack dismissed the notion as nothing but another in the long line of aberrations that was Las Vegas. How could a guy not get all hot and bothered in the presence of so much bare flesh? He was in the land of little costumes, big breasts, and bigger fantasies, a place where everything was designed to titillate, and the fact that it did, the fact that it had, and the fact that it still was, proved nothing at all except that he was human.

Mack's conscience prickled, and he pushed his scruples back into place and reminded himself that he was supposed to be working.

"Speaking of which . . ." They hadn't been talking about it

at all, but the thought occurred to Mack and he pulled a slip of paper out of the pocket of his jeans. "I'd like to take a closer look at some of the dancers at the theater." As soon as the words were out of his mouth, he realized it was a very bad pun. Before Everett could say a word, he stopped him with a look. "One of them is Tatiana Solvinesky. She's from Minsk originally, and while it probably doesn't mean a thing, it won't hurt to double-check. I'd also like to know more about a dancer named Julie. She snorts cocaine every night before the show and could probably use the kind of cash she would make dealing guns."

"You think it's a woman behind this thing?"

As much as Mack hated to admit it, he honestly didn't know. "Anything's possible," he reminded Everett. "You know that as well as I do. Especially when there's money involved. Or maybe it doesn't even have anything to do with money. There might be politics at work or some type of revenge or—"

"Know just what you mean." Everett nodded solemnly. "I got an ex-wife and there are days . . ."

If Mack wasn't so busy trying to work his way through the problem, he might actually have commented on Everett's attempt at levity. He'd never realized the Enforcer had a sense of humor. If Everett was trying to be funny.

He held out the paper where he'd written a dozen names. "There are some other names here, too. If you could run some background checks—"

"Me?" Everett poked one finger into the center of his shiny black tie. "I look like a cop to you?"

"No." It was the absolute truth and Mack didn't mind admitting it. "But I know you could make some calls. I doubt there's anything there, but it's worth a try." Even before he saw Everett's almost imperceptible nod, Mack pressed the piece of paper into the big man's hand.

"In the meantime, you keep your eye on the bottom line."

Everett glanced at the paper before he tucked it into his pocket. "You'll watch your spending?"

"Are we making a deal here?" Mack laughed. He honestly couldn't believe how ridiculous the whole situation was. He needed information. Legitimate information. And here he was, making deals with the Enforcer to get it. "Because if we are, you know what I'm going to say. I will be the ideal Boy Scout." He crossed his heart. "If that's what's going to get me the information I need, you know I'll cooperate."

"Right." Everett waited while the clerk brought Mack his bullets and Mack paid. When the kid walked away, he turned back to Mack. "You got a reputation, Mack. You don't play well with others. That makes me unhappy. It's not something I want to have to deal with." He tapped his breast pocket and the paper where he'd scratched down his figures. "Don't make me have this talk with you again."

"You'll get me the info on the workers at the casino." It wasn't a question. They had struck a deal. It was only right to remind Everett that he had a part to play in the bargain, too. "Personnel records? Addresses? Phone numbers?"

"Phone numbers?" Everett made a sound that might have been a snort of laughter. "I thought getting women's phone numbers was your specialty." His enormous grin didn't make his face any more attractive. "Just like taking off your clothes."

"Yeah. Right." Watching Everett go, Mack tossed the box of cartridges into his shopping cart. "Just like taking off my clothes."

He had a roll of paper towels and a box of Wheaties in his cart along with the cartridges and he'd already turned to head to the main checkout when he caught sight of a flash of color from the corner of his eye. The flash was headed in the direction of the pet department. The color reminded him of the landscape in Red Rock Canyon.

"No way," Mack told himself and the wayward fantasies that apparently had no compunction about sneaking up and biting him when he was least expecting them. "No way Rosie is hanging out in Wal-Mart."

He slipped the cartridges beneath the box of Wheaties, where no one could see them, and headed toward the pet department anyway.

Just in case.

5

Rosie wasn't the type who usually talked to herself.

At least she never had been.

But lately, she caught herself mumbling a lot when nobody else was around. At least nobody else who wanted to listen.

"Yeah, like about fingerprints?" She grumbled the words while she cruised the Wal-Mart aisles looking for the display of Super Glue the woman behind the service desk had assured her was in Aisle 15. The fact that not one of the people passing by looked suspiciously at a woman talking to herself was a tribute to the city where the bizarre was the norm. The fact that she was talking to herself in the first place was enough to make Rosie mumble even more.

She'd been doing fine, she reminded herself, until she called the local ATF office that afternoon and told them about the toolbox and the keychain she'd found inside the plastic bag. Until she asked them to check it for fingerprints.

Somewhere deep down inside, she must have known the request made her look like an overanxious rookie; she wasn't surprised when they told her exactly what she was afraid they were going to tell her.

"The chain of evidence is compromised. The toolbox was left lying around. Anyone could look in it. Anyone could have put the keychain in it. Which means it isn't even worth checking. Blah, blah, blah." Rosie spotted the Super Glue and tossed one blister-wrapped container into her shopping cart, where she'd already put a small hot plate and a piece of glass to cover the aquarium she was on her way over to the pet department to find.

She looked over her purchases and nodded grimly. Once she got the aquarium, she'd have everything she needed. If the local ATF folks wouldn't check for fingerprints, she'd do it herself. The technique was simplicity itself. She'd heat the glue inside the closed aquarium and if there were finger-prints on the bag, the glue would adhere to the enzymes left behind.

If she found something, she'd talk to folks at the local of-fice again.

And if she didn't?

If she didn't, no one ever had to know that she was an overanxious rookie.

Her mind made up, she headed over to take a look at the aquariums.

She was also not the type who usually bucked the system, and while she looked at a five-gallon model and decided it was too small and a fifty-gallon size and decided it was way too big, she wondered why she'd chosen this time and this place to show a side of her personality that was just slightly left of the nice, comfortable, right-wing position she'd estab-lished early on in life and had refused to budge from since.

She didn't need to remind herself that she already knew the answer.

Thinking about the keychain gave her something to ob-sess about.

Something that wasn't Mack.

Wondering if the keychain might have belonged to Gus gave her something to focus on.

Something that wasn't Mack.

Speculating about whether there might be fingerprints on the keychain or the plastic bag it was stored in gave her something to be curious about.

Something that had nothing to do with the way Mack peeled out of his clothes.

Which made her wonder why, when she wasn't supposed to be thinking about him, she was thinking about him. And why, when she swore she'd be better off putting Mack out of her mind once and for all, she imagined she saw him wheeling past the dog food and headed her way.

There was no way he could figure out what she was up to by looking at the items in her shopping cart, but she wasn't about to take any chances. On instinct, she grabbed the Super Glue and slipped it onto the nearest shelf, right between the cat toys and the gerbil kibble.

As if he weren't the least bit surprised to see her standing there with a 20-gallon aquarium in her hands, Mack slowed down and allowed himself to take a long look at Rosie. His gaze skimmed her sandals and up her legs. It grazed her short denim skirt and brushed her yellow T-shirt. When it got all the way to her lips, he allowed himself a slow smile. "You must live around here."

Not something she particularly wanted to share. Especially when she was working undercover. Rosie ignored his comment. It was harder to ignore the way Mack's abs strained beneath his T-shirt. "Princeton, huh? You don't look like the Ivy League type."

"You don't look like the goldfish type."

"Goldfish? Oh." Rosie set the aquarium back on the shelf and shrugged. "I was just thinking. About getting a pet. Dogs need too much attention and cats are too picky. I thought fish . . . well, fish seem easy. And it would give me something to take care of."

He let his gaze wander over her again and for once, she wished she were wearing a T-shirt with some school name emblazoned on it. Or some silly saying. Or some company logo. At least then she could pretend he was reading her T-shirt instead of admiring everything underneath it. Just like she'd pretended she was reading his.

He leaned against the shopping cart and aimed a megawatt smile in her direction. "If you're looking for something to take care of, I'm taking applications."

Rosie was too smart to be fooled. Not by the smile that went along with the comment. Or by the heat that rippled the air between them. She wasn't about to be fooled by the mind games her own head was trying to play on her, either. She was way too smart for that. And way too determined to do what she had to do, get out of Vegas and get back to her real life. A real life that—as far as she could remember, anyway—did not include handsome strippers with smiles that could melt glaciers, bodies that were made for action, and the kind of charm that even a levelheaded woman found impossible to resist.

Which didn't mean she couldn't enjoy it while it lasted. After all, she was also too smart not to recognize a twenty-four-carat golden opportunity when it smiled at her and turned her insides to mush.

She gave Mack a teasing little smile. "Were you taking applications from Angela and Tiffany and Julie, too?"

His expectant expression fell like a bad soufflé. He rubbed a hand over the late-in-the-day stubble of beard that brought out the planes and angles of his face. "So I guess you heard I've been out with a couple of the dancers."

"A couple is two," Rosie reminded him. "And so far, you've been out with three."

"Three. Yeah." Mack did his best to look sheepish about the whole thing. Not exactly an easy thing considering modesty, embarrassment, and bashfulness didn't exactly play into the whole male-stripper persona. If for nothing else, Rosie had to give him points for trying. She made a mental note that he was quite an actor. She made another mental note not to forget it.

"How'd you find out, anyway?" Mack asked. "I mean, about Angela and Tiffany and—"

"Julie," she reminded him, even though he didn't need it. "Word has a way of traveling pretty fast backstage. And the word on you is that you're out for a good time. Apparently with anyone you can find to go along with the plan."

Mack might have gotten away with embarrassed, but even he wasn't bold enough to try to get away with contrite. He shrugged and his T-shirt strained over his shoulders. "What? What's wrong with a guy wanting to have fun? You don't like to have fun? You don't like good times?"

"I'm crazy about good times."

"Which means we should have a drink together. Or dinner."

"You guaranteeing me a good time?"

He grinned. "Signed, sealed, and delivered," he promised.

"When?"

Mack glanced in her shopping cart. "You haven't bought the fish yet. Which means you're under no obligation to get home. How about right now?"

"Now?" Rosie wasn't about to lie to herself; it was exactly what she wanted. But somehow, she'd thought she'd have a little more time to plan her strategy. A little more time to try and get rid of the nervous energy that built up inside her like steam in a kettle whenever she thought of being close to Mack.

She glanced over his shopping cart. "You're not anxious to get home and eat your Wheaties?"

"Nope." With one hand, he pushed away his shopping cart and let it roll. It landed next to a display of bird seed and Mack brushed his hands together, disavowing all knowledge of it. "I'm new in town and I'll tell you what, spending time with you sounds way better than spending time with a box of

Wheaties. Maybe you could suggest a good place for dinner? Your choice, Rosie. What do you say? Your favorite food, your favorite place. I'm in your hands."

There was no way he could have known it, but the comment fed right into the fantasies that had been playing around in her head since the moment she saw him step on stage for the first time.

The realization flashed through Rosie's consciousness with all the subtlety of a well-placed jab to the solar plexus. Her cheeks got hot and she tried to drown out the words she fought to keep buried in her subconscious every time she watched him rehearse and saw him whip off his pants: Big Mack.

No way, Rosie told herself.

No way it was the reason she accepted his offer. She wasn't that easily swayed by a handsome face and a great body and the memory of the way he moved around on stage like sin incarnate. She wasn't that shallow. She wasn't that horny.

She watched Mack head out of the store a couple steps ahead of her and her gaze automatically went to the nice, snug fit of his jeans over his butt.

Then again, she admitted to herself, maybe she was.

"It says no food or drink allowed." Just as she was about to step off the elevator, Rosie hesitated, her gaze on the sign right outside the door.

"No food or drink allowed?" At her side, Mack looked at the sign, then down at the bag of burgers and fries he held in one hand. "And we're going to let that stop us because . . ."

"Because it's what the sign says." It was as simple as that. At least to Rosie. Which didn't explain why Mack looked like he thought the whole thing was pretty funny.

Her jaw stiffened and her shoulders went back. She held on tighter to the cardboard tray she was carrying, where her iced tea and Mack's coffee cup sat side by side.

"I like to follow rules," she told him, and she recognized the echoes of the past in her voice. It was a line she'd used dozens of times while she was growing up. The line that explained to her parents why she insisted on a plaid-skirt, white-shirt, all-girls private high school instead of the progressive, open-classroom environment they thought would be just the place to free her spirit and expand her mind. The line that explained to them why she felt so comfortable with her job and the nice gray-suit life she'd made for herself.

With a lift of her chin, she dared Mack to try all the same arguments her family had used on her over the years, and before he could, she asked him the same question she was fond of asking them. "What's wrong with following rules?"

"What's wrong with breaking them?"

Rosie knew the answer to that one by heart. "If we all broke the rules . . ." The door was still open and the elevator buzzed, reminding its passengers to make up their minds. She hit the DOOR OPEN button just to show it who was really in charge. "If we all made our own rules," she said, "there would be chaos. People driving through red lights. People robbing banks. People—"

"Eating burgers and fries in a place they're not supposed to."

When he said it that way, it did sound pretty trifling.

Which didn't mean Rosie was about to give in. At least not easily.

When Mack realized it, he shook his head. It was a side of her he hadn't expected and with a half-smile that was tolerant even if it wasn't patient, he told her that while it wasn't exactly a problem, it would take some getting used to. "You don't take many chances, do you?"

Another echo from the past. Only this one was a replay of the statement that had come at her dozens of times from her parents over the years. Now, like then, she bristled. "Do you?"

"Every time I step on stage."

The elevator buzzed again and, again, Rosie hit the button. "That's different," she told him.

"Is it?"

"Sure. That has very little to do with chance. You never know how an audience will react, but if you're smart and if you're a professional, you've done all you can to make sure things go well. You've rehearsed. You've studied. You've trained. You depend on your talent and your experience, just like I do every day." There was no way he could know she wasn't talking about dancing anymore, but it really didn't matter. No one was more surprised than Rosie to realize there were a few things a federal agent actually had in common with a showgirl. And a stripper. "Performing isn't a chance, it's a calculated risk. And I'm all for taking calculated risks."

"Then let's calculate this risk." Mack glanced around the elevator. They were the only two people on board. "Nobody here to report us to the food police." He leaned over and looked around outside. "And not too many people out there, either. Which seems strange, but since it plays into my plan of eating dinner sometime in this lifetime, I'm not about to argue with it. Not much risk. And besides, if we turn around and go back downstairs, we're risking the money we paid to get up here in the first place. So, what do you say?"

He didn't give her a chance to say anything. Before she could, he stepped outside and took her double cheeseburger and fries with him.

Rosie had no choice but to follow.

Like every time she set foot on the observation deck of the replica Eiffel Tower that stood just about in the center of the Vegas Strip, Rosie's breath caught. It was just after dark and the view from more than three hundred feet above the ground was nothing less than spectacular. One look made her forget that her conservative propensities had been offended, affronted, and challenged by Mack's devil-may-care disregard for the right order of things. Except for a Japanese couple taking pictures out the south windows and an elderly couple using the high-powered lenses for a better look at the mountains to the east, the place was empty. She pretty much had her choice of windows, and she hurried over to her favorite, the one that overlooked the fountain show at the Bellagio.

"So, what do you think?" she called to Mack over her shoulder. "Can I pick a dinner spot or what? Isn't it gorgeous?"

Mack supposed she was talking about the view that spread out around them like a neon carpet. He supposed she meant the altitude and the perfect night and the stars he could see flickering above the mountains.

He wondered if she had any idea that she was more gorgeous than any of it.

He came up behind her, letting his gaze skim her fantasy-long legs and the short denim skirt that showed them off to best advantage. Against the backdrop of Vegas lights, Rosie's profile was no less marvelous than the scenery. Her breasts were lush and her hair was down around her shoulders. In this light, it looked as if it had been touched with fire.

At the same time Mack promised himself he was going to kiss her before the night was over, he twitched away the funny little feeling that crawled through him like ice water.

He knew the sensation was due at least in part to the time and the place and the crazy atmosphere of Vegas. The city sparked a certain wild energy that tingled through him like a shot of single-malt scotch. The neon made his blood buzz. The excitement made his heart beat faster. The sense of possibilities (both good and bad) was as heavy in the air as cheap perfume and the smell of a million gamblers' high-rolling dreams. More than anything else, it was the realization that the unexpected might be right around the corner that gave Las Vegas its punch.

Hell, he even recognized—and admitted—that part of

what he was feeling was plain, old-fashioned lust. An hour with Rosie and his libido had already kicked into overdrive.

It was harder to come to grips with the realization that he was also feeling as guilty as hell and hoping to dispel the notion. He reached into the bag he was carrying, gave Rosie her burger and one of the little cardboard boxes of fries, and accepted the coffee she passed to him.

He wasn't used to feeling guilty. Not about anything. All his life there were folks who had warned him it wasn't a good thing; that it could turn into a real problem. He'd heard it from teachers in high school on those few and far between days when he'd bothered to attend. He'd heard it from counselors when he'd been dragged kicking and screaming into therapy. He'd heard it from social workers and from a variety of priests, ministers, preachers, and do-gooders who'd shown up on the streets of El Paso to try and save his soul.

None of it made any difference. Early on he'd learned that guilt was as useless as longing for a family. Which was why he didn't feel guilty about taking Angela and Julie and Tiffany to dinner.

After all, that was business. And this?

Rosie took a bite of burger and grinned, enjoying every morsel.

This was one hundred percent pure pleasure.

Rosie grabbed three little bags of sugar and dumped them in her iced tea. "Bad for you," Mack told her, and though he was talking about the sugar, he knew he was giving himself a little reminder, too. Letting himself get too caught up in Rosie's smile, that could be as bad for him as the sugar was for her. Especially if he didn't remember where to draw the line.

"I know." Rosie gave the tea a quick stir and took a sip. She looked at him over the rim of her cup. "Refined sugar. The scourge of the universe. My mother—" She made a face and drowned the rest of her words behind another, larger swallow. "You don't really want to know."

"Actually, I do." Which surprised Mack more than he could say.

Rosie set her iced tea down and grabbed a couple of French fries. "My mother is a staunch crusader in the name of brown sugar, brown rice, and brown bread."

"And you like burgers and fries." Mack felt a smile tugging the corners of his mouth. "Who says you're not a rebel?"

He was teasing. Rosie knew that from the sudden knot in her throat and the way her stomach jumped around as if it were filled with butterflies. She knew it because of the heat that built inside her and seeped through her bloodstream like the smooth, heavy syrup her parents had once tapped from a stand of maples in Vermont.

If they were alone, the look he gave her and the sensations it sparked would have jolted her imagination into high gear. If they were someplace private, it would have been a clear invitation and she would have been more than happy to accept.

But they weren't. She didn't need to remind herself of that. They were nearly four hundred feet above Las Vegas, and at the same time she realized there was nothing she wanted more than for him to kiss her, a feeling very much like panic made her think about hopping the next elevator and getting out of there before her baser instincts could get the best of her good intentions.

Because she couldn't tell him any of it, she decided it was better—and safer—to rely on small talk. At least until her heartbeat throttled back and she came to her senses. "You like the view?" she asked.

He nodded. Which didn't make a lot of sense, considering he was looking at her and not out the window.

"I mean this view." Rosie grabbed his hand and tugged him closer to the window just vacated by the elderly couple.

"You asked to see my favorite place in town. Now you know why this is it. Over there are some of the big resorts. The Monte Carlo, the Luxor, Mandalay Bay." He didn't look where she was pointing. He looked at her. At her lips. At her eyes. At the way her breath caught and her breasts strained against her shirt.

Not about to give up, Rosie tried again. She took his hand and hauled him over to another window. "And from here you can see the mountains. And from here . . ." She dragged him back to where their burgers and fries were waiting. "From here you can watch the fountains. They're beautiful. Especially at night."

"You're beautiful."

Modesty demanded that she at least tell him he was crazy. She would have, too, if it didn't make her feel so good to hear it.

She took another bite of burger, and ketchup oozed out of the sandwich and dribbled down her chin. Before she could grab a paper napkin out of the bag, Mack got one for her. He skimmed his thumb across her chin and the thanks she knew she should have given him never had a chance to materialize. Not in the wake of the heat that shot through her.

"Tell me . . ." He unwrapped his own burger—no cheese, no pickles, extra mustard—and took a bite. "How did you become a showgirl?"

Rosie sighed and was instantly angry with herself for doing it. There was no use regretting the past. Especially when the things that happened had been out of her control. "I got too tall," she said, and though it wasn't the full story, it was at least part of it. "The whole time I was growing up, all I ever wanted to be was a ballerina. I got too tall."

He let his gaze skim from her toes to the top of her head. "You're nice tall."

"Most guys don't think so." Rosie rolled her eyes. "Most

guys are intimidated by a woman who can look them right in the eye."

"Good thing I'm not most guys."

"Good thing."

When he shuffled closer, Rosie set her burger down. He didn't need to look up at her the way some guys did. He didn't need to look down. The realization made her think of Goldilocks.

Not too tall.

Not too short.

Just right.

Rosie braced herself against the rush of good old-fashioned lust that made her knees feel as if they were melting in the desert heat. When Mack smiled again, closer and more warmly this time, she couldn't help but smile back.

"What makes a guy like you become a stripper?" she asked.

"You got too tall to be anything but a showgirl?" One corner of his mouth twitched. "Maybe I got too big to be anything but a stripper."

As much as she was hoping it was true, she groaned just to let him know it was a lousy joke. "Good thing it didn't affect your ego."

"Hey, half my blood is Mexican and I was raised in the two-fisted, he-man, hairy-chested culture of the Lone Star State. Ego has never been one of my problems."

"Which doesn't explain why you chose a profession that requires you to strip nearly naked six nights a week."

"Or maybe it does."

"So you're doing the women of the world a favor, is that what you're saying?" He was kidding. At least Rosie hoped he was kidding. "You're giving us the opportunity of a lifetime to—"

"Watch me strut my stuff. Yeah, something like that."

"And you learned this . . . where? I don't think there's a Stripper's Academy. Or maybe there is. In Texas."

"The truth?" Mack backed up a step and the dreamy, here-comes-trouble look that had sparked in his eyes and made an answering spark kindle deep down inside Rosie disappeared. He looked away. It was the first time she'd seen him look anything but cocky, comfortable, and in control, and it was that more than anything that made her more anxious than ever to hear the story.

When he looked back at her, his shoulders were stiff and his jaw was steady. As if he were just daring her to be shocked. "I got started stealing cars."

Rosie's eyebrows slid up. "Great experience for a stripper."

"Actually, it was. Great experience, that is. Taught me early that I couldn't afford to be nervous. Taught me to concentrate on what I was doing and not worry about what was happening around me. But that's not what I meant. I really did start out stealing cars. Then one day when I was hot-wiring an '86 Monte Carlo Aero, I got interrupted by a cop who had seen one too many smart-ass street kids get in trouble."

"He busted you."

"He took me home."

"The cop talked you into becoming a stripper?"

"He talked me into staying in school. I was young, I was full of myself, and I didn't have any qualms about ripping off my clothes in front of screaming women. Stripping made it possible for me to support myself."

One look at the solemn expression on his face was enough to tell her that it wasn't a story he shared with most people. Which only made her feel worse about goading him into doing it. She reached for his hand and gave it a squeeze. "That's remarkable. I mean, really. That really says something about your grit. About your determination. About your—"

"My love of having women ogle me?" Mack laughed. "Don't be too impressed, *chica*. It wasn't that big of a deal.

Stripping paid the bills. It still pays the bills. And it pays them nicely. So you see, I'm just as superficial as everyone else in this town. Out to make a quick, easy buck."

She didn't like to think about him that way. Rosie turned to the window and looked at the rainbow of colored lights below. "Except that nothing in this town is easy."

"Nothing?" He leaned over her shoulder and the stubble on his cheeks and chin scraped her neck and cheek. The roughness should have been irritating. Hell, it was irritating. Almost as irritating as the fact that Rosie's nerve endings sat up and begged for more.

"I was talking about it in a sort of cosmic way," she told him.

"Uh-huh." His hand skimmed her ribs and came to rest on the curve between her waist and her hips. With his other hand, he lifted her hair and kissed her neck. He trailed a series of kisses along her jaw.

Rosie leaned against him, her back to his chest. He was aroused, and just thinking that he wanted her kicked her desire up a notch. So did the fact that he skimmed a hand over her shirt and across her breasts.

"Mack!" As much as she wanted him to keep touching her, Rosie's sense of propriety was as strong as her sense of justice. She stood up straight and looked around. "There are people here."

"Nice try, Rosie." His words were a low rumble in her ear. "While we were talking, they left."

He was right. The Japanese tourists were gone. So were the old folks.

"Which means . . ." Mack pressed her back against him and rotated his hips. "It means we could just stand here all by ourselves and look at the scenery."

She knew exactly what he had in mind. "Oh, no." The laugh she managed didn't sound any more convincing than it felt. "We're practically out in public," she said. "You wouldn't—"

"I would." He slipped his hand under her shirt. He dipped it into her bra and stroked her nipple, and he didn't stop until he heard her breath catch.

"What do you say, *cariña*?" He leaned in close and tugged up one side of her skirt. "You don't think this is what happened with those other girls, do you? With Angela and Tiffany and—"

"Julie." The name barely made it past the moan of pure pleasure that rose from deep in her throat. "No way. No way they would have kept it a secret. No, if you did—"

The words were smothered in a rush of desire when he hooked a finger around the elastic band at the top of her French-cut panties.

"If you did . . . this . . ." She heard him unzip his jeans. Felt him move against her. "They would have been shouting it from the rooftops."

"You won't." Mack nibbled her earlobe. "You're not that kind of girl."

"I'm not this kind of girl, either." She was pretty sure it was true. At least it always had been before. Which didn't explain why her voice sounded faraway and breathless, even in her own ears. "I'm sensible."

"You're gorgeous." How he managed it so smoothly or so quickly, she wasn't exactly sure, but the next thing she knew, he was inside her. Rosie hauled in a long, shaky breath.

"We're taking a chance," she said, even though she knew they were long past the point of talking.

"It's not a chance." Mack pushed farther into her and she moved against him, riding to the rhythm that fired her blood and sent her gasping for breath and spinning out of control. "It's a calculated risk."

Rosie tensed and shuddered against him just as he did against her, and she knew he was right. It was a calculated risk, all right.

And she couldn't believe that she—of all people—was taking it.

6

It was so much like the live-for-the-moment, don't-worry-about-tomorrow viewpoint her family espoused, Rosie couldn't even think about it without feeling a little queasy.

Which didn't keep her from thinking about it.

Which only made her feel queasier.

What had happened the night before on the observation deck of the Eiffel Tower was completely out of character and in complete defiance of the orderly, conventional, predictable life she'd made for herself. Not to mention stupid, irresponsible, and reckless enough that it could have landed both of them in jail.

And she was damned if she'd risk her career or her old-school values—not to mention her sanity—by ever letting it happen again.

Outside the dressing room Mack shared with some of the guys from the chorus line, Rosie stopped and told herself to relax. There was no use panicking. What was done was done, and because she couldn't change anything, all she could do now was what she'd been so good at doing all her life: looking at a situation logically and rationally. Handling things calmly and sensibly. Getting over it. Getting on with it. Getting a grip.

Her mind was made up, even though her body was telling her that she was crazy.

She had to give her body credit. It knew all the right arguments.

There was the faster-than-a-speeding-bullet heartbeat argument. The can't-catch-a-breath argument. Even the most-incredible-orgasm-ever argument.

Luckily for her, her head wasn't listening to any of them.

Shoulders back and head high, she rapped on the door of the dressing room, to give the guys fair notice that she was there. When there was no answer, she pushed the door open and went inside.

Like the women's dressing rooms at the Swan, the men's was no great shakes. The room was long and narrow and probably hadn't been painted since the last time Sinatra played the Sands. On either side of the center aisle were eight makeup tables, complete with above-mirror lights and straight-backed chairs Rosie knew for a fact were as uncomfortable as they looked. At one end of the room was a set of lockers.

The place was empty.

"Doesn't it figure?" Rosie grumbled to herself. "All set with the what-a-mistake, never-want-to-make-it-again speech and no one to give it to."

Convinced that if she didn't do it there and then, she might never do it at all, she decided on a note. There was a pad of paper in her purse and she pulled it out along with a pen.

It wasn't an easy thing to put in writing, and rather than lay it on the line and risk sounding anything less than level-headed and thoughtful, she told Mack instead that she'd like to see him so they could talk.

Now the only thing she had to figure out was which locker to leave it in.

Though Emery Carpathian liked to pretend he was doing his employees a favor by providing them with lockers where they could keep their personal property while they were working, it was common knowledge that the combination locks were more for show than security. There was a trick to opening a Swan locker—any of the Swan's lockers. When she first heard about it from the other girls in the show, Rosie thought it might come in handy. But she'd never anticipated that she'd be using it for something like this.

She went over to the nearest locker and got to work. "Spin the dial once, twice," she told herself, and did just that. "Give the locker a punch . . . right . . . here!" She bumped her fist into the metal door, right above the handle. "And voilà!" Just like Angela and the others had promised, the lock opened without a hitch.

Rosie swung the locker door open. "Bingo!" For the first time since she'd come to her senses and realized what she and Mack had done four hundred feet above Las Vegas, she smiled. First try and she'd found the right locker.

There was a pair of tear-away jeans hanging from a hook inside, and she recognized them immediately. "Biker boy stripper." She did her best not to think about the slick moves of Mack's routine or about that black leather G-string that was the only thing he was wearing by the end of the number.

On another hook was the pair of black, skintight pants Mack was wearing the first time she'd met him, the day he stepped out of the heat of the Las Vegas back alley and into a million different fantasies that hadn't stopped since.

She refused to think about those, either.

Instead, she bent to prop her note where Mack was sure to see it, against the duffel bag that sat on the bottom floor of the locker.

When she did, she stopped cold.

There was a .38 Smith & Wesson Superchief Special in Mack's locker, and for a couple of seconds, the sight of the gun where she'd never thought to see one caught her by surprise.

"Lots of people carry guns," she told herself. "Hell, this is Nevada. Everyone has a gun. Everyone has—"

Something else caught Rosie's eye and she stooped down for a closer look. Beneath the gun and tucked under the duffel bag was a folded piece of paper. It never would have attracted her attention except that one corner of the paper was turned back and on it she saw a bit of a drawing. She couldn't tell exactly what it was, but it looked familiar and, curious, she slid the paper out of the locker and unfolded it.

"What the hell?" Stunned, Rosie stared at a schematic that was as familiar to her as her own face in the mirror.

It ought to be. For the last few months, she'd been seeing it in reports. And in meetings. Even in her dreams.

"9A-91."

The queasy feeling was back in spades. This time, for all different reasons.

Her hands trembling, she refolded the paper and put it back exactly where she found it. She grabbed her note so Mack wouldn't know she'd been there, closed the locker and headed for the door, her mind furiously working over the possibilities.

The way she figured it, there weren't many options, and no good reason for Mack to have a picture of a Russian assault rifle in his locker.

Which didn't mean there weren't plenty of bad ones.

Outside the dressing room door, Rosie steadied herself, one hand against the wall, and waited for her heart to stop beating so hard it felt as if it would pound its way right out of her chest.

As complicated as the whole thing seemed, she knew it really all boiled down to two things.

Who the hell the man she'd let make love to her the night before really was.

And what he knew about the guns.

If there was one thing Mack learned early, it was that emotions weren't just something that got in the way out on the streets, they were a one-way ticket to psychological annihilation.

Which made him wonder why he'd succumbed so quickly and so easily when his emotions got the better of him up there on the Eiffel Tower observation deck.

"Mistake, pal," he mumbled to himself. He walked around the stage, collecting the pieces of clothing he'd discarded during the last run-through of the construction worker stripper number. "*Muy grande* mistake."

A big mistake he was about to put right. As soon as he found Rosie and explained—

What?

Working the problem over in his head, he slapped on the pieces of his tear-away khakis and slipped on a sleeveless undershirt.

Rosie was terrific. Rosie was beautiful. She had a great sense of humor, a body that didn't quit, and enough brains to make her stand out from the other chorus girls he'd wined and dined.

And because she was terrific and beautiful and intelligent, and mostly because she was trusting enough to put herself in the hands of a guy who apparently wasn't bright enough to get out of the way of his own baser instincts, it wasn't fair to pull a love-her-and-leave-her number on her.

But whoever said life was fair?

The thought sat on his shoulders like the touch of cold fingers and, no matter how hard he tried, Mack couldn't twitch it away. He knew one thing for sure: just because the thrill of Las Vegas was hot in his veins, and the sun and the sin had caused the new Mack to take a hike and the old Mack to take his place, didn't mean he was willing to risk everything he'd worked so hard to achieve.

If he was as smart as Dom and Lenny and even the Enforcer thought he was, he wouldn't forget it.

"Did you see it?"

The voice right behind Mack surprised him and he spun around. He found Warren shuffling from foot to foot and looking worried.

"What's that, Warren?" Mack caught the towel Tatiana tossed to him and draped it around his neck. "What's the matter?"

"My toolbox." Warren scrubbed one finger under his nose. "Missing," he said.

It was on the tip of Mack's tongue to point out that he had more important things to worry about. One look at the misery that misted Warren's eyes and crumpled his expression and Mack didn't have the heart.

"Missing, huh?" He clapped a hand on Warren's shoulder. "If you wait until I'm dressed, I'll help you look for it."

"You will?" A smile like sunshine brightened Warren's face. "Julie, she wouldn't help me. She said I was stupid. She told me I just didn't remember where I left my toolbox. And that Angela . . ." Just to be sure no one was around, Warren glanced over his shoulder. "She called me a bad name."

"She did, huh?" Mack wasn't surprised. Of all the chorus girls, Angela seemed to be the one with the most clout and the least patience. "I promise not to yell or call you any names." It went without saying, but the assurance was exactly what Warren needed. "Just give me a couple minutes, OK? I've got to get over to my dressing room and—"

"If you help me, I'll tell you a secret." Warren's eyes lit with pleasure and a sly smile teased the corners of his mouth. "You're nice to me, so I'll tell you that girl is here again."

"Girl?" Warren changed subjects as fast as the gamblers around town went from winning to losing. It took a second for Mack to collect his thoughts and change course along with him. "What girl are we talking about?"

"That one." Warren glanced toward the back of the theater, and Mack looked that way, too. "That's her. That's the girl."

The woman standing in the shadows at the back of theater looked vaguely familiar.

Long brown hair.

Hair that wasn't nearly as spectacular as Rosie's.

Short, short skirt.

A skirt that showed off legs that were bony and not nearly as shapely as Rosie's.

Flat chest and no curves to speak of.

A shape that wasn't nearly as luscious as Rosie's.

Mack dashed the thoughts and those damned unruly emotions that threatened to topple all the promises he'd just made to himself. He got himself back on track and, not in the mood to be bothered, he almost told Warren that he really didn't care.

Almost.

He squinted past the stage lights for another look at the woman and something in his brain clicked.

"It's the woman from the alley."

"No, Mack." Warren made sure he emphasized his point by shaking his head vigorously. "She's not in the alley. She's right there." Warren pointed straight at her, and if Mack wasn't suspicious of the woman before, he would have been then. When she realized they were watching her, the woman turned on her heels and headed out of the doors of the theater and into the lobby at something close to a run.

There was no use going after her; Mack wasn't wearing any shoes, and besides, he knew how congested the casino downstairs could get. By the time he was off stage and out the door, she'd be long gone.

He glanced at Warren who, though he saw the brown-haired woman hightail it out of the theater, had no idea of the significance. "Who is she?" Mack asked.

"The girl. The girl I was thinking about. You remember,

Mack." Mack headed over to retrieve his shoes, but before he could, Warren had already picked them up. He handed them to Mack. "You think I don't remember, but I do. When you first came here. You asked me if anyone ever came around looking for Gus."

"Of course." Mack knew he was off his game and he didn't have one ounce of doubt why. If his head wasn't so full of Rosie, it would have been on his work where it belonged. "Gus Friel. Sure. The guy who got whacked."

"He didn't get whacked, Mack. He got killed."

"I'm sorry, Warren. You're right. That woman . . ." Though he knew she was long gone, Mack scanned the back of the theater again anyway. "That woman came here looking for Gus?"

"That's right." Warren followed along after Mack, through the back hallway. "Once before. She came here. Only I didn't remember. I'm not going to get in trouble, am I, Mack? I'm not going to get in trouble because I didn't remember, am I?"

Mack gave Warren a smile and hoped it didn't look nearly as distracted as he was feeling. His mind racing a million miles an hour, he tried to make sense of everything Warren had said. "Of course not. You remembered now, didn't you? That's what counts."

Warren smiled and nodded. "When I saw her, I remembered. She was here once before. And she told me she was Gus's sister and I thought maybe . . . I thought maybe she was going to ask me to give the toolbox back, only she didn't. And now I can't find my toolbox and I thought maybe she took it, but she says she doesn't know what I'm talking about. She didn't ask about Gus, because Gus is dead. And she didn't ask about my toolbox. This time the girl asked for Rosie."

"Rosie?" Mack scraped a hand through his hair. As if that would help make some sense of Warren's disjointed conversation. "But that would mean—"

Just thinking what he was thinking made him feel as if he'd been hit in the head with a two-by-four, and he sucked in an unsteady breath. "That might mean that Rosie had something to do with—"

"Rosie. I like Rosie." Warren grinned. "She doesn't yell like the other girls. And she likes my salad. Do you like salad, Mack?"

"I love salad," Mack answered automatically. Already his brain was filled with likely scenarios. And he wasn't liking any one of them.

"That woman . . ." Though they were far from the stage by now, Mack looked back that way anyway. "The woman you pointed out, you're sure she was here today asking for Rosie?"

"Her name is Neeta. Neeta said she had to talk to Rosie. Said she needed to tell Rosie something important."

"Which makes me wonder what that something is." At the door of his dressing room, Mack stopped and gave Warren a smile he hoped was friendly enough to convince Warren to do exactly what he asked. "Do me a favor, will you, Warren? Don't tell Rosie any of this."

"Don't tell Rosie?" The concept seemed a little tough for Warren to understand. He got it, finally, and a smile broke over his face. "You're being sneaky, Mack." He wagged a finger in Mack's direction right before he laughed and headed down the hallway. "You want to surprise her!"

"Surprise her? Oh, yeah." Mack wiped the smile off his face and headed into the dressing room.

Surprising her was the least he could do for Rosie.

Because paybacks were a bitch.

And something told Mack that Rosie had already surprised him.

"You're looking a little green around the guts." Her eyes on Rosie, Angela Andrews stripped off her T-shirt and jeans and reached into the locker next to her dressing table for a black leotard. "Something happening with you?"

"It's gills. Green around the gills. And nothing's happening with me." Rosie glanced at herself in the mirror above her own dressing table. Angela was right. She looked as if she'd been hit upside the head and she told herself to get her act together. Before anyone else noticed. "Nothing new, anyway."

"Except that you had dinner with Mack last night."

Rosie spun around just in time to see a satisfied little smile come and go over Angela's face. "It wasn't exactly dinner," she told Angela. "It was burgers and fries. And how did you know about that, anyway?"

"Word travels fast here at the Swan." Angela allowed herself a full-fledged grin. "Did you have fun?"

"We didn't—" Rosie stopped herself before she started into an explanation that was sure to sound lame. She wouldn't exactly call what had happened the night before *fun*. Almost the second it was over, she knew that *reckless*, *mistake*, and *crazy* would better describe what had happened than *fun*. And now that she knew that there was more to Mack than she ever imagined, she was thinking that *dangerous* might be a real possibility, too.

None of which she was about to share with Angela.

She propped one foot up on the chair in front of her dressing table to unlace her sneakers. "What do you know about him?" she asked Angela.

"Know? About Mack?" Even for rehearsal, Angela refused to go on stage without makeup. She leaned closer to the mirror and applied a wide swathe of liner to her eyelids, then grabbed a tube of mahogany-colored lipstick. "I know he's hot."

"How hot?"

"Jealous?" Lipstick in hand, Angela spun around and leaned against her own table. "You know I went out with him the other night."

"I know." There was no use denying it. Everyone was talking about Mack's no-holds-barred dating habits. Just as they were, no doubt, already discussing the fact that Rosie was the latest conquest on his hit list.

Rosie kicked off her sneakers and shoved them into a metal locker exactly like the one in Mack's dressing room. *Hit list* wasn't something she wanted to think about. Not in light of the things she'd found in Mack's locker. Because she refused to let Angela think her interest was anything more than the curiosity of an in-lust woman, she shrugged. "I just wondered—"

"He was a perfect gentleman." Angela turned back to the mirror and made a face at herself. "Unfortunately." She tossed down her lipstick and ran a brush through hair that was almost as dark as Mack's and long enough that it touched her butt. "All we did was talk," she said. "You, too?"

"Talk? Sure." Rosie knew her expression would give her away, so she made sure she didn't look at Angela. "We talked about burgers and fries and . . . What did you talk about?"

Angela shrugged. "About the Swan. About what it's like to work here. About who he should watch out for and who he can trust. I warned him that Carpathian could be a picky little son of a bitch. I told him about Greg and what a weasely stage manager he is. I told him lots of stuff, but I guess that's only natural. Mack listens more than he talks. Now that I think about it, you don't talk about yourself much, either."

Angela paused as if she expected Rosie to do that now. But if that's what she was waiting for, she was disappointed. "He's gorgeous. He's available. He takes off his clothes at the drop of a hat. Why are you asking questions, Rosie? What isn't there to like about Mack? If he's interested, girl, don't look a gift horse in the face."

"Mouth," Rosie corrected her. "Gift horse in the mouth."

"Mouth. Face." Angela shrugged off the slipup. "What difference does it make when it's that mouth and that face?

Go with the flow, girlfriend. Lucky you, you'll have a chance to get up close and personal."

"I'm not planning on getting that personal." Rosie didn't bother to add that she already had. Way more personal than Angela could have imagined.

Angela shook her head. "Haven't you read the bulletin board today?"

Rosie had to admit she hadn't. Though each of the dancers was supposed to check the board every day for the latest about program notices, costume changes, or added rehearsals, she seldom did. Greg, the stage manager, had a habit of mixing his business messages with everything from off-color jokes to his own equivalent of a dating service. She simply wasn't interested and besides, if there was news to be had, she knew she'd hear it from one of the other dancers. Looked like a case in point.

"They want to see you in costume shop before you head out on stage for rehearsal," Angela explained. "Something about doing a number with Mack."

"Number?" The word fell dead against the knot that suddenly wedged in Rosie's throat. "What do you mean, *number*? Mack doesn't do numbers. He's not a dancer. He's a stripper."

"All I can tell you is what I saw on the board. You're supposed to get a costume fitting at three, which means"— Angela glanced at the clock on the wall and headed to the door—"you'd better get moving. Hey, look at the bright side. This will give you a chance to get to know him better."

"Maybe," Rosie answered automatically.

What Angela didn't know was that there was no *maybe* about it.

1

By the time Rosie was done in the costume shop and got out on stage, she was still trying to decide if spending more time with Mack was a gift from the gods.

Or one straight from the hottest fires of hell.

The way she figured it, she knew the answer. Or at least she ought to by now. Which didn't explain why, when Mack stepped onto the stage dressed like a cop, she felt a little winded.

Mack in crisp navy slacks, a long-sleeved navy shirt, a set of handcuffs hanging from his belt, and a badge pinned over his heart. . . .

She gulped down a little noise of surprise and dashed away the thoughts that threatened to smother her common sense.

Mack knew more than he should, she reminded herself.

She'd better not forget it.

Before Rosie had time to think about it, Tatiana walked out on stage and took over like a general in command of war-hardened troops.

"You," she said, pointing to Mack, then down at the stage near where she stood. "Here. You can pretend to be policeman? Out on street with cars. Only with the little hip . . ." She swiveled her hips in a passing imitation of the move Mack used in his strip act.

Like he was directing traffic, Mack did a couple of quick hand gestures and added a pelvis roll that would have done Elvis proud. "Like that?" he asked.

"Perfect." Tatiana grabbed Rosie by the arm. "Now you . . ." She looked at Rosie's new costume. The short-sleeved, floor-skimming white dress was just about the most elegant thing Rosie had ever seen. Which didn't explain why Tatiana's expression soured. "Where is veil?" she yelled. "There is supposed to be veil. Greg, where the hell is veil?"

As if she'd been waiting in the wings for the cue, Betty from the costume shop ran out on stage carrying a floor-length veil attached to a sparkling tiara. "Sorry." As if she'd run all the way from the costume shop, she dragged in a breath. She was winded. "I wasn't done with the beading. I—"

Never one for excuses or delays, Tatiana grabbed the veil and set it atop Rosie's head. "All right. Picture sparkling lights. Flowers. Bride is headed to church and needs to cross street. Here." She motioned to the stage at her feet. "Right at corner where police officer is directing traffic and . . ." She swiveled her hips.

Rosie ignored the swivel Mack gave in response and concentrated on getting through the basics. She knew that later, music and choreography would be added to the scene. For now, they'd go through the blocking once, maybe twice, before Tatiana demanded any more. Just as she was instructed, she walked across the stage and toward Mack.

"Policeman!" Tatiana turned toward Mack. "You see bride. And she is the most beautiful woman in the world. You are dumbstruck. You are enchanted."

"Like this?" Not surprisingly, Mack was a pretty good actor. He pretended to be waving a long line of traffic past him, then held up one hand, stopping the rest of it. He turned toward Rosie to wave her across, stopped dead, and stared at her.

The night before, Rosie had learned that it was just about impossible to ignore that look and the little tingle of antici- pation it started inside her, but that was then and this was now. After the no-nonsense lecture she'd given herself (not to mention all she'd seen in Mack's locker), hot looks and the hotter sensations that erupted because of them were the least of Rosie's worries.

"You're hamming it up just a little, don't you think?" she asked when she was close enough for Mack to hear.

"Oh, I don't know. You're looking mighty fine." He looked her up and down with a glint of lust in his eyes, but there was something else there, too, an emotion Rosie couldn't name.

If she didn't know better, she'd think it was suspicion.

Before she could work through the problem, Tatiana called out more directions. "Now, policeman, you are realiz- ing this is most beautiful woman you have ever seen and she's on her way to marry another man. And you—"

"I stop her." In one fluid movement, Mack moved to block Rosie's path. He faced her full-on, a smile playing around his mouth that didn't exactly go with the glitter of de- termination that suddenly sparked in his eyes.

"Perfect," Tatiana purred.

Not so perfect, Rosie decided. Unless perfect included more cockiness than it was good for any man to have and more secrets than she ever would have suspected from a stripper. She raised her chin and traded him look for look.

"This policeman, he gets in your way and you don't like it. You try to go around him . . ."

Rosie did just that.

". . . and he steps in your way again."

Mack followed Tatiana's instructions.

"You go left . . ."

Rosie did.

". . . and he moves to his right."

Mack angled himself in front of her.

"You go right."

Rosie moved just as she was told.

"And he goes left."

So did Mack.

"Around each other. Around and around," Tatiana called out, and Rosie and Mack circled, as wary as opponents in a Smack Down championship.

"So . . ." Moving as smoothly as a jungle cat, Mack gave her a long, careful look. "Do you know how to use it?"

Rosie gave him a sleek smile. "Thought I proved that last night."

"I'm not talking about that." His gaze flickered up from the plunging neckline of the gown to her face. "I'm talking about the .38 Ruger in your purse."

It took more willpower than Rosie knew she possessed not to rise to the bait. Back in San Francisco, she had been issued a .38 Ruger revolver, a gun that didn't scream federal agent like the .40 Sig she usually carried. She kept it in her purse. And her purse was on the floor in her locker. Which meant—

Apparently she wasn't the only one who knew the locker trick.

She reminded herself not to forget it.

"It's licensed," she told him.

"Seems a funny thing for a woman like you to be carrying."

"No funnier than you poking around in my locker while I'm getting a costume fitting. Which, by the way, I'm thinking is not very funny."

Which didn't explain why Mack was smiling.

Exasperated and tired of moving around and around to the incessant instructions tossed at them by Tatiana, Rosie raised her chin. "Who are you?" she asked.

"Mack." He stuck out his right hand, then just as quickly

pulled it back to his side. "But we've met, haven't we? More than met, if memory serves me right."

She refused to get distracted. Not by the smile. Not by the memories. Not by the raw sexuality that rose off Mack like heat from a fire.

Not again, anyway.

"Oh, yeah. That's right. Mack without a last name."

"Rosie without a driver's license."

Rosie stopped dead and propped her fists on her hips. "You looked in my wallet? You had the nerve to—"

"Just wondered whose locker it was. That's all." He gave her a look that might have been conciliatory. It was hard to tell with the stage lights reflecting in his eyes. "I wanted to leave a note for you. To tell you how much I enjoyed our . . . dinner . . . last night. And just so you know, I didn't pick the lock, your locker was open when I got there. Had to make sure it was the right one. Seemed like a driver's license was the easiest thing to look for. You don't have one. But you do have your Swan employee ID card in your purse."

It was a turned-on-its-head version of why she'd been looking through his locker earlier. Which should have made it a great story.

If she believed a word of it.

She figured a fair warning was in order.

"By the way . . . the Ruger . . ." She started up again when Tatiana told her to. "I do know how to use it. And I'm a damned good shot."

A shiver snaked over Mack's shoulders. "A woman with a gun . . . That's a pretty big turn-on to some guys."

"Good thing you're not just some guy."

"Glad you noticed."

"If you were smart, too—"

"This is perfect." Tatiana stepped between them, cutting off Rosie's comment. "All the while, bride is dancing. And policeman . . . you just move like you always move."

Mack locked his fingers together, put his hands over his head, and did a slow grind.

"Perfect," Tatiana cooed. "Perfect."

It was obvious the last thing she was thinking about was the blocking, and Rosie let her know it. She grumbled her annoyance.

"That is perfect, too," Tatiana said. "That is exactly reaction bride should have. You are angry. You are anxious to get to church. Policeman"—she pointed at Mack—"you grab her."

"You wouldn't dare." The words were out of Rosie's mouth before she even realized it. For a second, they were enough to stop Mack in his tracks. As if she thought it was part of the act, Tatiana applauded. Mack knew better. No doubt he saw the flash of anger in Rosie's eyes. Too bad it wasn't enough to stop him.

He clamped one hand down on Rosie's arm.

"Yes. Yes." Tatiana nodded. "And you, bride . . . you pull away."

"You don't have to tell me twice." Rosie yanked her arm out of Mack's grip.

"And you—" Tatiana began.

She never had a chance to finish. As if he'd been doing it all his life, Mack moved like greased lightning. He reached around to the back of his belt and unhooked his handcuffs. There was a flash of let's-see-you-top-this-one exasperation in his eyes when he clamped one of the cuffs on Rosie's left wrist.

"Perfect! Perfect!" Tatiana shouted. "Now you pull at policeman."

Rosie did.

"And policeman—"

As if Mack needed to be egged on. Rather than risk the chance of Rosie pulling out of his grasp, he slapped the other handcuff over his right wrist and held up his hand, bringing hers up with him, as if to show the world that he was in control.

"Yes!" Tatiana shouted.

"No." Rosie tugged at her arm. The uniform might have been nothing but a costume, but the cuffs were real.

She glared at Mack.

Mack glared back.

"Now, bride." Tatiana pointed. "Your one hand is free. Tug his sleeve."

"Sleeve?" Rosie didn't know what was happening. She didn't much care. At this point, all she wanted was to get this rehearsal over and get off stage. Using her free hand, she did as she was told, yanking at Mack's left sleeve.

It wasn't until she was standing there holding the bottom half of the sleeve that she realized what was going on.

And by then, it was too late.

Mack was already giving her a look that told her he had the upper hand and he wasn't going to let her forget it. Tatiana was already yelling at her to tug the other sleeve off, too. Angela and some of the other girls were already calling out their encouragement and reminding Rosie that if she didn't want to do the honors, they'd be only too thrilled to take her place.

"Get these things off!" Rosie jangled the handcuffs. The only thing she got for her efforts was a sore wrist.

Mack didn't wither under the look she shot his way. "Can't," he said matter-of-factly. "Part of the act."

"There is no act," she said, and the tone of her voice brought an instant hush to her audience. She glared at Mack and at Tatiana and at Angela. "There is no way in hell I'm going to be part of an act that involves taking off anyone's clothes."

"It's all in good fun," Angela called out.

"And it is not vulgar," Tatiana added. "You are not going to take *all* the boy's clothes off. Though I have to admit . . ."

Good thing whatever she was going to admit disappeared on the end of a long sigh.

Rosie looked at Mack in wonder. "You'd let this happen?" Her words were tight against the ball of outrage that blocked her breathing. "You'd actually come out on stage in front of an audience and let a woman you don't know—"

"Not true. We do know each other. Pretty well, as I recall."

A pertinent fact Rosie didn't need to be reminded of. When Tatiana clapped her hands to get things going again, Rosie stood her ground.

"No," she said. She didn't bother with Angela or Tatiana. She didn't spare a look for Greg who was having a full-fledged hissy fit at the front of the stage. She squared her shoulders, set her chin, and looked Mack in the eye. "No," she said again, just so there was no mistake about it. "I'm not going to do this."

"Don't worry, I won't let you take all my clothes off." Mack's eyebrows rose and a smile like lightning flashed through his eyes. "Unless you want to."

She didn't need to be reminded of what she'd done the night before. Her conscience prickled like the strange, not-known-to-modern-medicine rash she'd gotten the summer her parents took her hiking through the Andes in search of an endangered species of condor. Her conscience nudged her professionalism. Her professionalism kicked her ethics in the butt. Her ethics reminded her that what she'd done with Mack had put her in far over her head.

She wasn't going to take the chance again.

Before anyone could stop her, she stomped off stage and, like it or not, Mack had no choice but to tag along.

"Rosie . . ."

She marched through the theater and out into the wide foyer.

"Rosie . . ." Mack tried again to get her attention, tugging her arm. "Rosie, you can stop now. I'm getting the picture. Something tells me you don't want to do the act."

"You think?" Her blood pressure ready to rocket through the roof, her breaths coming fast enough to make the tight bodice of the wedding gown squeeze the life out of her, Rosie kept right on walking. Down the sprawling, curved stairway decorated with swans that led to the first floor. Right past the registration desk where this day, like every other day, there weren't nearly enough people checking in. Through the doors that led into the casino.

She had a vague impression of Mack stumbling along beside her, doing his best to keep up with each agitated step, trying hard to make his way around the small groups of gamblers congregated in front of the blackjack tables and the roulette wheels and the crap tables. When Rosie's arm jerked, she knew Mack had had enough, that he'd stopped cold. She didn't much care.

"I'm leaving. Right now." She glanced back and saw him trailing an arm's length behind, doing his best to hold her in place without causing too much of a scene. The little bit of chain between the two cuff bracelets was the only thing that kept his hand from touching hers. That, and the incredible annoyance that was building inside her like the lava in the phony volcano that exploded over on the Strip a couple times a day.

"Come hell or high water, I'm not doing it. I'm getting out of here." Just to prove her point, she yanked at the handcuffs, and Mack's arm along with them, and started walking again, this time toward the slot machines that beeped and rang and flashed and buzzed in row after endless row.

"Rosie!" Mack's left arm was free, and he hooked it around her waist and hauled her to a stop alongside a slot machine that promised fifty-to-one odds and a payout every day. How he managed it one-handed, she wasn't sure, but he turned her enough to pull her against him. He opened his mouth to speak, but he never had the chance.

Something whizzed through the air between them and *pinged* into the front of the slot machine on Rosie's right. The glass on the front of the machine cracked right down the middle.

There was nothing like getting shot to clear a person's head.

In the heartbeat it took for both of them to realize what was going on, Mack watched the anger evaporate from Rosie's expression. It was replaced with one moment of pure astonishment. The next second, awareness flooded through her. Just as it did through him. They both hit the floor at the same time.

"What the hell . . ." Rosie craned her neck to try and see where the shot came from.

"Are you *loco*?" Mack slid his arm from her waist and up to her shoulders, dragging her back into what little cover the slot machines afforded them. "Do you have any idea what that was?"

"Small caliber. Probably automatic. From the sound of it"—Rosie squirmed out of his grip and looked around again—"there's a silencer on the gun." She dropped back down to the floor beside Mack. "Sure wish I had my .38."

"You're not the only one who wishes you had your .38." Mack didn't bother to add that he wished he had his .38, too. Though he wasn't about to let Rosie try it again, he sat up and looked around. Aside from the fact that they were in danger, so were the rest of the folks in the casino. All it took was one stray bullet . . .

Mack looked toward the doors that led outside. "Think you can make it?" he asked Rosie.

"I know I can," she answered. "How about you?" And before either of them could change their minds, they got to their feet and took off running.

Outside, the afternoon heat hit like a physical force. They ran into the crowd of tourists that, day and night, seemed to be as much a part of Vegas as the cheesy shows, the neon signs, and the ungodly heat. When he spotted a large group of people across the street waiting to board a bus, Mack headed that way.

"Turnaround bus," he told Rosie, and before she could ask what it meant or what it had to do with them, he pushed his way to the front of the line.

He found two empty seats about halfway down the bus aisle and Rosie dropped into the aisle seat next to his.

"Smart." She hauled in breath after breath, and for the first time, Mack realized he was doing the same. They had barely slowed down since they left the casino, and he'd barely had time to think about anything but the fact that someone was trying to—

"Who wants to see you dead? Rosie, someone was taking shots at you. Someone was—"

"Me? What makes you think it was me?" With her right hand, Rosie whipped off the veil, rolled it into a ball, and stuffed it into the small space that separated the two of them. Not exactly adequate in the keeping-them-apart department, but with the veil there, no one could see the handcuffs.

She pulled in a long, calming breath and let it out slowly. "Maybe," she said, "they were after you."

It was possible.

Even before the thought had a chance to fully form, Mack dismissed it. He wasn't the one who knew Gus Friel's sister. Or the one who'd nearly gotten creamed by an SUV with attitude.

"I don't think so," he told her. "And just remember, if it wasn't for me back there—"

"If it wasn't for you . . ." The bus door *whooshed* closed and when the bus started into traffic, Rosie jerked back against her seat. "If it wasn't for you, none of this would have happened in the first place. You were the one who went along with that ridiculous excuse for an act."

"So now it's my fault?"

"Absolutely." She nodded, satisfied that it was as much of an answer as she would ever need.

And even though it wasn't, Mack didn't have a chance to argue. The bus turned a corner and Rosie popped out of her seat. "Come on," she said, heading for the door.

As if Mack had a choice.

Between the two of them, they managed to hold the veil around their hands as they jerked their way toward the front of bus.

"You can let us off here," Rosie told the driver when he stopped at a red light. "This will be fine."

The driver gave her a look over his shoulder, but he didn't say a word. The light changed and they started up again.

"I said—" Rosie began.

"I know what you said, lady." The driver kept his eyes on the road and his hands on the wheel, but there was no mistaking the fact that he wasn't about to take any lip. At least not from a passenger in a fluffy white wedding gown.

Mack figured he'd have better luck. "She's right," he said, infusing the words with the kind of can't-we-all-just-get-along tone he knew could defuse just about any tense situation. "You can just pull over and—"

"Ain't no pulling over. Ain't no stopping." How he managed it, Mack wasn't sure, but the bus driver aimed a glare at the two of them at the same time he gave a less-than-polite hand gesture to a guy in a minivan who cut them off. "At least not until we get to Fresno."

"We can't go to Fresno," Mack told the driver. "You'll have to stop. We'll just—"

"Look, pal, rules is rules." The bus sped toward the interstate. "I've got to report to my boss. And if that son of a bitch hears that I let anyone off this bus, he'll be all over me like flies at a picnic. This ain't much, but it's my job, you know?

And I'm not losing my job over some two-bit jockey playing cop with his girlfriend." He gave Mack a quick once-over before he touched a hand to the two-way radio that hung on a metal hook near his left hand. "You try anything while we're on the road and I'm calling the state police."

Mack honestly didn't understand why a guy who obviously didn't enjoy his job would care about losing it.

He did, however, understand about the state police.

"Come on," he said, giving Rosie's hand a tug. "We'd better sit down."

She didn't look any happier, but she didn't argue. She made a move, then realized she had to wait for him to go first or risk having her wrist broken. They ended up turning around pretty much at the same time.

And found the entire busload of people staring at them.

There were old people standing in the aisles for a better look, old people half out of their seats, craning their necks. There were old people leaning forward, as if they didn't want to miss a moment of the excitement, old people grinning from ear to ear and poking their seat partners.

As if there were any doubt what all the staring was about, the lady in the seat closest to them jumped to her feet and pointed to them with a flourish.

"Look," she called out, loud enough for everyone on the bus to hear. "Newlyweds!"

8

An old lady leaned over and congratulated Rosie. The man nearest to Mack clapped him on the back. The good wishes were repeated as they sidestepped their way down the aisle and toward their seat, jolting and swaying with the movement of the bus.

It was an amazing show of affection—even if it was not only misplaced but also misbegotten, misdirected, and just plain mistaken—and Mack did his best to pretend he was enjoying it. At least if he were busy accepting wishes for a long and happy life with Rosie, he didn't have to think that he was heading for a long and probably not-so-happy road trip with Rosie.

Then again, a long road trip might give him a chance to find out a little more about what was going on behind that beautiful face.

Before the thought had a chance to fully materialize, the guy three seats up from Mack and Rosie's seat got to his feet, signaled the crowd for silence, and raised his bottle of Rolling Rock.

"This calls for a toast," he yelled, and the other passengers hooted their approval. All around them, brown paper bags crinkled open. Someone shoved a can of Bud Light into Rosie's right hand and someone else handed Mack one of those tiny airplane bottles of vodka.

"Here's to the bride and groom," the Rolling Rock man called, and, as if the movement had been choreographed by Tatiana herself, every person on the bus raised a can or a bottle or a coffee cup in a toast.

Automatically, Rosie reached to pop the top on her beer can.

And her bridal veil fluttered to the floor.

It took a second for Mack to realize that everyone was suddenly deathly quiet. Every eye on the bus—including, he suspected, the driver's—was on the handcuffs. At his side, Rosie was as red as a beet and as breathless as she had been after they made love. A collective gasp escaped the crowd and a couple of hoots of approval went up along with a smattering of applause. In the midst of it all, Mack managed a knock-'em-dead smile. He held up his right hand for silence and muttered a curse in Spanish.

"It's not what you think," Mack told them. "It's a religious sort of thing."

"And how!" a lady nearby called out.

Mack slid Rosie a look that told her to just be quiet and go along with the story. "That's not exactly the kind of religious experience I was talking about," he said. "It's a symbol." He raised his hand higher, and hers along with it. "It's a symbol of our commitment to each other. When we exchanged our wedding vows, we promised not to take the handcuffs off right away. Just to show how much we love each other."

There was a murmur of consent all around and another burst of applause, and when it died down, Mack started toward their seat.

"This love thing is hell on my wrist," Rosie muttered through clenched teeth.

Mack beamed a smile over his shoulder at her, but behind it, his jaw was tight and his teeth were gritted. "It's not doing a lot for mine, either," he admitted. He slid into the seat first and Rosie dropped into the one next to his. She shot him a look.

"I think we've pretty much proven our commitment to each other," she told him. "Time to get the key, Dick Tracy, and get these things off."

"An excellent idea." Mack's smile was brittle around the edges. "Except that the handcuffs weren't really supposed to be part of the act." Even if he did have to admit the truth, he wasn't about to admit that back at the theater, his temper had gotten the best of his better judgment. "I don't have a key."

"You don't have—"

It was probably a good thing that at that moment, the two people sitting in front of them decided to stand up and peer over the backs of their seats at Mack and Rosie.

"Aren't they the cutest things, Sid? Remember when we were first married?"

"Who could forget!" Sid wrapped an arm around his wife's shoulders and pulled her close. "We're still as happy now as we were then. I don't know, Gloria. . . ." Sid shook his head but there was a smile puckered around his mouth. The overhead lights gleamed off his bald head. "These kids don't look like they're having a very good time. Not like we did on our wedding day."

Gloria wasn't taller than five feet, and almost as big around. She twinkled like a beauty pageant contestant. "Oh, Sid, that's because they're not alone. They haven't gotten to all the really interesting parts yet."

"I don't know. . . ." Sid's gaze strayed down to the hand-cuffs, and, automatically, Rosie burrowed her hand beneath the folds of her gown. When she realized Mack's hand was along for the ride, she yanked it out, hauled down the arm-rest in the middle of the two seats, and plopped both their hands on it.

"I think these kids know exactly what's in store." Sid gave Mack a wink. "Go get her, tiger."

"Now, Sid . . ." With a grandmother's benevolent smile, Gloria leaned forward, and in spite of the fact that Mack reminded himself that he was supposed to be playing along with the role of newlywed, he wondered what Sid and Gloria would have said if they knew the groom was more comfortable packing heat than being on the receiving end of their good wishes.

He pulled himself out of the thought just in time to see Sid nodding at whatever it was his wife had said. "You're absolutely right." While Sid reached for Rosie's free hand, Gloria grabbed onto Mack's. Together, they tugged them to their feet.

"Traditions, people!" Sid had to raise his voice to be heard above the noise. When that didn't work, he reached across his wife and rapped his knuckles against the window frame. It worked like a charm and once it was quiet, he started again. "Toasts are fine, but we can't let these kids start off on the wrong foot. Go ahead, young fella." Sid made a sweeping motion toward Mack at the same time he pulled Gloria close to his side so everyone around them was sure to have a good view of the action. "You've got to kiss the bride!"

Give Rosie a bad guy with a Magnum and an itchy trigger finger and she knew for a fact that she could take care of him. Give her a nutcase with a pound of explosives strapped to his chest and she was pretty sure she could talk him out of whatever crazy plan he happened to have, or at least get in close enough to incapacitate the guy before he did any damage.

Give her Mack standing close, with the kind of body language that just screamed *go ahead and make my day*, and she couldn't catch her breath.

Definitely not something the federal government had ever prepared her for.

Rosie swallowed hard and pulled back her shoulders. "This isn't a good idea," she said in a voice only Mack could hear.

"You thought it was a good idea last night."

"Last night . . ." She glanced away. This wasn't the time or the place to tell him that she wasn't really the sex-charged she-devil he knew from the night before. Rather than try, she swallowed a breath for courage. "A little peck ought to be enough to keep them happy."

"Think so?" He didn't sound any happier about it than she did, but that didn't stop him from tugging her close.

Rosie narrowed her eyes and gave him the look that had had been known to send fear into the hearts of bad guys from San Francisco to New York. "You wouldn't dare," she shot back. "Not here."

It was the wrong thing to say to a guy who stood up in front of a crowd of screaming women and took his clothes off for a living.

Because Mack didn't need to remind her, he kissed her instead. It started out pretty much like the peck she was hoping for and for a second, Rosie relaxed. So far so good. She could handle the warmth of his lips, just like she could handle the slight pressure of his mouth against hers. Maybe not easily, and maybe not for long. Definitely not if she allowed herself to think about burgers and fries and the Eiffel Tower. But for now, Rosie had everything under control.

She should have known that the same guy who was crazy enough to rip off his clothes and toss away his discretion wouldn't stop with something as humdrum as a peck. He would milk the situation for its full theatrical potential. And in this case, that theatrical potential was all about making their fellow passengers believe they were the hottest couple since Jennifer and Brad.

Good intentions or no good intentions, by the time Mack deepened the kiss, Rosie was completely defenseless. She tipped her head back and even above the murmur of appreciation she heard all around her, she heard something else. If she didn't know better, she would have said it was a moan that rose from deep in her own throat, one that was answered by a rumble from Mack.

She parted her lips and his tongue traced the outline of her mouth, and she didn't do anything to stop him. She couldn't.

Mack slid his hand up from her wrist to her elbow and from her elbow to her shoulder, and Rosie shivered at the touch. He moved a hairsbreadth nearer and in spite of the fact that the bridal gown was, like most theatrical costumes, built like a fortress to stand the test of time and the stress of repeated wear, she swore she could count the number of places their bodies touched. Each and every one of them was suddenly so hot that she was sure the little pearls and the tiny sequins that encrusted the gown were going to burn right through the fabric and brand her skin.

For just one terrifying, logic-defying second, she knew that if they weren't surrounded by a busload of old folks, there would have been a repeat performance of what happened up in the Eiffel Tower. The mind-numbing realization left her as breathless as his kiss.

Another round of applause went up. Thank goodness. It was the perfect opportunity for her to break off contact.

"That was wonderful, dear. So romantic!" On the other side of the high-backed seat in front of them, Gloria pressed both her hands to her heart and beamed at the happy couple, her expression as bright as the yellow sweatshirt she was wearing. "You two are just perfect for each other."

"Perfect." Rosie echoed the word and dropped into her seat fast, before anyone else could get any other ideas about wedding traditions and how they should be observed.

"For the happy couple." A woman leaned across the aisle and offered them each a paper cup of champagne, and for just a moment, Rosie was tempted to ask who the hell she was talking about.

Happy?

Happy sure didn't describe the way Mack looked, because now that the kiss had ended, he was looking both shaken and stirred.

Then again, it didn't describe the way Rosie was feeling, either.

Happy sure didn't fit with the way things were going, because as far as she could remember, *happy* was all before she met Mack. All before she'd let down her guard and let herself act like some kind of crazy, raised-by-hippies wild child who let her heart rule her head and her lust run rampant. All before she realized that great kisser or not, Mack just might be the key to her case.

Happy?

Rosie grumbled a word she shouldn't have used on a bus full of senior citizens.

She was feeling a lot of things, but *happy* sure wasn't one of them.

"Fresno!"

The sound of the bus driver's voice over the loudspeaker made Rosie jump. She hadn't realized she'd dozed off. She craned her neck and looked past where Mack was staring out the window, but there wasn't much to see this late at night.

"All set to start the honeymoon?" Gloria popped up from the seat in front of them and beamed them a smile that wasn't the least bit sleepy. "I suppose you have something wonderfully romantic planned." It wasn't exactly a question, but there was no doubt she was fishing for information.

When neither of them answered, Sid stood up and peered over the seat at them. Behind his thick glasses, his pale blue eyes honed in on Mack, and he looked as fierce as a federal judge. "You do have something romantic planned, don't you? You'd better, young fella. If you're lucky, you're going to spend the rest of your life with this beautiful girl.

And that means this is the only honeymoon you'll ever have. The only first night of the only honeymoon you'll ever have."

Lucky for them, at just that moment the bus stopped and the front door *whooshed* open. Neither Mack nor Rosie wasted any time. Rather than listen to any more lectures or risk any more advice on how to ensure their happily-ever-after, they hopped to their feet and headed for the door.

Once they were out in the parking lot, Rosie looked around. All around them, old people were hobbling off the bus and shuffling toward their cars. But other than the bus and those cars, it looked like they were in the middle of nowhere.

"We could call a cab," she suggested.

"Not in this neighborhood," Mack said, and she had to agree with him. If the hubcap outlet and the boarded-up store across the street meant anything, something told her they weren't exactly in the best part of town. Not the kind of place any cabdriver would want to collect a fare.

There was a pay phone hanging from the wall of the abandoned store and for a second, Rosie brightened. There had to be an ATF field office somewhere nearby. She'd make a phone call and explain the situation and some nice special agent whom she never met before, but who would be her best friend from that moment on, would come and get them and take them someplace where some other new best friend would get these handcuffs off her wrist and—

She glanced at Mack only inches away and her hopes plummeted right along with her mood.

There was nothing to say. Mack realized it, too. As if the handcuffs linked their minds as well as their bodies, they started walking, heading who-knew-where.

They never made it out of the parking lot. Before they got to the sidewalk, a car slowed down beside them and Sid rolled down his window.

"We finally figured it out," he said.

"You kids should be ashamed of yourselves," Gloria added, leaning across him.

"You should have just told us you didn't have the money for a hotel room. Come on." He leaned over the seat and opened the back door. "Get in. You're coming home with us."

It probably wasn't the best idea. Hell, it probably wasn't even a good one. But it was late, and Rosie's feet hurt, and she was cranky and achy and just plain disgusted with the way her investigation was going nowhere but places it should never have gone in the first place.

She slid into the car, dragging Mack in behind her. She didn't bother to look at him to see if he thought it was a good idea or not. The way she figured it, it didn't make a whole bunch of difference. Sleeping on the couch with Mack at Sid and Gloria's was a way better proposition than sleeping in some no-tell hotel with Mack.

Besides, Sid and Gloria were just a couple of nice old folks who were generous enough to open their homes and their hearts to two young strangers.

What could possibly go wrong?

Mack supposed that someday he'd laugh about the whole thing.

This wasn't the day.

He paused in the doorway of the bedroom Sid and Gloria insisted they use, and he had to give himself credit. At least he waited until the two old folks had disappeared down the hallway, their arms looped around each other's shoulders, before he allowed his mouth to drop open. "*¡Carajo!*"

"My thoughts exactly." Wide-eyed and disbelieving, Rosie stepped over the threshold and while Mack swung the door shut behind them, she inched her way toward the round bed that sat against the far wall of the room. It was covered with a sleek bedspread and enough plush pillows to make it look as if it came straight out of a whorehouse where the madam traded favors in return for bolts of cheap red velvet. The bordello motif was echoed in the gold headboard (complete with leering cherubs), the black-and-red-flock wallpaper, and the black marble hot tub that took up one entire corner of the room. Gloria had taken the time to light red candles all around the tub and a few more that floated on the musky-scented water. The candles and the single stained-glass lamp next to the bed that featured a bronze casting of a very voluptuous, very nude, and very naughty-looking lady were the only lights in the room.

There were three containers of what looked to be flavored massage oil on a table nearby, a bottle of low-priced champagne in a holder beside the tub, and a big wicker basket at the foot of the bed that was filled with things like feather boas, an assortment of scented cocoa butters, and a board game that, if Mack's eyes weren't playing tricks on him, was called Around the World in Bed.

All of which was reflected in the room's mirrored ceiling.

Rosie dropped her head into her hands—or at least into one hand—and Mack saw a shiver skitter across her shoulders. "I don't know whether I should laugh or cry," she said.

"Something tells me laughing and crying isn't exactly what Sid and Gloria are going for here." Looking around, Mack gave a long, low whistle. "I haven't seen anything like this since the time I was in Juarez and—" Catching sight of the disgusted look that dashed across Rosie's face, he shrugged. "What? I was just saying that I was in Juarez once and there was this place called the Kitty Cat Club that—"

"Spare me the details." Rosie marched over to the hot tub with Mack in tow, and blew out the candles. Little by little, the darkness grew. Soon the side of the room where the water bubbled merrily in the tub was bathed in a twilight relieved only by what little light seeped from the stained-glass lamp.

The gathering darkness should have made the place more romantic. Or at least more interesting, in a tawdry, tasteless, and totally indecent sort of way. Instead, all it did was make Mack feel uncomfortable.

This was not the right time, he reminded himself. It was late and it had been a long day. A long day that had started with the discovery that Rosie just might know something about his guns. A day that had been capped off with him finding a loaded Ruger in Rosie's purse, not finding the driver's license he'd hoped would give him more information about her, and getting shot at.

And maybe because of the handcuffs—or maybe in spite of them—this was not the right place, either. Sid and Gloria's little love nest wasn't exactly his idea of the perfect place for a seduction. Sure it held a certain kick-in-the-pants erotic charm few guys would be able to resist. Sure there was something about Rosie's clipped, precise, very unconcerned movements that told him she was thinking exactly what he was thinking.

But there was also something about the nasty prickling in the pit of his own stomach. Something that reminded him that though he'd gone along with the game enough to kiss Rosie in front of a bus full of on-the-edge-of-their-seats seniors, he was not about to hop into bed with her.

No matter how much he wanted to.

Wrong time. Wrong place.

The words marched through Mack's head with all the refinement of a herd of marauding elephants.

Wrong woman.

And didn't it figure? For the first time in as long as he could remember, he'd found a woman he wouldn't mind kissing silly and she was so far off-limits, he didn't even want to think about what might happen if he made love to her again.

If Rosie was the one he'd been sent to Las Vegas to find . . .

Mack banished the thought with a twitch of his shoulders that traveled down his arm and made the handcuffs rattle.

"Aw, come on, Rosie." Because he couldn't let her know what he was really thinking, he gave her a lecherous smile instead. "Are you telling me you don't think this is romantic?"

"Romantic?" Rosie glanced around and her lips thinned. "Reminds me of a truck stop I was at once outside Stockton. There was this truck driver, you see, and—"

As if she just realized what she was saying, her cheeks shot through with a color as dusky as the red in the stained-glass lamp. In spite of himself—and the advice he knew he should follow about not getting involved, and not getting too interested, and not getting into a place he knew he'd never be able to get out of—Mack couldn't help but want to know more.

"Stockton, huh?" His eyebrows did a slow climb along with his runaway imagination. "Or should I say . . . truck driver, huh? Because obviously, the fact that there was a truck driver involved is way more interesting than the fact that there was a truck stop."

"The truck driver was a ham-handed, big-bellied, beer-guzzling goofball who happened to have the inside of his cab done up in red velvet. Not a pretty combination, so don't get any ideas that it was any more interesting than that. And my brief and not very happy relationship with him? That was strictly business."

Now Mack wasn't just interested; he was downright curious. "What kind of business does a showgirl have with a truck driver from Stockton?"

Rosie's shoulders went back a fraction of an inch. Her chin came up. "I didn't say the truck driver was from Stockton," she reminded him. "I said—"

"Yeah, yeah. You said you met him at a truck stop in Stockton."

"I didn't say that, either. I said there was a truck stop outside Stockton. And I said there was a truck driver. And oh, by the way, did I mention the part about how I shouldn't have mentioned it in the first place and how it doesn't matter anyway so why don't we just change the subject?"

"Subtle but effective." Mack grinned. There wasn't much else he could do. Rosie was delicious when she was being assertive. He wondered if she knew that. He also wondered why he was torturing himself thinking about it.

Rather than try and work through the problem that was better left alone, he turned and surveyed the room. "At least it's clean."

Rosie was close enough that her sigh ruffled the air between them. "Look . . ." She turned to face him. "This is probably as good a time as any to tell you this. About last night—"

"You're thinking it was a mistake." Funny, Mack was thinking the same thing. Which didn't explain why, when he put it into words, it made his insides feel so empty. "You're sorry we—"

"Not sorry. Not exactly. It's just that . . ." Whatever she was going to say, she seemed to think better of it. "I'm exhausted. And these handcuffs feel as if they weigh about a thousand pounds. I'm tired and I'm cranky and I'd just like to get some sleep. Sleep. That's all."

"Fine." The word came out a little too forced. As if in addition to convincing her, he had to talk himself into it. "We're both adults, Rosie. Sensible adults. And this sensible adult is just about wiped out. I'm looking to sleep, too. Just because we're sharing a bed doesn't mean—"

"Good. Fine." Rosie frowned. "It's just that this dress weighs a ton and—"

"Really?" Now that she mentioned it, Mack saw that the wedding gown wasn't a typical woman's dress. There was more weight to it, more substance. It didn't move naturally with Rosie's body. In fact, the dress didn't move much at all. It looked stiff, as if there were some kind of metal framing inside it. And considering it was meant to stand up to the punishing abuse of two shows a day, there just might be.

"Hell, Rosie, you must be dying in that thing. You should have said something sooner."

"And what? Taken it off on the bus? That's just what those old folks were waiting for!" She glanced around the room and shook her head in disgust. There was no sign of the kind of furniture usually found in a bedroom. No dressers. No chest of drawers. Not even a closet, which had apparently been removed to make room for the hot tub. "I'd love to take it off now. Don't Sid and Gloria know you're supposed to keep clothes in your bedroom?" Her jaw tensed and, even in the dim light, he could see she was resigning herself to the situation. It wouldn't be easy, but Rosie was tough. In spite of how well she kept secrets, Mack knew that much about her.

"I guess it doesn't matter anyway." Tough or not, she sounded exhausted. "I'd never get my left sleeve off over these handcuffs."

"Unless we ripped it." Rosie looked so shocked by the suggestion, he scrambled to justify himself. "I mean, just a little. Just the sleeve. Just so you could slip it over the cuffs."

The very idea rankled at Rosie's right-wing conscience. It offended her sense of justice. Destruction of property. Somebody else's property. Not exactly something she had ever endorsed.

Funny how much her notion of justice could change after more hours than she cared to remember in a dress so tight that she had to fight for every breath. Her breasts were squashed. Her waist was pinched. The gown was gorgeous, but it also weighed at least twenty pounds. By this time of the night, if felt more like two hundred.

Before she even realized she was doing it, Rosie's shoulders drooped with fatigue. "I'd really like to get out of this god-awful gown and get some sleep," she admitted.

"Then turn around." Mack motioned her to twirl so that he could get to the zipper at the back of the gown. "Come on. You want out . . . ." He beamed her a smile as bright as the tail of a comet. "I happen to be an expert at getting women out of their clothes."

It was something Rosie didn't want to think about. Because when she did, the very thought zipped through her like the kick that comes from a shot of Jack Daniel's. Zipping and unzipping, and Mack unzipping her out of what she should have stayed zipped into was something she couldn't afford to think about. Not if she was going to maintain any sense of integrity and avoid a repeat of the night before.

"Thanks for the offer but truth is, I don't have much on under here." She glanced down to where the top of her breasts showed above the low neckline of the gown. "I may be willing to sleep on the same bed with you, but I'm not willing to do it wearing nothing but a smile and a look of gratitude."

Mack barked out a laugh. "And that's supposed to talk me out of this?"

Was it?

Rosie could barely pull in her next breath, much less think clearly. Not with Mack only inches away in the warm half-darkness and the memory of the way he moved inside her still fresh enough to make her tingle.

"It's not that I don't want to." That much was true. Every inch of her body ached for his touch. Every beat that slammed her heart against her ribs reminded her how it felt when he pulled her back against him and inched up her skirt and . . .

Every scrap of self-control she had reminded her that doing it again was a sure invitation to disaster. At least until she knew what Mack did—and didn't—know about the Russian assault rifles.

"If I wasn't so tired." She gave an exaggerated yawn that she hoped wasn't too phony. "This dress is really dragging me down."

"I get the message." Maybe it was a trick of the light. Rosie could have sworn Mack looked a little more relieved than he did disappointed. "I'll tell you what, I'll help you get out of the dress. I'll rip it just enough to get it over the cuffs. And then—"

"And then?" Rosie didn't like to think about the *and then* part because when she thought about the *and then* part, her cheeks shot through with fire and her heart raced as fast as it ever did when she was trying to outrun her latest 5K times. She didn't want to think about the *and then* part because she was afraid when she did, Mack would realize that her breaths were coming just a little too fast and her voice was just a little too breathy and it was all she could do not to jump him right then and there. And then . . .

"And then . . ." Mack glanced toward the basket of sex toys at the foot of the bed. "Pink feather boa?" he suggested with a one-sided grin.

"Not exactly what I had in mind." Eager to keep herself from quivering at the suggestion, Rosie tried to cross her arms over her chest. Failing that, she tapped one foot against the plush, very red carpet.

Mack's expression brightened. "How about a policeman's shirt?" He glanced down at the navy shirt with the badge pinned over the heart and the American flag sewn on one sleeve. "It's one of my costumes. Which means it—"

"Falls apart at the slightest touch. Yeah, I remember that part."

"So if I get it off—"

"I can wear it." It sure beat spending the night in nothing but the purple French-cut panties she had on under the built-in bra dress. "Deal," Rosie agreed. "Where do we start?"

"*We* don't start anywhere." Mack looked down at the handcuffs. "I've only got one hand to work with, remember? And it's my left hand. And while I've got a whole bunch of talents you haven't even imagined yet, being left-handed isn't one of them. So *you* start. And you start by pulling off my clothes."

It wasn't the most outrageous offer Rosie had ever had. That had come from a six-foot-six, three-hundred-and-sixty-pound, back-to-nature whacko up near Merced who had a warped imagination and a grudge against a developer who was putting an upscale housing development a little too close to the wilderness for his liking. The way Rosie remembered it, that same whacko had a shitload of weaponry in his mountain cabin, and he was more than happy to show it to the woman he thought was nothing more than a waitress at the local greasy spoon. Once they got to know each other a little better, he made her an offer, too. Only his had to do with them teaming up to blow away not only the development but the developer.

Of course, that was before Rosie pulled out her Sig. Before he found out, much to his chagrin, that she was a federal agent.

That was the most outrageous offer she'd ever had.

This one was running a very close second.

Before the thought could upend her, or do to her insides what it was very close to doing, Rosie nodded and motioned Mack to stick out one arm. "You're right." She sounded calm. She sounded in control. If she could keep her hands from shaking, she might actually get through this with her pride intact. "It's a good idea and it sure beats trying to sleep in this sparkling suit of armor. I'll wear your shirt. Thank you for the offer."

She tugged at his right sleeve. No problem with the handcuffs; the two pieces of fabric fell off right around them.

She raised her eyes to find Mack staring at her. "Now you need to do the rest of the shirt." His voice was hushed against the heavy wallpaper and the red velvet pillows. His eyes were wide and in them, Rosie saw a reflection of her own slightly dazed look. He drew in a breath that shuddered through him and vibrated through Rosie's fingers. If she didn't know better, she would have said that he was just as nervous as she was. Just as unsure. Just as convinced that in a relationship that had been like a minefield from the start, they had to tread more carefully than ever. Or risk getting blown to smithereens.

"So far so good." She gave Mack a smile that probably looked as forced as it felt, and before she could talk herself out of it, she bunched a hand around the front of his shirt.

"Whoa! Wait a minute there!" Mack backed up a step and Rosie was left holding nothing but air. "What kind of guy do you think I am?"

For a second, she was too stunned to think it might be a rhetorical question. "You're a stripper. You strip. For a living. Remember? And if you can take off your clothes in a room full of howling women, I'm guessing you can take off your clothes just as easily for me."

"You're wrong."

Rosie's eyes must have been fooling her. She swore that, just for a second, the shimmer in Mack's eyes settled into something warmer. That, just for a second, the smart-alec smile that was apparently as much of his personality as the sex appeal, throttled down into something much more.

The next thing she knew, Mack was as smug as ever. "That's not what I was talking about," he said. He looked down at the line of navy buttons that marched down the center of his chest and disappeared where the shirt was tucked into the waistband of his blue slacks. "You can't just rip apart the rest of the shirt. Not until you unbutton it. It's designed that way. You know, to drag out the expectation. Titillate the audience."

She took a step back, away from the suggestion and the warm ripple of awareness it caused to fizz through her. "No audience. No expectations. No titillation. And since you're a big boy, I think you can handle your own buttons."

"I could, but . . ." He rattled the handcuffs. "It's tough one-handed. And tougher when the one hand you can't use is—"

"Oh, all right." Rosie sighed and stepped forward. Better to get it over with than to stand there and act as if just the sight of a half-naked Mack was enough to send her common sense out the window and her hormones into overdrive. Rosie undid the button at Mack's throat. A simple enough procedure with two hands, but with one, it required a little more finesse and time. When that one was taken care of, she moved to the one below. And the one below that.

As each button slipped from its hole, the shirt opened just a little more, and Rosie watched the mellow light caress Mack's bare chest. It spotlighted his Adam's apple, then slid down, touching his breastbone, stroking a body that looked as if it had been sculpted by an artist with a taste for the sublime and a penchant for temptation. It wasn't until she undid the fourth button that she realized Mack hadn't moved since she started. He hadn't said a word. Hell, she didn't think he was even breathing.

Rosie glanced up to find him looking a little like that back-to-nature whacko had looked when she whipped out her badge and told him he was under arrest. A little stunned. A lot tense. A little like there was too much happening for him to take all of it in at once.

And for once, she knew she had the upper hand.

The thought hit out of nowhere and Rosie knew she didn't have time to second-guess it. She wanted to get her case off dead center? Well, this was as good a time as any to start.

"So . . ." As lightly as if it were a mistake and not a well-thought-out plan, she brushed one finger over his bare chest. It was completely free of hair and as hard as granite. "You know a lot about guns, huh?"

If nothing else, the question started him breathing again. He glanced down at her, his look suddenly wary. "Guns? What are you talking about?"

"Guns. You know." Rosie grabbed onto the shirt and tugged it out of his pants. When she undid the button close to the very bottom, she made sure she leaned in to give him a good look at her breasts. "You didn't say *gun*. You didn't say *weapon*. You didn't even say *piece*. You said *Ruger*. You knew my gun was a Ruger. So . . ." There was one more button to take care of and she took her time, dragging out the expectation. "So the way I figure it, you must know something about guns."

He glanced down to where the silver badge pinned on his shirt touched the bare flesh exposed by the low neckline of her gown. "Double-action revolver. Five rounds. Stainless steel finish. I know a Ruger when I see it. Kind of a no-brainer."

"Like . . ." Rosie gave the shirt a little tug and was rewarded with the *rip-rip* sound of strips of Velcro separating. "A no-brainer like the fact that you knew someone was shooting at us down in the casino? It's not the first conclusion most folks would have made, but you . . ." She tugged again, just a little, and the shirt loosened a bit more. "You didn't look surprised."

"You didn't, either."

"It takes a lot to surprise me."

"Yeah." A smile broke through his expression. "I found that out up in the Eiffel Tower. Up there, you even surprised yourself. But down in the casino . . ." He looked her over as carefully as she was studying him. "You didn't look surprised and you didn't look scared."

She shrugged away the comment, as irritated with the way their relationship had gone from hotter-than-hell to dodging-and-feinting in record time as she was with the wayward urges that had a way of sneaking up and sidetracking her. Just so she wouldn't forget who she was and what she was supposed to be doing, she forced herself to keep up her questioning.

"What else do you know about guns?" This time, she gave the shirt a yank strong enough to make it come apart in three separate pieces. She gathered the fabric in one hand at the same time she gave Mack's chest a slow and careful look, then slid her gaze down even farther. "Bigger guns."

Mack knew better than to take the bait. He wasn't ready to commit himself. Not on unfamiliar territory. Not when he was handcuffed to a woman who was looking more and more like the person Dom had sent him to Las Vegas to find. And deal with.

He traded Rosie look for look, wondering what was going on behind the seduction that simmered in her eyes and the questions that sounded so innocent.

Lucky for him, though he didn't have an ounce of patience, he had plenty of staying power and enough stubbornness to make it possible for him to outlast just about anybody. No matter how long she looked, he refused to answer, and when she realized he never would, she gave up with a little grunt of annoyance and got to work on putting the pieces of Mack's shirt together.

Watching her toss the pieces of the shirt on the bed and run her fingers over the spots where Velcro met Velcro, he waited for the right moment to initiate a little foray of his own. When she was done with the body of the shirt and stepped back to admire her handiwork, he knew it was time to get started.

"OK, you've got your shirt. Now"—he motioned for her to turn around—"let's get you out of that dress."

Now that the moment had arrived, Rosie didn't look nearly as sure of herself as she had when she was stripping off Mack's clothes. She took a deep breath and held it in for a couple of seconds. She didn't let it out again for a long time and when she finally did, it seemed to come all the way from her toes.

"You always practice deep-breathing exercises at times like this?" he asked. "I thought that was just for stressful moments. You know, like getting a speeding ticket or having a baby."

"This qualifies as a stressful moment." She swallowed

hard and turned around and, though he suspected he wasn't supposed to see it, she squeezed her eyes shut.

Before he could talk himself out of it, Mack found the tiny white zipper tab among the pearls and sequins on Rosie's dress. Once he did, there was nothing to inching it down. He found himself staring at the long sweep of Rosie's bare back and just enough of a hint of her purple panties to send his heart pounding against his ribs with enough force to shatter them.

It took more willpower than he knew he possessed to force his mind back where it belonged.

"So . . ." Mack took hold of her left sleeve and gave it a yank that should have been powerful enough to rip it. He might have accomplished his mission except for the fact that when he tugged, the dress drooped over her shoulder. Too late, he realized the whole thing would have been easier if the dress was zipped. No time for second-guessing. And no way he was going to zip the dress. That would mean he'd have to unzip it again, and though Mack was good at a lot of things, being too wholesome for his own good wasn't one of them.

"Hold still," he advised her. "And grab onto the top of the dress. I need a little leverage."

She did as she was told and this time when Mack yanked the fabric, he was rewarded with the sound of ripping cloth.

He didn't let go of the pieces right away. "So . . ." He inched his way back to the matter at hand. Or at least the matter that should have been at hand if his hands weren't on Rosie's silky skin and his body wasn't on the verge of a full-scale meltdown. "You know a lot about guns, too."

She glanced at him over her shoulder. "What makes you think so?"

He shrugged as if it were no big deal. "You said it. Back at the casino. You said *small caliber*. You said *probably automatic*. You mentioned a silencer."

"I watch a lot of Court TV." She had the nerve to smile

before she glanced down to where he was holding the pieces of the ripped sleeve in his hands. "I think I can handle the rest of this myself," she told him. She reached for his shirt and she had it in her hands when she threw him another look. "Eyes closed," she said.

"Eyes—"

"Closed. I want your eyes closed."

"You've got to be kidding! We're both adults. And way past the stage of being shy with one another. You don't think I'm going to—"

"I sure as hell do."

"I didn't tell you to close your eyes when you took off my shirt."

"You could have."

"And you would have listened?"

"If you asked. I would have respected your privacy and your needs."

"Look, if we're talking about needs—"

"Not those kinds of needs."

"Right." Mack backed away, too, until the chain that linked the two cuffs was taut between them. Not that the distance helped a whole bunch. Something told him that even a chain of a couple miles wouldn't do that. It was enough to remind him that he was swimming in deep waters. And that if he wasn't careful, he'd be in over his head soon. "All right." He surrendered without a fight because he knew he didn't have a choice. "You want me to close my eyes, I'll close my eyes."

"Then do it."

"I am."

"If you are, you're doing it with your eyes open."

"Oh, yeah." He got a grip and closed his eyes, and when Rosie slipped the pearly dress over her shoulders and down her bare torso and to her waist, when she slid one sleeve over one hand and the ripped sleeve over the handcuffs, when she slithered the dress over her hips and stepped out of it and stood there in absolutely nothing at all but those damned purple panties and a glaze of light that brushed against breasts that were nothing short of astonishing, he kept his eyes closed.

Almost all the way.

9

"You have to admit . . ." Behind the wheel of his big-as-a-boat Buick, Sid adjusted the rearview mirror and glanced back at his passengers. He gave them the once-over, Mack in his navy police uniform trousers and the I LEFT MY HEART (AND WALLET) IN LAS VEGAS T-shirt he'd borrowed from Sid, and Rosie in the police shirt and the pair of too-wide, too-short pink sweatpants she'd gotten from Gloria. Sid smiled and sighed his contentment. "This is a whole bunch more comfortable than the bus."

"Comfortable." Rosie managed to choke out the word. Which wasn't as easy as it should have been, because while she was doing it, Sid changed lanes in front of an eighteen-wheeler, sped up to eighty-five to get around another truck, and ducked into the right lane in front of a third truck.

"And much more fun!" Apparently unconcerned by her husband's driving skills (or lack of them), Gloria turned and offered a bag of brightly wrapped hard candy. When both Mack and Rosie declined, she dug one out for Sid, unwrapped it, and reached across the front seat to pop it in his mouth. She unwrapped a red-and-white-striped mint for herself. "And a little more relaxing than the bus, too."

Comfortable was one thing. But as much as Rosie appreciated the fact that Sid and Gloria had offered them a ride back to Las Vegas, she wasn't about to call it relaxing.

She glanced to her left and found Mack looking way more calm than she felt. The road from Fresno back to Las Vegas was—thanks to the Sierra Nevada Mountains—anything but direct. While the shortest distance between the two points might have been a straight line, a straight line was nearly impossible to follow. Rather than try, Sid decided to follow the route the bus had taken in the opposite direction the night before. They were headed south to Bakersfield, then east and north back to Las Vegas.

It was, apparently, a popular route.

"There are an awful lot of trucks on this road." As if it were the most natural thing in the world to pass the time of day while they were breaking land speed records, Mack looked out the back window on the driver's side of the car. He didn't cringe like Rosie did when Sid took a bend in the road on two wheels. He didn't seem to mind the breakneck speed. When they cut into the right lane, sped past a semi, and then cut in front of the guy without so much as a flicked turn signal, Mack simply took a look at the truck and the brightly painted LETTUCE HEADS sign on its side, then turned around and settled down.

"Of course there are a lot of trucks." Gloria laughed, the sound as lighthearted as a girl's. "You know how they call Kansas and Nebraska the country's bread bowl? Well—"

"We're the salad bowl," Sid chimed in. "Lots of produce coming out of these parts. Headed all over the country."

"Plenty going right to Las Vegas, too, I think," Gloria added. "You know, for all those fancy restaurants." They zoomed by another truck that was puttering along in the right lane at a relatively conservative seventy, and Gloria cocked her arm and pumped her fist. The driver gave her a blast on his air horn and, giggling, Gloria sat back, satisfied.

"You know," she said, "Sid and I were married in Vegas. Of course, that was a long time ago, but . . ."

Rosie supposed in some corner of her mind, she was actually listening to Gloria's story. At least she was trying. But it seemed the longer Gloria talked (about what she wore and how Sid looked in the blue suit he had borrowed for the occasion and what the weather was like the day they were married), the faster Sid drove. They made Bakersfield in what she suspected was record (and completely illegal) time and got off at the exit that would take them east toward Nevada.

Every time she saw a truck on the road up ahead, Rosie's stomach bunched in anticipation. Just as she expected, Sid always gunned the motor. He never once failed to take an opening—no matter how small—to make his way around the truck.

And every time, Rosie's breath got wedged behind a ball of panic in her throat. And her hands got clammy. And her heartbeat sped up, nearly as fast as it had between the burgers and the fries and the careless abandon of making love to Mack.

It wasn't that Rosie was a chicken. There was no way she could do her job and do it well if she didn't have at least a splash of daring in her blood. But daring was one thing. And risky was something else. Rosie was known to take chances in her work, even if she hardly ever took them in her personal life. But she knew better than to rush in where angels feared to go. Not unless she could rush out again just as safely.

Which, now that she thought about it, was probably the reason Mack scared her even more than Sid's driving did. Then again, maybe it wasn't the speed she minded so much with Sid or with Mack. Maybe it was the sensation of being out of control.

As if on cue, Sid hit the accelerator to make his way around a tanker truck, and Rosie found herself automatically digging her nails into the strip of plush velvet upholstery that separated her left hand from Mack's right.

Maybe Mack had heard some silent signal. Or maybe he was just good at picking up the scared-silly-and-hoping-to-make-it-back-to-Las-Vegas-alive vibes Rosie was sending out like radio waves.

He didn't look at her and he didn't say a word. He simply covered her hand with his and held it. All the way back to Las Vegas.

"This is fine. You can let us out right over there." Mack leaned forward and pointed Sid to a street corner not far from his Las Vegas apartment building, and he hoped he didn't sound, or look, too eager. It wasn't that he didn't appreciate everything Sid and Gloria had done for them. (Even though what Sid and Gloria had wanted to do for them wasn't anything Mack wanted. Or at least nothing he wanted to want.) But he suspected that the longer they stayed with the two old folks with the hearts of gold and the staying power of two seasoned and serious partiers, the harder it would be to get away from them.

After hours in the car, he was getting antsy. And maybe not just because of Sid's less-than-stellar driving. Or Gloria's nonstop stories.

There was only so long any man could sit in close proximity to Rosie in the sweatpants she'd borrowed from Gloria, the shirt she'd literally taken right off Mack's back, and her white satin pumps. The look would definitely not start a trend, but there was something about it that tugged at his heart as well as other, more sensitive and far more vulnerable, portions of his anatomy. Half showgirl sparkle, half bag lady chic, Rosie looked rumpled and mussed. She looked tired, frazzled. And completely irresistible.

And it was well past time to stop thinking about it and find out what she was really up to.

As soon as the car slowed, Mack popped open the back

door. "Thank you," he told Sid and Gloria, and he honestly meant it. "This is terrific. Really. What you did for us is—"

"You two just have a beautiful life together." Gloria turned and gave them the kind of grandmotherly smile that didn't jibe with the decadent bedroom, the hot tub, or the black satin sheets. "That's the only thanks we need."

"Good luck, kids," Sid called to them, and before they were all the way up on the sidewalk, the Buick rocketed into traffic, heading toward the Strip.

"You can let go of my hand now."

The sound of Rosie's voice was enough to pull Mack out of the too-long-in-the-car, too-much-Sid-and-Gloria, too-close-to-Rosie-for-comfort thoughts that were busy trampling through his head. "What?"

"My hand." To demonstrate, Rosie lifted her left hand, and when Mack's right hand jerked up along with hers, he realized he was still holding on to it. "You can let go now," she said. "I'm a big girl. Perfectly capable of getting out of a car on my own. Perfectly capable of going . . ." She looked around and shook her head, and the long, fat braid that Gloria had help wind into the back of her hair, twitched. ". . . wherever it is we're going."

Mack gave her a quick once-over, forcing himself not to linger (at least not too long) at the place where she'd left the top button of the shirt undone. The hollow at the base of her throat looked pale and soft against the dark blue fabric, too vulnerable and way too feminine for a shirt that by its very nature stood for something tough and more than a little macho. He didn't dare let his gaze drift farther down, either, because when he did, he couldn't help but think of the way he'd watched her slip out of the wedding gown that she was now carrying slung over her right arm, the way the soft light of the multicolored lamp next to Sid and Gloria's bed stained her skin and caressed her bare breasts, or the way talking himself out of not making love to Rosie again was one of the hardest things he'd ever done.

He ditched the memory before it got the best of him. "You're a big girl, all right. Which is exactly why I think we'll cause less of a commotion if we hold hands. Less chance of anyone seeing the handcuffs."

His logic was, as always, indisputable. Which didn't mean Rosie was going to accept it at face value.

"Look . . ." When Mack started walking, Rosie yanked him to a stop. "There's something I need to say and if I don't say it now, I might not have a chance later. That would offend my sense of neatness, my sense of the way the world and everything in it should be orderly."

"Except that it isn't."

"That doesn't mean I can't try to make it that way." As if she were ready to give a speech, she cleared her throat. "You're holding my hand," she said. "You held my hand."

"So? I did way more than that to you the other night and I didn't hear any complaints."

"That's not what I mean." Rosie's expression softened, and Mack couldn't help but bristle.

"I don't need your sympathy," he told her.

"Good thing I'm not offering any. Get with the program, pal, and quit thinking that spotlight that's trained on you when you're on stage follows you around when you're off. This isn't about you. It's about me. What I'm trying to say— and apparently saying very badly—is thank you."

It wasn't exactly what he was expecting, and it took a couple seconds to process the information. "Thank you? You mean—"

"I mean, I'm not mad at you for holding my hand. And I'm not criticizing you for doing it. I'm not even going to get all crazy and accuse you of coming on too fast or too much or too strong. It's a little late for that." Rosie sucked in a deep breath of heated air. "I'm saying thank you. You picked up on the fact that I was scared. Back there with Sid, the Popeye Doyle clone. You knew I was afraid and you did your best to comfort me, and I have to admit, it surprised me.

Let's face it, I knew you could be a lot of things, but warm and fuzzy wasn't one of them."

Mack cringed. "You even make compliments sound like insults."

"I know." Rosie heaved a sigh that did remarkable things to the police shirt. "I'm not very good at compliments. I'm afraid I don't always expect the best of people. I don't usually expect them to be so decent. Or so kind."

Kind?

Mack couldn't remember the last time someone had used the word to describe him. Maybe because no one ever had.

He warned himself not to be too pleased by the sudden flush of satisfaction. "It was no big deal," he told her.

"It was a very big deal. And in case you haven't noticed, it's a big deal for me to admit it. I'm not supposed to be scared. Not of anything."

The statement was so out of left field, it made Mack laugh. "Says who?"

"Says me," she replied, and she was darned serious. He wiped the smile off his face and fought to keep it off. "I mean, this is the twenty-first century. Women are strong. They're equal. They're up to any task. Any challenge."

"And some of them don't like to drive with crazy old guys who have lead feet."

"And some of them don't like to drive with crazy old guys who have lead feet," she conceded. "But that doesn't mean I should have caved."

"What could you have done? Bailed? Jumped out of the car while we were roaring down the highway? That might have proved how brave you are, but it wouldn't have done much for your pieces and parts. And in case I haven't told you lately . . ." He gave her the hot-as-a-firecracker look that he usually reserved for the stage and the one woman in the audience who looked to be the most susceptible to being embarrassed by a little extra attention. "You have very nice pieces and parts."

"But you weren't scared."

So much for hot looks. Which was probably just as well. Mack turned his attention away from Rosie's delectable pieces and parts just in time to realize that her jaw was firm, her chin was steady, and her shoulders were as stiff as a Marine's. Which, now that he thought about it, made her look pretty delectable, too.

He brushed aside the awareness that flooded him and dismissed what she made sound too much like a heroic deed. "Definitely not a big deal," he told her. "Just a personality sort of thing. Nothing I like better than ripping down the road as fast as I can. But then . . ." Hoping to coax a smile out of her, he gave her a wink. "I thought you knew I was a fast guy."

"That's morals. This is relative velocity."

He started walking, tugging her along with him. "Look," he told her, "take it from me, if there's one thing I've learned, it's that the only time you're really at risk is when you're not scared."

It was Rosie's turn to laugh. "You're kidding, right? You? Scared? I can't believe you're scared when you're out there on stage ripping off your clothes."

"Terrified." Although it was the first time he'd ever admitted it, Mack realized it was true. "Each and every time I step out on stage," he admitted. "I'm afraid the audience will laugh. I'm afraid they won't appreciate the fantasy. Or the slick moves. Or the abs. I'm afraid one of these days, it will all be gone." He made a face. "I guess it's something I've been afraid of ever since the first time I stepped on a stage."

Now that it was out in the open, it was nearly impossible to shove the thought out of his head. Where it belonged. And since he couldn't, he handled it the way he'd handled every other unpleasant thing in his life. He faced it head-on. "It never hurts to be afraid. It only hurts when your fear causes you to panic and the panic freezes you. That's what really hurts. When you don't do what you're supposed to do because you're afraid."

"Like going out on stage and stripping?"

"Like going out on stage and stripping," he said, because even though it wasn't what he was talking about, it would have to be enough to satisfy Rosie.

Knowing the truth and figuring out why it bothered him so much were two different things. Two different things Mack didn't want to stand out on a street corner and try to figure out. He shook off the thought. "Come on," he said. "We're going to my place."

Rosie didn't look like she thought it was the greatest idea in the world. Then again, right about then, he didn't much care. He was hot. He was tired. And though the prospect of being cuffed to Rosie might have held a certain amount of charm at the right time and in the right place, after twenty-four hours, that charm was fading. Fast. He needed to ditch the handcuffs—the sooner, the better. Almost as much as he needed to take a break from the too-hard-to-control ideas, emotions, and urges that swamped him every time she was around.

He did a quick mental inventory of his apartment, considering what she might see when they got there. Satisfied that it wouldn't be anything that might give him away, he gave her a little tug and they started walking. "The way I figure it, we've got to do something with these things." He gave his hand and the cuffs a shake. "I just might have a handcuff key in my—"

"Tell me you're kidding me." Rosie stopped so fast, the heels of her high shoes scraped against the sidewalk. In spite of the early evening heat, her cheeks went pale. "On second thought, don't tell me you're kidding. You don't really have a key to hand—"

"I might." Mack gave her a sleek smile, glad for once that she'd made the wrong assumptions about him. "You never know."

"Oh, I know, all right. I'll tell you what," she said, glancing back the way they came. "Let's go to my place. I think maybe I have a couple of handcuff keys and—"

"Whoa! Wait just a minute." Mack refused to budge another inch. "Are you telling me—"

"I'm telling you exactly what you just told me. And I don't see why you should be allowed to say it and not expect the least little flicker of a reaction from me. But then when I say it—"

"When you say it, *dulzura*, it gives a whole new meaning to the conversation."

"Which is not at all what I intended to do." She eyed him levelly. "We need to get out of these things."

"Agreed."

"And . . . now don't take this the wrong way, it's not like it hasn't been fun . . . but to my way of thinking, that can't happen soon enough."

"Agreed again."

"So what do you say? My place?"

Mack should have said yes. Right then and there. He knew better than to allow strangers into his home, even when that home was simply a rented apartment filled with rented furniture in a city he would probably never visit again. Even back in Seattle, where his apartment might have been rented but the furniture—at least—was his, he didn't accept people lightly into his inner circle. Years on the streets had taught him that at their worst, people had their own reasons for getting close and getting friendly. They had their own motives and, sometimes, their own agendas. It was one of the reasons he didn't have many friends and certainly one of the reasons he didn't (except on rare occasions and with the occasional rare woman) invite them to glimpse a part of his life that was too hard-won and far too personal.

But though his instincts for privacy might have been well developed, his survival instincts were even keener. And he knew he'd feel far safer on his own turf. At least until the handcuffs were off.

"My place." He hung on tight to Rosie's hand and turned to the left. "Although if we have time a little later, maybe you'd like to show me those handcuffs of yours and—"

"Didn't say I had handcuffs." She stood her ground. "Said I had a key. Two different things."

"Got me there," Mack gave in, but only because he knew it wouldn't do any good to argue. "Look, we're wasting time. And I don't know about you, but I've just about had it with these handcuffs." He looked at the red tile roof of his apartment building where it showed over the tops of a fast-food burger joint, a car wash, and a mom-and-pop place that advertised cold beer and red-hot odds at a couple dozen slot machines. "My building isn't far."

"And my building . . ." Rosie turned in the other direction, stretching the chain that linked her cuff to his. "My building is pretty close, too."

So much for appealing to Rosie's smart side. Mack grumbled his displeasure. "We're not going to fight about this, are we?"

"Of course we're not going to fight." She looked at him as if he'd just suggested they knock over the local Federal Reserve. "We're just going to go to my place."

"Rosie!" Mack rolled his eyes. "You're being unreasonable."

"And you're being pig-headed. My place is just as close as yours."

"My handcuff key is just as good as yours and there's no reason you shouldn't want to head to my place—"

"Unless you're—"

"Scared."

"Scared."

The single word rang through the evening air like the echoes of a thrown gauntlet. If thrown gauntlets echoed.

Which Rosie doubted they did. Echo or not, Mack's message was loud and clear. So much for thinking of him as kind.

Her spine went rigid and her shoulders stiffened. Better to be angry than to allow the cold chill of disappointment that settled inside to get the best of her.

"Nothing like taking advantage of the fact that I confessed a personal and humiliating secret to you."

"Which I definitely was not." Not one to be intimidated, Mack stood straight and tall, too. "I wasn't making fun of the fact that you were afraid back there in the car. Although I suppose if I wasn't such a nice guy, I'd point out that Sid is nothing but a little old man and—"

"Oh, make it worse. Call him a little old man. Make me look like a wimp."

"I was simply pointing out . . ." He dragged in a deep breath and let it out slowly. "I was simply pointing out that my plan has advantages."

"Name one."

"It's my apartment."

"Funny, my plan has that same advantage."

"Which doesn't mean—"

"Which shouldn't—"

Though Rosie was as sure of the righteousness of her position as she was of the fact that she didn't want to venture into Mack's apartment, where he had the advantage of knowing the lay of the land and she had the definite disadvantage of being handcuffed and pretty much helpless, she wasn't at all sure what she could say to make him see things her way. She didn't have to. Before she could think of a way to convince him, Sid's Buick raced up to the curb and jerked to a stop.

"Glad you didn't get too far," Sid said, even before he had the window rolled all the way down. "We've been thinking, you know, about what you said about your commitment to each other and then—"

"That you didn't even have the money to stay in a motel,"

Gloria added. She popped out of the car and came around it to stand on the sidewalk. "It took us a while but we realized you probably don't have the money for a locksmith, either, and—"

"We want you to have this." Sid gave Gloria the high sign and she held up a tiny silver handcuff key.

"How—" Rosie stopped short of asking. For the first time in twenty-four hours, she was about to be free of the handcuffs—and of Mack—and right now, that was all that mattered. The *how* and *why* of Sid and Gloria owning a handcuff key wasn't important.

And besides, she honestly didn't want to know.

10

Enough was enough. And Rosie had had enough.

She'd had enough of wasting her time and her talents—not to mention the government's money—on a case that was going nowhere. Enough of wasting her brain cells and her energy—not to mention her fantasy life—sparring with a too-hot-to-handle stripper who didn't know when to quit. Her investigation was stalled, her real life was on hold, her neatly organized world threatened to go into nuclear meltdown whenever Mack was around and—damn it—her wrist still hurt.

Automatically she massaged her left wrist where the skin was pink. At the same time, she consoled herself with the fact that at least the numbness had gone away. That didn't stop her from shaking her hand. Force of habit. She'd spent the better part of the last thirty hours trying to get her circulation moving again, and if there was one thing she'd learned (aside from the fact that handcuffs were a whole bunch more uncomfortable than she ever imagined), it was that she'd had enough and she knew it.

In her bones. In her head. Even in her heart.

Now if only she could convince the rest of her.

As if some force in the universe were out to remind her that her bones, her head, and her heart were on the wrong side of a losing cause, she caught sight of a poster hanging outside the door of the Silver Swan's human resources department and stopped dead in her tracks. The rest of her—the part that was trying to forget the heat of Mack's body against hers, and the touch of his hand, and that little zip of adrenaline that shot through her every time they were together—responded in exactly the way her head had warned her was nothing short of asking for trouble.

Then again, she couldn't imagine any woman, anywhere, who wouldn't be wide-eyed, open-mouthed, and awestruck by the almost-big-as-life image of Mack staring back at her from the poster.

Mack with his chest bare. Mack with his jeans unbuttoned and slung low over one hip. Mack with that look in his eyes. The one that made a woman feel like she was seconds away from self-combusting.

Rosie ought to know. There were a few times she'd been pretty close to calling the fire department herself.

There was a note taped to the wall next to the poster, one written in bright pink ink. "Tonight's the night, girls!" it said. "Be there!" The note was positioned just above the fiery red lettering that crawled across the top of the poster and announced the first-time-in-Las-Vegas, live-and-in-person, hot-hot-hot appearance of the Saint.

A welcome, chilly thread of cynicism sneaked in to smother the heat.

"The Saint?" The words pushed out of Rosie along with a breath that felt as if it had been lassoed and yanked from her lungs. "If you're a saint, pal," she told the picture of Mack, "I'm the pope."

OK, she'd give the photographer credit. It was a clever enough shot. Mack had been photographed on a bare stage against a black background. His body was lit from the front by a muted orange light, one that looked like it was leaping off a fire. The only other light in the picture was a very white, very bright light behind his head. It looked like a halo, all right, but Rosie barely needed to glance down at the rest of the poster to know that was where the saintly comparisons ended.

Unless saints had bodies that could tempt the angels, the devils—and federal agents who should have known better.

Rather than think about it and risk getting her head, her heart, and her bones all tangled up with that part of her that found Mack impossible to ignore, she reminded herself that she didn't have much time. If she was going to do what she had to do and get out of here before the staff got back. . . .

Reassuring herself, Rosie glanced over her shoulder.

Just as she planned, just as she'd hoped, there was no one around.

Which only went to prove that saint or no saint, Mack was tempting enough that even the skeleton staff that worked the late shift in the HR department had been taken in by the hype. Apparently, the gossip Rosie had heard backstage was true: The HR staff (three women and a guy named Trevor) was planning to duck out on their break and watch Mack's first show.

If the crowds she'd seen entering the theater just as she was leaving it meant anything, a lot of other people had been drawn into the Swan by the publicity, too. For that, at least, Rosie was grateful. The theater was packed. Which meant the staff up there was plenty busy. And if the staff down here was really gone . . .

She hauled up the sleeve of her billowing clown costume and glanced at her watch. Mack's show was scheduled to start in just twenty minutes and she knew it wouldn't last long. After all, how long did it take for a guy to rip off his clothes? Especially when those clothes were held together by nothing except Velcro.

She punched open the swinging double doors that led into the HR department reception area and clumped inside,

her clown shoes entering the room a couple of seconds before the rest of her. There was no one behind the counter
that took up the far wall of the room. So far so good.

"Anybody home?" she called out.

No answer.

That was a good thing, too, but she wasn't about to take
any chances. Rosie opened the door that led into the area
where a small army of clerks worked processing time sheets,
issuing checks, and doing whatever else had to be done to
keep a place like the Swan running day to day. The room was
at least thirty feet wide and just as long. This late at night, it
was as quiet as a tomb. Most of the lights were off, but a couple of overhead fluorescents had been left on and in their
frosty light she could see that the room was divided by cubicles with head-high walls, open doorways, and no ceilings.
On the far wall, there was a second door with a glowing, red
emergency exit sign over it.

"Hey! Anybody around?" she called out again, just to be
sure.

And again, there was no answer.

Satisfied that she was alone and fully aware that it might
not last, Rosie *thumped* her way into the room and hurried
down the long aisle on her right, the slap of her shoes echo-
ing back at her in the dark. She found a likely looking cubicle and, flattening her red wig to fit through the narrow
doorway, she ducked inside. She didn't dare flick on the
lamp above the desk. Instead, she tapped the computer
keyboard that sat on the desk and the computer screen
flicked on.

It took what seemed like forever for the desktop to show
on the screen, and when it finally did, she bent closer for a
better look and quickly read over the folders displayed
there. "Benefits, vacation, employee records. Bingo!" She
punched one fist into the air and double clicked the records
file.

After that, it didn't take long to find Mack in the employee database. Prospective employees filled out their applications right on the computer, and Rosie zipped past the screen that showed Mack's original employment application, annoyed in spite of herself that he'd somehow managed to type *Mack* so that it filled in a little of the section marked *first name* and a little of the section marked *last name*.

"Not a problem," she consoled herself. Because she really didn't care if he wanted to play games. Mack's full name wasn't what she was after.

Lucky for her, the lines set aside for experience were filled in. So was his list of references.

"Looks like you need experience even when you've got a body to die for and an ego as big as your—"

Rosie dashed the thought. She scrolled down until she found the line where his Social Security number was listed. Though the Powers That Be might be forgiving when it came to the first and last name department, at least they hadn't been willing to let a little matter like a Social Security number go unnoted. She rummaged through the desk, found a piece of scrap paper decorated with sunflowers, and scrawled the number on it. She stuffed the paper down the front of her costume until it nestled between her breasts, then backed out of the computer program as carefully as she could. No use letting anyone know she'd been there.

"Quick and easy," she told herself, and she clicked the computer off.

She had just stepped out of the cubicle when she heard the emergency exit door swing open.

Rosie cursed herself and her bad timing. It was all she had time to do before she had to dart back into the cubicle.

She stood and waited, her heartbeat the only sound she could hear over the constant buzz of the overhead fluorescent lights. One minute melted into two and she had just convinced herself that she was being jumpy and completely irrational when she heard the unmistakable *beeps* and *clicks* of a computer turning on. She bent her head, listening, and was rewarded by the sounds of a keyboard and the quiet tap of a mouse.

"You'd better hurry up."

A man's voice broke the silence, and Rosie jumped. Careful not to make a sound, she inched her way toward the cubicle opening and peered around the wall. Farther up the aisle and six cubicles away, a light was on above one of the desks. She saw a shadow move in the cubicle and she knew someone was in there. The man whose voice she'd heard was standing outside it, his massive shape nearly blocking the aisle.

Flattening her wig, Rosie leaned forward for a better look.

The guy was well over six feet tall and had shoulders that would have made a linebacker green with envy. When he moved toward the light, she saw a face that looked as if it had been chipped from a block of wood by a carver with little patience, no talent, and not much in the way of taste. Heavy jaw. Crooked nose. Bristling eyebrows. The man was wearing a dark, pinstriped suit and a tie that blended with his dark shirt.

"You know," he said, juggling a pair of sunglasses in nervous fingers, "they're going to have your head if they find you in here."

"Relax."

Even though the voice from inside the cubicle was muffled, Rosie recognized it instantly. Which was the only reason she wasn't at all surprised when Mack stepped into the aisle. "First of all, they're not going to find me." As if he had every right to be there and all the time in the world, he paused outside the doorway and leaned back, and Rosie saw that he was wearing one of his stage costumes, the way-too-tight-for-any-woman's-sanity tear-away slacks and the silky red-and-black shirt he'd been wearing the day they met.

"Second of all . . ." He shrugged and the silky shirt slid over his shoulders. "Well, maybe there isn't a second of all.

Let's just settle for they're not going to find me. Not a problem, my friend. Never is."

"Don't know how you do it." The big guy scraped one beefy hand through hair that looked like it had just been buzzed with a lawnmower. "But then, I never did understand you daredevil types. Not for me, I'll tell you that. Give me a clear-cut job any day. Doesn't this stuff make you nervous?"

"No more nervous than you following me around with that damned calculator of yours."

"Now, Mack . . ."

Though the big guy sounded like he wanted to be conciliatory, Mack was apparently not in the mood. He ducked back into the cubicle and, again, Rosie heard the computer clicking and grinding its way through its cyber-gyrations.

"All I said was that I found a better supplier."

Supplier?

Rosie's ears pricked and her heart sped up, just as they did every time she was closing in on an important bit of information that eventually led her to solve a case. If Mack and his big friend were talking suppliers . . .

Too practical to let her imagination run away with her, but too smart not to consider all the places it might take her, Rosie shuffled as close to the doorway of the cubicle as she could without letting her shoes hang out into the aisleway.

"My supplier is cheaper than the one you're using," she heard the big guy tell Mack. Over the top of the cubicle, the big guy watched whatever it was Mack was up to. "See? You're a computer literate sort of guy. And I found this supplier on the Internet. That ought to make you plenty happy."

"This makes me happier." Mack emerged with a single page of paper in his hands. He waved it under the big guy's nose. "Got what I wanted," he said. "And if you'll spare me the lecture about financial responsibility, I really do have to get back upstairs."

"All right. All right." The big guy may have known how to

sound like he was cooperating, but it was clear, at least to Rosie, that he wasn't about to give up. "But if you'll just consider my people."

"Right." Mack was busy looking over the paper in his hands. "Whatever you say."

"Cheaper, Mack. Way cheaper for those . . . whatever it is you call them."

Rosie held her breath. What did she expect, that they would give her details? That they would explain in living color where they got the 9A-91s, who was selling them, if there were any more?

Damn straight.

"Most people call them thongs," she heard Mack say, and her hopes for cracking the case fell at the same time that her fantasies soared. "Or gripper thongs. Or G-strings. And the price I'm getting is more than reasonable."

"Yeah, but—"

"But we'll talk about this later. I'm set to go on in just a couple minutes. Right before the circus number." Mack turned back toward the cubicle. "I'll just turn this off and—"

A sound from out in the reception area stopped both Mack and his friend in their tracks. The big guy instinctively stepped into the shadows but Mack didn't waste an instant. He moved quickly and quietly toward the door on the other side of the room, and the big guy followed.

Rosie stood perfectly still and listened as the door whispered closed behind Mack. She could have sworn she'd heard something from out in the lobby, too, but the only sound she could hear now was the pounding of her own heart. She listened to it for another minute before she decided she was being too jumpy. It was time to get moving.

Rosie slid out of her hiding place and headed for the cubicle Mack had vacated. The computer he'd used was still on, and she scuttled into the rolling chair in front of the screen and took a look at what Mack was looking at.

Rosie's breath caught in her throat. Her hands clenched. Her stomach turned.

Because while she was looking up Mack's personnel file, Mack had been busy looking up a personnel file, too.

Rosie's.

"What are you trying to say, Chuck?" Rosie shifted the phone from her right ear to her left. As if that might make a difference. No way would it be that simple to change what her boss back in the San Francisco office was telling her. "Are you saying there's no such person as—"

"I'm not telling you there's no such person." She heard Chuck Orlowski's desk chair squeak and pictured him leaning back in his neat-as-a-pin, everything-in-its-place office. "Obviously there's such a person, because you've met him. What I'm telling you, Malone, is that the Social you gave me doesn't match. Not with anyone with a name even close to Mack."

Rosie had just stepped out of the shower when her phone rang. Normally, she would have let the call go to her answering machine, but Chuck had promised her an answer ASAP on the Social Security number she'd called in to him the night before. She raked her fingers through her sopping hair. "I know I got the number right. I saw his employment application. If the human resources department is supposed to check out every employee like they say they do—"

"If everybody checked out everybody like the say they do, the world wouldn't be as messed up as it is." Chuck held his hand briefly over the phone while he said something to someone who walked into his office. "Besides . . ." Rosie heard him shuffle through a stack of papers and the scratching sound of him signing his name.

"Besides," he said again when he was finished, "it's not a phony number. It's legit, all right."

"It's legit, it's just not Mack's."

"You got it." Chuck's chair squeaked again and Rosie pictured him spinning it toward his window, the way he always did when he was thinking through a problem. "The number you gave me belongs to J. J. Harrigan."

"J. J. Harrigan? That's Mack's real name?"

"Only if he's a little over ninety-three years old, died back in the seventies, and is a woman from Sheboygan."

Even long distance, she knew sarcasm when she heard it. She also knew what it meant. "What you're telling me is that the Social belonged to this Harrigan woman. And that somehow Mack got it and—"

"Somehow?" The single word contained all the cynicism a man with Chuck's easygoing personality could manage. "You know there's a market for this kind of thing. That shouldn't be a big surprise. Sounds to me like your stripper—"

"He's not my stripper, Chuck."

"Doesn't change a thing. Still sounds to me like he's—"

"Hiding something."

"Big time."

Rosie chased away a chill she was sure had something to do with the fact that she was dripping all over her bedroom rug. At the same time she reached for her white terry-cloth bathrobe, she told herself she should be feeling jazzed. She was looking for progress in her case? Well, she'd just gotten it.

Which didn't explain why she felt so hollow.

She cinched the tie belt of the robe around her waist and flopped down on the edge of her bed. "He says he's from El Paso. What are the chances he's from the other side of the border? Trouble with the INS?"

"Already ahead of you there." Of course Chuck was already ahead of her. Chuck had spent the better part of a long and illustrious career with the ATF one step ahead of everyone. It was one of the reasons Rosie admired him so. One of the reasons she was hoping to be just like him someday. "It's the first thing I thought of, too," he told her. "But we ran a computer check against INS files and, while there are a couple of names that might fit the bill, none of the descriptions are even close."

Somehow, Rosie wasn't surprised. A simple computer check that turned up simple information would be too easy. Too damned ordinary. Leave it to Mack to be anything but.

"Let me guess, those references he had listed on his employment application haven't turned up anything, either."

"Oh, they've turned up plenty." She heard Chuck shuffle through a stack of papers. "They check out as much as they can. He says he started stripping at a place in El Paso called the Studs Corral." Rosie didn't have to see Chuck to know he cringed at the very mention of the name. Chuck was nothing if not straightlaced. It was another reason Rosie admired him. "It went out of business years ago, so we didn't have any luck there. The second club he listed is long gone, too, but one of the guys here in the office had heard of it. A place called the Kitty Cat Club."

"The Kitty Cat Club." Rosie grumbled the name, remembering, in spite of herself, the tacky bedroom at Sid and Gloria's: the satin sheets, the red velvet pillows. "Let me guess. It's in Juarez, right? Or was he lying about that, too?"

"You talked about Juarez?" There was the tiniest bit of laughter in Chuck's voice. Rosie decided to ignore it. Her boss knew that she didn't often indulge in idle chitchat with suspects. It was one of the things that made her a crackerjack special agent. She didn't waste time. And she didn't mince words. He knew that if Rosie and Mack had traded personal information, it was for a good reason.

And if she hadn't bothered to mention the Eiffel Tower? Or Sid and Gloria's? If she hadn't bothered to let her boss or anyone else from the office know that she'd been handcuffed to Mack for twenty-four long hours?

Rosie discarded the thought as immaterial, irrelevant, and just plain too embarrassing to share. Especially with the man who would be doing her next performance evaluation.

"So he's hiding something," she said, and she hoped she

sounded as if she was reasoning her way through what little information they had. And not trying to make excuses. "Plenty of people are hiding something. I'm hiding something."

"True." She had seen Chuck in enough meetings to know that by now, he'd picked up a pencil from his desk and was tapping it thoughtfully against his chin. "But—"

"But it doesn't prove anything. I know. I know. Even though back there in the Human Resources Department, I thought he was going to turn out to be just what we're looking for. My bad luck. He and the big guy, I thought they were talking guns. They weren't. They were talking G-strings."

"You talked about G-strings?"

"Not me. Not us." Rosie shrugged away the roar of supercharged awareness that shot through her at the very thought. "They were talking G-strings. Mack and the big guy."

"Don't ask, don't tell. Sounds like a sound policy in this instance."

Rather than even think about it, Rosie went through the kind of careful analysis that had always impressed her superiors. It was a skill she prided herself on, one that was hard-won through years of trying to keep on an even keel in the bedlam of the Malone family.

"He's not a dumb guy," she told Chuck. "Though he doesn't strike me as the brightest bulb in the box, either. I mean, instead of getting the hell out of the way when that SUV nearly mowed me down—"

"He's got a lot of nerve."

Chuck had no idea just how right he was.

Rather than telling him and risking having to explain a whole bunch of stuff she didn't want to confess to anyone, she got the conversation back on track. "When that SUV was headed right for me, he actually stepped into its path and pulled me to safety. And when that shooter was after me . . ." Another thought occurred to her and she sat up, something so much like hope blossoming inside her that she refused to even consider what it might mean.

"What are the chances he's one of the good guys?" she asked Chuck.

"Good guys?" It took a little longer for Chuck to work his way through what she was getting at. But then, Chuck didn't have a vested interest. Not like Rosie did. "You mean, like us?"

"I mean like us. I mean federal. Or at least local. What are the chances that he's Vegas PD? Or how about the Gaming Control Board? Or—"

"Slim to none." There was enough confidence in Chuck's answer to dash whatever hopes she might have had. Which wasn't such a bad thing, Rosie consoled herself while she slumped back down on the bed. No hopes, no reason to wonder why she was hoping. Or why her hopes were *whooshing* over her head like a balloon that had just been pricked with a pin.

"The old days of turf wars are over, Malone. We don't spar with the FBI anymore. We don't wrestle with the locals to see who's going to come out on top and get all the attaboys on a case. We're all one big, happy family now." If she didn't know Chuck better, she might have suspected him of being pessimistic. But she did know him better. And she knew he was a Boy Scout, a cheerleader in the cause of truth, justice, and the American way. She also knew that as a conscientious and able administrator, Chuck made sure all the *i*s were dotted and all the *t*s were crossed. Which meant he actually practiced what he preached.

"If there was someone else in on this case, we'd know about it." Chuck put into words exactly what she was thinking. "Believe me, I'd be swamped in miles of red tape. And hours of interagency meetings. I'd know all the players. And I'd for sure remember one who just so happens to have the added talent of taking off his clothes to music."

"Which means he was checking my employee records for the same reason I was checking his. He's suspicious."

"Or it could mean you've got a stalker on your hands." Chuck didn't sound any happier about saying it than hearing it made Rosie feel. "You haven't had any problems with this guy, have you?"

"Problems?" Rosie was tempted to ask for a definition. She decided against it. There was that performance evaluation to consider. "Not those kinds of problems."

"Keep your eyes open." He didn't have to tell her it was all the advice he would give her. And he wasn't about to patronize her by reminding her to be careful. Which was another reason she thought a lot of Chuck.

"I know. I will. I just . . ."

Just what?

The question skidded over Rosie's still-damp back like icy fingers and she hopped off the bed and did a turn around the room. Better to get her brain in gear than to wonder why she was feeling as if the beige Berber had been pulled out from under her feet.

"You don't sound happy."

Understatement of the year. "I'm not happy, Chuck. Someone is onto me."

"Or onto your friend, Neeta, and trying to get at her through you."

"And you haven't—"

"Got anything on her? Not for sure. Not yet. But we're checking. I've got that new guy doing a check on every Neeta in the Vegas area. He's not happy about it."

"I don't imagine he is." It was Rosie's turn to chuckle and she was grateful for that. Leave it to Chuck to find the one thing that would make her laugh in a situation that was anything but funny. She remembered being the new kid on the block at the office, too, and getting the kind of learn-the-ropes assignments Chuck always saved for the newbies. "When you get something—"

"Of course you'll be the first to know." She heard Chuck's desk chair squeak and she knew their call was just about over. "In the meantime, Malone, let me remind you that it sounds to me like you've got your most solid lead yet."

He didn't need to remind her. Rosie would have done that on her own. Eventually. As soon as getting confirmation of everything she suspected stopped churning through her like the god-awful sushi her parents insisted on serving every time Rosie went back East to visit.

She set the thought aside with the same determination she used when she was faced with a plate of sushi. Chin up. Stare it in the eye. Face the facts and deal with them. In the case of sushi, it meant reminding her parents (again) that not only was it not her favorite food, it was something she didn't touch. Ever. In the case of Mack, it was more like reminding herself (again) that hard bod or no hard bod, face of a god or no face of a god, sexy or not . . .

The memory and all the sensations that followed it were nearly enough to upend her, and she sucked in a breath and got herself back on track. Feet on the ground. Head out of the clouds. Wasn't that the lesson she'd learned in spite of her family while she was growing up? Now more than ever, she needed to remember it. She needed to be a grown-up. And being a grown-up meant facing the facts. Even when they were as stomach churning as sushi.

"This means I'm going to have to stick to our little stripper like a tattoo on a sailor's bicep," she told her boss.

Good thing Chuck was satisfied with that and hung up without saying anything else. Because there was the Eiffel Tower to consider. That, and the fact that Mack had held her hand all the way back from Fresno.

"A nice, conservative, hardworking federal agent does not let herself get waylaid by feelings," Rosie reminded herself. "Not the scorching-enough-to-do-serious-damage kind. Not the warm-and-fuzzy kind."

Which was a great theory.

But still didn't explain why she couldn't decide if sticking to Mack was good.

Or bad.

11

"Do you know how many Rose Malones there are in this country?"

"That's not what I asked, Lenny, and you know it." Mack shifted the paper cup Lenny had given him from hand to hand and leaned against the slot machine where Lenny was feeding nickel after nickel. He was impatient, edgy, and just a little tired after last night's opening, the encore that followed, and the mob of frenzied, hopped-up-on-sex-fantasies women waiting for him outside the stage door when he left for the night.

"I asked if the Social Security number I gave you matches the one I found in Rosie's employment records."

"In a word?" Lenny pulled the lever and watched while the pictures of bars and bells and cherries rolled and shifted and came to rest in a pattern that won him absolutely nothing. He glanced at Mack out of the corner of his eye. "No."

Mack was surprised. And he wasn't. Rather than puzzling through either scenario, rather than trying to decide which made him feel better and why he was worried that one option actually might make him feel worse, he stuck to the matter at hand. Safer that way. More to the point. Less unsettling than trying to figure out why a Rosie Malone who wasn't the Rosie Malone she said she was, bothered him as much as it did.

He shifted his stance and moved the tall paper cup from his right hand to his left. "Who does the Social Security number belong to?"

"Knew you'd ask." Lenny reached into the pocket of his plaid sport jacket for a piece of paper torn from a spiral notebook. He handed the paper to Mack before he dropped another nickel into the slot.

Mack read over the name scratched out in Lenny's spindly handwriting. "Zachary Folsom?"

"Died back in the twenties." Lenny pulled the lever and this time three bars came down in a row and the little tray at the front of the machine filled with nickels. "See what I mean about this?" He scooped up his winnings and dropped the coins into the paper cup Mack was holding. "There's a method to the madness. A pattern. Know what I mean? Three nickels in, three no-wins. But the fourth one always—"

Mack's grumbled curse cut Lenny short. "I really don't need a lesson in gambling."

"Maybe you do." Lenny plucked one nickel out of the cup and held it up between his thumb and his forefinger for Mack to see. He dropped the coin into the slot and pulled the lever.

Nothing.

"Maybe you need to step back and take stock of the situation," Lenny said. "You know, study the thing a little harder. The way I've been studying this slot machine when I hang around here keeping an eye on you. You know, look at the situation from every angle, and while you're waiting, maybe things will fall into place, just like they did for me. You'll see the pattern." He repeated the procedure with a second nickel.

Nothing.

"Maybe you need to realize that there's a pattern to things other than nickel slot machines," Lenny said.

"If the Gaming Control Board knew, they wouldn't be happy campers."

"Of course not." Lenny removed a third nickel from the cup, inserted it in the machine, and pulled the lever.

Nothing.

"But then again, maybe if someone was looking into gambling irregularities and took a close look at this machine . . . maybe they'd never find anything because the pattern of wins and losses isn't consistent."

"Which means it isn't a pattern."

"Which means it's a pattern that's only a pattern sometimes." Lenny inserted a fourth coin. He pulled the lever and the red light at the front of the machine flashed. The tray filled with nickels. "See?" He gave Mack a smile while he piled the nickels into the paper cup. "Pattern. Everything has a pattern."

"In this case—if it's true—it's completely illegal."

"Absolutely," Lenny agreed. "But in this case—if it's true—that doesn't make it any less of a pattern." He started the process all over again, inserting one nickel, a second, a third. He came up empty every time.

"So I'm asking myself . . ." Lenny reached for a fourth nickel and inserted it in the slot. He pulled the lever.

Nothing.

"Moral of the story." He gave the slot machine a dirty look before he turned to Mack. "So I'm asking myself, if a pattern with a slot machine is a pattern only sometimes, then why can't a pattern with other things be a pattern only sometimes?"

Mack glanced around at the sea of slot machines that surrounded them. Across the few feet of worn carpet with its busy design that separated their row of slot machines from the ones across the aisle, a middle-aged woman hit the jackpot and whooped. "This place is giving me a headache." He ran a hand through his hair and realized it was the same headache he'd had since Dom sprang the news that Mack— and his singular talents—were needed in Las Vegas. "Maybe we could go outside and get some air?"

"Sure." Lenny clapped him on the back and grabbed his cup of nickels, leading the way through the doors that led out to the Swan's less-than-spectacular outdoor swimming pool.

It wasn't until they stepped out into the bright sunshine and the searing heat that Mack was able to take a deep breath; cigarette smoke was as common in Vegas casinos as escorts in short skirts and too-tight tops. He followed Lenny over to a corner of the pool area that was separated from the Swan's back parking lot by a wall of head-high tropical foliage.

"You're talking about Rosie."

"Obviously." Lenny pulled a fat cigar from his pocket and when a cocktail waitress in tiny white shorts and a white cropped top that tied under her surgically enhanced breasts walked by, he rattled the paper cup.

"What will you have?" The waitress didn't give Lenny a second glance. She smiled at Mack.

"Corona."

Lenny added a scotch and water for himself. "I don't usually drink this early in the day," he told Mack. "But"—he jingled the coins—"we are celebrating."

"Are we? Celebrating what?"

Lenny waited until the waitress sashayed away, her white, feathery swan wings swaying with each roll of her hips. "You're not getting discouraged, are you?" he asked Mack.

Mack crossed his arms over his chest. "No," he said, because giving up wasn't an option. "Not discouraged. Confused. I'll admit to confused. Hell, I'll even admit to mystified. She's not who she says she is. Or she is, and she's not who her Social Security number says she is. She carries a .38 revolver. She's got some connection with the sister of the guy who was intercepting our guns and selling them. She's got someone after her who drives like a lunatic and someone else—or the same someone—who, fortunately for me, can't shoot very straight. And whoever that someone is, he looks real serious about whacking her."

"And she's got you all mixed up."

Mack didn't think it showed. Which was all the more reason he jumped in with a denial. "Not mixed up," he told Lenny. "Never mixed up. Going around in circles, sure. But I know what I have to do, Lenny. I haven't forgotten that."

"Knew you wouldn't." When the waitress came back, Lenny grabbed the beer off her tray and handed it to Mack. He took his own drink and deposited the entire cup of nickels on the tray.

"You're the Saint, aren't you?" The waitress batted her mascara-veneered eyelashes at Mack. "Saw your show last night. Going back tonight. I don't suppose you—"

"Not a chance, *chica*." Mack softened the news with a smile that made the woman shiver. "Saving myself for the paying customers."

She grinned. "Me, too."

Lenny watched the waitress leave, his gaze sliding from the mane of bleached blond hair that hung to the center of her back, down to where her shorts hugged curves that were nothing less than monumental. "Some assignment, huh? Women throwing themselves at you. Never had that problem myself. Bet you never would have guessed." He was smart enough not to give Mack a chance to answer. "So what do you think?" he asked. "About this Rosie."

Mack sipped his beer. It was his usual brand and it was icy cold, but suddenly it didn't taste as good as he remembered. Even after a long drink, his mouth was dry. "I think she's smart. I think she's got guts. And a hell of a left hook. I think if someone was looking for an undercover cop, she's just the type they'd choose. She's way too pretty. Not a chance anyone would suspect her. Not a chance anyone would take her seriously." He braced himself against the memories. "Not with a body like that."

"Which doesn't keep you from taking her seriously."

"I'm smart, too." Mack's smile lasted just about as long as the little puff of a cool breeze that came and went before it had much of a chance to do any good. "Anything more on this Neeta?"

"She's not a Friel, but hell, that would be too easy, wouldn't it?" Lenny held his drink up to the light and made a face. "Watered down," he said, which probably explained why he was able to toss it back in one motion. "I'm working the Neeta angle. I'll leave you to take care of Rosie."

Lenny's choice of words didn't sit particularly well with Mack's conscience.

Maybe Lenny noticed. Maybe he just had an uncanny way of getting to the heart of a matter. "You ready to commit yourself?" he asked. "Try a buy and see if she jumps at the chance?"

It was a question Mack had asked himself more than once in the past few days. Once he made the move, he couldn't retreat. Once he started, there was no going back. "It might help clear the air." He wondered if Lenny noticed that he hadn't answered his question.

"Afraid she won't bite?" Lenny gave him a look that was way too razor-sharp to go along with his nickel-slot persona. "Or are you afraid she will?"

It was another question Mack wasn't about to answer. "At this point," he told Lenny, "everything I have is circumstantial. That's not good enough. Before I start talking Russian assault rifles, I want to know more. I want to be sure." Even while he'd been working his way through the problem, another thought had been tickling at the back of his mind. Without another taste, Mack set his beer bottle down on the nearest empty table. "So if Rosie isn't Rosie," he asked, "who is she?"

"I was kind of hoping you'd find that out." Lenny set

down his glass and turned to head back into the casino. "Who does she hang out with? What do they know? Who does she talk to? What does she say? You know the routine, Mack. Go on a little fishing expedition and see if it gets us anyplace."

Mack wasn't about to argue. The only thing he was worried about was that the *anyplace* he was headed was someplace he didn't want to be.

"We need to talk."

Apparently, women in various stages of undress weren't enough to throw Mack off his game. But then, that shouldn't have surprised Rosie. A guy who took off his clothes for a living obviously wasn't as worried about modesty as most of the other folks she knew.

He strolled into the dressing room Rosie shared with some of the other chorus girls and flashed a smile at Angela, who was across the way pulling on her clown costume over a sparkling G-string, a pair of high heels, a dusting of sparkles in her hair—and absolutely nothing else. He smiled at Julie, too, who was down at the far end of the row of dressing tables, tugging on her clown shoes, and at Tiffany, who wasn't wearing anything except her red clown wig, a towel, and the biggest come-and-get-it smile Rosie had ever seen.

Mack acted like he didn't notice. Or at least like he didn't care. He grabbed the chair that Rosie had just gotten out of, flipped it around and straddled it, and she thanked her lucky stars that she was already dressed.

If a bikini encrusted with red sequins and a pair of fishnet stockings could be considered dressed.

Rosie reached into her locker for her red plastic clown nose and tossed it on her dressing table, where her clown wig sat like some kind of pampered Pekinese gone bad.

"Did you hear me?" Mack asked. "I said we have to talk."

"Which begs the question, about what?" Another time, another place, she might have come right out and asked the questions that needed to be asked: *Who are you, Mack?* *Who are you really?* But this was the wrong place. And it was certainly the wrong time.

Which didn't mean she was about to let Mack off easy. Just to let him know she hadn't forgotten how he'd looked through her purse, she slammed her locker closed and made sure she turned the combination lock three times. "So, what will it be? Trips to Fresno? Handcuffs?"

"Handcuffs?" Her eyebrows raised, Angela walked by and purred the word, ignoring Rosie completely and focusing her attention on Mack. "Something you want to share?" she asked.

"Handcuffs?" Julie was headed for the door, too, and she gave Mack a pout of epic proportions. "You never said anything to me about handcuffs."

"Handcuffs?" Tiffany's face went a little pale under her plastic nose and the blotches of bright red greasepaint on her cheeks. "Isn't that a little—"

"Come on." Angela grabbed Tiffany's arm and hauled her out of the room. "You can get your costume on in the dressing room next door," she said. She scooped up her own red clown wig from her dressing table at the same time she plucked Tiffany's clown costume off the wardrobe rack. She stepped out into the hallway and closed the door behind her.

"Nothing like having cooperative roommates." Rosie wondered if she was trying to convince Mack or herself. It was suddenly awfully quiet in a room that only seconds before had been bustling with activity. Awfully quiet and awfully close quarters. A combination that spelled trouble. Especially when Mack was around.

Rather than think about it, she turned toward her mirror and reached for her own jar of red greasepaint. It wasn't until she bent close to the mirror to slap the color on her cheeks that she realized she'd just given Mack a perfect look at her other cheeks. She set the jar down and grabbed for the blue-and-white clown jumpsuit she'd left on the back of her chair.

Was it her imagination, or did Mack look just a little relieved to see her step into the clown costume and poke her arms into the sleeves? Deciding it wasn't possible, not for a guy whose *modus operandi* was all about flesh and sex and the kind of heat that flashed through Rosie like a mushroom cloud over some faraway Pacific atoll, she gave Mack the quick once-over.

"The police uniform again, huh?" She rolled her eyes. "You're not really going through with that tacky excuse for a peep show, are you?"

He glanced down at the blue uniform and gave the police officer's hat he was holding a twirl. "Looks like it," he said. "And it's not exactly a peep show. Not technically. Angela's doing the number with me now. Did she tell you? When you backed out of the act, she talked Greg and Tatiana into letting her take your place. And all she takes off is my shirt. After that, she moves aside and I've got center stage all to myself. At least until the end of my act when she shows up again and we walk off to live happily ever after." He grinned. "Interested in a second chance?"

"Not on your life." Rosie barked out a laugh. "I've got my standards, pal, and they don't include undressing you in front of a crowd of drooling women."

"How about if we were all alone?"

"How about you say what you came in here to say and then get out so I can get dressed and get on stage in time for my number. Unless . . ." Another thought occurred to her and Rosie automatically reached for the zipper at the front of the clown suit and pulled it up to her chin. No use letting him see that she blushed all the way from where her breasts spilled out of the sparkling bikini top, up to the roots of her hair. In the hopes of covering, she gave him a sassy grin. "Unless that is what you came to say?"

"Nope. We found out the undressed part wasn't exactly necessary. Remember?"

As if she could forget. As if Mack would ever let her. As sleek as a tiger on the prowl, he stood and set the chair aside, putting his hat on his head as he did.

"You don't look like a cop." He didn't look like a saint, either, but apparently those kinds of technicalities weren't enough to stop Mack.

"That's because I'm not a cop." Mack grinned. "The hat, it's all part of the costume. You know . . ." He did a couple showy dance moves that she knew came straight from his act. As he did, he pretended to take off his shirt and throw it aside. After that, he slipped the hat off his head, tossed it from hand to hand, and held it in front of his crotch while he pretended to peel away his pants. "Nothing like prolonging the anticipation of the audience," he said, and he gave her a wink.

"If they're anticipating anything." As if Rosie weren't. As if each of the moves he made didn't sizzle through her like lightning on a hot summer night. As if he didn't notice.

Mack danced closer. "They're anticipating, all right. Anti-ci-pa-tion." He lowered his voice. "My stock-in-trade."

"That and sex." Rosie couldn't help herself. Even though every piece of his clothing was right where it was supposed to be—at least for now—she skimmed a glance down his body to where the hat was strategically placed. "Doesn't it bother you to prance around naked on stage?"

"Doesn't it bother you?" He gave her the same kind of look she had just given him, and he didn't let the clown outfit stop him. Then again, he didn't have to. He knew exactly what she had—and didn't have—on underneath it.

"I'm not hearing any of that talking you were talking about," Rosie said. "That is what you came in here for, isn't it?" She gave him a big smile. "Or were you planning on picking the lock on my locker again?"

"I didn't pick the lock on your locker. It was open and I just looked, remember?"

"So you're here just to look?"

Mack's gaze slid down the baggy clown suit. "I was. You ruined the view."

"Tell you what, I'll ruin it some more." She twirled toward the mirror and slapped on some of the sticky stuff that held her red clown nose in place. She let it dry the required twenty seconds, then set the plastic nose over her own. "So what do you think?" She glanced at his reflection in the mirror, her voice suddenly nasal thanks to the plastic ball on her nose. "Better? Or worse? No. Don't tell me, let me guess. You're going to say I'm gorgeous either way. But then, that's all tied in with that anticipation thing, isn't it? Just practicing for later when you're out on stage?"

"Not practicing." Rosie whisked her red wig off the table and Mack set his hat down. "Talking. Which is exactly what I came in here to do."

It *was* what he'd come to the dressing room to do, and Mack told himself not to forget it. Not again. It might have been easier if he hadn't been faced with so much bare flesh the moment he stepped inside the dressing room door. It wasn't Angela or Julie or Tiffany he was worried about. Hell, he'd barely noticed. At least not any more than any red-blooded guy would have noticed three good-looking women in various stages of undress. OK, so Tiffany had great legs. And Julie had buns of steel. And Angela's breasts . . . well, there was a reason she'd been tapped to expose them in the glittering production number right before intermission. But it wasn't any of that that had nearly done him in. It was Rosie's costume. Downright demure when compared to Angela's, but still tiny enough to show off curves that were luscious enough to stroke. And that little spot right below her belly button. The one that looked soft and silky enough to—

"Talk. That is what I'm doing." With a cough, Mack

cleared away the tight knot in his throat. Too bad it wasn't as easy to unknot the tension that built inside him.

An ill-advised reaction considering the situation. Almost as stupid as the way he was letting emotion cloud his reason. And his mission.

Time to find out what was really going on behind that clown nose of Rosie's, and that clown wig and that body that was scrumptious enough to—

He yanked himself away from fantasy and back to reality. "I was just wondering . . ." Just wondering what? Now that it came down to crunch time, Mack tussled with the best way to say what needed to be said.

I was just wondering if maybe, since you've been around here longer and know the ropes better than I do . . . I was just wondering if maybe you knew where a guy could buy certain things that aren't found on the open market? Strictly on the QT, of course. Under the table. Behind the scenes.

A little beat-around-the-bush and really not his style.

I was just wondering about how a fellow—or in this case, probably a group of fellows—I was just wondering what kind of network they might have that allowed them to smuggle certain merchandise through a place like the Swan? Not that I'm accusing anyone of anything. Just theoretically. Just wondering. Just interested in hearing your opinion.

A little more to the point, but it was missing the finesse that was Mack's trademark.

I was just wondering if there's any chance of you knowing where I could spend three thousand bucks? And not just on anything. I'm looking for high quality and a decent price. I'm also looking to avoid any unwanted publicity, if you know what I mean.

Not subtle, but it might do the trick.

And doing the trick was what Mack was all about.

Which didn't explain why the words came out sounding suspiciously like "I've been thinking, Rosie. About that person who took a shot at us down in the casino. And the one who was driving that SUV that tried to make mincemeat out of you." Even as he said the words, he wondered what the hell was wrong with him. Rosie's safety—or relative lack of it—wasn't what he came in here to discuss. It wasn't his problem. And besides, he didn't have the luxury of caring.

Great argument. Irrefutable logic. Flawless reasoning. So why was there a little gnawing somewhere way deep down inside him that wouldn't leave him alone? Some gut feeling that tugged him toward the slippery slope where emotion was sure to lead?

He slid a look at her locker and felt himself skid a little more. "I've been thinking about that .38 you carry around in your purse. If you're in some kind of trouble . . ."

"Does this look like a face that's worried about being in some kind of trouble?" She jabbed one finger at her clown nose.

Mack shook his head. "Nice try," he said. "But if that was an attempt to distract me, I'm not buying it. And it's not going to work anyway. There's something going on, Rosie, and whether you admit it or not, I think it's something you can't handle on your own."

"Really?" Her jaw tensed and her eyes narrowed. "And you're what, now? Psychic? Actually, that would be a pretty good thing. We could probably find a job for you at that place over on the Strip where—"

"Cut the crap." Mack was angry. He was tired. Tired of the bullshit and the hedging. Tired of second-guessing himself and his methods and the life he'd managed to build for himself, one hard-won inch at a time. Tired of wondering if he should allow himself to be turned on by Rosie. Or be just plain scared to death of her.

"If you're in some kind of trouble," he told her, "there are people you can talk to. People who would be willing to help."

"Like you?"

It wasn't the first time he'd wished he could know what

was going on inside a woman's head. But this time, more than ever, it seemed not only important but critical to know what Rosie was thinking. Was she as cocky and unconcerned as she appeared to be? Or did the flush that raced across her face mean something else? Did the way she gulped down a tiny breath betray an emotion he wasn't supposed to notice? And the way she rolled her fingers into her palms, the way she straightened them again, did that mean something, too? Did it mean she was afraid?

Mack braced himself against the wave of concern that enveloped him. Not a good idea, he reminded himself. Not a good idea to get involved. Not a good idea to care. The only thing caring had ever gotten him was kicked in the teeth. The only thing it had ever done for him was left him on the outside looking in.

Damned good advice.

Kind of tough to follow when he was already stepping closer to Rosie. When already, though he had no intention of doing it, he found himself with his hand on her arm.

"Hell, yes, like me. I can help you, Rosie. I know some people who—"

"Who what?" Her gaze skimmed down to where his hand lay against the sleeve of her clown costume. When she looked up again, there was something very much like suspicion in her eyes. "What kind of people do you know, Mack?"

"People. You could talk to them and—"

"Tell them what? No, thanks. In case you haven't noticed, I can take care of myself."

As if her clown suit were suddenly the temperature of molten lava, Mack dropped his hand and moved back a step, and if he wasn't so damned pissed, he might have remembered all the things he'd heard from the therapists and the counselors and the do-gooders who had passed into—and mostly out of—his life since he was a kid. All that stuff about retreating. And emotional withdrawal. All the times they'd told him that no man—no matter how well intentioned, no matter how strong, no matter how smart—could ever completely stand on his own.

Then again, maybe he did remember it all. Maybe that's why he was so damned pissed.

"You think you can take care of yourself? Well, here's a news flash for you, *dulzura*. I don't think you have a clue what you're involved in."

"No. You're the one who needs the news flash." Rosie moved back, too, widening the gap between them. "I'm not your *dulzura*. And I'm nobody's *chica*. And I know exactly what I'm doing. Stay out of my way, Mack." She spun around and headed for the door. "Before you end up knee-deep in problems you can't handle. Or maybe you've already got problems. Maybe you're the one who should—"

"Me? That's a laugh." Which didn't explain why Mack wasn't laughing. "Maybe the same goes for you. You've had your chance. I offered some protection, but now—"

"Protection?" Rosie stopped so fast her red wig bucked. When she turned to face him, her expression was perfectly composed and her voice was as calm as the hush that settled right before a full-blown Texas twister hit. "Are you threatening me?"

Mack knew better than to take the bait. "I'm talking sense," he told her. "That's all. I'm reminding you that whatever the hell you think you're up to, it might just land you in a heap of trouble. And if you were smart—and at this point, I'm beginning to think that's a big *if*—you'd be thanking me."

"Thank you." She grabbed for the doorknob. "Thank you for threatening me? A little twisted, don't you think?"

"As twisted as working under some dead geezer's Social Security number?"

Just as he expected, his words stopped Rosie cold. He hoped they'd also catch her off guard enough that she might spill something she otherwise might not have said. He should have known better. Even though she was wearing a plastic clown nose, her expression was deadly serious. As if the bombshell weren't much of a bombshell at all.

"I've been wondering when you'd bring that up. . . ." She eyed him coldly, her eyes dark against the contrasting bright red nose. "J. J. Harrigan."

"How—" Mack swallowed the rest of the question. No use sounding too surprised. Something told him his expression had already given him away. But then, the revelation that she knew as much about him as he knew about her was nothing if not surprising. "When—"

"The same night you were down in Human Resources checking on me. Who are you really, Mack?"

"Who are you?"

"Why do you care?"

"Why shouldn't I?"

"Because it's none of your business."

"But see, that's where you're wrong. It is my business. Because—"

He never had a chance to tell her and it was just as well. Even Mack wasn't sure what he was going to say.

Before he had a chance to say another word, they heard a crash from the direction of the stage. It was followed by the frightened shrieks of a dozen chorus girls. The heart-stopping noise built like a wave. Until it was shattered by the gut-wrenching sound of a woman's terrified scream.

12

It wasn't often that one of the overhead lights came loose from its wiring and crashed down on the stage like a sparking, eighty-pound, demolish-everything-in-its-path bat out of hell.

Which was precisely why Rosie thought it was so damned odd that it happened. Odd and mighty suspicious. Especially considering that when the light came down, it came down on a stage full of clowns.

She didn't have a chance to consider what it all might mean. She didn't have the time or the opportunity to stand in the wings and gawk, either. By the time she and Mack got to the stage, the place was in chaos and someone needed to take control. At least until the Swan's security team arrived. Didn't it figure? Mack decided he was going to be that someone.

"Stay back." He stiff-armed her before she could step onto the stage. "No use making things worse by—"

"By me being there?" She gave him an acid glance that was wasted; he didn't notice. He was looking over the scene. "Thanks for the vote of confidence," she told him, and she ducked under his arm, headed onto the stage.

It didn't take long to size up the situation. Near the center of what would have been the chorus line just a couple minutes later, the light sat on its side in the crater it had gouged into the stage. Not three feet away, surrounded by a crowd of sobbing clowns, lay one of the girls, her left leg tucked up under her and her right leg cocked at a peculiar angle. Impossible to tell who it was because of the wig, the makeup, and the red nose. Not so impossible to see that it didn't matter. Whoever it was, she was in a world of trouble. The clown's eyes were closed and even with the coating of makeup, Rosie could tell that her skin was bluish purple. Her wig was soaked with something dark and even redder than the mile-wide fuzz.

Kneeling next to the injured woman was a clown Rosie recognized because her nose had gone flying. Julie's wig sat at a funny angle and she was holding the injured clown's hand, which, Rosie supposed, was a thoughtful, comforting, and supportive thing to do. Too bad Julie ruined the tender moment by screaming her lungs out.

"Like that's going to help." Grumbling, Rosie made a move to get past the clowns blocking her way. She needed to get Julie the hell out of there before her histrionics turned what was already an emotionally charged situation into a full-scale panic.

She actually might have accomplished her mission if Mack hadn't pushed past her. Her mood teetering between thankfulness and anger, she watched him haul Julie to her feet and hand her over to the clown who was closest.

"Get her out of here," he told the clown, and though it looked like she was on the verge of going into shock herself, the clown didn't argue and Rosie couldn't blame her.

Maybe it was the police uniform. Or the traditional and annoying tendency most women had of turning to a man in a crisis. Maybe it was because, of everyone there—everyone except Rosie—Mack was the one who seemed to keep both his head and his cool. He took over like a trained professional, and within just a couple seconds, he had the clowns moved back so they weren't crowding the woman who was hurt, yelled for someone to call 911 and call them fast, and knelt down at the injured clown's side.

Which, now that Rosie thought about it, all sounded like her job.

Of course, just because Mack looked the part didn't mean he knew what he was doing. Not willing to waste another precious second on the chance that he didn't, she knelt down across from Mack.

"Is she—" Rosie placed two fingers against the injured clown's neck, feeling for a beat in the carotid artery. "There's no pulse," she said, and she slid her gaze to the front of the blue-and-white clown suit. No movement there, either. "She's not breathing. Any sign of EMS?"

Apparently Mack wasn't in the mood to waste any time, either. He didn't bother to glance over his shoulder to check. He scooted up to kneel next to the clown's head. Her mouth was ringed with foam and Mack tugged at his shirt until the Velcro gave way. He used the front of the shirt to wipe off the clown's mouth, then tilted back her chin. "How good are you at CPR?" he asked Rosie.

"How good are you?" she countered.

Neither one of them bothered to answer. While Rosie moved the woman's right arm aside and positioned herself next to her chest, Mack yanked off the woman's plastic nose.

"Tiffany," Rosie said, and she glanced up at Mack. She didn't need to point out that Tiffany stood right next to her in the chorus line. If Rosie had been out on stage and exactly where she was supposed to be . . .

Rosie swallowed down the feeling that bubbled up in her stomach. "Two breaths," she told Mack. "And then I'll do—"

"I know the routine," he shot back, and after he'd given Tiffany two breaths, Rosie started the first chest compressions.

"One. Two. Three . . ." She counted under her breath,

making sure each push was even and centered over Tiffany's chest. "Thirteen. Fourteen. Fifteen. Now you—"

Mack was already giving another two breaths.

"Come on, Tiffany." If Tiffany could hear her was anybody's guess, but Rosie figured it was worth a try. "Start breathing, honey," she told her. "Nice and easy. You can do it. Hey, how often do you get Mr. Sexy to help you out?"

Mack angled her a look but he didn't say a thing. He didn't have the time. Or the breath.

It couldn't have been long before the paramedics arrived along with the Swan's security team. It felt like forever. When Rosie finally moved aside so that the professionals could take over, her arm muscles felt as if she'd just bench-pressed a couple hundred pounds, and her breaths were coming hard and fast. Adrenaline pumping full speed, she paced over to where an old-fashioned popcorn cart was overturned, right behind where the EMTs were working. She leaned back against it, and it wasn't long before she saw Tiffany's chest rise and fall to the rhythm of a couple of shallow breaths. Not much, but it was something, and when one of the paramedics looked over his shoulder and gave Rosie the thumbs-up, her throat closed over a ball of emotion and her eyes misted.

While the paramedics loaded Tiffany onto a stretcher and carried her off the stage, Mack came up next to Rosie. Call it a fallout of the crisis, or the result of too much nervous energy, but she barely noticed the way his bare chest gleamed in the stage lights or the slight sheen of sweat that highlighted his abs and his pecs so perfectly, she could have sworn it was sprayed on in the makeup department.

Or maybe she did notice. And maybe she was too jazzed to care. Saving a life worked that kind of magic.

Then again, so did working side by side with someone who didn't panic. Even when he could have. Someone who stepped in and got the job done. Because he knew that was the kind of above-and-beyond that set heroes apart from everyday people.

As if he'd been reading her mind and thinking all the same things about her, Mack slapped her a high five. "Good work."

"Thanks. You, too. You looked like you knew what you were doing."

"Hey, mouth-to-mouth . . . it's my specialty."

It was the kind of black humor she'd heard from firefighters and police officers and rescue personnel at a dozen different disaster scenes, and Rosie let it roll off her back. Sometimes black humor was the only thing that kept them all going. And since Mack was in uniform . . . well, she figured she'd cut him some slack.

"Where does a stripper learn CPR?"

"Hey, strippers have hearts."

"Which doesn't answer the question."

Mack shrugged and the light slid across his shoulders. "You pick things up. You know? And you—"

"I was a lifeguard." It was another little piece of her past and she didn't mind sharing it. She glanced over her shoulder at the place where the stage was stained with Tiffany's blood. "She's lucky she wasn't killed."

"Exactly what I was thinking." When Rosie started to pull herself up, Mack offered her a hand. His skin was warm and his fingers wrapped around hers with a touch that told her he was surprised by what she'd just done. Surprised and impressed. His reaction went to her head, and acting on instinct, Rosie gave his hand a squeeze.

Right before she reminded herself that when it came to Mack, acting on instinct meant acting like a lunatic.

She didn't have the luxury. Or the inclination.

Not when someone had just tried to kill her.

As soon as she realized what she'd done, she yanked her hand out of Mack's and used it to dust off the seat of her clown costume. As if anyone would notice a dusty butt in the midst of the wreckage on stage.

When the light came down, it brought a lot of the stage infrastructure down along with it. Its moorings cut, a huge bunch of helium-filled balloons went flying up in front of Rosie and floated to the rafters. The red-and-white-striped tent through which the clowns made their entrance drooped precariously behind them. Even the gigantic and very phony-looking elephant that stood in a pen at center stage looked much the worse for wear. Its trunk flopped and its stuffing—like that Thanksgiving turkey she'd never had at home because her family believed the holiday marked the beginnings of the destruction of the indigenous Native American culture—oozed from a hole in its side.

A few of the hands had come out on stage to try and get things back in order. Not an easy thing to do considering that there were pieces of smashed scenery scattered around, members of the security team talking to the clowns who were still on stage, and a photographer Rosie recognized from the security department who was taking pictures of the fallen light.

"Doesn't look like there's much for us to do around here," she told Mack.

"No. Doesn't look like there is."

But neither one of them made a move to leave.

A guy from maintenance arrived with a roll of wide yellow plastic tape like the kind the cops used at crime scenes, and Rosie knew she couldn't wait for Mack to make the first move. If she hung around doing nothing until he finally decided to leave, she might not have a chance to take a closer look at the fallen light.

There didn't seem much point in making up a story to explain what she was up to. Rather than try, she walked across the stage and stopped next to the light. She looked up.

"Nothing much to see up there, I don't suppose."

"Is there a reason I'm not surprised you followed me over

here?" She glanced at Mack, who was standing at her side. Another not-so-big surprise. He was doing exactly what she was doing. He was looking up, past the metal catwalk that spanned the stage, and over to where a whole army of stage lights was hanging side by side, looking stable and blessedly secure.

"Guess that's the end of the excitement."

Mack was right. The end of the excitement, but Rosie knew it wasn't the end of the evening. At least not for her. As soon as she ditched Mack and the costume from hell, she was planning on climbing up to the catwalk and taking a look around. If the stage light had been tampered with—and even this early in the investigation, she was willing to bet it had been—she wanted to get a good look at what had been done to it before the maintenance crew and stagehands showed up and messed up whatever evidence might have been left behind. After that, she needed to talk to every stagehand she could find. And try to determine who was on stage at the time of the accident. And who wasn't.

"Think it was an accident?" Mack's question broke through her thoughts.

"Think I'm that dumb?"

Good thing Warren raced out on stage before Mack had a chance to answer.

"Rosie! Rosie!" His cheeks flushed and his mouth opening and closing over words he just couldn't seem to get out, Warren looked all around. "Rosie, where are you?"

"Here!" Rosie waved. "It's me, Warren." Just to prove the point, she plucked off her nose. "See?"

A wave of relief washed over Warren's face. "That's good. That's good, Rosie."

"Hey, Warren!" Mack smiled and glanced down at the toolbox Warren was carrying. "I see you found it."

"Found it?" Rosie wondered what she'd missed and how significant it might be. "Warren, was your toolbox—"

"Right where I left it." Warren nodded so vigorously, his

shaggy hair flopped over his forehead. "Right where I left it. I found it. But when I found you, Rosie, I thought you would be—"

"Mashed like a bowl of Thanksgiving potatoes?" Not that Rosie knew exactly how a bowl of Thanksgiving potatoes was mashed. Even after she moved away from home and established her own holiday tradition, she had never gotten the mashed potato part down right. Which didn't mean she didn't understand the concept. Or the fact that in the case of potatoes, mashed was a good thing. And in the case of clowns, it was very bad, indeed.

"Mashed. Yeah." Warren looked at the fallen light and at the spatters of blood on the stage. "I don't like Mr. Carpathian."

Neither did anyone else, but what that had to do with the fallen light, Rosie couldn't say. Not that she was about to question it. Whatever he was worried about, it made sense to Warren. Enough sense to make his eyes fill with tears.

He dashed them away with the back of his hand. "When I heard what he said to that Angela, that girl who yells and tells me to mind my own business and asks too many questions, I thought you would be mashed."

"You heard Angela and Mr. Carpathian talking about the accident? No wonder you were upset, Warren. Everyone was after the light came down. But see, I'm fine. No mashed Rosie."

"I'm glad, Rosie. I was worried. I ran all the way here because I was worried. I was going to tell you. About the light."

"Thanks, Warren." Rosie gave him a reassuring pat on the arm. "Why don't you help—"

She didn't get a chance to suggest that Warren help with the cleanup. Before she could, Warren's mouth dropped open and his face went pale. She looked over her shoulder and saw Emery Carpathian headed their way. When she turned back around, Warren was gone.

"Thirty minutes." His expression blank, Carpathian

looked over the scene before he turned his attention to Mack. "You're on in thirty minutes."

So much for fanfare. Or even a little oh-my-god-how-are-you-and-did-you-get-hurt-and-aren't-you-the-two-who-saved-that-clown. Every hair on his head in place, every whisker of his skinny little mustache impeccable, Carpathian lit a slim brown cigarette and tossed the match down on stage. "You'll be ready," he told Mack, and without another word, he spun around and started issuing orders for getting the smashed scenery, the mashed costumes, and the mangled clowns off the stage.

"Heartless bastard."

Rosie didn't even realize she'd grumbled the words until Mack responded. "No. It's OK. Really. I understand where he's coming from. He's got patrons out front and from what I heard earlier, they sold a lot of tickets for tonight's show. Sorry to burst your bubble, but I think it's safe to say that they're not here to see you chorus girls, they're—"

"Here to see you." She gave him a sour smile. "Neither snow, nor rain, nor falling light fixtures can stop a stripper, blah, blah, blah."

"Something like that. Though in this case . . ." He glanced down at the pieces of his police shirt that he still held in one hand. The shirt was wet and stained with Tiffany's blood. "I guess we'll have to put the bride and policeman act on hold for tonight and come up with a Plan B pretty fast. That gives you another day to think about it. Another chance to change your mind. You could still be my bride."

It wasn't something Rosie wanted to think about.

She watched Carpathian make his way over to where the head of security was supervising the removal of the broken light, at the same time she wondered what he was trying to cover up and why the cops hadn't been called. "Patrons or no patrons, he could cancel the show. He could offer everybody out front a couple free drinks and tickets to tomorrow night's performance."

"He could, but if he does, a whole lot of people are going to be unhappy. And Carpathian's too smart a businessman to make people unhappy. It's not personal, Rosie. It's business. Just like I was telling you back in the dressing room." He looked up at the place high over their heads where the wires that had once held the light fixture dangled like black spaghetti. "Something tells me this is business, too." He let his gaze wander over to the crater at their feet and then over to Rosie. "If you're smart, you won't forget it."

"Not forget it, huh? How can I?" Rosie grumbled the words under her breath. "Kind of hard to forget an out-and-out threat. Especially when that threat—"

She didn't dare utter the rest of what she was thinking.

Especially when that threat was tossed at her by the man she'd made love to.

"Yeah," she reminded herself, "and don't forget the part about how he never would have had the chance if you didn't let your professionalism slip along with your panties." She mumbled the words. Not that anyone would have heard her even if she yelled at the top of her lungs. On the other side of the blue velvet curtain that separated the stage from the audience, a crowd of a thousand screaming, clapping, stomping women was making enough noise to wake the dead.

Anticipation. Wasn't that what Mack called it?

Well, they were well into the anticipation thing. After the delay caused by the accident and the time it took to put the stage into some semblance of order, Mack's show was about an hour late starting. And anticipation was as heavy in the air as the mixed scent of a couple dozen different perfumes that wafted backstage from out front.

"We want the Saint! We want the Saint!" A high-pitched voice toward the back of the house got the cheer going, and the rest of the audience took it up.

Anticipation.

Apparently, Mack knew what he was talking about. By

the time he got on stage, the women in the audience would be so worked up, they probably wouldn't care if he was over-weight, balding, and as homely as a basset hound.

Which he definitely was not.

Rosie dashed aside the thought and the heat that flooded through her along with it. From the other side of the curtain, she saw the houselights dim. The chant quieted and a buzz of expectation shivered through the crowd.

This was her opportunity and she knew she had to take it. It was time to get moving before the stage lights came up and the spotlight hit.

She glanced around to make sure no one was watching. Just as she'd hoped, everyone was as busy as they always were right before the curtain went up. The stage was empty and nearly dark except for the dim blue stage lights on the overhead track.

Keeping to the shadows and congratulating herself for being smart enough to slip into black slacks and a black sweater, she ducked under the yellow tape that had been strung up to limit access to the place where the light had crashed onto the stage. The metal ladder that led up to the catwalk wasn't far away, and she hurried over to it and caught the bottom rung. Like a fire escape, the ladder was designed so that it wasn't easily accessible from below, and she had to haul herself up, hand over hand, until she could find a foothold. Piece of cake.

As long as she didn't look down.

Rosie reminded herself that she didn't have time for half-baked psychodrama. She wasn't exactly afraid of heights, she just didn't like the way her stomach swooped and her head spun anytime she was up higher than the four-inch heels she wore for the last production number of the night. Moral of the story: get the job done fast. Before she could convince herself not to do it at all.

She scurried up the ladder, her sneakers providing just the right traction and making her climb completely quiet.

"Ladies and gentlemen . . ." Out front, the announcer's voice boomed over the sound system. Starting and stopping and starting again. "Ladies and ladies . . ." he corrected himself.

The crowd cheered.

"The Silver Swan Casino and Hotel proudly presents . . ."

"Just get on with it!" someone yelled.

"Yeah, just get him out here so we can get it on," another voice called out.

Though Rosie knew for a fact that there was supposed to be more to the announcer's shtick—some nonsense about the eighth wonder of the world and a gift from heaven above—the announcer knew a losing cause when he was smack dab in the middle of one. His sigh rippled over the sound system, a sure sign that he was ready to give up.

"The Saint!" he shouted and although Rosie knew it was his job, she wondered why he bothered. There was no way on earth anyone heard him. Not with all the applause and the high-pitched shrieking that started up even before he got the words out of his mouth.

Noise was a good thing, she reminded herself. Lots of noise down in the audience meant no one would notice a little noise high above the stage. Rosie sprinted up the last ten rungs of the ladder. Just as she got to the place where the ladder met the catwalk, the stage lights went out completely and she was plunged into darkness.

"Shit." She was thirty feet up in the air with nothing to hold on to but the metal rungs of the ladder. She held her breath and waited for the curtain to rise, sure that when it did, at least some of the stage lights that were computer-operated from a booth at the back of the theater would come on. It wouldn't give her perfect light in which to work. But it would be better than nothing. And right now, what she had was a big old, very dark nothing.

Nice plan. It might even have worked if, when the curtain slid up, the light that came on wasn't a strobe.

Glaring light pulsed through the theater, its brightness a sharp contrast to the throbbing blackness that punctuated it and the sweep of a spotlight that arced across the stage. For just a couple seconds, the light show mesmerized Rosie. It took a couple more seconds to get used to the flashing pattern of light and shadow. Just about as long as it took for the audience to take up the rhythm. Pretty soon they were clapping to the rhythm of a drum that started a pounding and furious beat.

The sounds echoed until Rosie's head pounded along with them. She didn't need to look down to know the exact moment Mack walked out onto the stage. A searing guitar joined the drum and the decibel level rose to something rivaling the takeoff of a 747. The noise that before now had been a cheer of anticipation, turned into something else altogether. Something that rose from a thousand female throats like a growl.

As much as she told herself it probably wasn't a good idea, Rosie couldn't help herself. She had to look down.

She was right. It wasn't a good idea.

The rungs of the ladder were slender bars of metal, and other than that and the thin metal rails that ran perpendicular to them for handholds, she was floating through a world no more solid than the pulsing lights and flickering shadows. Instinctively she tightened her grip on the rails but by that time, it was too late. That one instant of looking down was enough to throw her equilibrium out of whack. Her right foot slipped. Her body jerked forward. Her chin slammed into the one of the ladder rungs.

If she wasn't so busy hanging on for dear life, she might have found the time and energy to let loose with another curse.

Rosie pulled in a deep breath. She needed to get her bearings, and if the noise in her head and the slow roll in her stomach meant anything, she needed to get them fast. She needed some grip on reality. She sure wasn't going to find it in the swirl of lights in the air around her, or in the first few rows of upturned faces she could see from her vantage point. The ones that smiled and screamed and swooned on the other side of the stage lights. She sure wasn't going to feel any better if she watched the way the audience picked up the beat, until every person she could see was swaying to the pounding rhythm of Mack's music.

The stage was the only solid thing she had to focus on. Like it or lump it, it looked like Mack was destined to be her grip on reality.

Rosie swallowed hard and wondered if she was bracing herself against the height or against the drumming she knew would start in her bloodstream the moment she looked at Mack. She looked down, anyway, and just as she did, he dance-stepped into the spotlight.

And Rosie saw what all the fuss was about.

Mack in black slacks and a silky red shirt was delectable. Mack in a police uniform was a sight to behold. But this Mack was Mack in dusty khakis, a sleeveless T-shirt, a tool belt, and a yellow hard hat. And Mack as a macho-man construction worker was nothing short of mouthwatering.

Too bad she couldn't forget that this was the same man who just a short time before had threatened her.

The one who knew more than he let on. About a whole bunch of things he shouldn't have known about.

Feeling a little steadier and a whole lot more sure of herself, Rosie swung over to the catwalk. After the sensation of floating she'd had on the ladder, it was heaven to have something more solid under her feet. Even when *more solid* meant a metal plank no more than eighteen inches wide. At least there was a metal railing running along the entire length of the catwalk and, holding onto it like the lifesaver it was, Rosie scooted to her right, scanning the stage lights that hung just above her head both in front and behind the catwalk.

From down below, she heard a shout of approval. The

tool belt or the hard hat? Rosie weighed the possibilities while she scuttled over to where there was a gap in the row of stage lights. If she had to bet, she would put her money on the tool belt. It made the most sense that Mack would jettison that first. After all, as he'd demonstrated with the police officer's hat, he'd need his hard hat for the grand finale.

The picture that flashed through her mind blindsided her. So did the heat that erupted along with it, and before she even realized what she was doing, Rosie found herself with both hands clutched to the metal railing, her knuckles white. By now, she was just about center stage and Mack was directly below and just a little in front of her. Call it curiosity or just plain old lust gone out of control, she couldn't help but watch.

Just as she'd guessed, he'd tossed aside the tool belt and was working on the T-shirt while he worked the audience. It couldn't have been easy. But Mack made it work like magic.

When he danced toward the front of the stage, dozens of hands reached out for him. One lady leapt out of her seat and started up on stage. She would have made it if not for the fact that there was a bouncer nearby. Other women tossed little gifts to Mack, pieces of paper where they'd (no doubt) written their phone numbers, and silky panties.

Something else she didn't want to think about.

Not in the same context as Mack.

Keeping the thought firmly in mind, Rosie leaned out over the metal hand railing, searching for the dangling wires. What she got instead was a better look at Mack. Just as he whipped off his khakis.

The next thing she knew, Mack was down on his knees on the runway that extended out into the audience, and the women nearby were tucking messages and dollar bills into the strap of his yellow, silky thong.

Even thirty feet above the action, Rosie realized how lucky the women down in the audience were. They were having the time of their lives, completely oblivious to the fact that Mack was—

What?

A stage light next to her flashed on and Rosie jumped. It was part of the special effects designed to whip the audience into even more of a frenzy. Next to her, a yellow light flashed on. Farther down the line, a red one flicked on and off. All around her, the lights snapped on and off until the stage looked as if it were in the center of a fireworks display.

With all the light, it was easy to find the wires she was looking for. Rosie stopped and examined the wires left dangling when the stage light fell. It didn't take a forensics specialist to see that they had been cut. There was no fraying, none of the hit-and-miss splitting of wires that was the telltale sign of an accident. These wires were cut clean and, if she had to guess, she would have said it was with something as simple as a pair of garden shears. Or a stagehand's tools. Even the kind of long-tipped scissors she'd seen in Warren's toolbox.

Rosie wanted to take a closer look but just as she leaned forward, the lights closest to her turned off. Too bad. There was something odd hanging from the edge of the catwalk just to her right. She stooped down, but in the dark, it was impossible to find it again. She had just about convinced herself that she'd imagined it when the light came on again. Rosie got down on her knees and leaned over the catwalk. There on the edge of it, caught on a scrap of sharp metal, was a piece of blue-and-white-striped cloth.

Right off a clown costume.

Rosie grabbed for the scrap of cloth, tucked it in her pocket, and stood. Just as she did, the light directly behind her turned on and her shadow—big as life and twice as hard to miss—fell right on Mack.

The light went off again just as quickly, but by that time, it was already too late.

Mack froze, one arm up in the air, one hand out to a

sweet young thing in the first row who looked like she was going to melt right on the spot. He swung around to give the audience a look at his well-shaped behind. Lucky them. And lucky for him, too, because when he did, he had the chance to glance up at the catwalk.

Rosie stood stock-still. Though there was no way he could miss the fact that there was someone on the catwalk, from the angle he was at, he might not be able to tell exactly who that someone was.

Then again, maybe he could.

Her heart thudding against her rib cage, Rosie watched Mack slip his hard hat off his head. Just the way he'd done with the police officer's hat back in the dressing room.

She watched him do a couple of showy dance moves, the hat held out in front of him in both hands. His back still to the audience, his gaze on the catwalk high above his head, he held the hard hat over his crotch. Just like he'd done in the dressing room.

He did a couple of slow hip gyrations and aimed a smile at Rosie that was brighter even than the stage lights. In one slick move designed to coincide perfectly with an earth-shattering guitar chord, he spun around toward the audience, whipped off the neon-yellow G-string, and tossed it up and over his shoulder.

Perfect three-point landing.

Right on the catwalk at Rosie's feet.

She didn't wait to see any more. With the crowd still screeching its approval and the lights still flashing and the music still booming, Rosie raced back over to the ladder and climbed down. She was halfway to the bottom when the curtain closed. She was on the last rung of the ladder when she realized Mack was waiting for her.

Like it was the most natural thing in the world, she hopped off the ladder and landed lightly on her feet.

She looked Mack up and down, her gaze resting just a little longer than it should have on the yellow hard hat he held right below the belt. If he was wearing a belt. "Nice show."

"You, too." He glanced up at the catwalk before he let his gaze settle on Rosie. "You didn't happen to bring my thong down with you, did you?"

Rosie snapped her fingers. "Forgot." She moved to get around Mack at the same time he moved to block her path.

"You want to explain what you were doing up there?"

"To you?" OK, so Rosie admitted it. She was shallow. Her gaze flickered down again. Over the shoulders. And the completely-free-of-hair chest. And the flat-as-a-board stomach. Down to the hard hat. She looked up again. "Doesn't look to me like you're in any position to be asking questions."

"What? A guy can't ask questions when his clothes are off?" There wasn't the least bit of amusement in the grin Mack aimed at her. "Seems to me, that's when he should ask more questions than ever."

"Not in this case." Rosie smiled back. "In this case, I'd say you need to get back . . ." She let her gaze slide to the closed curtain. From the other side of it, a thousand women were screaming for an encore. "Sounds to me like they want more, more, more."

"They can wait." Mack shuffled close enough for his hard hat to touch Rosie's thigh. "I've got more important things to worry about."

"Like . . ."

"You hurt your chin." With one finger, he grazed the spot where her chin had banged against the metal ladder rung.

It must have hurt more than Rosie remembered; she winced at the contact. "It's nothing," she insisted.

"Like the nothing you found up there?" Mack's gaze left hers only long enough to skim the catwalk. "Were the wires cut?"

"What do you think?"

"Was there anything else? Anything—"

"Telltale evidence?" Rosie laughed. "What do I look like,

Nancy Drew? You want to find out what's up there, go on up and see for yourself. Only you might want to put on some clothes before you do."

His smile sparked up a notch. "I do my best work without."

"They certainly think so." Again, she glanced toward the curtain. It was getting nosier out front. The audience was getting even more insistent. "Something tells me you'd better get out there or we're going to have a full-scale, hormone-induced riot on our hands. They want their money's worth. Go on out there"—she nudged his arm—"and take off your clothes. Oh, but wait." Rosie allowed herself a look that was half surprise and half wide-eyed innocence. She glanced down at the hard hat. "Looks like you can't. You don't have any more clothes to take off."

"Oh, I don't know about that." In one quick movement, Mack lifted the hard hat, spun it in his hands, and plopped it on his head.

And Rosie couldn't help herself. She gasped and stepped back.

It wasn't until she saw him laughing that she dared to look down. He was wearing a black leather thong, one that was even smaller than the yellow one he tossed up to the catwalk.

"Not funny." Rosie glared at him.

"Neither is this." Mack glanced behind Rosie toward where the crater was left when the stage light hit. "So not funny that it nearly killed Tiffany. Only something tells me Tiffany wasn't the target."

"And you think I was. That's not funny, either."

"Not supposed to be." He leaned in close, his voice no more than a murmur that whispered over her cheek. "It's all about anticipation," Mack whispered, right before he headed around the curtain and to the front of the stage. "Remember that, Rosie. An-ti-ci-pa-tion. Time to ask yourself when it's going to happen again."

13

"You think maybe you were a little hard on her?"

It wasn't the response Mack expected from Lenny and, for a couple of seconds, he found it impossible to answer. Hard? On Rosie? After all he'd told Lenny about what had happened at the theater the night before, he was surprised Lenny would even consider it.

"You're kidding me, right?" Mack congratulated himself. It was a better response than the "hell, no" he was tempted to give Lenny. "If that's what you think, I must not be explaining myself very clearly."

"Oh, you're clear all right. Like crystal." Lenny adjusted his stance and glanced across the street to where the volcano in front of one of the Strip's more popular hotels was about to pop. He tipped back his head, watching the plume of smoke that rose in the cloudless sky. "Sounds to me like you were trying to intimidate the girl."

"She's not a girl. She's a woman." Not that it mattered a whole bunch in the great scheme of things, but Mack thought it was important to get the facts straight. "And I wasn't trying to intimidate her. You know I wouldn't do that. Besides, I was doing it for her own good. I was trying to make her realize what she apparently doesn't realize. Or at least what she doesn't want to admit."

"And that is . . ."

"That she's in danger." Mack stuffed his hands into the pockets of his jeans and turned his back on the spectacle going on across the street. He was always antsy when things weren't progressing as quickly as he would have liked, and he knew that watching a crowd of wide-eyed tourists goggle at a bogus volcano shooting out phony lava would do nothing to improve his mood. "That light fell at just the right time. And at just the right place. If it was the only thing that's happened, I might not be suspicious. But let's face it, Lenny. We put two and two together and we're going to come up with four. If Rosie had been out on stage where she was supposed to be . . . if I hadn't pulled her out of the path of that SUV . . . if we hadn't been so quick down there in the casino . . .

"Plus, she knows Gus Friel's sister. It all adds up, Lenny. It has to. Rosie knows something. And the fact that she's carrying a Ruger proves it. I thought if I could shake her up a little, you know, get her thinking about how dangerous things are, I thought I could get her to talk."

Lenny glanced his way. "You sure?" he asked.

"Sure?" Mack wasn't certain where the conversation was headed, and not knowing made him edgy. Unless Lenny was talking about—

"You don't think I'd let the fact that she's attractive get in the way of—"

Lenny shook his head and the small yellow feather in the band of his fedora quivered. "Look, Mack . . ." Even though Mack hadn't budged, Lenny held up one hand. As if that would stop him if Mack decided to make a move.

"It's my fault," Lenny said. "I should have had this conversation with you a long time ago. Back when I realized you were attracted to the girl."

It was the perfect opportunity to jump in with a protest,

but somehow, Mack just couldn't make himself do it. There was no use lying. Not to Lenny. There was no use making up excuses, either. The only thing excuses would do was get him in deeper. And he was already in plenty deep enough.

When Mack didn't jump in with an objection, Lenny continued. "Then again, I guess I can't blame you. She's a looker, all right. I didn't bother to lecture you about how dangerous it is to get too involved, to take your work too personally. You're a professional. As good as any I've worked with and better than most. I didn't think you needed to be reminded—I don't think you need to be reminded now—about stepping over the line. But listen up, Mack: if you think you can play knight in shining armor—"

"I'm not trying to save her. Not the way you think." The suggestion made Mack bristle. "You know me better than that. I don't get involved. Not like that."

"Not much point in getting too close to people."

Mack didn't bother to wonder if Lenny was being facetious. "Damn straight," he told him, and he knew it was true. Getting close meant getting hurt. Always had. There was nothing and no one who could convince him that this time was any different. Rosie was the perfect case in point. Get close—real close—and find out the woman you got close to—real close—was also close to Gus Friel's sister. And Gus Friel was close to the 9A-91s.

Mack twitched away that thought along with the one that reminded him that Rosie was determined, smart, self-sufficient, and cool in a crisis. In spite of the fact that she liked to hide behind a straight-arrow suit of armor, she was also far more daring and more fiercely sexual than she was willing to give herself credit for.

She'd proved that up in the Eiffel Tower.

Maybe that's why this time, Mack knew that getting close meant getting his teeth kicked in and his heart ripped out and his gut sliced in two. And that this time, it was going to hurt more than it ever had before.

"All I'm trying to do is get her to talk," he told himself and Lenny. "If that means scaring her a little, then so be it. It doesn't mean I'm trying to scare her so she comes running to me and I can play hero. Rosie doesn't need that kind of protection."

Before he even realized he was doing it, Mack touched a finger to the bridge of his nose. This far removed from the incident, his nose no longer hurt, but he didn't need to remind himself of the force of her punch.

"All right," he admitted to Lenny and to himself. "So she's tough. So she's got this ridiculous don't-stop-until-you-win attitude. And the annoying tendency to be way too secretive. Even so, it shouldn't take much to get her to listen to reason. To get her to open up and maybe tell us something that will lead us to the guns. You think she'd be pretty scared already."

"Which makes me wonder why she's not."

It had made Mack wonder, too. Plenty. "I think she is and she just won't admit it," he told Lenny. "I think she's just stubborn and proud and way too independent for her own good."

"Or in too deep and not willing to back out."

"Or in too deep and not willing to back out."

As much as the thought made him uneasy, Mack knew he owed it to himself to consider it.

"Maybe she's just being cagey." Lenny walked up to a newsstand and paid for a copy of the day's paper. He glanced over the front page while he walked. "Maybe she's waiting for you to make the first move. Ever think of that?"

Mack had thought about it, all right. But something told him the first move that sprang to his mind wasn't the same first move Lenny was talking about.

As fast as he could, he doused the emotions that threatened to overwhelm him. "I'm not ready to lay my cards on the table, if that's what you mean, Lenny. I don't want her to know who I am. Not yet."

"Agreed." Lenny read down to the end of one article, then flipped the newspaper pages to find its continuation inside. He folded the paper open. "Believe me, I'll let you know when I think the time is right for that. But I do think there's something else to consider. I know you're not going to agree with this, Mack, but maybe you're being a little pig-headed, too? Maybe you aren't willing to admit that you might be in as much danger as Rosie? What if you tell her who you are and what if she—"

"Comes after me with everything she's got?"

The words settled inside Mack like ice.

"I know. I've thought of it. You don't think I'd let that stop me, do you? You don't think I'm afraid?"

"Afraid? You? Not of anything, kid. Which, frankly, is one of the reasons I worry about you. But I also know that no matter what, you'll do what you have to do. Even if it hurts like hell."

"Which it most definitely won't." Mack grumbled a word in Spanish that Lenny shouldn't have known. From the look the older man gave him, it was clear Mack needed to remember that there was a whole lot more to Lenny than met the eye. "Nothing's going to stop me from doing my job," he assured Lenny.

"I know that, too." Lenny gave him a friendly slap on the back. "So what do you say, Mack? How about we try a little more productive approach? Like, say you had more information to work with?"

"If I had even a little useful information, I'd be a happier man."

"Then I have some good news for you." With a smile, Lenny reached a hand into the pocket of his sport coat, pulled out a single, folded piece of paper, and handed it over to Mack.

Even before he unfolded it, he knew what was inside. Mack's mood brightened. "Neeta. You found her?"

"We found her." Lenny nodded. "That's a phone number

where she can be reached, but it looks like she's not always there. Unlike Rosie, she seems to understand the importance of working with us instead of against us. Only she's not exactly ready to come in out of the cold. Not yet. She's pretty jumpy. She wants to keep this very low key and I can't say I blame her. She says you shouldn't try to contact her. She'll get in touch with you. Soon."

Finally they were getting somewhere. Finally he was on the verge of getting some information that was less smoke-and-mirrors and more solid and maybe even helpful.

For a second, Mack allowed himself the luxury of wallowing in the news. For another second, he wondered why it didn't leave him feeling very happy.

For a third second, he told himself not to stop and consider it. Or to look for the sweetness and light in any situation. No matter how it was accomplished, he had a job to do.

Satisfied things were finally moving in the right direction, he pulled himself back to the matter at hand. "Did she say how?" he asked Lenny. "This Neeta, did she say how she was going to contact me?"

Just as he turned to walk away, Lenny shook his head. "She says you'll know," he called over his shoulder. "She says there's no way you'll miss it."

Mack had to give Neeta credit. When she promised an impossible-to-miss message, she wasn't kidding. She might have made him wait a few days, but she came through like a trooper.

At first he didn't recognize her. Neeta's hair was pulled back from her face and wrapped into a prim-as-a-school-teacher bun. Her clothes were far more conservative than the ones she'd been wearing the afternoon he saw her race out of the alley. Her makeup was toned down.

And he couldn't blame her.

If she knew something about Gus Friel and the 9A-91s,

the last thing Neeta needed to do was call attention to herself.

Even with the makeover, he noticed her soon after he dance-stepped his way onto the stage. It didn't take a degree from Princeton to figure out what she had in mind. Somehow, Neeta had managed to wangle a ticket for one of the most coveted tables in the house, one right next to the runway. Perfect. For her purposes. And for his.

Like he did every night, Mack threw himself into his strip routine with the kind of mindless abandon that had worked so well for so many years back in El Paso. He waited until the audience was worked into a frenzy before he ventured onto the runway, and like they did every night, the women who had come to watch him bump and grind his way into their daydreams showed their appreciation with nothing less than wild enthusiasm. They grabbed for him when he danced by and fought to snatch up the articles of clothing he discarded. They threw little gifts into his path. They tossed flowers at him and begged him to come closer so that they could tuck their messages and their dollar bills into the strap of his thong. They screamed his name and begged him for dates. A couple came right out and told him they'd meet him after the show and that if he was ready, they were more than willing and able to oblige.

Like always, it all left Mack feeling more disconnected than ever. And grateful that somehow, he'd found another path in life. One that didn't lead straight up a runway and toward the outstretched hands of a horde of women whose sex drives were in overdrive and whose inhibitions had been checked at the door. One that didn't gyrate to the music.

The thought was enough to remind him that he had more important things to do than indulge in self-analysis or self-pity.

As he danced by, Mack glanced at Neeta, telling her with a look that he'd be back when the time was right. A few minutes, eighty-seven dollars, and a couple dozen messages later, he got down on both knees in front of Neeta and tossed her the kind of hot-as-hell-and-twice-as-dangerous smile he'd given every other woman who had the nerve to get close enough to nudge aside the thin strap of spandex over his hip.

Neeta was as jumpy as a cockroach and she looked like she hadn't slept in a couple of days. She didn't look quite convinced that the mostly naked guy on stage in front of her could possibly have been the same guy Lenny had set up a meet with. But she didn't hesitate. Her nicotine-stained fingers shaking, she tucked a small slip of folded paper into Mack's G-string. She didn't wait to see the end of the show. As Mack danced back to center stage, he saw her hurry out of the theater.

And he knew he needed to get a move on, too.

Which made the call for an encore not as much of a compliment as it was an irritation.

Mack got his second number over fast and, back in the dressing room, he moved quickly. Like he always did, he put aside the tip money that had been thrust at him to give to Lenny the next time they got together. Like he never did, he glanced through the notes that had been tucked into his G-string. And he realized why he never usually bothered with them.

"Meet me at the bar after the show and we'll—" Even Mack, who had pretty much seen everything there was to see out on the streets, was speechless at the suggestion. He crumpled the note in one hand and tossed it into the wastebasket at the same time he reached for another one. That one ended up in the circular file, too, as did the next dozen or so.

Disgusted, Mack shook his head. Something told him he'd know Neeta's message when he saw it. The same something that told him it wouldn't have anything to do with black leather, late-night trysts, or invitations to strip privately.

He was right. Neeta's message stood out from the pack by its very simplicity, not to mention the fact that there wasn't one four-letter word in it. Mack read it over twice, committing the words to memory before he tore the paper into a dozen small and unreadable pieces and dropped it into the trash. He threw away the rest of the messages, too, showered, and pulled on a pair of jeans and a black T-shirt. He dug his shoulder holster out of the duffel bag in his locker and slipped it on, made sure his .38 was loaded and that he had extra ammunition, and shrugged into a leather jacket.

He was out the stage door and onto his Harley in a matter of minutes. As he'd been instructed to do by Neeta, he stopped the bike at the mouth of the alley that led back to the Swan's loading dock and waited.

Just like she promised she would be, Neeta must have been watching and waiting. She came out of the casino directly across from the Swan and headed up the street. There was a beat-up green Toyota Corolla parked not too far away, just like she said there would be, and he waited until she started it up before slipping into traffic to follow her.

After a hell of a long time in traffic congested enough to induce even the most mild-mannered driver into a full-fledged case of road rage, they were out of Vegas and headed into the desert.

"The desert, huh?" Rosie shook her head, unsure at this stage if this was good news or bad. They were finally out of the god-awful Las Vegas traffic, and that was a good thing, she supposed. But the desert? The desert sounded dark. And mighty lonely. Exactly the kind of place she would have chosen for a meet.

Not exactly the kind of place she wanted to walk into without backup.

Just to reassure herself, Rosie touched a hand to the shoulder purse she'd brought along with her and the revolver that fit into a compartment at the bottom. It wasn't the first time she wished she had her Sig. Overkill? Maybe. But there wasn't a cop alive who didn't believe that too much firepower was better than too little.

She just prayed she wouldn't have to use it.

Hoping to get some sense of the lay of the land and at least some idea of where they might be headed, Rosie took a quick look around. Already, the glaring lights of Las Vegas were no more than a gleam in her rearview mirror. On either side of her, the Nevada desert was barren and, at this hour of the night, pitch-black. Luckily, there were a few other cars on the road, headed who knew where, so though she hung back from Mack's motorcycle and hoped he hadn't noticed when she headed out of her parking place and into the traffic behind him, she didn't have to worry about following from too far. Now and again, a car came the other way on the two-lane road and Rosie squinted against the brightness of the headlights. Now and again, another set of headlights flickered in her rearview mirror.

Even so, when Mack turned onto a dusty side road, she slowed down. There was no use letting him catch on, not at this stage of the game. Besides, she didn't have to worry too much about losing him. The farther they got from Vegas (Las Vegas, she reminded herself), the sparser the traffic got. Out here, forty-five minutes from the city and about a million miles from nowhere, it wouldn't be hard to catch up with Mack again. All she needed to do was listen for the purr of the motorcycle engine or watch for the single headlight that illuminated the road in front of Mack's bike.

Before she even realized what she was doing, Rosie caught herself hauling in a deep breath and letting it out slowly. The habit had less to do with the yoga classes she'd taken as a child than with the routine she'd established before each and every bust, each and every big meet, each and every important new phase of each and every case she'd ever been in on. Breathe in. Breathe out. Focus. Concentrate. Think. Calm down.

Too much nervous energy meant too much excitement, and too much excitement caused slipups. When the stakes were high, there was no margin for error.

Which didn't mean she wasn't itching to get on with it.

Impatience building, Rosie shifted in her seat and covered her eyes against the bright lights of a dark-colored Suburban behind her. She pulled to the side of the road to let the truck pass. Sure, she was eager to get going. Sure, she was anxious to cut to the chase and get in on the action. But her mind was made up. And her mind was telling the impatient part of her to sit down and shut up.

She cut her engine and rolled down her window, listening as the sounds of the country music blaring from the Suburban's radio grew fainter and the growl of Mack's motorcycle faded bit by bit.

And not for the first time since she threw on a pair of jeans and a red, button-down cotton shirt and raced out of the Silver Swan twenty feet behind Mack, she wondered where the hell he was headed and what the hell his connection was to Neeta.

Like it had every other time she'd stopped to consider the questions, a tingle of expectation tickled up Rosie's back and across her neck. And to think, she would have missed the whole thing if it wasn't for a few feathers.

She was already in the dressing room after the second dance number of the night when she realized the fluffy puff of red feathers on the back of one of her bikinilike costumes was missing. No big deal, really, but it was no big deal to retrace her steps back to the stage to find the feathers, either. Besides, the process of locating what was lost and putting it back where it belonged, like dovetailing the pieces of a puzzle, fit well with her everything-in-its-place view of the world.

As she suspected, the clump of bright red feathers was

sitting in the wings. Just as she bent to retrieve it, she heard Mack's familiar introduction ring through the theater. Of course she had no intention of watching his show.

Not that she wasn't tempted. But after the way he'd bullied her the night the overhead light had made an unexpected appearance center stage, Rosie had decided that she didn't need the aggravation. Which didn't mean she didn't have her eye on Mack. Or that she wasn't looking into his connections to the stage crew, the other showgirls, and everyone else at the casino from the pit bosses to the cocktail waitresses.

What she'd learned could be summed up in a couple of terse words: absolutely nothing.

And the way she figured it, that was pretty much all she was going to learn.

Until she saw Neeta sitting in Mack's audience.

As she leaned against the stage wall and peeked out at the audience from behind the curtain, Rosie felt the rush that told her she was finally making some headway.

More interested than she could say, she watched Neeta of the pink fingernails and the pink lipstick and the outfit that made her look like a cross between a Salvation Army major and a dime-a-dance hostess tug down the strap on the side of Mack's thong just enough to nestle a little note next to his skin.

If she wasn't the suspicious type, she would have assumed that Neeta—like every other howling, shrieking, hot-enough-to-melt woman in the place—had lost her senses and was throwing herself at a man who was a sex fantasy come to life. But Rosie was suspicious. Always had been. Always would be. She knew better than to second-guess the gut instinct that told her there was more to this whole thing than met the eye.

She had every intention of asking Mack what the hell was going on. And she would have done it, too, if not for the fact that by the time she begged off the rest of the show on the pretense of a migraine, changed, and got to his dressing room, she caught sight of him slipping out the stage door. Was he meeting Neeta? She thought he might be, but that was before she saw him hop on the Harley that had been parked out in the alley behind the casino. Was he following Neeta? She wasn't sure, but she wasn't willing to take a chance that she was wrong. Especially when she flew to her car and inched into traffic thirty feet behind Mack and saw him make every move a green Corolla up ahead of him made. Even when that green Corolla left the bright lights of Las Vegas and turned into the desert.

After waiting a couple of minutes, Rosie swung back onto the road. Just as Mack had done, she turned onto the dirt road and when it dead-ended at a place where the landscape looked as if it had come straight from the Moon, she hung a left at the only road in sight. For a long while, there was nothing to see and nothing to hear but the buzz of the Harley engine somewhere up ahead. After what seemed like forever, she came to the top of a small rise, and from there it was easy to spot the headlight of the Harley sparkling down below. Mack turned into a long driveway and headed up to what looked like a motel. He cut the engine and, against the light of the pink neon sign that blinked on and off just over his left shoulder, she saw him swing off the bike and head inside.

The single-floor building was long and low, not much more than a smudge in the pitch-dark landscape. But the closer Rosie got, the more she could make out. There was a courtyard of sorts near the center. Right above it hung the neon sign, but since most of the lights were burned out, it was impossible to read what it said. She slid her gaze left and right from the central portion of the building. There were lights in some of the windows, others were dark. There were cars parked outside, including the green Corolla. Mack's bike was there, too, close to the center door where she'd seen him enter. She cut her headlights, parked her rental car on the side of the building, and made her way around to the front entrance. From inside, Rosie could hear the combined sounds of eighties' disco music and static playing over a radio. There were double glass doors at the front, and through them, she saw a woman sitting behind a desk.

No sign of Mack.

Before the woman caught sight of her, Rosie straightened her red shirt, lifted her chin, and punched open the doors.

"Good evening!" The woman behind the desk offered Rosie a wide smile, but her expression teetered between wariness and disbelief. "Can I help you with something?"

Rosie considered pulling out her badge and thought better of it. It was too early in the game to tip her hand, especially when she didn't know what she was getting herself into. Though it rankled, she knew there were times when playing dumb was smarter than acting tough.

"Lost." Rosie shrugged and gave the woman the kind of aren't-I-just-the-silliest look she'd seen some of the chorus girls use to such great advantage. "Headed out of Vegas a while ago and just got all turned around. I was following a biker. . . ." She looked over her shoulder at the Harley parked out front. "I was hoping he was headed. . . . well, headed somewhere other than nowhere. But then he turned in here and—" She glanced around the small lobby with its understated tile floor, pale wallpaper, and pots of fake ficus. "Where'd he go, anyway?" she asked. "I pulled into the parking lot right behind him and I swear I saw him walk in here."

The woman behind the desk stood. "If you've been referred here by someone . . ."

"Not referred. Lost." Rosie grinned and took a quick look around. There were two corridors heading off in either direction from the main lobby. Down both of them, she could see what was pretty standard motel scenery: a long expanse of burnt-orange carpet, a couple dozen closed doors, some pretty generic-looking artwork hanging on walls that were paneled with fake wood. To the right of the desk and the woman was a closed door and from behind it, Rosie heard a bark of laughter.

"Not lost anymore," she told the woman, and before she had a chance to move out from behind the desk, Rosie was around her and had the door opened.

She stepped into a room that looked like it had come straight out of the bargain-basement version of one of Sid and Gloria's crazy fantasies. No red velvet, but then, this place didn't need it. Not when it had so much ambiance of its own. The walls were papered in imitation pink silk. The furniture was pressboard painted white and gold. French provincial on a really bad day. The carpet was white, stained here and there. With what, Rosie didn't even want to know. The curtains that covered each of the room's three windows were heavy gold cloth accented with tassels. There was a bar at the far end of the room and at it were seated three women, each of them talking to a man.

Not exactly Better Homes and Gardens, but not so unusual. Until Rosie registered the fact that one of the woman at the bar was wearing a see-through negligee, one was wearing a black leather bustier and biker boots, and one was wearing pretty much nothing at all except black, high-cut thong panties, a pair of mules, and a gap-toothed smile.

"Shit." Rosie's heart plummeted into her stomach, then lurched back up again and nearly choked her. If she had known what she was getting herself into, she would have been a little more discreet.

"We don't let guests back here." Behind her, the woman from the front desk sounded royally pissed. "Not without an appointment."

"And a credit card number, right?" Rosie shook her head, astounded by her own naiveté. "Not that I'm criticizing, mind you. After all, we're in Nevada and it's all perfectly legal."

"Perfectly." The woman's voice was icy and the fact did not go unnoticed. On the other side of the room, the tall, broad-shouldered bartender—who was obviously also the muscle whose job it was to keep visitors in line—stepped out from in back of the bar. He crossed his arms over his chest and gave Rosie the quick once-over, and one corner of his mouth lifted into a sneer. Lucky bastard. At least he figured he was. He was used to dealing with a rougher crowd, and no doubt he pegged Rosie as a piece of cake.

She didn't intend to let things get far enough out of hand for him to find out how wrong he was.

"Let me guess," she said, "Neeta's a hooker."

"We prefer to call our employees escorts."

"All right, then. Neeta's an escort and she works here and—"

Reality hit and the blood drained from Rosie's face. Mack and Neeta arranged a meeting. And Mack followed Neeta to her place of business. And her place of business was—

"Double shit." Rosie groaned at the sensation that coursed through her. The one that made her feel as if a bucket of ice water had been dumped down her back. No time for soul-searching, she told herself. No time for analysis or the kind of get-in-touch-with-what-you're-really-feeling psychobabble her mother would have suggested if only she'd been there.

There would be time for all that later, along with a big dose of calling herself every name in the book. Not to mention a big session of wondering why she suddenly felt so disappointed.

"Look, I'm sorry if I interrupted anything," she told the woman. She backed toward the door, suddenly as desperate to put some dark and lonely desert miles between her and this place as she had been eager to close in on Mack only a short time before. "I'm just going to head on back outside and—"

Before she could get as far as the door that led back into the lobby, one of the sets of gold curtains parted and Rosie saw that there weren't three windows in the room, but two.

The third pair of curtains covered a kind of alcove and when the curtains parted, Mack stepped out.

"Rosie?" Without missing a beat, he stalked over to where she was standing and before she could move to get out of his way, he grabbed her by the arm and tugged her toward the door. "I thought I heard your voice! What the hell are you doing here?" he asked, but just as he didn't give her a chance to move on her own, he didn't give her a chance to answer. "This is no place for a woman like you and—"

"Look, I'm sorry, all right?" Rosie did everything she could to wiggle out of Mack's grasp, short of getting him in a headlock and knocking him to the floor. Once she was free of him, she sidestepped the woman from the front desk, circumnavigated Mack, and headed toward the lobby, her head down, her arms tight against her sides, and her sneakers pounding against the threadbare carpet.

"I got mixed up." It was the understatement of the century, made all the more apparent when Neeta stepped out of one of the rooms in the hallway, her hair down and her prim-as-a-schoolmarm blouse unbuttoned enough to show the lace teddy she wore underneath. Rosie wasn't about to get herself in any deeper by trying to explain herself. She didn't need to announce to the world that her imagination had run away with her, that she'd assumed Neeta and Mack were up to something illegal when all they were really up to was—

Well, something that was legal. At least in most of the counties of Nevada.

A rush of heat raced up Rosie's neck and into her cheeks. "I'm sorry. I didn't know. I thought—"

"Threesomes are extra." With a look that was nothing short of blasé, the woman from the front lobby pushed her way back to the reception desk. "We take Visa, MasterCard, and—"

"Oh, no! Oh, my God!"

At the sound of Neeta choking out a cry, Rosie turned

and found Neeta with her face pale and her eyes wide. She was pointing toward the front window. Rosie spun around to see what was going on at the same time Mack did. Together, they watched a dark SUV pull into the parking lot.

"That's it!" Neeta's voice trembled. Her hands shook. "That's the truck. The one that's been following me. Outside my apartment. Outside my kid's school. That's the one. Oh, shit! They're here," she said. "They followed us. They followed you." She swung her terrified gaze from Mack to Rosie, apparently unsure who to blame. "What are you going to do about it?" she asked, and this time, it didn't seem to matter whom Neeta was talking to; Rosie knew exactly what she had to do.

She nudged Neeta toward the back barroom at the same time she reached into her purse and pulled out her .38. It would have been a hell of a lot easier to take charge and keep an eye on the three burly guys who got out of the SUV if Mack didn't push her out of the way and get between Rosie and the front door.

14

Mack was only two feet from the front glass doors when he wondered if it was the smartest move he'd ever made. Not that he was afraid. The three guys who pounded across the parking lot and headed straight for the lobby looked plenty tough, but that was hardly enough to intimidate a guy like Mack. He'd seen worse odds at a Vegas blackjack table.

What worried him wasn't his own safety, it was the safety of the civilians in the building.

With a practiced eye, he glanced around, quickly assessing the risks and weighing the possibilities.

Of all of them, Neeta was the smartest. She took off like greased lightning. So did the other people who were in the bar, including the bartender who was, apparently, not enamored enough of his tough-guy image to put his money where his mouth was. He got wind of the commotion, peeked into the lobby, and hightailed it down the hall in the direction of a door marked EMERGENCY EXIT. The madam who worked the front desk was apparently no fool, either. She followed the bartender out of the building.

Which left only Rosie.

As tempted as Mack was to figure out why her safety was

so much more vital to him than the safety of the others—or of himself—he knew he didn't have the luxury. For now, his reasons weren't nearly as important as the facts. And the fact was that Rosie was—

"Holding a gun. You're holding a gun." He stared at the revolver in Rosie's hands. At the way she braced herself and readied the weapon.

"No shit, Sherlock." Rosie gave him a look he suspected might have been a sneer if she wasn't so busy keeping an eye on the three goons who were closing in on them. "You knew I had it. You looked through my locker and—"

"And that doesn't mean I knew you carried." Mack tried to get the picture straight in his head. Rosie in feathers. Rosie in sequins. Rosie with a deadeye aim, a steady hand, and a look in her eye that told him she wasn't fooling?

As impossible as it seemed, the image almost made sense. Or at least as much sense as anything could under circumstances that might be called, by the kindest of interpreters, stressful.

"Come on." He grabbed Rosie by the elbow. "We've got to get you out of here."

She clutched her weapon in both hands and held it alongside her ear. She didn't budge an inch.

"Are you crazy?" Mack tugged her toward the hallway where the bartender and the madam had disappeared. "You're going to get yourself killed."

"Am not." Rosie's glance was level, and as steely as any he'd ever seen. "If you'll just get the hell out of my way."

"OK, so you're not crazy. You're stupid. If you think you can take these guys—"

"I don't think it. I know it."

If he had more time, he would have told her that he knew he could take these guys, too. Knew it as surely as he knew his own name. While he was at it, he would have pointed out what it had taken him a lot of years out on the streets to learn: that knowing you could do something didn't mean you had to try. That when it meant putting other people at risk, discretion really was the better part of valor. It took him until that very moment to realize that was especially true when *other people* was Rosie.

He braced himself against the bolt-from-the-blue awareness and decided on a conciliatory response. It was all he had time for. "We'll talk about it later."

"No." Rosie gave one shake of her head. "We need to talk about it now. You need to know something."

Both Mack and Rosie noticed the movement from outside, and what they saw wasn't pretty. In fact, it was downright ugly enough to rob Rosie of her voice and to make Mack more sure than ever that discretion, valor, and the whole host of other emotions that were racketing through his insides weren't going to be worth very much. Not if he didn't live to see the next day.

The guy on the left (a heavyset fellow in a dark suit that made Mack think he and the Enforcer must have frequented the same tailor) whipped out a nine-millimeter semiautomatic. He went around to the left side of the building. The guy in the middle (a tall, lean cowboy wearing brown boots, a flannel shirt, and a skinny string tie) whipped out a nine-millimeter semiautomatic. He went around to the right side of the building. The guy in the middle worried Mack the most. He was wearing a full-length black leather coat and when he reached inside and pulled out a shotgun, Mack knew they were in trouble. Rosie's peashooter .38 was no more match for these three guys than . . . well, than the peashooter .38 he was carrying.

Which didn't mean he wouldn't have at least tried to get the situation under control if a Dodge Ram pickup didn't squeal into the parking lot and slam on its brakes. Three more guys got out and they looked just as tough, just as determined, and just as well armed as the first batch.

"Reinforcements," Rosie said, and he knew she was right. There was no use waiting around to see any more.

Mack hooked one arm around her shoulders and yanked her down the hallway. Just as he did, a blast from the shotgun hit, and the front window shattered into a million tiny pieces.

The emergency exit led out to the front of the building, and right about now, that was the last place they wanted to be. There didn't look to be a whole lot of other options. Mack tried the first door on his left. It was locked. So was the second door. And the third. By the time he got to the fourth, he wasn't about to take no for an answer. He tried the handle and when it didn't turn, he hauled back and kicked open the door.

No doubt, the two people on the bed had already heard the racket out in the lobby, but just as surely, a little commotion was par for the course and not nearly enough to interrupt what they were doing. Having the door kicked in was something else.

"Do you mind?" The woman raised herself up on her elbows and glared at them over her partner's head. "We're doing business here."

Mack didn't bother to say he was sorry. Instead, he raced over to the window, wrenched it open, and punched out the screen. He helped Rosie out and slipped out behind her.

When he settled himself on his feet, he was grateful to find her with her back against the wall and her .38 still in her hands. He unholstered his weapon and signaled her to head toward the squat, low-slung building about thirty feet away.

"You go," Rosie told him. "I'll be right behind you."

"Like hell," Mack growled. "Let's face facts here. Those guys followed you."

"Or you."

"All right. They followed me. They followed you. It really doesn't matter. What does matter is that as long as we stay here, everyone in the place is in danger."

Damn but she hated it when other people were right. Especially when *other people* was Mack.

She nodded her agreement and took off running toward what looked to be a garage. Once they had some solid walls between themselves and the gorillas who had them out-weaponed and outnumbered, she'd take some time to think about how she planned to handle the situation. For now, what seemed most important was getting far from the building, as fast as they could.

That, and keeping Mack safe.

It wasn't exactly an epiphany as much as it was a wake-up call.

A nice, conservative, hardworking federal agent did not fall in love with a suspect, she reminded herself in no uncertain terms.

Good thing a shot whizzed passed her head and snapped Rosie out of her reverie. Otherwise she might have been tempted to figure out how the falling-in-love part had somehow happened when she wasn't looking and when she definitely knew better.

Rosie zigzagged her way over to the garage and signaled to Mack to do the same. He was a quick learner. When another shot zinged by, he dropped and rolled and came up running. He got to the building at the same time Rosie did and, on her signal, waited, his back to the wall and his weapon in his hands. Together they flung open the door, and together they stepped inside, feet apart, arms extended, guns ready.

In the light of the single bare bulb that dangled from the ceiling, they found only Neeta. She was standing at the bottom of a rickety wooden ladder that led up to a kind of sliding trapdoor in the ceiling and she was shaking so badly, it was a wonder she could keep on her feet.

No sign of cowboys with automatic weapons, and Rosie breathed a sigh of relief. But that didn't mean she thought they were home free. "Hands," she ordered Neeta. "Out at your sides. Where I can see them."

Neeta obliged, stepping to her right as she did. As if she were trying to hide something. Or someone.

It wasn't until she heard a small, whimpering sound from behind Neeta that Rosie realized exactly who that someone might be.

Her stomach suddenly as cold as the temperature in the garage was stifling, Rosie gave Mack a look. The nod he returned told her he knew what she had in mind. He closed the door and while he covered her, she lowered her weapon. Her worst fears materialized along with the little boy who stepped out from behind Neeta.

"Your kid?"

Neeta nodded.

"Shit." Rosie scoured a hand across her forehead. It did nothing to still the pounding that had started up inside her head sometime between when the simple act of following Mack and Neeta had escalated from major embarrassment to major trouble. "Not the best place for a kid."

"Never been a problem before. Not like this. Not until you two showed up." Neeta's voice lurched to the tempo of the same cha-cha that was pounding through Rosie's head. With one hand, she pushed the kid farther behind her. The move was instinctive, like a mother lion doing what it could to protect her cub. It was that more than anything that convinced Rosie she wasn't going to let Neeta down.

"What if we weren't here?" She wasn't sure if she was asking the question of Neeta. Or of Mack. Or of the universe in general. She only hoped that somebody came up with an answer—fast—before the rumble of voices she heard outside and the sounds of boots crunching against the dusty Nevada soil got any closer. "When they followed you the other times, Neeta, did they ever cause trouble?"

Neeta shook her head.

"Then it's us they're after."

"No kidding." Mack didn't sound any more cheered by her line of reasoning than he looked. His expression grim and determined, he lowered his weapon and looked around. There was a wooden tool bench close by, and he hauled it in front of the door they'd just entered. It wasn't much in the keep-the-bad-guys-away department, but Rosie knew that for now, it would be enough. It would have to be. It was all they had.

That done, Mack did a quick turn around the sprawling garage. On the wall opposite from where they stood were double doors that slid to the right to open. Each door had a window in it. He stood with his back to the wall next to the door, drew in a breath, and in a movement as graceful and as polished as the ones he used on stage, he pivoted, glanced outside, and moved back again and out of range. Apparently satisfied that they had at least some time to try and find some way out of a situation that looked more than somewhat hopeless, he hurried to the other side of the garage.

There was a beat-up pickup parked over there, and though she was no expert, Rosie knew the truck wouldn't do them any good. One wheel was missing, it didn't have a driver's door, and the front end was all but gone. Just beyond it was something covered with a green plastic tarp, and Mack went over to it and pulled the tarp away.

"Eighty-three Honda Shadow 750." Mack whistled low under his breath and gave the motorcycle a quick once-over. "Does it run?" he asked Neeta.

Before she could answer, they heard a shout from outside. "What good's a bike going to do, anyway?" Neeta asked, her voice teetering between reason and full-fledged panic. "You can't get us out of here."

"No, not all of us. But we can get *us* out of here. It's what you're thinking, right?" Rosie turned to Mack only long enough to see him moving the bike toward the double doors that opened toward the back of the building. Knowing there was nothing she could do to help him, she turned her attention back to Neeta and the dark-haired little kid who peeked up at her from behind his mother's knees. "We need to create a distraction. That way, they'll follow us and leave you alone. Do you understand that, Neeta?" Rosie didn't wait for her to answer. She looked at the ladder and the door into the attic. "Is that someplace you can hide?"

Neeta nodded. "There's a room," she said. "And the ladder, you pull it up once you're up there. It's corny, I know. Like some old movie. But . . . well . . . we keep it in case there's ever any trouble. You know? I mean . . ." She looked in the direction of the brothel. "Some of the customers are . . . well . . . you know."

They would discuss the sociology of the issue some other time. For now, it was more important to keep Neeta and her son alive. "Go," Rosie said. Hands on her shoulders, she turned Neeta toward the ladder and gave her a nudge. She watched her climb and slide the door at the top open. When all was ready, Rosie bent so she was eye-to-eye with Neeta's son.

"So what's your name?" Rosie asked.

"Brendan." Though he clearly had no clue exactly what was going on, it was also clear he'd been through this drill before. Trouble in the cathouse. Hide in the attic. Just the thought of it was enough to make Rosie's heart squeeze and her breath catch behind a funny little lump in her throat.

She coughed away the tightness. "Hey, Brendan. You ever play firefighter?"

This was a new game, one he wasn't familiar with. Unsure if he was supposed to say yes or no, Brendan glanced up to where Neeta waited for him at the top of the ladder.

"You get to be the firefighter." Because Rosie knew they didn't have time to wait, she scooped Brendan into her arms and hoisted him up the ladder "There you go, Firefighter Brendan." She patted the back of his pint-size jeans. "Up the ladder. Scoot!"

Rosie waited until the kid was sitting on the floor next to Neeta, then ventured a few rungs up the ladder herself. "Pull the ladder up and get that door closed, and try to be as quiet as possible." She reached into her pocket, pulled out her cell phone, and stretched to put it in Neeta's hand. "And while you're at it, call the cops."

For a couple of seconds, Neeta looked at the phone as if she'd never seen one before. "You mean, you're going to give this to me and leave yourself without—"

Rosie motioned her to close the trapdoor. "You can thank me some other time. Like by sticking around long enough to talk to me one of these days." They heard the sounds of men's voices outside, louder this time. Closer. "Only this isn't the time."

"Here." Neeta had her purse slung over one shoulder. She reached into it, pulled out a pressed powder compact, and tossed it down to Rosie. "There's a trailer," she said, her voice sharp, her gaze darting to the door. "About six miles from here. Through the little town down the road and on toward Pahrump. There's a place where the road divides and there's a trailer park there."

Mack came over and when Rosie lifted one side of the ladder, he grabbed the other. Together, they boosted it into the attic. "I know the place," he said.

"Second one from the end," Neeta told them. "It's got red-and-white curtains in the windows. It's mine and no one else knows about it. It's for him." She looked at her son. "And me. The key's in there." She pointed to the compact. "If you can lose them—"

"Consider it done." Rosie stuffed the compact into her pocket while she gave Neeta what she hoped was a smile confident enough to calm her fears. "Only now—" Something banged against the garage door and Neeta slid the trapdoor shut.

"You ready?" Mack asked, and he must have figured she was. Before she even had a chance to answer, he grabbed her hand and, together, they raced to where the red motorcycle waited. "It's got gas. Let's hope it's got some pick up, too," he said.

Though Rosie was no expert when it came to vehicles of any kind, there was no doubt what he was doing when he yanked off a piece of metal near the handlebars, pulled out a couple of wires, and wound them together.

When the engine caught, she smiled. "Nice work," she told him.

Mack apparently didn't think his hot-wiring skills were any big deal. He climbed onto the motorcycle and looked toward the sounds of the voices. "We're going to have to let them see us both."

It wasn't a question, but Rosie knew he was waiting for an answer. She nodded, letting him know she understood, and on his signal, she slid open the door and when she hopped onto the back of the bike, he raced out of the garage and headed around to the front of the building. Right toward where six goons with big guns and bad attitudes were waiting to blow them both to kingdom come.

Though the guys out front didn't expect anyone to be gutsy enough, daring enough, or stupid enough to attempt what was pretty much an impossible escape, they didn't stay too surprised for too long. When the motorcycle screamed out from behind the garage, they stared in wonder for a few open-mouthed seconds.

Right before they decided this was the next best thing to a county fair shooting gallery.

Fortunately, Mack knew what he was doing when it came to both motorcycles and defensive driving. When the guy in the dark suit unleashed a hail of gunfire, Mack swerved and swung the bike around. When the cowboy wearing the string tie aimed and fired, Mack slowed down and sped up and slowed down again until the shooter was so disoriented, he didn't know which end was up.

Rosie got off a few shots of her own. Between the speed they were traveling, the potholed terrain, and the sheer concentration it took to not take a header off the bike, she knew

she didn't have a snowball's chance in hell of hitting anything. But that didn't mean she was going down without a
fight.

When they screeched around the far corner of the
cathouse and nearly into the front end of Rosie's rental car,
Mack slammed on the brakes. "Ready?" he called to her
over his shoulder, and because she couldn't have made
words come out of her mouth if she'd tried, Rosie nodded.

At her signal, Mack revved the engine and took off toward the front of the building. He raced through the parking
lot, rocketed around the far side of the whorehouse, and by
the time the gorillas with the arsenal and the itchy trigger
fingers got their acts together and were headed toward the
parking lot to follow them, he was already coming up behind
them.

It was a repeat performance. One they survived only
barely and only because Mack knew exactly what he was doing. They did another turn around the six stunned gunmen,
just to be sure there was no mistake about who was on the
bike and heading for parts unknown. Unknown parts plenty
far away from Neeta and the little kid with the big eyes.

It didn't hurt that the maneuver gave Rosie another
chance to take as close a look as she was able to in the dark
and at sixty miles an hour. Not much to go on, but more than
she had before. She'd call the sketch artist in the San
Francisco office when she got back to Las Vegas and get him
hopping on the faces of the six shooters. With any luck—

The motorcycle kicked up a rock and bucked forward,
and Rosie uncoiled her fingers from around the sissy bar and
grabbed onto the back of Mack's jacket.

With any luck, she'd live long enough to make it back to
Las Vegas.

As if he were thinking exactly what she was thinking—
which was all about how skill was great but luck didn't always
hold—Mack raced out to the parking lot. This time, the
shooters weren't taking any chances. Three of them stayed

at the back of the building. The other three ran after the motorcycle, and when Mack hit the long, dusty driveway at full throttle, Rosie saw them hop into the SUV and start off after them.

Just as she'd hoped.

For a millisecond, a feeling like satisfaction settled inside her. Or maybe it was just the mouthful of gritty air she made the mistake of gulping down. She coughed and swallowed another mouthful of dust and decided it was a lost cause.

At the place where the long drive met pavement, Mack slowed down just enough to glance back and make sure the SUV was following. A couple of seconds later, so was the Ram. In the dim halo of light thrown by the single headlight of the bike, Rosie got a quick look at him. His eyes were narrowed against the flying dust and the headlights of the SUV, which were getting dangerously closer by the second. His jaw was set.

And she knew exactly what he had in mind.

She loosened her hold on Mack's leather jacket only long enough to wrap her arms around his waist and hang on for dear life. Something told her they were in for a hell of a ride.

The two trucks followed them for another ten minutes or so. Which mustn't have been easy for the drivers or their passengers, considering that Mack flew across the paved road and hit the open terrain on the other side at breakneck speed. He drove a reckless, staggered pattern, zipping right, then left, slowing down and speeding up until the engine strained and sent up waves of heat that roasted Rosie's legs and thighs. In the crazy quilt of light thrown by their own headlamp and the high-intensity lights of the two trucks, Rosie could just make the scenery as it zipped by: boulders and scrub grass, rocks and broken fences that Mack maneuvered around like some sort of Evel Knievel understudy with attitude.

Rosie held on tight and hoped against hope that when

they went flying off the bike and into some ravine lined with razor-sharp rocks, she would land on top and he would cushion the fall.

Mack glanced over his shoulder. The brief smile he gave Rosie was nothing compared to the glare he aimed at the guys in the two trucks. In spite of the bumpy terrain, the ruts and the stunted vegetation, they were closing in. Fast.

He drove even faster, and Rosie's stomach swooped. Her breath came in gasps that rasped over the heat and the dirt and the hundreds of bugs that hit her in the face every time she was crazy enough to peek over Mack's shoulder to see where they were headed.

"Hang on," he yelled to her, and when she nodded (as if she could hang on any tighter), he cut the headlight and they rushed headlong into the desert in total darkness.

For a while, the SUV and the Ram kept pace, but Mack had a couple more tricks up his sleeve. He squealed into a turn so low to the ground that Rosie's knee scraped the soil. He doubled back the other way and ran right between the SUV and the pickup. Behind the two trucks now, Mack headed for the road.

Rosie might actually have breathed a sigh of relief if she didn't hear the trucks grate to a stop and turn. Their lights hit the terrain just up ahead, and Rosie braved the bugs and dared a quick look over Mack's shoulder. A hundred feet in front of them, the dark desert landscape looked even darker, an inky patch against the rest of the gloom. Like a black hole in a sci-fi space movie, the blackness seemed to swallow everything. She couldn't see scrub grass. Or boulders. She couldn't see anything but an outcropping of stones that looked to be level with the place the blackness deepened.

And something told her they were in for trouble.

"You ready?" Mack called to her over his shoulder. But he didn't wait for her to answer.

A second later, the ground fell away and the bike went airborne. Time stood still. So did Rosie's heartbeat. It wasn't so much that she minded flying through the air with her arms around Mack and her thighs so tight around his hips that her muscles ached. It was the thought of landing that scared the hell out of her.

It came with exactly the kind of jolt she expected. Her teeth smacked together. Her head snapped. The shock got her heart going again with a thump hard enough to make her chest hurt.

Even then, he didn't slow down. He took one more look at the place where the two trucks had screeched to a stop at the top of the elephant-high outcropping they'd just flown over, and he turned on the afterburners. The headlight still off and their pursuers left literally in the dust, Mack took off overland, in what Rosie could only hope was the direction of Pahrump.

Just as Neeta promised, her place was easy to find. But while she'd been good about directions, she wasn't exactly accurate when it came to a description. Neeta's home away from the whorehouse wasn't exactly a trailer as much as it was (at least in better days) a motor home. Then again, maybe the fact that the entire thing was missing its wheels and was propped up on cinder blocks meant the motor part didn't apply.

"Second from the end. Red-and-white curtains." When Mack cut the motorcycle engine, Rosie went through as much of Neeta's description as fit the bill. "Looks like the place."

His expression grim, Mack nodded. He took one more look over his shoulder toward the road. For as far as the eye could see, it was empty. Just like it had been since they left the SUV and the Dodge Ram high and dry on that rocky hill. The same place where Rosie was convinced she had also left her stomach.

Apparently, even an empty road and miles of desert weren't enough when it came to Mack's comfort zone. He swung off the bike and motioned Rosie to get moving. "You get inside," he told her with a look at the rusted trailer door. "I'll stash the bike around the back where nobody can see it."

She wasn't about to argue. She was certain that he was right, just as she was certain that the whole experience of outmaneuvering the bad guys made her feel as if she could take on the world. She hopped off the bike.

And realized too late that her knees felt as if they were made of jelly.

Automatically, Rosie grabbed for the handlebars. Too late, she realized it was just the kind of weakness Mack would glom on to and never let her forget.

"A little shaky?" he asked.

"Not at all." Rosie drew in a breath that calmed her racing heart. She pulled back her shoulders. She backed away from the bike. "I'm fine," she told him. "As a matter-of-fact, I've never been better."

"Right." If Rosie had the nerve to tell such a colossal lie, he could at least have had the decency to sound like he believed her. Instead, Mack shook his head and wheeled the bike toward the far side of the trailer.

While he was gone, Rosie headed up the two creaky steps that led to the trailer door. The compact Neeta had given her was in her back pocket, and she pulled it out and snapped it open.

The powder on the inside of the compact had been carved out, and nestled in the spot where it used to be was the key. She inserted the key into the lock.

"Take it easy, OK?"

Mack's suggestion as he came around to the front of the trailer was enough to make Rosie bark out a laugh. She threw a withering look at him over her shoulder and somehow managed to keep her voice down. No use causing any more commotion than they already had, chugging into the Desert Cactus Trailer Park at the crack of dawn.

"Take it easy? You mean like, take it easy opening the door? Like I can't handle a wanna-be Winnebago in the middle of Nowhere, Nevada? What do you think I'm going to do, kick down the door and go in with guns blazing?"

"It wouldn't surprise me." Mack didn't look especially pleased at the prospect.

"Are you telling me I'm careless?" she asked, and maybe if the sound of the motorcycle engine wasn't still buzzing in his ears the way it was in hers, he would have realized she wasn't being literal.

"Not as careless as you are stupid." Mack folded his arms across his chest. "Are you just one of those people who always seem to be in the wrong place at the wrong time? Or are you actually trying to get yourself killed?"

"I didn't exactly issue those goons an engraved invitation. And as much as I was tempted, I didn't think it was right to take off like everyone else did and leave you out there all by yourself." She turned the key, shoved the door open, and stepped inside. "Like it or not," she told him, "somebody had to protect you."

"Me?" Mack shot up the steps and into the trailer. He slammed the door behind him. "Protect me from what? A ditzy chorus girl who thinks she's a cross between Miss Marple and Buffy the Vampire Slayer?"

The trailer was shabby, cramped, and no better looking on the inside than it was from out front, where yucca and scrawny sagebrush grew around the steps. There wasn't a whole lot of room to move around. Rosie positioned herself in what looked to be the roomiest spot, a foot or so of brown indoor/outdoor carpet between a battered stove, a half-size refrigerator, and the two dilapidated captain's chairs in what had once been the cockpit of a good-to-go motor home. She propped her fists on her hips.

"What am I trying to protect you from?" she echoed. "How about yourself? What the hell did you think you were doing back there at the whorehouse? You should have taken a clue from Neeta and gotten the hell out of there before the shooting ever started."

"Yeah. Right." There was a slim strip of grimy carpet between them and Mack closed the distance in one step. "And leave you on your own? Not a chance!"

"Well, thank you very much. That's sweet. And very macho, in an I'm-from-Texas sort of way. But I'll tell you what . . ." Rosie spun toward the back of the trailer. There was no place to go in that direction, nothing there but a bathroom that didn't look big enough even for little Brendan, and a battered mattress that had been thrown on what there was of a bare spot on the floor. She twirled back around.

"You want to take care of something, Mack, buy yourself a puppy. Don't you ever . . . ever . . ." The thought of the way he'd put himself at risk back at the brothel nearly choked her, and Rosie coughed away the sudden tightness in her throat. "Don't you ever put your neck on the line for me. I don't like that kind of me-Tarzan-you-Jane bullshit. I don't need it. I don't want it. And I don't want to have to worry about getting my butt shot out from under me because I'm so worried about you that I lose my concentration."

"That's a laugh." Which didn't explain why Mack wasn't laughing. "That's a real laugh. You? Worried about me? Maybe you should listen to a little of your own advice." Before Rosie had a chance to step out of range, he grabbed her arm. "You think I was going to stand by and watch something happen to you? That I was going to turn tail and run and let you take the fire instead?"

"Yes!" At least he was finally getting the picture. "That's exactly what I expected you to do. And if you were smart, you would have. Why didn't you, Mack? Why would you be that stupid?"

"Why?" The single word sounded like sandpaper scraping metal. "You want to know why, Rosie? I'll tell you why."

He didn't. He showed her instead.

Before Rosie could even think about moving, he pulled her into his arms and brought his mouth down on hers.

There was nothing gentle about the kiss. Or about the way he snaked one arm around her waist and held her against his chest so tightly that she could feel his heart beating wildly against hers. Then again, Rosie figured they were even. There wasn't anything gentle about the way she responded, either. Her teeth nipped his lips, her arms went around his neck, and when he forced her lips apart, she was the one who took the initiative, deepening the kiss until his knees buckled and his breath caught.

Just like hers did.

When he broke off the contact, Mack didn't look any happier than when he started. Which, now that Rosie thought about it, wasn't any more happy than she was feeling.

Mack's breaths were ragged. His expression was fierce. "Any more questions?"

"Lots." Rosie sucked in a shuddering breath. "But why bother? Something tells me I'm not going to get answers."

"Something tells me you're right." As fast as he'd grabbed her, he let her go, and Rosie staggered back.

"Which doesn't mean I can't ask anyway."

"Which doesn't mean I'm going to answer."

"Oh, how did I know you were going to say that?" He was just as angry as she was, so angry that she doubted he caught the thread of sarcasm that laced her voice. It didn't stop her.

"Let's start with your visit to Neeta's place of business."

"Jealous?"

Rosie's mouth dropped open. Her stomach turned to ice at the same time her face got fiery hot. "Hell, no!"

Mack wasn't convinced. He crossed his arms over his chest and settled back, his weight against one foot. "So not jealous that you followed me all the way out there? What were you planning to do, Rosie, rush in just as I was down to my skivvies and declare your love?"

"Love?" The word would have choked her if Rosie wasn't

feeling so angry. Angry, outraged, too livid to keep her head in the face of a realization that left her feeling completely out of her league.

"Is that what you think?" Because she couldn't admit the truth—not now, not ever—she knew she had to disagree with him, instead. "You think I went through all that trouble just so I could throw a kink into your romantic fantasies? Or was it the kinky part I was ruining?"

"You weren't ruining anything, kinky or otherwise." He dismissed her accusations with the sharp sweep of one arm. "That's not what I was there for."

"Right." Rosie managed a smile that was a little stiff around the edges. "I know a lot of guys who go to whore-houses not to have sex."

"And why do you care anyway?"

"Why?" The word escaped her along with a breath of surprise. "I'll tell you why, Mack."

It was Rosie's turn to catch him off guard. Before he saw it coming and before he could move to get out of her way, she bunched one hand around the front of his T-shirt and pulled him close. She kissed him—hard—at the same time she reached for his belt and unbuckled it. She popped the button at the waistband of his jeans and he fumbled with the top button of her shirt. She skimmed her hand across the front of his jeans, searching for the zipper while she tested the length of him against her fingers, and he gave up on the buttons. One hand over her right breast, one hand over her left, he grabbed the red shirt and pulled. Rosie's buttons went flying and landed on the floor. Her shirt followed in record time.

She didn't wait for Mack to strip off her bra. There didn't seem to be much point, so she did it herself. Besides, she couldn't wait to feel his palm against her skin and his mouth tugging at her nipples.

Rosie arched her back and when he pressed her back to the wall and bent to take her into his mouth, she braced herself, her fingers digging into his shoulders, her breaths coming as hard and as fast as they had when they were racing through the desert at seventy miles an hour.

"Mack." She breathed his name at the same time she skimmed off his jeans and his close-fitting briefs. "This isn't a good idea." Her words sounded like they were coming from a million miles away. From a place that wasn't here. From a woman who wanted this more than she'd ever wanted anything. Or anyone.

"I know." Mack undid the button at the waistband of her jeans and yanked them off. He skimmed a finger beneath the lace that edged her white panties, and she caught her lower lip in her teeth and moaned.

"As a matter of fact . . ." He nibbled her breasts. Kissed her throat. Fighting for breath and for control. "It's probably the worst idea I've had in as long as I can remember."

"Thanks." She almost managed to sound like she meant it. "Which means we should really—"

"We really should shut up." He kissed her again. Longer this time. Harder. And when he lifted her in his arms and she wrapped her legs around his waist and he thrust inside her, Rosie knew he was right.

Shutting up was the best thing she could possibly do.

15

When Rosie came to her senses, she was straddled across Mack's lap in one of the chairs that used to constitute the front seat of the motor home. Her hands on his chest, her body still shuddering from the orgasm that had just ripped through her, she fought to catch her breath.

"That was . . ."

"I know." When he caught the tip of one breast in his teeth, she groaned. "It was—"

Where she found the strength—physical or emotional—to push away, even Rosie wasn't sure. Maybe daylight did the same thing to crazy fantasies that it did to vampires. Just like the undead, her lust went up in a puff of smoke and the cold reality of the situation seeped in to freeze the places that had been as hot as the fires of hell. And just as dangerous.

"It was a mistake," Rosie said, and she congratulated herself. At least she sounded in control. Even if she didn't feel like it. "All of it. It was all a mistake."

Mack tensed, and for a couple seconds, she didn't dare breathe. It was too sobering to think about all they'd done, too painful and far too intense. Rosie concentrated instead on the way his head nestled between her breasts, on the play of the light that accented the inky highlights in his hair and the pinpoint, knock-her-socks-off (if she happened to be wearing any) pressure of his teeth against her skin.

"I was going to say incredible." Mack glanced up. It was impossible to tell what he was feeling, but there was no mistaking what he meant when he loosened his hold on her and made a gesture that was part shrug, part twitch. Rosie wasn't one for missing the point. She slid off his lap.

She stepped away from him just as he leaned back in the passenger-side chair that was looking a little more lopsided than it had when they fell into it together. He propped his hands behind his head and raised his chin, his jaw so rigid it looked as if it might snap. "I guess what I meant to say was that it was an incredible mistake."

"You know it was." Rosie didn't mind the way he looked at her. She didn't care that his gaze raked her breasts. She didn't feel self-conscious when it danced over her hips and down even lower. In the last hour, he'd seen everything there was to see of Eleanor Roosevelt Malone. He'd touched and tasted and tempted his way through a world tour.

It didn't change a thing. There was nothing between them but the wild heat that built whenever they were in a room together. That and suspicion. Nothing now but the blistering memories she knew would drive her crazy every time she was weak enough to allow them to creep into her head or lonely enough to think that things might have been different if only . . .

Standing in the front window of a motor home stark naked and with the sun shining full on her didn't seem to be the solution to the problem. Ever practical, Rosie got herself moving. Her panties were hanging from one corner of the Lilliputian countertop, and she snatched them up and stepped into them. "You know I'm right. How can there be anything between us when there isn't even honesty?"

"Honesty?" He laughed, and if she didn't know better, she would have thought it sounded just a little too forced, just a little too confident. "Is that what you're looking for?" He got up and reached for the briefs that had somehow landed on top of the refrigerator. He twirled them in two fingers, as cool and as cocky naked as he was when he was nearly naked on stage, daring her with that little half-smile he used so effectively on the women in his audience to take just one more look. "You want to start first?"

When she didn't answer, he nodded grimly. "I thought so," he said. "I guess we can chalk the whole thing up to an adrenaline rush."

"Yeah. I guess we can." The sun was coming up fast and the sky outside looked clear. The temperature inside the little trailer would go from comfy to stifling in just a couple of minutes. Which didn't explain why Rosie's insides were touched with frost.

She pulled on her jeans and looked around for her bra. It was lying on the shabby mattress at the back of the trailer, and she plucked it up with two fingers and turned her back on Mack to slip it on.

When Rosie turned away from him, Mack wasn't sure if he should be offended. Or relieved. At least with her back to him, he didn't have a view of those breasts, full and luscious enough to make a man lose his mind. Or that silky little triangle of cinnamon curls between her legs.

He braced himself against the rush of desire that even now threatened to rob him of his common sense, and reminded himself that he was lucky. He was lucky that Rosie had a brain in her head when he'd apparently lost his. Lucky that she was talking reason and logic after an hour that had included absolutely none of either. When he still wanted her so much that every inch of him ached and every beat of his heart was like fire in his chest.

He was lucky because one of them needed to act sensibly, but for once, he thought that job was going to fall to him.

"Hey . . ." Just so his body didn't get any ideas about what he intended to do when he got close to her, he reached for his jeans and slipped them on before he risked walking up to Rosie. "No regrets, huh?" He put a hand on her shoulder and was grateful when she didn't pull away. "I'm willing to blame the adrenaline if you are. We'll say it was the excitement, what do you say? We'll say it was the fault of an emotional high. Or stupidity. Does that work for you? We could just chalk it up to two really smart people being really stupid."

"Stupidity, yeah." Rosie turned and gave him a smile that, while it lasted, lit up the little trailer like sunshine. "If you're willing to forget it . . ."

"Forgotten." Mack backed away from her, both hands in the air in a gesture of surrender. "Can't even remember what we're talking about."

She would have been more convinced if he wasn't staring at the place between her breasts where her skin was rubbed red from the chafing of his beard.

Her cheeks suddenly as hot as her insides were icy, Rosie teetered on the brink of a full-scale meltdown. Mack was the most incredible lover she'd ever been with. The most inventive. The most responsive. He was also a suspect in her case, she reminded herself.

"It was a mistake." She found her shirt and shrugged into it, but it wasn't until she tried to button it that she remembered how Mack had torn it off and how the buttons had gone flying. She tugged the shirt over her chest and held it there with both hands. "We got carried away. That's what happened. Carelessness. Adrenaline. Heatstroke. Call it whatever you like. What it all boils down to is a—"

"Mistake. You bet." She watched Mack zip his jeans. "Forgotten." His shirt was hooked on one corner of the bathroom door and he whipped it down and tugged it over his head. "You want to go back to Neeta's place for your car?"

One look at her ripped shirt was all it took for Rosie to make up her mind. She knew the routine, and she knew the whorehouse would still be crawling with local police. The last thing she needed to do was walk into a group of good ol' boy country cops with beard burn, a ripped shirt, and a stripper in tow, and announce that she was a federal agent and this was her case.

Just thinking about it made Rosie's stomach turn.

"I think I'd rather go home and get cleaned up before I head back for my car," she said, and before Mack could get the crazy idea into his head that she might actually be fishing for an excuse to see him again, she added, "I can get someone else to drive me out there later. If you could just get me back to Vegas—"

"Las Vegas," he corrected her. "And don't worry about it. I'll borrow a car and drive you back out tonight after my last show. That way, you can get your car and I can get my bike."

"Forget it." Rosie congratulated herself. This time, she added just the right oomph to the statement. She sounded forceful. In control. Completely unlike the woman who only a short while earlier had abandoned her common sense and her principles along with her clothes and clear head.

One look at Mack and she knew that her head had not— for even one moment—entered into the equation.

Rosie curled her fingers into her palms and held on tight to her good intentions. "I appreciate the offer," she said. "I really do. But I think we both know it's not a good idea. There's no use—"

"What? Tempting fate?" Mack's laugh didn't contain the least bit of humor. "You think I'm looking for an excuse to get you alone so we can go at it again?"

"Aren't you?"

It was an unfair question and besides, Rosie didn't want to know the answer. Damned if she did. Damned if she didn't. And she'd be damned if she'd stand there and listen to which Mack thought she was. Before he could say a word, she hurried out of the trailer and bounded down the steps, and even when she heard him come outside and snap the door closed behind him, she didn't turn around.

"I'm not any more proud of what happened than you are." Mack's words died against the wall of heat that rose off the desert floor.

She tried to make her voice match the cocky smile she gave him when she did turn around. "That bad, huh?"

"No. That good." He reached out a hand, and for one second, she thought he was asking for a second chance. For one second, she actually thought about giving him one. The second dissolved and she realized he was waiting for the key. She got it out of the compact and handed it to him and, for one more second, his fingers closed over hers. "You don't have to worry, Rosie," he said. "I swear, it will never happen again."

Just as quickly, he loosened his hold on her hand, locked the door, and headed around to the other side of the trailer for the motorcycle.

Rosie swallowed hard. Mistake or no mistake, great sex or not, it didn't change a thing. Mack knew exactly what she knew, and she knew they'd overstepped the line.

She also knew they were both too smart to ever let it happen again.

The last thing Mack needed was for some hot-to-make-a-bust state trooper to pull them over. Especially on the off chance that someone at the whorehouse had reported the Shadow stolen.

He drove like a poster boy for Motorcycles Anonymous, which might not have been such a bad thing if the snail's pace didn't prolong their trip. He didn't need more of Rosie, he needed less. As far as he could tell, *less* didn't include her tucked up against his butt, with her arms around his waist and the image of her naked body moving against his so clear

in his head that he was tempted to pull over at the first motel they came to and beg her to change her mind.

He didn't. Not the easiest thing he'd ever done, but then
again, who said anything in life was going to be easy?

Fortunately for him, before his thoughts could get too
maudlin or too philosophical—there was no way he could
keep them from getting way too graphic—they hit Vegas
traffic and there wasn't time to do anything more than worry
if they were going to live long enough to regret everything
they'd done.

"Here is fine." They were idling at a red light and Rosie
leaned over his shoulder and shouted. She pointed to the
left, to where there was a space to park between a red
Corvette and a black sedan. "I can walk from here."

"Dressed like that?" OK, Mack had to admit it. Here in
Vegas, where sin was as common as playing cards and flesh
was just a commodity like poker chips, a woman in Rosie's
state of almost-dressed would barely cause heads to turn.
That didn't mean he was going to let anybody and his
brother ogle her when she walked the two blocks to her
apartment. He shook his head, and when the light changed,
he gunned the engine and zipped between the two lines of
traffic waiting to make the turn onto Las Vegas Boulevard.
He didn't need to ask Rosie where she lived; he remembered the address from when he'd taken a look at her personnel file. Apparently she remembered that little detail,
too. She didn't question him when he turned down the
correct street and burned rubber into the parking lot of
the four-story apartment building. There was a space near
the front door, and he parked the bike and made a move to
get off.

"Don't." Rosie stopped him, one hand on his arm. "I can
find my way upstairs all by myself."

"Right." He wasn't about to fight with her. Not out here
in a parking lot with a senior citizens' van letting its passengers out on one side of the parking spaces set aside for the

handicapped and a vintage Volkswagen bus filled with what looked to be escapees from the Flower Power generation on the other. He slid off the bike, firmly ignoring the way his thigh brushed Rosie's and the way his blood caught fire.

He stepped back, waiting for her to dismount, crossing his arms over his chest before he was tempted to help. "You think I'm going to let you walk in there all by yourself? After what happened last night?"

Her eyes flashed with the kind of quick, brilliant light that reminded him of the little snap fireworks he used to toss around when he was a kid. Her cheeks turned a nice, dusky shade of pink, like the sensitive skin around her nipples. "We said we were going to forget last night. Remember? We said we weren't going to let what happened last night influence anything we did from now on. We said—"

She was so darned sincere, so darned determined, he couldn't help but smile. So, he wasn't the only one thinking about everything that had happened in the trailer.

"I was talking about the cathouse." Mack reminded her— and himself—that it wasn't safe to talk about anything else. Not for his peace of mind. Not for his body. Not for the unruly and just-about-uncontrollable urges that even now invited him to forget everything he should have remembered and remember everything it was better they both forget. "You remember. Six big, bad bruisers? Automatic weapons? Bullets flying?"

She let go a shaky breath and turned toward the front door. It wasn't until her shirt flapped open that she remembered it was torn, and she clutched it around herself with a vengeance, her knuckles white against the bright red fabric. "Of course I knew that's what you were talking about. What else would we be talking about?"

"Exactly." He fell into step beside her. "Which is exactly why I'm not letting you walk into your apartment all alone. If someone's there—"

"Ellie! Is that you, Ellie?"

The sound of a voice calling from across the parking lot stopped Rosie in her tracks. Every drop of that nice dusky color drained out of her face.

While Mack had noticed the man and woman who stepped out of the VW bus, Rosie apparently hadn't. She took one look at them and grabbed Mack's arm. She tugged him toward the building. "Inside," she said, then just as quickly changed her mind. She pushed him away. "You have to leave. Now."

"But, I—"

Mack took a good look at the man who was headed their way. He was middle-aged, tall, reed thin. He had salt-and-pepper hair that was scooped back into a ponytail that dangled to the middle of his back. The woman who got out of the passenger side of the van looked like a piece of a matching set: flowing skirt, sandals, hair that was the same color as Rosie's. It was frizzy and swung down to her butt. When she saw Rosie, she smiled and waved.

Her stomach clenched, her mind suddenly completely blank, Rosie stared at the couple across the parking lot and at the three younger men who got out of the van with them.

All the way back to Vegas, she had been consoling herself with the one and only comforting thought to come out of the last few hours: Things couldn't get any worse.

Well, she'd been wrong.

Dead wrong.

Because bad had just gone right past worse. And the worst had just materialized. Live and in color.

There was only one word Rosie could even imagine that was appropriate enough to describe the situation. She dropped her head into her hands.

"Shit."

If she'd been staked out on the desert sand and covered with flesh-eating ants, Rosie couldn't have said how she got through the next few minutes. She remembered babbling excuses to Mack, excuses that didn't sound very plausible, even to her. If the look on his face meant anything, they weren't very convincing to him, either, but as he had made so apparent back in the trailer when the cold light of reality was staring them both in the face, he knew a losing cause when he saw one. He didn't look as unhappy as he did simply perplexed. And if there was one thing she'd learned about Mack in the weeks she'd known him and the time they'd spent together, it was that though he didn't often play by the rules, he liked to at least know what they were.

Not her fault, Rosie consoled herself, and when Mack hopped on the motorcycle and headed out of the parking lot, she breathed a sigh of relief. He was not her problem, either. At least not for the moment.

She would have felt a whole lot better if he was the only thing she had to worry about.

She remembered the looks she got from the neighbors she'd been unfortunate enough to run into when she tramped into the building followed by two aging hippies and three young men with shoulder-length hair, wire-rimmed glasses, and bell-bottom jeans.

Once she was inside her apartment, she remembered that her shirt was torn and that her bra was showing, so before she did anything else, she headed into her bedroom. She stripped off the shirt and tossed it into a nearby wastebasket, wishing that it was as easy to toss aside the memories it conjured.

"Not a chance." She sighed, and she reached into her closet for a sweatshirt. Once she put it on and combed her fingers through her hair, she ducked into the bathroom to brush her teeth. Finally, she felt a little more like herself. It wasn't until she did that she dared to glance in the mirror.

Considering the fact that she hadn't slept, that her insides were twisted inside out, and that her career might very well hang in the balance of what Mack chose to say—and not say—about what the two of them had done the night before, she didn't look any worse for wear. It wasn't much, but for now, it was better than nothing. A little more calm and in control, Rosie threw back her shoulders and walked into her living room to face her family.

She glanced from where her father and mother were sitting on the couch holding hands to where two of her brothers, Hubert Humphrey Malone and Pete Seger Malone, were sorting through the small collection of CDs she'd brought with her from San Francisco. From the slightly sour looks on their faces, it was obvious they didn't approve. In their book, Dvorak would never compete with Dylan, Beethoven was a poor substitute for Baez. And as for the Barry Manilow collections? Well, something told her they just didn't get it, which was fine with her. The day her tastes—in anything—meshed with theirs . . .

The thought was too terrifying to consider, so it was a good thing she was distracted by the sounds of cupboards being opened and closed out in the kitchen. She knew exactly what was going on in there. The youngest of the clan, John Kennedy Malone, hadn't wasted any time looking for something to eat.

Rosie drew in a deep, calming breath. There was no use beating around the bush. Not with this bunch; her family was never much for subtlety.

"I'm working undercover," she told them, letting her gaze rake them over one by one. "Would you mind telling me how the hell you knew where to find me?"

Francine Mercedes Malone bounced up from her seat on the couch and her tie-dyed, ankle-length skirt billowed around her. She waved her hand dismissively. "Anyone can find out anything," she said. Convinced of the righteousness of her argument, her face split with a beatific smile that made her look younger than her fifty-four years. "You should know that by now, honey. Freedom of information. We fought for it for years. If our Big Brother government can know every little thing about every little person—"

A lecture on the American political system was the last thing Rosie needed. Instead of listening, she waved a hand, cutting off her mother's words, and realized, too late, that it was the same gesture her mother had used. Horror-struck that an old-fashioned traditionalist like she was could have even so small a thing in common with the free-thinking, free-spirited, freewheeling liberal who had given her birth, Rosie slapped her hand back to her side and kept it there.

"News flash, folks," she told her family. "These days, Big Brother has more important things to worry about. And that wasn't the question, anyway. This has nothing to do with Freedom of Information or freedom of anything else. You knew I was in Vegas—"

"Las Vegas," Daniel Malone corrected her.

Rosie gritted her teeth. "Las Vegas. You knew I was here. You knew my address. You were lying in wait. The concept of undercover . . . that means . . . what to you folks?" She glanced toward the kitchen when John appeared with a Dove Bar in one hand and a bag of rippled potato chips in the other.

"No tofu?" John asked.

"No tofu." Rosie stalked across the room and relieved him of the Dove Bar. If ever a situation called for chocolate, this was it. She ripped off the wrapper and bit into the ice cream bar.

"Not good for you," her mother declared. "Too much processed sugar."

"I'll tell you what's not good for me." Rosie swallowed a mouthful of chocolate and used the ice cream bar to point at her family members, one by one. "Having you and you and you and you and you show up here unannounced. I am supposed to be *undercover*." She pronounced the word carefully, as if that might make them realize its importance. "There I was, with someone who could be a suspect and—"

"Give me a break!" Leave it to Hubert to call her on that one. He was only a year and a half older than Rosie and they had always been close. Though he wore the same rose-colored glasses that tended to blind the entire Malone family, Hubert was more inclined than the rest to realize that rose-tinged or not, things weren't always what they seemed. "That guy? A suspect? If I had to suspect what you two were up to—"

"Didn't look too suspicious to me." John joined in the fun at the same time he wrinkled his nose and set down the bag of potato chips, as if just holding it would make the saturated fats inside migrate into his bloodstream and destroy what was, no doubt, a perfect balance between his good and bad cholesterol.

"Didn't look like anything to me. Not anything but good times," Pete added.

"Well, you're wrong." Rosie crossed her arms over her chest. At the last second she realized the pose was far too defensive and she brought her arms to her side, her fists clenched. "Good times implies a certain unethical—"

"Now, now." Francine took charge the way she always did, a move that should have annoyed Rosie the way it always did. Instead, she felt a rush of relief. At least if she wasn't busy trying to rationalize her behavior to her family, she wouldn't have to rationalize it to herself.

As if she could read every thought pounding through Rosie's head and the GUILT SPOKEN HERE sign she had no doubt was flashing over her in neon letters ten feet high, her mother gave Rosie one of her patented peace-love-and-brotherhood, nothing-ruffles-my-feathers, live-and-let-live smiles. Arms open, she hurried across the room and folded Rosie into a hug.

"Ellie's an adult and as an adult, she can make her own choices," she said, stepping back but keeping an arm around Rosie's shoulders. "If we question those choices—like I'll admit we were tempted to do when she surprised us all by announcing she was going to work for the government—we need to question our own ability to allow other people to live the kinds of lives they choose."

"Thank you," Rosie grumbled. "I think." Too edgy to stand still, she eased away from her mother's embrace. "Would somebody please tell me what's going on?" she asked. "No. Don't tell me. Let me guess." Though no one had made a move to explain, Rosie held up one hand, suggesting they let her take a stab at it. Actually, it really wasn't very hard. Like politics, a lifetime of activism had given the Malone family, en masse, some pretty strange bedfellows. They numbered an assortment of like-minded journalists, politicians, and entertainers among their friends. It wasn't hard to see how the network could work to their advantage.

"You found out where I was from some contact on the Hill, right? Somebody who knows somebody who knows somebody who—"

"You got it, Sunshine." Her father pulled a pipe out of his back pocket, tapped it against the edge of Rosie's oak coffee table, and reached into the hand-knit bag he had slung over one shoulder. She'd hoped he'd learned his lesson just a few months earlier when he led a protest aimed at legalizing marijuana and ended up spending three days in jail for his efforts, but Rosie couldn't help cringing. The day was already bad enough without introducing illegal substances into the mix.

Fortunately for her, Dan's weed of choice (at least for the moment) was nothing more mind-expanding than tobacco. He filled his pipe, lit it, and puffed on it thoughtfully. "We were headed this way anyway," he told her. "And then when we heard you were here, too. . . . Well, we couldn't pass up the opportunity. It's been a long time since you've been home, Ellie."

She couldn't deny it. And why would she try, anyway? Rosie shrugged away the twinge of guilt that threatened to sidetrack her. "I've been busy," she told them, and if nothing else, they were kind enough not to point out that it was the same excuse they'd been hearing since the day she packed her bags and left for college and the wonderful, quiet, tofu-free life she'd always dreamed of. "Besides, I was just there. To see you. I was just—"

"Two years." Francine held up the appropriate number of fingers, and it was no coincidence that she looked perfectly at home making the peace sign. "Not that we're judging or criticizing. After all, you are an adult. And you do send cards and gifts for birthdays. And you did call on Mother's Day—"

"The machine picked up the message." Rosie remembered the incident clearly. "Something about a protest in the South Atlantic. Whales?"

"Penguins," Pete corrected her. "Threatened by the collective greed of developers, global warming, and—"

"Yeah, yeah, yeah." Rosie finished the last bite of ice cream and headed into the kitchen to get rid of the wooden stick. "So what is it this time?" she asked when she was done. "There's not a whale or a penguin within miles of here. No spotted owls, either. At least I don't think there are any spotted owls. Hell, this is Las Vegas. There's nothing here but gamblers, pimps, and hustlers. And as far as I know, none of them are endangered species."

"*Cricetidae.*" Francine plunked back down on the couch and leaned forward, excitement sparkling in her eyes. "Voles. Specifically, the mine vole. No one knows for sure, but we suspect that there are only—"

"A dozen or so left in all the world." Dan warmed to the subject. "A dozen! Do you know what that means?"

Rosie shrugged. "Pretty soon, no more mine voles?"

"You got it!" Never one to recognize sarcasm when he heard it, Pete nodded enthusiastically and went to join their parents on the couch. Hubert pulled up a chair from the dining room table. John went to do another recon of the kitchen, confident, no doubt, that in the time he'd been gone, a whole host of healthy, unprocessed, and additive-free foods might have appeared to replace the less-than-organic selection

Rosie had gone out of her way to purchase the last time she'd visited the grocery store.

She paced the length of the living room and back again. "Look, I really am happy to see you. Honest. It's just that . . . well, you picked an inopportune time and I didn't know you were coming and—"

"And there was that hot guy she was with." Francine elbowed her husband in the ribs and gave Rosie a wink. "Glad to see you're loosening up a bit, Ellie. It's about time."

"No. It isn't about time." Rosie looked at her mother in wonder. "Don't you get it? Don't any of you get it? This is my job, and I can't risk it by—"

Just listening to her own words made her stomach clench. Not risk it by what? By leading on a man who had no idea who—and what—she really was? By not giving in to the baser urges that had been more urgent than any she'd ever had before? By stepping too close to the edge? Risking her case and her heart over some good-time guy who could blow the whistle and stand back to watch her career go up in smoke?

"Are you all right, Sunshine?"

Her dad's voice snapped her out of a place she knew it was better not to go. "I'm fine," she said, and though she knew it wasn't true, she knew it had better get true. Fast. She would be fine because she was going to put Mack and everything that had happened between them completely out of her mind. She would be fine. She had no choice.

"I'm just a little tired," she confessed. "Maybe we could spend some time together on your way back from . . ." Instinctively she looked to John for the answer. He was the unofficial family tactician: part travel agent, part navigator, part social secretary.

"Rhyolite," he said. "We're headed to a place called Rhyolite, about a hundred and twenty miles northwest of here."

"Funny name, huh?" Pete scratched a hand through hair

that was long and silky enough that even Rosie envied it. "I mean, rhyolite . . . it's a rock, a kind of granite, and it's not what they mined in Rhyolite. They mined gold."

"And when the gold was gone," Hubert added, "the town was deserted and there's nothing left there now but the ruins of a few buildings and the empty mines and—"

"Mine voles." Rosie nodded. She was starting to get the picture. "So you're headed to Rhyolite and once you get there you're going to . . ."

"Count the voles. Study the voles. Save the voles." His mind as firmly made up now as it had surely been back home in New England when he first heard about the plight of the unfortunate critters, Dan Malone got to his feet.

"We've organized a protest." Smiling, Francine got up, too. She headed toward the door, stopping only long enough to give Rosie a kiss on the cheek. "There's talk about closing up the mine shafts for safety reasons, you see, and if that happens—"

"It will disrupt the voles' natural habitat." Her father kissed her, too, and after Rosie hugged him back, she opened the door.

"They'll lose accessibility to the surface and their ability to get back and forth for food," Pete said. He added a hug to the kiss he gave Rosie.

"And a vital component of the ecosystem will be eliminated." Hubert, always the big brother, ruffled a hand through Rosie's hair. "We've got to stop this before it has a chance to start. We've got to convince the community—"

"That while safety is of some importance, it's immoral and just plain environmentally irresponsible to allow the concerns of one species to take precedence over the interests of another." John gave Rosie a peck on the cheek and headed out into the hallway. "We've got the placards all printed up and a dozen different environmental groups meeting us there. *National Geographic* is going to be there, too. And the Discovery Channel. The rally is the day after tomorrow if you're interested, Ellie."

"I'll check my schedule. Promise." She would, too, even though she knew there was no way in hell she was ever going to make an appearance at one of her family's protest rallies. Not for love. Not for money. Not for saving the whales or rescuing the spotted owls. And certainly not for counting mine voles.

She watched her family walk down the hall to the elevator and when the door opened, she waved. They would be back. Just like they promised. She was sure of that. As soon as the rally songs were sung, the protest signs were flourished, and all dozen of those voles were safe.

By the time she got to the theater, Rosie was running a half-hour late. She'd already missed the afternoon's rehearsal and she knew that when she ran into him, Greg was going to be one unhappy stage manager. She'd missed warm-ups, too, and because of that, there would be hell to pay with Tatiana and demands for explanations (reasonable or otherwise) from the other dancers. When she raced into the dressing room, the other girls were already dressed for the first number. Angela gave her a pointed look, one that wasn't as concerned as it was simply curious.

"Rough night?"

"Does it show?" Back at her apartment, Rosie had thrown what she needed for the night into a backpack and she set it down on the dressing table and glanced at herself in the mirror. After seeing her family again, she'd felt the urge to remind herself of who—and what—she was, and she was wearing a neat black pantsuit and a conservative French braid. There was no mistaking the slightly drawn look on her face or the smudges of dark color under her eyes. "Guess I'll need some extra makeup tonight, huh?" she asked no one in particular.

"I don't think anyone in the audience will notice." Julie hauled up the top of the sparkling costume she was wearing and checked the mirror to make sure her breasts weren't too exposed. Or too concealed. Satisfied, she reached around Rosie for a container of powder and a large, feathery puff, and dabbed powder across her shoulders and the tops of her breasts. "No one back here would notice, either," she said, "if it wasn't for Mack."

Rosie's stomach flipped. Halfway to her locker to stow her stuff, she stopped and turned, backing up a step and forcing herself to meet the curious stares of the women in the room. "Mack? What do you mean *if it wasn't for Mack*? What did he say?"

"Say?" Angela laughed. "Honey, he didn't have to say anything. He walked in here this afternoon looking like the cat that ate the parakeet."

"Canary." Rosie automatically corrected her. "Cat that ate the—"

Angela clucked her tongue and tucked a long curl of hair beneath the feathered headdress she'd just put on. "Parakeets. Canaries." She barely controlled a wicked grin. "It doesn't much matter who's eating what—or who—does it?"

"Mack practically ran out of here after his show last night and you were nowhere to be found. Now the poor boy's looking worn and frazzled." The glance Julie gave Rosie was nothing short of green-eyed envy. "You must have been awfully hard on him."

"I wasn't . . ." Rosie swallowed the rest of an explanation that was bound to sound lame. To them. To her. This was just what she didn't need, a starring role in what would soon be—if it wasn't already—fodder for every rumormonger at the Swan. She didn't need it, her case didn't need it, and as much as she hated to admit it, she knew Mack didn't need it, either. Even if Mack was a bad guy, it wasn't fair to him.

It was the *wasn't fair* part that made Rosie feel so rotten.

The self-reproach that had been poking at the corners of her conscience reared its ugly head, and it was probably no accident that it was not only live but in psychedelic color. If nothing else, her let-it-all-hang-out family had always been big on responsibility. Responsibility to the environment. Responsibility to society. Responsibility to self. Whatever else she thought of them, she would give them credit for that. Seeing them again had reminded her of what she'd been trying to forget since she unzipped Mack out of his jeans. And she knew she wouldn't rest easy until she put things right.

It sure wouldn't be good for her chorus-girl persona and it probably wouldn't be all that good for her case, either, but she knew what she had to do. She had to talk to him. She had to give him a chance to come clean and confess. It was time to tell Mack who she really was.

She owed him the truth. Because like it or not—and with every minute that went by she liked it less and less—he meant a lot to her.

Discreetly, Rosie reached into her backpack, fished out her ATF ID, and looped the chain around her neck. She tucked the ID into her shirt. "Is he in his dressing room?"

"Can't wait, huh?" Angela squealed with laughter.

Julie sighed. "You are going to tell us everything there is to tell, aren't you?" She pouted nicely, the effect made more complete by the bright red lipstick she'd just applied. "If you're going to keep him to yourself, the least you can do is share the details."

"All I'm going to share with anybody is the truth." Rosie yanked open the door and headed into the hallway.

"You're going to be late getting on stage," Angela called after her.

Rosie didn't much care. She knew what she had to do and she intended to do it, and if that meant she was going to be late for the show, so be it. Besides, if what she thought was going to happen really happened, it wouldn't matter because she wasn't going to be in tonight's show or any other show. Ever again.

Her mind made up, she went in search of Mack and peace of mind, determined to find both. Even if it meant blowing her cover.

16

She didn't bother to knock. She knew the guys from the chorus were already in the wings waiting for their cue to hit the stage and she wasn't worried about walking in on Mack when he was half dressed. The way she figured it, they were way past the blushing stage.

Which didn't mean Rosie wasn't surprised when she pushed open the dressing room door and found Mack on one knee, bent over someone who was lying facedown on the floor.

And even more surprised when she recognized the T-shirt that advertised the latest and greatest resort up on the Strip, and realized that someone was Warren.

"What the hell is going on here?" Before she could decide if it was smart or not, she hurried into the room and swung the door closed behind her. "What happened to Warren? Is he all right? Have you called—"

"It's too late." The way Mack was positioned, she could see only his profile. She didn't need to see any more to know that his face was pale and his eyes were bright. Or that he didn't look surprised to see her. "It's too late to call anyone. But then again, maybe you already knew that."

"Knew what?" When Mack turned a little, Rosie was able to get a better view. There was something dark and wet matted in the hair at the back of Warren's head. Her stomach swooped and her knees nearly gave out. "What happened?"

"I was hoping you'd tell me." There was a shimmer of some emotion in Mack's eyes that Rosie couldn't read. He didn't look angry, but there wasn't a shred of doubt that he wasn't about to give an inch. His shoulders were rock steady. His jaw was tight. He didn't look shocked or afraid, either. He looked disillusioned. And very sad. "I thought maybe you could explain why you'd want Warren dead."

"Want—" Her voice refused to work. Her mind couldn't form the words. She gulped down her outrage and tried to rein in her confusion. "You want to tell me why you're assuming I'm the bad guy here? From where I'm standing, you're the one with the dead body on your hands and Warren—" She blinked back a wave of emotion that threatened to topple what was left of her self-control. "Poor Warren."

"Poor Warren has what looks like a hole from a .38 slug in his head."

"And I'm the only one who owns a .38? Maybe *you're* the one who put the .38 slug in Warren."

She should have known Mack wouldn't respond. Rosie glanced down at Warren's lifeless body and something very like regret clutched at her heart. She'd gone out of her way to make sure Warren was never directly involved in her investigation and, damn it, it looked like even that hadn't been enough to keep him safe. "Did he say—"

Mack's voice was calm; the look he aimed in her direction was as cold as ice. "He said something about a keychain."

The pieces of the puzzle started sliding into place. Too bad it wasn't in time to save Warren. Rosie thought about the keychain she'd found in the toolbox and how she'd turned it over to the evidence room when she didn't find any useful fingerprints on it or the bag it was stored in. She thought about Warren's missing toolbox.

There was no use explaining. Not to Mack.

Especially if Mack already knew.

A sick sensation filled Rosie's insides and her heart banged against her ribs. The room spun and she reached for the back of the nearest chair, clutching it to steady herself. Mack was a lot of things. He was brash. He was nervy. He was—at least when he thought no one was looking—kind and considerate. He was also suspicious. She hadn't forgotten that.

But she had never pegged him for a murderer.

A nice, conservative, hardworking federal agent did not—

But a nice, conservative, hardworking federal agent already had.

And it hurt like hell to find out she'd been right to suspect Mack all along.

"He said your name."

Mack's words intruded on the lecture she was about to give herself. Through the tears that misted her eyes, she glanced his way.

"It was the last word he said. He said *Rosie*."

"And that makes you think that I did this?" The disappointment that filled Rosie's insides dissolved beneath a healthy dose of anger. "Don't be ridiculous. And don't think you're going to talk yourself out of this by talking me into it. If he did say my name"—she glanced down to where Warren lay—"if he mentioned me, it was because he wanted me to know. That this is all about the keychain. All about the toolbox. And just so you don't get any ideas that I'm as stupid as you must think I am, let me tell you that I've already figured that part out. You didn't find the keychain in Warren's toolbox because I've got the keychain." She raised her chin. "I know exactly why Gus had it. I know exactly what it means."

Exactly was probably the wrong word, but the way she

figured it, Mack didn't have to know it. At least not at this stage of the game.

Watching her carefully, he got to his feet, and when he did, Rosie realized he was holding something in his left hand. Something that looked a whole lot like one of the small-size assault rifles she'd been trying to track down since the moment she set foot in town.

"9A-91. That's it!" If the gun was loaded, she didn't stand a chance. Rosie was beyond the point of caring. In one fluid movement, she reached behind her back for the .38 she'd clipped into a paddle holster at the back of her slacks before she left her apartment.

Slick move.

Except that Mack made the same one. At the same time.

In less than a heartbeat they were squared off, Rosie staring down the barrel of Mack's .38 and Mack down the business end of hers.

At least he'd dropped the Russian assault rifle.

"This is crazy." Mack's eyes flashed green fire. His aim never wavered. "You don't want to go here, Rosie. You want to drop your weapon. Now."

"Good idea." She remembered what she'd learned at the academy: never put your finger on the trigger unless you planned to shoot. She slipped her finger over the trigger. "Such a good idea, why don't you show me how it's done? You drop your weapon. Now."

"Can't." A vein knotted at the side of his throat and she noticed that Mack's finger was on his trigger, too. "Not smart."

"Not smart for me, either." Rosie wasn't sure how she managed to talk when she could barely breathe. She glared across the dressing room at the man who only twenty-four hours earlier had folded her into his arms, enfolded her in his embrace, and introduced her to sensations she had thought were only possible in the pages of romance novels.

Even those thoughts couldn't manage to take hold in the

harsh light of reality, and she got rid of them with a little grunt of disgust. "You're not leaving me with a lot of choices here, Mack," she told him. "And it's making me grumpy."

"You're not leaving me with a lot of choices, either. Please don't make me do anything we'll both regret."

"I thought we already did that." She gave herself points. Cold steel staring her in the face and one hot bullet in the chamber and at least she could still get in a zinger. Which wouldn't be much consolation if she didn't talk her way out of a bad situation that was looking worse by the second.

"I'll tell you what . . ." His gaze drifted from the gun and her finger, still firmly on the trigger. It rested on her eyes. "I'll put down mine. You put down yours. We'll—"

"We'll what? Wait for me to make the first move and take me out with one shot? Just like you did to Warren? I don't think so." As crazy as it was, as impossible as it seemed to even consider, Rosie knew she couldn't take the chance.

Apparently Mack did, too. Though it lasted no more than a heartbeat, she swore she saw a look of admiration in his eyes. Just as quickly, it shuddered and changed, flash frozen into a look of pure determination.

"If you won't listen to reason, Rosie, listen to this. I'm an FBI agent. And you're under arrest."

Something told Mack he was supposed to feel better once the words were out. He'd needed to get them off his chest for a long time, and now that the truth was out in the open . . .

Well, now that the truth was out in the open, he felt like hell.

Which wasn't exactly the best way to be feeling when Rosie's aim was still square on him. And his was on her.

The whole thing might have been a whole lot easier to work through if, like most sensible suspects, Rosie would just back down and back off. Instead, her hold on her .38 never wavered, her gaze never flickered, her shoulders never lost one bit of the starch that kept them back and steady. She never moved her finger off the trigger, either.

In fact, the only suggestion of emotion from Rosie was the frown at the corners of her mouth and the way her eyebrows slanted down over her steady gaze. "Hey," she said. "That's my line."

"Line?" Mack glared at her, trying for that just-hard-nosed-enough look that usually intimidated the hell out of the folks unfortunate enough to be on the business end of his weapon. It wasn't working on Rosie. "What are you talking about? What do you mean that's—"

"My line. Well, not the FBI part." Rosie kept her weapon up, too, and her sights trained on Mack. "My line. I'm a federal agent. ATF. And I've got news for you, pal. You're the one who's under arrest."

"Bull."

OK, so it wasn't a classic comeback. So it didn't carry a lot of weight. Or a lot of authority. Or anything more than the whole lot of the incredulity Mack was feeling. He wasn't about to be outfinagled by some hot little number who'd discovered there were quicker ways to a man's heart than through his stomach, and wasn't afraid to use them. Last night, her quick way of choice had been all about sizzle, all about sex, and all about taking care of both.

And today she had the nerve to lie to him.

Even Mack, who had seen a lot and been fed plenty of lines of hooey in his years with the government, had never come up against anything this outrageous. A fact he would think about later, he reminded himself. After he dealt with the problem at hand.

The problem was Rosie, and the nearly imperceptible movement he saw her make with her left hand.

"Reaching for my ID." As if she knew exactly what he was thinking: that in a situation like this, an agent couldn't be too careful or too slow to react, she unpeeled her left hand from around her gun. Being sure not to make any quick moves, she reached for the silver chain Mack could see dangling inside the yellow shirt she was wearing under her black blazer. "I'll show you mine," she said, "if you show me yours."

The ID badge she pulled out looked authentic, but Mack was enough of a veteran to know it didn't prove a thing. He'd seen bad guys go to a lot more trouble to get what they wanted.

For just a second, he let his gaze shift from Rosie to the 9A-91 he'd dropped on the floor. "There's plenty at stake here, Rosie."

"Don't offer me a cut." Her teeth clenched and her cheeks went ashen. "Don't you dare offer me a bribe to turn my back on this. I swear, if you do, Mack, I won't be responsible for what I'll do to you."

He controlled the burst of anger that threatened to get in the way of the self-control that was the only thing that stood between him and disaster. "I'm not offering you a bribe. That's not what I meant at all. I meant just what I said: There's a lot at stake. Enough to make a phony ID worth your while."

"Which isn't exactly telling me why *you* haven't pulled out your credentials. Unless you don't have any."

"Credentials." Mack grumbled the word while he dug into his back pocket and flipped open the leather wallet that contained his gold badge and ID picture.

"Living proof," he said. "You'll excuse the picture. It's a few years old."

"And it doesn't prove a thing. Like you said, there's a lot at stake here."

"And did I mention the part about how, if we don't come to some kind of compromise, we could end up standing here all night?"

"You didn't, but we could. And while we're at it, maybe you could mention the part that explains what an FBI agent is doing with a dead body. Or for that matter, what the hell you're doing with my 9A-91."

"Your 9A-91?" Mack glanced at the assault rifle he'd dropped to the floor when he pulled his weapon. "It's my 9A-91. It looks like Warren had it hidden here in the dressing room. He must have been coming to get it when—"

"When some son of a bitch shot him in the back of the head."

Rosie didn't have to remind either of them that she was pretty much convinced that the son of a bitch in question was standing across from her. And that he was thinking the same thing about her.

Her gaze flickered down to the leather wallet that contained his credentials. "And I should believe what you're saying . . . why?"

"Because if you don't and if we go on facing off like this, somebody's going to get hurt." His gaze flashed up from where her finger sat poised on the trigger of her .38, to her eyes. "I don't know about you, but I'm only willing to risk so much for the federal government."

Rosie's voice hardened. "Which just goes to prove your line about the FBI is bullshit. If you really were an FBI agent, you'd be willing to put your life on the line for your job."

"It's not my life I'm thinking about."

She pulled in a sharp breath. It was the first time in as long as he'd known her that he'd seen her at a loss for words, and didn't it figure that it came at a time when he couldn't do anything about it. Nothing but wait and see what her next move was going to be, and hope that he wouldn't be forced to counter.

She ran her tongue over her lips. "That doesn't change a thing."

"Didn't intend it to."

"And I still want some corroboration."

"Which is exactly what I was thinking." With his left hand, Mack reached slowly toward his back. "Phone," he explained, even though he apparently didn't need to. At the same time he pulled his cell phone out, Rosie got out the one the local office had issued her to take the place of the phone she'd given to Neeta. They dialed in unison, their gazes locked, their weapons still at the ready.

"Dom." When the special agent in charge of the Seattle office answered his phone, Mack didn't bother with the preliminaries. There didn't seem to be much point. "Yes, I know it's late, but I knew you'd still be at the office. I need information. Fast. Positive ID on a Treasury agent. Woman by the name of Rosie—"

"Eleanor." Rosie interrupted both Mack and the conversation she was having with someone named Chuck. "My name is Eleanor. Eleanor Roosevelt Malone. I'm out of the San Francisco office. I've got my boss here on the phone if you'd like—"

The sour look Mack gave her stopped her midoffer. Like he'd believe a voice on the phone. Like he'd expect her to. "He's checking," Mack told her, and Rosie took the opportunity to ask some questions of her own.

"FBI agent," she said into the phone. "Or at least that's what he says. His name?" The question seemed simple enough, but it caused a rush of color to streak her neck and stain her cheeks. "Chuck wants to know your name, and something tells me he's not going to settle for just plain Mack. Then again, that might explain why he's the boss and I'm not."

"Santos." It was a vital statistic he didn't share with many people, and something about doing it now made Mack feel more nervous than staring down the barrel of Rosie's .38. He twitched the thought away and tried to ignore the muscles in his shoulders that were beginning to remind him that he'd been standing for far too long. "Santos MacDougal."

"Santos. The Saint." Rosie nodded. She repeated the name into the phone along with a "Something tells me there won't be two of them."

While she waited for the person on the other end of the

phone to get her the information she needed, Dom was back on the line with Mack. "She's genuine," he told him. "Or at least an ATF agent named Eleanor Roosevelt Malone is genuine. She's the daughter of those famous activists. You know, the ones who are always up in Washington leading protest rallies. They're on the news all the time. The whole tribe of them. Father, mother, sons."

"Three sons." Mack filled in the blanks. "They're hippies, down to the sandals and the VW bus."

The remark was more gut reaction than commentary and Mack hadn't meant for Rosie to hear it, but in the close confines of the dressing room, it was pretty impossible for her not to. She gave him a smug smile, one designed to say something pretty much like *I told you so*.

He still wasn't willing to throw in the towel. If there was one thing a life on the streets, a stint with the El Paso Police Department, and a six-year tenure with the Feds had taught him, it was that nothing could be taken at face value. "Picture?" he asked Dom.

"Just coming over the fax." He heard the sounds of papers shuffling. "Nice-looking. You didn't tell me—"

"Not what we're talking about."

"Yeah, right." Dom got down to business. "Five-ten. About a hundred and thirty pounds. Redhead. No identifying marks, but then, I don't suppose you'd know about that anyway, would you?"

Mack grumbled a few choice words in Spanish. "Social Security number?" he asked, and at the same time that Dom was reading it to him from the sheet of vital statistics sent over by the ATF, Rosie said the number, too. It was the last bit of proof he needed. Mack let go a long breath, slid his finger off the trigger of the .38, and lowered his weapon. He listened to Dom give him a few last-minute instructions, then set the weapon down on the nearest dressing table. "OK. So you're the real thing. You're an ATF special agent and an ATF special agent wouldn't shoot an unarmed man."

Another thought occurred to him and he gave her a quick look. "Would you?"

"I'm not going to shoot you." Rosie shook her head. She was listening to what the person on the other end of the phone was saying. "Social?" she asked, and when Mack supplied the information, she lowered her weapon, too, and slipped it back into the paddle holster she was wearing under her blazer.

She flipped the top of her cell phone closed. "Great," she said. She sounded anything but.

"Fantastic." Not that Mack felt it. "Which means—"

"We're—"

"—working together?"

The acid look Rosie tossed him spoke volumes. Now that the guns were lowered and the situation diffused, she went over to the dressing table where Mack had tossed his credentials. She held the leather wallet and his picture up to the light and wrinkled her nose. "Santos, huh? Let me guess, your mother thought you were a real little saint."

"My mother was a *callejera* who really didn't give a damn." It was another one of those vital statistics that he didn't share. Not with friends. Not with acquaintances. And certainly not with fellow federal agents who only moments before had pretty much accused him of murder. Rather than think about how he'd let it slip and why, he plucked his credentials out of Rosie's hands and tucked them in his back pocket.

Her ID badge was still hanging around her neck and he'd always believed that turnabout was fair play. Especially when he was the one who'd been seduced, lied to, and bamboozled. Before he could remind himself that it wasn't too smart to get close to a woman who was too hot not to handle, he reached out and tugged at the silver chain. Rosie came along with it. Her thigh brushed his. His arm touched her breast. He refused to give in to the sensations that erupted through him, and in the long run, he supposed that was a good thing. Because it looked like Rosie was all for not giving in, either.

Her gaze steady, her breathing as controlled now as it had been when she stared at him over the barrel of her gun, she never flinched.

"Lousy picture," he told her. It wasn't, even if it did show a Rosie who was more straightlaced and buttoned-up than the woman he was used to seeing sashay around the theater in little more than a wisp of feathers. But then, he figured he owed her for the *little saint* comment. Which might have been part of the reason he didn't drop the badge.

"Thanks." She didn't step back.

"You know I never meant anything by it."

He had to give her credit; a lot of women would have asked him to elaborate. But then, if he didn't know it before, he sure knew it now: Rosie wasn't like a lot of women. She knew exactly what he was talking about. Which didn't mean she was going to let him—or herself—off the hook.

She gave him a cocky half-smile that told him she wasn't exactly serious. And not exactly kidding. "I never meant anything by it, either. It was just something that happened."

"I wouldn't have used it against you."

"Really?" She tipped her head and gave him a penetrating look. "If you really were a lowlife hit man and you found out I was a federal agent, you never would have told a soul that we'd been to bed together?"

"Not technically to bed." If the catch in her breath meant anything, Mack didn't need to remind her. Just like he didn't need to remind himself. "And if I was a hit man and you had me jammed up on charges . . . yeah, I guess I might have mentioned it."

"And since you're not?"

"Since I'm not and you're not . . ." There was only one thing to do, only one way to handle the situation, and Mack knew it. Just like he knew that sometimes the right thing, the one thing, and the only thing wasn't the easy thing. He dropped her ID badge and stepped away.

"Dom wants us in the local office," he told her. "The sooner the better. But we'd better get the cops in here first to take care of Warren. We've got to figure out how things got so screwed up."

Rosie reached for the 9A-91. "I assume you're talking about my investigation."

She sounded so matter-of-fact, so one-hundred-percent sure of herself, Mack couldn't help but bristle. He stowed his weapon and punched 911 into his phone.

"Actually, Special Agent Malone . . ." He waited for the dispatcher on the other end to answer. "I was talking about *my* investigation. And I'll be damned if I'm going to let you take it over."

"Really?" As instinctively as a mother held a baby, Rosie tucked the assault rifle into the crook of her arm. She flashed Mack a look that was every bit as tough as the one she'd given him when she thought he posed a different kind of threat. "We'll see about that, won't we?" she asked, but it was clear she didn't much care what his answer was going to be. Before Mack could say a word, she turned on her heels and headed out the door.

It wasn't until she was gone that he allowed himself the luxury of pulling in a shaky breath.

ATF?

Of all the things he'd imagined about Rosie (and he'd imagined plenty), this was not a scenario that had ever entered his mind. Rosie, a Fed? A professional? A peer?

He should have been breathing a long sigh of relief. But part of him—one he'd spent years trying to deny, one he still had trouble bringing out into the daylight and acknowledging—knew what he was feeling went a lot deeper than that. Old habits died hard and this was the hardest one of all to kill.

The thought made Mack's stomach go cold and he pulled

in another breath, this one deep enough to make his lungs ache.

When he thought Rosie was nothing but a hot little number who would help him pass the time he'd been condemned to Las Vegas . . .

When he thought she was a suspect in his case . . .

Even when he knew he couldn't stop himself from making love to her any more than he could stop the world from spinning . . .

He'd thought something else, too.

He thought he was safe.

Because this time—like every other—he thought it was going to be easy to walk away.

17

For a split second, Rosie didn't recognize the man standing near the windows in the conference room of the local FBI division headquarters office. The navy suit made a dressed-for-success fashion statement, but as far as she knew, it wasn't a language spoken by anyone she'd met in Las Vegas. The white starched shirt didn't exactly go with the local flow, either. Kind of like the basic-issue maroon-and-white-striped tie and the shined-to-within-an-inch-of-their-lives wing tips.

Then again, there was no mistaking the width of the shoulders. The tapering hips. The confident tilt of the head. Or the rock-steady jaw.

FBI Special Agent Stripper.

The thought hit her like an explosion and she paused just inside the door, grateful that she'd been quiet and that Mack seemed so deep in thought that he hadn't noticed her. He was standing at a right angle to the windows that took up most of the far wall of the room, his body silhouetted by the first light of another crystal-clear Nevada morning, both his hands wrapped around a Styrofoam coffee cup.

"Special Agent Malone." He didn't look at her, just tipped his head in a kind of greeting.

"So much for being unobtrusive." Rosie plunked her briefcase down on the conference table and tugged the boxy jacket of her gray suit into place. "We beat everyone else?"

"They're in Brian's office." Mack glanced toward the closed door on the other side of the room. "Ironing out the kinks. Or at least trying to." He turned and Rosie braced herself against the sensation of a hand reaching inside her and grabbing her stomach. It held on tight. Twisted. And didn't let go.

Kind of like the thoughts that had been storming through her head ever since she finished with the local cops, watched Warren's body being carried away, and went home to try and get herself together for this meeting.

"We need to talk," she said.

Mack didn't flinch and something about his cool, calm, and collected demeanor reminded her of the way he'd looked at her from the other side of his .38. "I thought we did that already."

"We said we didn't have anything to talk about. We said we were all for forgetting the whole thing. But forgetting the whole thing . . . well . . ." Rosie shrugged. As if that might even make a start at explaining the emotions that were rioting through her. "You need to know that I never had any intention of taking advantage—"

"We already said that, too."

"Not exactly." She didn't mean to lecture, but she wasn't going to let him off the hook, either. It was way too early in the guilt game to forgive him. Or herself. "Actually, what you said was that you wouldn't use any of it against me. And I want you to know that I would never use any of it against you, either."

Mack drank down the rest of whatever was in his coffee cup and tossed the cup overhand into the wastebasket on the other side of the room. "There," he said. "We talked."

"I don't think that qualified as a talk. Not in the strictest sense of the word."

"You're not going to start analyzing me, are you?" She wasn't sure if Mack was kidding or not, until she saw a flash of green spark in his eyes. "You're not going to let it all hang out like your hippie family and—"

"My family has nothing to do with this." The statement came out just a little harsher than Rosie intended, but right about now, she didn't much care. If that's what it took to set Mack straight . . .

She pulled in a calming breath. "My family and who they are and what they are . . . They have nothing to do with this, nothing to do with me, and certainly nothing to do with my career. In case you didn't notice, we are not cut from the same cloth."

He let his gaze slide over her white cotton shirt, her tailored jacket, the straight-cut gray skirt that skimmed her knees. He twitched his shoulders in a sort of impatient half-shrug that told her he wasn't all that interested, anyway. "So all this means . . . what?" he asked.

"It means nothing except that I want you to know that even before tonight . . . last night." She glanced at the window and the quickly rising sun. "Even before last night, before I knew who you really were and what you really are . . . even before you knew about me . . . I want you to know, I never meant to take advantage—"

"Don't flatter yourself, Rosie." Mack walked as far as the conference table that separated them. He leaned forward, his palms flat against the tabletop. "No one takes advantage of me. Not now. Not ever. Not even a federal agent who thinks she's just playing with a handy boy toy."

"Which is exactly what I'm talking about." It was far too confrontational and she never meant to do it, but Rosie leaned forward, too. She couldn't help herself. Part of her reaction probably had something to do with basic science: magnet to metal, moth to flame. Another part was all about not backing down, about not giving an inch, about refusing to pull back because it was a sign of weakness. Even though the way she leaned over gave Mack a clear shot at looking down her blouse.

When she realized it—and that Mack was taking full advantage of it—Rosie still refused to move. "I never thought of it that way," she said, and it was true. "I never thought of myself as the major player and you as just some convenient way to while away the hours."

"But you did think of me as a suspect. And you might have thought that with a little of the right persuasion . . ." He let his gaze slide up from the open neck of her blouse to her chin and from there to her mouth. "You've got the persuasion part down pat."

"And you don't?" Enough was enough. Rosie stood up straight and tall in her sensible black pumps, her voice as sharp as the look she threw Mack's way. "Let me remind you that the same applies to you. You thought I was a suspect, too. You might have planned to get me to open up—"

The allusion was a little too right on the money, even for Rosie, who was never one to waffle. She forced herself back on track. Before thinking about everything that had happened between them made her forget what that track was and where it was headed and why she was on it in the first place.

"All right, so we're both as guilty as hell." She gave in with a sigh that had everything to do with surrender, even if it had nothing to do with weakness. There was pretty much nothing else she could do. Not when the truth was staring them both in the face. "You had your secrets and I had mine. Now that we've got everything out in the open—"

"Do we?" Mack didn't look convinced. "As long as we're talking about the truth, then we'd better go all the way."

It was another reference Rosie didn't much care for in this context, but rather than point that out and risk getting sidetracked again, she kept her mouth shut.

"This isn't about us, Rosie. It's about my case and you know it."

The hammering in Rosie's chest stilled. The rushing noise in her ears stopped. So that was the lay of the land, was it? And it had nothing to do with the lay Rosie had been thinking about.

Her jaw clenched. "You're worried I'm going to sabotage you and take credit for the case?" She could hardly believe her own words. "That I'm going to—"

"Would you?"

"Would you?"

He didn't seem any more inclined to answer the question than she did.

"I thought the old days of Justice and Treasury working at cross purposes were over." Because she had to do something to keep busy and to keep him from seeing how easy it was to push her buttons—and that he had found exactly which buttons to push—she unsnapped the lid on her briefcase and fished out a leather portfolio. She tossed it onto the table. "At least that's the party line I've heard at all those meetings I'm required to attend. Bet you're hearing the same thing from your side. We're all one big happy family."

"We are one big happy family." Mack stood ramrod straight, his arms close to his sides. He glared at her across what looked like an acre of polished wood. "And we'll stay that way. As long as you keep your nose out of my investigation."

"Your investigation?" Rosie laughed. "I haven't danced my feet off for the past couple months just so you can—"

"And I have?" Mack snorted. "I've been pawed and propositioned. Hell, I've even been proposed to. Do you think I—"

"I can't believe they sent you in as a stripper and you actually agreed to it." It was not one of the things Rosie had intended to bring up, but once the words were out, she realized it was something that had been bothering her since the moment Mack told her his Social Security number and Chuck confirmed that Mack was the genuine article. "Don't you think that's a little—"

"Sleazy?"

"I was going to say *sordid*. And point out that the heart-tugging story you made up, the one about the poor kid out on the streets who was forced to strip for a living was—"

"It was the truth." Mack's hands curled into fists. "And besides, look who's talking! What I did was no more sordid than you in one of those little costumes that showed off more of your—"

"Me?" It was a ludicrous comparison if ever there was one, and besides, she didn't need to be reminded of what she'd been showing off. Or who had noticed. Rosie plunked down into the nearest chair, grabbed a pen, and drummed it against the tabletop. "At least all I was doing was dancing. Not shaking my—" She raised her chin and gave him a level look. "Not shaking whatever I needed to shake just so a bunch of sex-starved, middle-aged, hyped-on-hormones women would give me tips."

"The only tips I care about are the ones from informants, and let me remind you, Special Agent Malone, if you hadn't lost your informant from the start—"

"Who I wouldn't have lost if every time we tried to get together, someone didn't try to kill us."

"Which is the reason I had to go out and find her again. And then you showed up at the whorehouse and nearly got us all blown to bits, just because you were so jealous—"

"Jealous?" The word froze in Rosie's throat. She set down her pen. "You're flattering yourself. I followed you and Neeta because I saw her in the audience at your show. And I thought you two had something planned. Something that isn't what you think I thought you had planned."

"Well, you almost planned all of us into early graves. You allowed yourself to be followed. And if it wasn't for the fact that I was quick enough to get us out of there—"

"All by yourself."

"You helped. Some." Something told her the barely per-
ceptible tip of Mack's head was as much recognition as she
was going to get. "What it all boils down to is that Neeta was
willing to talk. At least to me. Before you came in and ruined
things before we ever had a chance to start talking. Which
maybe explains why I never found out about that keychain
you and Warren seemed to know about."

There was no use keeping the information to herself. Not
anymore. She had pretty much let the keychain cat out of
the bag back at the theater, and besides, she would need to
share it eventually, anyway. She sighed. "I found a keychain
in Warren's toolbox. The toolbox that used to belong to
Gus."

She could tell it was news to Mack by the flash that came
and went in his eyes, and she congratulated herself. Nothing
like a little one-upmanship to lift a girl's spirits.

"And what's so special about the keychain that someone
would want to kill Warren for it?" The glint was back in
Mack's eyes, the guardedness so evident in his body language that he might as well have hung out a sign. *Guilt*
might have been the language Rosie was speaking, but
doubt, suspicion, and *distrust* were what Mack was all about.

And knowing he still didn't trust her made her feel as cold
as a New Hampshire January.

She shrugged in response to his question. "Nothing any
of our forensic people can find. No fingerprints that
shouldn't be there. No secret code or hiding places."

"Oh, come on!" If he thought the thread of exasperation
in his voice was going to talk her into anything, he was dead
wrong. "I've got most of it figured out already. Warren took
over Gus's job. And something they did in their jobs—someplace they went, someone they worked with—had something to do with the guns. I never met Gus, but I didn't have
to. I know he wasn't the brightest bulb in the box. He's not
the mastermind behind this. And I think it's safe to say that

Warren wasn't, either. Gus must have found the guns he sold on the street. Just like Warren found the one he hid in my dressing room. He told me where he hid it. Right before he died."

When the door across the room snapped open and they heard voices from the other office, Mack pulled a chair away from the conference table. "What that all means is that you should be thanking me, Special Agent Malone. If it wasn't for me, you wouldn't know nearly what you know. And one way you can thank me is by keeping your nose out of my investigation."

"Your investigation?" The voices from inside the office got a little louder. Which is the only reason Rosie didn't let out a laugh. Instead, she lowered her voice so that only Mack could hear it. "What makes you think you have any business in this investigation? ATF, Mack. Alcohol. Tobacco. Firearms. We're guns and bombs, and this case—my case— is all about some lowlife selling guns out on the street."

"Ever think about where those guns came from?" Mack sat down. "They were stolen from a Russian military base. The KGB asked for help getting them back. They asked us, Rosie, not the ATF. Which, to my way of thinking, means this is my case."

A group of men walked out of the office, and Rosie clasped her hands together on the table in front of her. Her jaw firm, her eyes narrowed, she took the time to give Mack one more look, daring him to continue his half-baked argument now that they weren't alone. "*My* case."

He looked like he wanted to say something. He didn't have a chance. A man in a well-tailored gray suit walked in and sat down. He was followed by the bulky fellow Rosie had seen Mack with the night she found him looking up her records in Human Resources. Behind them was a short, thin guy in a polyester sport coat, maroon slacks, and white patent leather shoes.

Mack took care of the introductions, and if any of the

others noticed that his voice sounded just a little too clipped, that he looked everywhere but at Rosie, they didn't show it.

"Brian Hayes," Mack said, and the man who'd walked out of the office first shook Rosie's hand. "Lenny Underwood." Mack gestured toward the man who looked like an escapee from a vintage Rat Pack movie. "Lenny is the case agent in charge of my undercover investigation, and Everett"—he turned toward the big man in the dark suit who had a pair of Ray-Bans peeking out of his pocket—"Everett Tancredi is my personal accountant." The look Mack gave Everett and the one Everett gave him back told Rosie there was nothing personal about it. "He's taking care of the financial aspects of this investigation."

Everett eased himself into a chair. "Which would be easier if you'd stay within budget," he grumbled.

And something told Rosie that it took a whole lot more willpower than Mack realized he had, not to answer him.

In addition to the FBI agents, the ATF had sent three of their own to the meeting. They filed in and took their seats, and it wasn't until everyone was settled around the table that Rosie realized how flimsy her cheerleading rah-rah about one big happy family really was. FBI on one side of the table. ATF on the other.

Whether or not it meant anything, the dividing line was impossible to miss.

"At least we figured out how you two didn't know about each other." Brian Hayes looked from Mack to Rosie. "Ever hear of a guy named Parmenter?"

"Parmenter?" It rang a bell for Rosie, but a very distant one. "Isn't he the dolphin guy? Well, tuna guy, really. At least that's what he'd like everyone to think. He owns one of the biggest tuna canneries in the country."

"Yeah." Hayes nodded. "And a couple years ago, your family got into it with him."

"What!" Paul Turner, head of the local ATF office, shot her an exasperated look.

Rosie bristled. "My family exposed the fact that what was in his cans was way more dolphin than it was tuna. You think he had something to do with this case getting so mixed up?"

"Don't think it. Know it. We've been looking into Parmenter's dealings for a while. Not the whole dolphin thing," Hayes added, as if he needed to distance himself from anything that was even vaguely associated with the Malones. "But there are rumors. Kickbacks and payoffs. Cooked books. You know, the usual thing. It's not surprising that Parmenter has some powerful friends. Apparently he was owed a favor by someone who knew someone who knew about this investigation and wasn't shy about leaking the information." He puffed out a breath of annoyance. "You know the drill. Politics stinks."

"Especially when it interferes with my case." Mack's expression was unreadable.

Which didn't stop Rosie from reading plenty into it. "So Parmenter's hobnobbing with his buddies and the Malone name comes up. And someone who wants to cozy up to him mentions that I'm in on this investigation. My family was responsible for getting Parmenter a whole bunch of bad publicity, not to mention some big, fat fines. He's still hot under the collar, and—"

"He convinces his well-placed friends to keep our investigations a secret from one another." Mack filled in the blanks. "Which means you were looking to find out who was selling the guns out on the street one at a time because you didn't know there was a whole stash of weapons. And we were looking for the whole stash of weapons because no one bothered to tell us they were being sold on the street, one at a time. Parmenter probably hoped the lack of information would make you fall flat on your face. That family of yours, they make a lot of interesting friends."

"Actually, they do." Rosie wasn't about to be drawn into a discussion about her family. Right or wrong, they still had rights. Even when they were wrong. "Maybe Mr. Parmenter never considered that by trying to make my job harder, he might have jeopardized the whole case. Sounds like obstruction to me."

"You bet it does." The way Paul said it, Rosie was glad she wasn't Parmenter. Then again, she supposed it was what the scumbag deserved for selling all that Flipper meat.

"It all makes sense." Rosie grabbed her pen and started scribbling notes. "So now that we're all on the same page, what you're telling me is that someone's got the guns. All the guns. And they're using the Swan as the distribution point."

The look she shot him across the table dared Mack not to see things exactly as they were. Black and white. Plain as day. No denying.

This was a firearms case. Start to finish. And it was all hers.

She knew exactly where she was going to start with it. With the keychain. She also wanted to talk to Neeta again and consult with Chuck back in San Francisco. She would need to put her head together with Paul and the other agents from the local office, and they would need to do a sweep of the casino and talk to staff and question management. They still had a long way to go, but at least they were moving. At least things were headed in the right direction.

Satisfied, Rosie set down her pen and sat back. Content and not above a little gloating, she smiled across the table at Mack.

And wondered why he was smiling back.

Brian Hayes stood. "It's obvious we've got overlap here," he said, though what was so obvious about it wasn't at all obvious to Rosie. It was apparently not obvious to Mack, either. At the same time Rosie's smile faded, she saw Mack's wilt.

Hayes glanced back and forth between Rosie and Mack. "That's why we've decided . . ." He looked at Paul Turner and at Everett and at Lenny Underwood, who, for some reason Rosie couldn't fathom, looked like he was enjoying himself way more than he should have. "That's why we've decided this will be a joint operation. From now on, you two will work this case together."

By the time the sun went down, the conference room was littered with sandwich wrappers, coffee cups, and empty soda cans. Though smoking was not allowed in the building, the agents gathered around the table took a vote and decided Lenny would be permitted one cigar after lunch and one right after they'd finished the three large pepperoni pizzas that were brought in for dinner. Rosie was no fan of cigars, but she couldn't argue with the call. In spite of the seventies-vintage wardrobe and an unfortunate penchant for calling her *babe*, it was clear from the start that Lenny was a valuable member of the team. He was a veteran, and he was on the ball. He offered more than enough insight into the case to make up for a little chauvinism, not to mention a little secondhand smoke.

Besides, concentrating on the cigar smoke that wafted by every now and then kept Rosie's mind in the game. And off the player who was sitting across the conference table from her, looking as focused and as pissed as he had when they started.

Fine with her—Rosie finished with one of the files the FBI had provided, set it aside, and reached for another— she was still feeling pretty pissed herself.

She flipped open the next manila folder and her mood went from pretty pissed all the way to livid.

"Pictures?" She stared at the eight-by-ten glossy photograph on top of the stack. It showed a panoramic view of the Swan's stage, complete with the chorus line: arms linked, right legs raised in a shoulder-high kick. The girls were wearing their red feathers-and-sequins costumes—the ones cut up to here and down to there—and until that very moment, Rosie had never realized just how mesmerizing all that glitter was. Not to mention how titillating a stage full of exposed flesh looked.

Though she warned herself she probably wouldn't like what she saw, her gaze honed in on her own image, there at the center of the chorus line.

Too much makeup. Too much bare thigh. Too much naked skin peeking out from the top of a too-small costume.

Before she even realized she was doing it, Rosie buttoned the top button on her blouse and pulled her gray jacket closer around her.

The smirk on Mack's face told her he had noticed.

With a muffled *harrumph*, she shuffled the photo to the bottom of the pile. Unfortunately, the next picture wasn't much better. It was a close-up of the chorus line. And there was a red marker circle around Rosie's face.

Mack was still watching her carefully. "That's when we thought you were worth keeping an eye on," he said.

"Oh, I don't know, Mack." Lenny leaned over and glanced at the picture at the same time he gave Rosie a good-natured pat on the arm. "I'd say she's still worth keeping an eye on."

"Nice to know someone cares." She turned back to the photographs. A dozen or so showed the chorus girls in the wings, leaving the stage at the end of the last production number of the night. Another few showed them in their clown costumes, waiting for their cue to dance onto the stage.

And it took that long for Rosie to realize what she should have realized when she saw the first picture.

Her head snapped up and she looked at her FBI counterparts. "You have hidden cameras." She tipped the photo so Paul could see it. "They have hidden cameras," she said. "Why do they have hidden cameras and we don't?"

"Funding." Mack got up from the table and stretched. He picked up the ceramic mug decorated with flowers that one of the secretaries had left for him to use and walked around to the other side of the room where there was a thermal carafe of coffee. "Proposals," he said, filling his cup and drinking it right down, hot and black and without sugar. "Reports. Meetings. When we're good little boys, they give us all the toys we asked for."

"And we're not good little boys?" Again, Rosie looked to Paul for answers. "I don't see why they should have top-of-the-line equipment and we—"

"It doesn't matter. We've got the pictures now." It was Paul's voice, smooth as glass and as reasonable as can be, that made Rosie realize she was overreacting. "We're sharing. Like good little boys." He smiled over at Lenny and Everett and the message was clear. They'd better be sharing, too. Everything.

While they were busy with the nonverbal sparring, Rosie glanced through the rest of the photographs. "There better not be any of the dressing room," she grumbled.

"None of my dressing room, either." Mack took the long way back across the room. He leaned over her shoulder, close enough for his breath to ruffle her hair. Near enough to heat the air around her. "If that's what you're looking for."

She gave him a sour smile. "I'm not. Trust me."

"I do."

"Bull." Rosie straightened the pictures into a neat pile and kept her voice down. There was no way the other agents present had missed the undercurrent of antagonism than ran like a riptide between her and Mack. But there was no use giving them a ringside seat at the fiasco that passed for their relationship, either. She tapped the top picture and her own image circled in red. "You didn't trust me. Ever. Not any more than I trusted you."

"I wanted to."

Before she had a chance to register the comment or to try and study the expression on his face when he said it, Mack went around to the other side of the table, grabbed one of the files he'd been looking through, and took it over to the window. His back to her, his posture completely unreadable, he flipped open the file and bent his head, reading.

And left Rosie to figure out what the hell he was talking about.

Too annoyed to play games, too involved in her case to allow herself to be involved in anything—or anyone—else, she got back down to business and back to the photographs.

Angela in the wedding gown and Mack in the police uniform.

Rosie shook her head, amazed that even a trained investigator could have been so easily bamboozled. One look at Mack in that uniform and she should have known. No stripper could be that comfortable in regulation dress. Not even when the dress was designed to undress.

She set the photo and the thought aside and went on to the others. There were pictures of Greg, the stage manager, and pictures of the stagehands. There were pictures of Emery Carpathian looking irked on the night the light had come crashing from the ceiling, and pictures of Emery Carpathian looking irked at rehearsals and before shows and after shows and down in the casino when one of the whales who gambled there regularly was winning more than he was losing. There were plenty of pictures of Rosie, too, but she refused to look at them, just on general principle.

The next photo was of the chorus girl clowns gathered around Tiffany the night the light fell onto the stage. She and Mack weren't in the picture; they obviously hadn't made their way to the stage yet, but it looked as if just about everyone else was. She recognized Julie right away because her clown nose was missing. She recognized Angela, too, because, though she couldn't possibly have known she was being photographed, Angela was looking right into the camera. No big deal, Rosie told herself, setting the photograph aside.

Except that Angela didn't look as upset as everyone else. As a matter of fact, she didn't look anything but mad as hell.

The thought washed over Rosie like a cold ocean wave and as quickly as she set aside the picture, she reached for it again.

"Paul." The urgency in Rosie's voice made Lenny and Everett look up from the files they were reading. Even Mack turned around. Rosie popped out of her seat and carried the picture over to where Paul Turner was sitting. "Look at this." She tipped the photo in his direction. "Notice anything?"

He didn't, at least not at first. And although Rosie knew he was too good an investigator not to eventually see what she was talking about, she also knew she didn't have the time for games.

"Her costume." Rosie pointed to the right sleeve of Angela's clown suit. "It's ripped. I found a piece of costume up on the catwalk."

"You did?"

Rosie didn't honor Mack's question with an answer. He had weeks' worth of photographs and he was quibbling about a little piece of fabric?

She grabbed her purse. "Warren knew it all along. That's why they killed him. He told me the night the light came down. He told me he heard Angela talking about the accident with Emery Carpathian. I assumed he meant he heard them talking after the accident, but—"

"He just as easily could have heard them talking about it before." Mack hurried across the room. "Which means the key to the whole thing just might be—"

"Emery Carpathian."

Brain Hayes must have recognized something in Rosie's voice that told him she was all set to make a move. As if that would be enough to stop her, he held up one hand. "I don't need to remind either of you that we need evidence," he said.

"Evidence." Rosie repeated the word and headed to the

door. "You'll get your evidence. And I know exactly where I'm going to start. I'm going to talk to Angela."

"Not by yourself." Mack yanked open the conference room door for her.

Rosie headed into the outer office. "Afraid I'm going to scoop you, Special Agent MacDougal?"

"Afraid you're going to get in some trouble you can't get yourself out of and screw up my case." Mack opened the door and followed her down the hall. At the elevator, he punched the DOWN button. "I don't suppose you'd like to share a ride?"

Rosie sidestepped the offer. "I'd rather meet you," she said. "Ten minutes ought to do it if traffic isn't bad."

"Then let's say fifteen." Downstairs, she headed for the car the guys from the local office had retrieved for her, and Mack hopped on the motorcycle she'd last seen parked outside the whorehouse. Mack glanced at his watch. "The first act has already started. I'll meet you in your dressing room?"

Rosie unlocked her car and got in. Mack hadn't noticed that she didn't answer his question and that, she told herself wheeling out of her parking spot, was just fine with her. Because she knew something Mack didn't know.

It was Wednesday, and a week earlier, Angela had mentioned she wouldn't be in on Wednesday. She was taking the night off.

Rosie watched Mack turn out of the parking lot and head toward Las Vegas Boulevard. She waited until he was far enough ahead, then followed, and it wasn't until she got caught at a light and he went on that she breathed a little sigh of relief.

He was headed over to the Swan and that was just fine with her. It meant he wouldn't get in her way.

She was going to head over to Angela's apartment, but first, she had a couple of calls to make. She grabbed her cell phone and called the local ATF office, and when she had made arrangements to pick up Gus Friel's keychain, she called the University of Nevada at Las Vegas. It was late but there were a few words that could work miracles. *Federal government* was tops on the list. *Special agent* was another phrase that never failed to work.

Before she knew it, she was headed toward UNLV and, she hoped, the answers to a few nagging questions.

"Rhyolite? Are you sure?"

As soon as she asked the question, Rosie knew it was out of line. Not exactly polite to sit across the desk from one of the country's leading geologists and second-guess what he had just said. Especially when he'd been nice enough to drag himself away from his home and back to the office.

She smiled an apology. "Not that I don't believe you. It's just that . . . well . . ."

"It's rhyolite all right, Special Agent Malone." Professor Victor Butterworth had enough initials after his name to fill a box of alphabet noodles. He was older than middle-aged, silver-haired, distinguished. Fortunately, he was also tolerant of ATF special agents who dared to call into question the wall full of diplomas behind his desk. He lowered his grizzled eyebrows and gave Rosie a penetrating look over the tops of his reading glasses. At least he had the good grace not to ask why, if she was such a know-it-all, she had come to consult him in the first place. He used the tip of an expensive ballpoint pen to point at the little rock mounted in the center of the keychain.

"Rhyolite comes in a variety of colors, sometimes light, sometimes more grayish, like the specimen you brought with you. It's closely related to granite, you know. They are both igneous rocks. The difference . . ." He pointed and though Rosie was less than a novice when it came to the earth sciences, she tried to follow along as best she could.

"You see the texture." He ran his pen just above the surface of the rock. "As it does here, it frequently shows slight differences as far as granularity and color. Flow banding is sometimes also evident but I don't think . . ." He bent closer and took a long look before he grumbled something under his breath that sounded scientific and incomprehensible. "Your specimen may contain spherulites but I cannot say for certain, of course. They're quite small and you'd need to leave the specimen with me long enough for me to—"

"I really don't think that will be necessary." Though the offer to check for spherulites was apparently a heartfelt one, Rosie declined. She didn't know what spherulites were, and besides, right about now, she didn't much care. The geologic composition of the little rock didn't seem to matter as much as what it was called.

"Rhyolite." Rosie scooped up the key chain. "It's the name of a town, too, isn't it?"

"A town?" His lips pursed, the professor sat back in his leather chair. "A ghost town. Somewhere west of here." He gestured toward the window on the far wall. "Heard of the place, though I've never been there. I doubt your rhyolite is actually from Rhyolite."

"No. I don't suspect it is." Rosie tossed the keychain up and down in one hand. She closed her fingers around it and held on tight. "And you know what? That's what makes it so interesting."

18

If the door to Angela's apartment had been closed, Rosie wouldn't have thought anything of it when no one answered. Angela was taking the night off. Which probably meant she had something special to do. And though Rosie had been hoping that whatever that something special was, it was happening in the high-rise Angela called home, it was just as likely that the something special meant someone special and someplace special, too.

None of which explained why the door swung open when Rosie rapped her knuckles against it.

"Angela?" She stuck her head inside, but since the lights were off, there was nothing to see. "Angela, it's me, Rosie. Are you there?"

No answer. But there was a sound from inside the apartment and Rosie strained her ears, listening.

"Running water," she mumbled to herself, and deciding that it was as probable a cause as she needed to search the apartment, she reached for her weapon and stepped inside.

Now that there was no reason to pretend to be Rosie the chorus girl any longer, there was also no reason for her to pack the .38. Rosie hefted the considerable, comfortable weight of her .40-millimeter Sig and did a sweep of the apartment. The living room was empty. The dining room was dark except for the glow of the computer terminal that sat on one end of an oval table. There was a light on in the kitchen just above the stove, and in it, she could see that no one was there and that nothing looked to be out of place.

The closer Rosie got to the back of the apartment and the long hallway that led to the bedrooms, the louder the sound of the water got. The bathroom was the first door on the right, and she paused outside.

"Angela?"

When there was no answer, Rosie braced herself, her back to the wall. She pushed the door open and went in with her weapon at the ready.

Apparently, Angela had never had a chance to turn off the water in the sink. It was running full force. Fortunately, the light in the room was still on, too.

Otherwise Rosie would have tripped over Angela's body.

By the time Mack got the call and drove across town to Angela's, the crime scene unit was already there and a team from a local funeral home was getting ready to carry out the body and deliver it to the coroner.

He squeezed around them and into the apartment, automatically searching for Rosie in a crowd that included everybody from uniformed officers to detectives and even Lenny and Brian Hayes.

He found her in the dining room. She was sitting on a wooden chair with a high, carved back and a pink brocade seat, clutching a pile of papers in one hand, staring into space, and looking far more fragile than he'd ever seen her look. Even when she was scared to death in the backseat of Sid and Gloria's car or dealing with the six guys who had ambushed them out at the brothel.

As much as he hated to admit it—and he hated to admit it a lot—the realization nearly made Mack feel sorry for her. A lot to fess up to for a guy who'd spent an hour at the theater getting madder by the moment and another he-didn't-know-how-many minutes on his way over to the apartment, reminding himself that if Rosie wasn't going to play by the rules, he didn't have to, either.

That, at least, made him feel better.

Or at least it should have.

It would have if Rosie's cheeks weren't pale. If the skirt and jacket of her well-tailored, neat-as-a-pin gray suit weren't smeared with blood.

Occupational hazard, Mack reminded himself. At the same time he reminded himself that one of the occupational hazards none of them had ever signed up for was finding the body of a friend.

It took more self-control than he knew he had not to put his arm around Rosie. Instead, he crouched down in front of her and touched her arm. "Hey."

"Hey." Rosie brushed a hand over her cheeks. "You heard, huh?"

"I heard you found her. That must have been tough."

"I tried CPR." Rosie looked down at the mess that stained her clothes. "But it was already too late. Somebody surprised her when she was washing her face. Somebody with a big knife and a bad attitude." With deep breaths, she pulled herself together the way Mack had seen law enforcement officers everywhere bounce back after some especially traumatic event. Dealing because they had to deal. Because it was their job. Even when it was rough.

"It wasn't pretty," Rosie said.

"I'm sorry." Mack squeezed her hand, then decided it was a mistake. There was no room in their relationship to get personal. Not anymore. Besides, something told him Rosie didn't need—or appreciate—the sympathy. Not when they had more important things to worry about. He backed off. "I know she was your friend."

"She was KGB."

Even Mack wasn't ready for that one. He stared at Rosie in wonder. "She was what?"

"KGB." She pointed to the papers she was holding and he saw that they were written in a language that definitely wasn't English. "I found these in her bedroom. My Russian is pretty much nonexistent but when Brian got here, he called Washington. They say it looks like a definite possibility. Angela was working undercover, too, Mack. She was KGB, and if I had to guess, I'd say she was looking for the stolen guns. Just like we were."

Mack whistled low under his breath. "Then why—"

"Weren't we all working together? Your guess is as good as mine. Aren't you the folks who are supposed to coordinate things with foreign agents?"

It was ridiculous to think of it as a personal indictment, but that didn't keep it from feeling like one. Mack stood, but before he could prepare a defense, personal or otherwise, Rosie massaged her left temple with the tips of her fingers.

"I should have caught on," she grumbled. "I should have paid more attention. Cat that ate the parakeet. Gift horse in the face." Mack had no idea what she was talking about, but one corner of her mouth crinkled into a cynical expression. "She was good, all right, but she wasn't perfect. I should have seen right through her."

It was self-indulgent to use the opening for a little gamesmanship, but then, Mack figured he owed her. For the foreign agents comment, for the weeks of lying. Hell, he owed her for a lot of things, some of them justified, most of them not. All of them eating away at him ever since he made the mistake of letting down his guard and letting Rosie worm her way into his heart.

"You didn't see through me, either," he told her.

"And that's supposed to make me feel better?" Rosie pushed herself up from the chair and tossed the pile of papers down on the bare dining room table. She propped her fists on her hips, tough and together in spite of (or maybe

because of) the bloodstains on her clothing. "This investigation has been screwed up from the beginning. Maybe if all
the players weren't working at cross purposes . . ."

"This from the woman who knew Angela had the night
off and sent me to the theater anyway?" Mack stepped back
and crossed his arms over his chest. He hadn't meant to
come in here and get into a pissing contest, but he'd been
holding in his anger since the moment he realized Rosie had
played him for a patsy. The fact that other emotions had gotten tangled with his anger the moment he saw her didn't
help. "You were trying to pull the proverbial rug out from
under my investigation," he reminded her.

"I was trying to keep you out of my way."

"My turn to ask . . . that's supposed to make me feel
better?"

"That's supposed to send a really clear message."

"At least your cards are on the table."

"I assume yours are, too." Rosie plunked back down in
her chair. "Great."

"Fine," Mack said, and satisfied that he'd had the last
word (even though it wasn't much of one), he left the room.

He had a quick conversation with Brian and took a look
around the apartment, being careful to avoid the dining
room. There wasn't much to see. If it was true that Angela
was a KGB agent, she lived like every other undercover
agent he'd ever met. The apartment was leased, the furniture was rented, her life was circumscribed in every way.
There were few personal items in the place, and though she
had a wardrobe that probably would have gone for a fortune
on the Russian black market, there was little else to tell him
what kind of woman Angela Andrews really was. Or for that
matter, who she really was.

Mack rifled through the dresser drawers in Angela's bedroom. Nothing unusual there, either.

"No help," Mack mumbled, and he headed out of the
bedroom and back to the dining room. By that time, Rosie

was already gone and it was just as well. Especially when, on a hunch, he decided to check out Angela's computer to see what Internet sites she'd been surfing in the past few days.

Clothes, makeup, cybersex.

None of it was especially interesting or revealing.

Until he stumbled on a site dedicated to the back-of-beyond, middle-of-nowhere ghost town on the edge of Death Valley.

"Rhyolite?" Though he'd never been there, Mack had heard of the place. It sure didn't sound like the kind of spot where a sophisticated woman like Angela would look to pass the time.

Which is why it struck him as odd. He didn't need to remind himself that anytime something odd popped up in an investigation . . .

Mack spoke quickly to Brian and headed for the door.

There was no use going anywhere when it was already well past midnight. There was no use heading out when she hadn't slept for longer than she could remember. Good advice, Rosie knew. She had to force herself to follow it.

She went back to her apartment and stowed her formerly favorite suit in a big black garbage bag, then took a very long, very hot shower. She set her alarm for nine o'clock, and though she thought she was too keyed up to sleep, too worked up about the case to put it from her mind, and too steamed about Mack and the way he was acting and the way he had acted and the way (damn it) that she caught herself wishing he would act, she managed to drift off for a couple of hours.

Good thing, too. By the time she gulped down a couple of bowls of Honey Nut Cheerios and half a pot of coffee and pulled on a dark-colored polo shirt, a pair of khakis, a lightweight jacket, and sturdy hiking boots, she was feeling a little more like herself.

And a lot less like the crazy woman who had nearly sabotaged her investigation, her career, and her peace of mind, all because of a stripper who wasn't.

By noon, she was almost all the way to Rhyolite.

She turned off Highway 95 at Beatty and headed west; after that, it didn't take long to find Rhyolite. Or at least what was left of it. Thanks to a gold strike in the early twentieth century, the place had once been the home of more than ten thousand people, complete with schools, a public swimming pool, more than its share of brothels, and, if what Rosie had read was true, no fewer than fifty saloons.

But when the Rhyolite gold petered out, so did the population. Now there was nothing left of the place but dusty streets and the shells of buildings baking in the desert heat and looking especially desolate against a sky that was as clear and as blue as any Rosie had ever seen.

Something told her that any other day, she would have had the place to herself. A scenario that would have been much more to her liking. Just her luck, she rolled into town in the middle of what had to be the biggest mine vole love fest of all time.

Rosie slowed her car and looked over the lay of the land. She had to give her family credit. When they decided to throw a save-the-endangered-species-of-the-day party, they did it up right.

The streets of Rhyolite were lined with cars, vans, and RVs. Here and there, the more enterprising of the socially conscience vole lovers had set up makeshift stores, some from the back ends of vans, and other, more sophisticated versions, on tables and carts. Along with gourmet coffees, vendors offered falafel sandwiches, yogurt smoothies, and posters of brown furry critters that looked a little like mice. Farther up the road and just outside a small clutch of tents, she noticed candles and incense for sale alongside jewelry and hand-carved wooden toys. Right next to a place that advertised palm readings, mind-expanding herbs, and a cookbook that, at least according to the sign that advertised it, was a surefire hit among the anarchist crowd.

Any other day, she would have loved to flash her badge and rattle some cages, at least as far as that last item was concerned. Instead, she parked her car next to a remote-broadcast TV van complete with satellite dish and a mannequin-handsome anchor and squeezed through a crowd of placard-carrying protestors singing something to the tune of "Blowing in the Wind" that was all about the plight of the endangered mine vole.

Safely on the other side of the tie-dyed crowd, she ran smack into her mother.

"Ellie!" Francine was so excited to see her, she apparently didn't stop to think that it was the first family protest where Rosie had ever made an appearance, that they were dead center in the middle of the desert wilderness where it wasn't just coincidence to run into a daughter who happened to have an unfortunate fondness for working for the government, or that Rosie should have been back in Las Vegas and not out here where the deer and the antelope didn't stand a chance in a sea of flowing Indian cloth, Birkenstocks, and tree huggers.

"I'm so glad you made it." Her mother folded her into an embrace that smelled of patchouli and pot. "And so quickly, too. We left our message not an hour ago."

"Message?" Rather than risk a contact high, Rosie pulled away. "I left Vegas a couple of hours ago," she explained. "I didn't get a message. Is something wrong?"

Francine looked over her shoulder before she pulled Rosie farther from the crowd. "Your dad's over there." She pointed across a wide-open area where nothing grew but stunted scrub grass and spiny yucca. Beyond it and the three-story skeleton of what once must have been an impressive place of business, the hills that ringed the town were bathed in squat, high-noon shadows. "It's killing him to miss out on all the fun." Rosie's mother shook her head and her cinnamon curls shivered around her shoulders. She sighed. "But he says it's his duty and I can't argue with that. He left me in charge of the media and took Hubert with him. They're waiting for you."

"Because . . ."

When someone called to Francine to hurry over so she could be interviewed by the anchor with the perfect smile and every hair in place, she headed back toward the TV van, but not before she lowered her voice and bent her head close to Rosie's. "Because of the guns, of course," she said. "We found them. This morning. That's what we called to tell you. We went down into the mine to count the voles and—"

Before she could disappear back into the crowd, Rosie grabbed onto her mom's arm with both hands. "You found them? The 9A-91s? They're—"

"Down in the mine." Francine nodded and waved at the anchorman, assuring him she'd be right there. "Dad and Hubert are standing guard. You'd better get over there."

No one had to tell her twice.

Because she knew she'd never get her car out of the parking space and through the crowd of chanting protestors, Rosie decided to walk. She kept her eye on the place her mother had pointed out and headed off across Rhyolite. She found out quickly enough that in the desert, distances are tricky to calculate, and landmarks can't always be trusted. By the time she found her dad and Hubert, the back of her neck was baked from the sun, her feet were on fire, and the shadows were inching west off the tumbledown entrance to what had once been a thriving gold mine.

"Knew you're come." Dan Malone clapped her on the shoulder and stepped away from the mine entrance where he'd been stationed with his arms crossed over his chest and his feet apart. "We figured you were the right person to call, Sunshine. Not that I like the idea of you being mixed up with guns, but—"

"It's OK, Dad." She kissed him on the cheek and headed

toward the pitch-black opening that led down into the mine. "It's my job."

"You're going to need this." Hubert tossed her a flashlight, but when he stepped up beside her, Rosie signaled him to stay back. "We were down there—"

"Counting voles. Yeah, I heard." Rosie gave them both a smile. "I appreciate it. Honest. Both of you . . . you're heroes."

"Not." Hubert blushed.

She knew Dan was about to say something about coming with her, and Rosie stopped him before he could. "You keep up the good work out here," she told them. "Make sure no one else comes down. I'll just look things over, see if it's what I think it is, then we can get the guys from the local office in to clean it all up."

"Which won't make the voles very happy." Dan shook his head.

"Sorry." Rosie honestly was. She knew her family's heart and soul went into each and every one of their crusades. "Tell you what, I'll be quick and quiet. And when the rest of them get here, I'll tell them to be careful. Wouldn't want a gang of angry voles on our hands. The rifles, they're easy to find?" she asked Hubert.

"Straight through the main shaft." He went as far as the mine entrance and peered inside. "There isn't another passage in this part of the mine, so you can't get lost. And it's a pretty gradual slope. Just keep heading down. This shaft ends in a big sort of room. That's where the guns are. From the looks of it, there are a lot of them."

That would be consistent with what she'd learned from the FBI files she'd read the night before. One hundred and sixty-three weapons. Each and every one of them stolen from a Russian army base somewhere between Moscow and St. Petersburg, and somehow smuggled into the good ol' U.S. of A. There were apparently three times as many silencers, too, as well as optical night sights and underbarrel grenade launchers.

A whole lot of firepower. And a whole lot of opportunity to cause a whole lot of mayhem out in the streets.

Just as her dad and Hubert had promised, it was easy to find the twenty-by-thirty-foot passageway where the weapons were stored. In the circle of light thrown by her flashlight, Rosie could see that she was at a crossroads of sorts. Ahead of her, another shaft led off into the darkness. To her right and her left, there might have been other openings into the mine. It was hard to say, because it was hard to see past the wooden shipping crates neatly stacked along the walls. One of the crates nearest to her had been pried open. She had no doubt it was John's handiwork. He never could resist anything as tempting as a wooden crate, especially one that was nailed shut and stenciled with Cyrillic letters.

But while John might have been nosy, he was smart enough to look, then leave well enough alone. Nothing else had been touched, and she peeked inside the crate and saw a folded butt stock she would have recognized anywhere.

"9A-91!" She punched a fist into the air, the only celebration she'd allow herself until the weapons were safely in storage. She was already heading back up the passage to the surface where she knew she could use her cell phone when she heard a noise behind her.

Rosie stopped in her tracks and turned slowly, being as careful as she could not to make a sound. She arced her flashlight around the room. From where she stood, she could see most of the passageway and the stacks of crates that contained the rifles. The longer she stared, the more she saw nothing at all, the more sure she was that her ears were playing tricks on her.

Because though not a creature was stirring, she swore she heard the faint sounds of scratching.

She'd just about convinced herself that her imagination was getting in on an act that shouldn't have involved anything but her common sense and her know-how, when she saw a movement in the shadows near the right-hand row of crates. She trained her light in that direction and a second later, a shape emerged from between the line of crates and the rough-hewn mine walls.

Rosie leaned forward and reached for her Sig.

Little by little, the view came into focus. What looked to be the slick bottoms of men's dress shoes. Two of them.

And a rear end clad in charcoal-gray wool.

It was another butt she would have recognized anywhere.

"What the hell are you doing here?"

The sound of Rosie's voice echoed inside the mine and Mack was so startled, he nearly clunked his head on the wooden crates. He grumbled a word that pretty much described how he was feeling about dark mine shafts, narrow spaces, and ATF agents who just happened to catch him at what was definitely not his best.

Not that he was about to let Rosie know it.

On his hands and knees, he carefully backed out of the space between the crates and the mine wall, stood, and brushed off the front of what had been, a couple of hours earlier, an immaculate and neatly pressed suit.

"What do you think I'm doing here?" He ran a hand over his hair and realized it was standing up at all angles. So much for playing spelunker between the stacks of wooden crates. "I'm looking for my guns, that's what I'm doing. Looks like I found them."

"Actually, it looks like I found them." Rosie stepped into the circle of light thrown by the flashlight Mack switched on. What had once been a neat braid in her hair was coming undone, and she was dressed in khakis, a dark shirt, and thick hiking books. Chalk one up for Rosie. At least she'd had the sense to realize that a desert ghost town was roughly the equivalent of the back of beyond.

Mack gave his suit jacket a tug, brushed off the elbows, and put away his Glock. "Hate to disappoint you, Special

Agent Malone . . ." He didn't, and he made sure he let her know it with a smile. "But I got here first."

Rosie nodded. "Which explains why you were hiding between the rows of crates."

"Which explains where I ducked when I saw your light." He brushed off the knees of his previously pressed trousers and straightened a tie that had once been blue. It was coated with dust and smeared with something dark and soft. "I didn't know it was you," he said. "And I wanted to make sure I wasn't outnumbered."

"So that explains why when you saw it was me, you didn't say anything?" As if she didn't believe a word of it, Rosie had the nerve to laugh. "What were you going to do, head outside as fast as you could and call the office? Scoop me in my own investigation?"

"My investigation." She was so right on the money about what he'd planned to do, Mack figured there was no harm in reminding her that he had a stake in this case. "That's especially true if we're taking the time element into consideration. You just got here. I've been all over these mines all damned night. Stumbled into this one about a half-hour ago and realized I hit pay dirt."

"You're not kidding, dirt." She looked him up and down and Mack automatically found himself scraping a hand across the grit that coated his cheeks. "Why the hell are you dressed like you're going to church?" She gave him a sour smile. "Unless you're planning on stripping your way out of—"

He puffed out a breath of annoyance. "You're never going to let me forget, are you?" Because he couldn't forget, either, he twitched the thought away.

Rosie backed up, her hands in the air. "Hey, I'm willing. If you are. I'll forget the stripping, if you forget the chorus line."

"Done." Mack nodded.

"I'll forget the the tear-away clothes, if you forget the sequins and feathers."

"A little harder," Mack admitted. "But doable."

"I'll forget that little strip of fabric you have the nerve to call a pouch when it barely held what it was supposed to hold, if you forget—"

"Can you?" Mack's question surprised even him.

It sure brought Rosie up short. She blinked at him and two spots of color appeared in her cheeks. "Can I—"

"Forget?"

It was a legitimate question, even if it did make Mack feel as uncomfortable as Rosie suddenly looked. Hard to face facts, especially when the facts that were staring him in the face were ones he would rather not deal with.

If the way his insides heated and his blood caught fire meant anything, it didn't look like he'd be forgetting, either. Not anytime soon.

The thought hit Mack right about at the Windsor knot of his tie. "I didn't think I was going to be crawling through the dirt," he said, coughing away his discomfort and firmly ignoring the unsettling thoughts that danced through his head in feathers and sequins one second, khakis and a polo shirt the next, and finally in nothing at all.

He loosened his tie. "When I left town last night, I thought I'd hit Rhyolite, ask some questions, get some answers . . ."

"And get back to Vegas again before I ever knew you were here."

"Las Vegas," he corrected her.

"Las Vegas," Rosie conceded. "Which doesn't explain how you got down here when my family—"

"Your family? They're part of that nonsense going on outside?"

"It's their show," she told him.

"Because . . ."

"Mine voles," Rosie said, as if that were much of an explanation. She rubbed a hand over the back of her neck. "And how did you know? About Rhyolite, I mean. How did you—"

"Angela." There was no harm in sharing the information at this stage of the game, especially when Mack hoped Rosie would do the same. "You didn't stick around long enough last night to check out her computer."

"And you did."

He nodded. "I didn't think a girl like Angela would be much of a fan of a dusty ghost town. And you?"

"The keychain, of course," Rosie said. "Turns out the keychain I found in Gus's toolbox—the one Warren died for—is made with a piece of rhyolite."

Before he could stop himself, Mack's voice rose. His muscles tensed. "And when did you plan to tell me about this?"

"Never." Chalk up another one for Rosie. Mack knew he could be intimidating. In fact, sometimes he even counted on it. At a show of temper from him, most people would have been shaking in their boots. All Rosie did was laugh. "Or at least not until I had to. Are we even now?" She apparently figured they were, because she breezed right on. "So here I am. And here are my guns." She laid a protective hand against one of the wooden crates. "Case closed."

"Not exactly. We still need to find out who put the guns here. And how they're getting to the casino."

Rosie nodded. "I hate it when you're right."

At least she was honest. The tension drained out of Mack's shoulders and he couldn't help but smile. "The first thing we need to do—"

She didn't let him finish. "The first thing I'm going to do is get these guns out of here so they don't end up on the streets."

"Agreed." Mack knew a momentous occasion when he saw it. It was the first thing they'd agreed on since they'd agreed to forget the night in the trailer.

"Once we've got the area secured," Rosie said, "we can

station a couple of agents down here to intercept whoever comes for the guns. That's how it works, don't you think?"

She was so wrapped up in her case, she didn't even realize she'd actually asked for his opinion. Which is the only reason Mack didn't bother to offer it.

"They must be coming for them one by one, getting them back to the city, selling them." Rosie nodded, convinced of the logic of her argument. "Now all we have to do is figure out how. And how Carpathian is involved."

Mack didn't believe in fate. Just like he didn't believe in coincidence. He didn't believe in fairy godmothers or genies in bottles or magic potions, either. All of which made him think he was imagining things when he heard someone coming down one of the passages behind where they were standing, the same passage he had followed when he found himself down here not an hour earlier.

At the same time he reached for his Glock, he signaled to Rosie to be quiet, take cover, and turn off her flashlight. The last he saw of her, she was ducking behind the long row of crates and whipping out her Sig.

Mack was closest to the second stack of crates. He crouched behind it, careful to keep himself hidden. And he waited.

After a minute, he wondered if he was imagining things. After two, he was pretty much sure of it. But not a second after that, he saw the jumpy beam of a flashlight snake over the walls of the passageway. A minute later, a man stopped at the doorway long enough to swing the light of his flashlight around the room.

Satisfied nothing was out of place, he grabbed two of the wooden crates, hauled them up on his shoulder, and, straining under the weight, headed back the way he'd come.

Mack took off after him.

A tactic that might have been a hell of a lot easier if, halfway there, he didn't bump into Rosie.

They didn't dare talk. Instead, Mack tried a kind of sign

language, hoping to convey what he was thinking. If they were quick and they were quiet, they could follow the man and find out where he was headed with the guns.

Apparently, Rosie understood. Except for the part about Mack going first. Before he could squeeze between her and the crates of weapons, she was already hot on the stranger's trail.

The passageway was as black as the inside of a licorice stick, and they didn't dare turn on their flashlights. Rosie paused just outside the room. She should have expected that Mack would run into her full force.

Her knees buckled and she would have gone down on her nose if Mack hadn't snaked an arm around her. He held her against him, his left hand just under her breast, his mouth so close she could feel the unsteady breath he sucked in to calm himself.

And she was glad she had more important things to worry about than the way her body responded instantly to his.

Rosie pushed away from Mack, following the faint streak of the flashlight she could see up ahead. This passage was longer than the one she'd followed when she went down into the mine, and though there was no doubt in her mind they were gradually heading to the surface, it was hotter than hell. A couple of times she heard the man up ahead grunt, and she knew he'd put down the heavy crates. When she saw the light of the flashlight moving again, she motioned to Mack and, together, they followed behind him.

After what seemed like a lifetime, she saw a small square of bright light up ahead. Another exit from the mine, not the one where her dad and brother stood guard. Little by little the light grew, and silhouetted against it, Rosie saw the man with the crates walk out of the mine.

This time she didn't need to signal to Mack. He was still behind her and he gave her what amounted to a little shove.

"Exactly what I was thinking," Rosie whispered. And she took off to see where the man was headed.

By the time they were nearly to the exit, the blinding light of the midafternoon sun was streaming into the shaft. Rosie pulled to a stop just where it met the shadows and pointed outside.

They were apparently on the other side of Rhyolite. No dusty streets here. No dilapidated buildings. It was an out-of-the-way mine entrance in an out-of-the-way part of town. And perfect for anyone interested in smuggling guns.

There was an eighteen-wheeler parked outside the exit, and Rosie committed the license plate number to memory. The back of the truck was already open, and the man loaded the crates next to what looked like oversized, heavy cardboard drums.

By that time, Rosie already had her cell phone in her hands. A quick call and her troubles were over. The local office could find someone nearby who would trail the truck all the way into the city. And a welcoming committee of ATF agents would be ready to intercept the truck at the other end.

Nice plan.

It actually might have worked if the truck driver did exactly what she'd hoped he'd do. If he stored the guns, closed up the truck, and hopped into the driver's seat, Rosie's troubles would have been over.

But then, she'd never counted on him turning around and coming back for another load.

19

Mack yanked her back against him so fast and so hard, Rosie almost lost her footing. For the second time in as many minutes, she found herself with her back pressed to his chest, his head on her shoulder, and her butt nestled up against—

Good thing she had other things to worry about.

When he stepped farther into the shadows, Rosie back-pedaled right along with him. Though she hadn't noticed it on the way up the shaft, there was a narrow passage that bisected the one they were in. Mack must have seen it on his way down into the mine. He tugged her into the passage-way and slipped his arm to her shoulders. Side by side, they plastered themselves against the jagged wall of the mineshaft.

Not more than a couple of seconds later, the man with the flashlight headed past them and back down into the mine.

Rosie was all for following him. When Mack stopped her, his arm tightening around her, his hand clamping on her shoulder, she gave him a dirty look.

"He's not going anywhere." He whispered the words

close to her ear. "He's not going to sneak out the other way. Not when his truck is back here."

With a look, Rosie told him she understood. Still side by side, they checked the passageway and when they were sure it was empty and the coast was clear, they hurried out into the blinding afternoon sunshine and the stifling afternoon heat.

While Mack sprinted around to the front of the truck to check out the cab and make sure the driver was working alone, Rosie looked over the truck. LETTUCE HEADS. She read the words painted in bright green letters on the side of the truck right above a cartoon of a head of lettuce wearing a smiley face. "Of course." She shook her head, amazed. "Remember what Sid and Gloria said—"

"The salad bowl of the country." Mack nodded. "Someone at the Swan orders produce from Lettuce Heads. All completely legitimate. Except every now and again, one of the trucks takes a little detour. Take a look at this." He pointed into the truck of the cab and Rosie took a quick look.

Dangling from the accelerator was a set of keys hooked to a chain that was a perfect match to the one she found in Warren's toolbox.

"Just like yours?" Mack asked.

"Just like it. Which probably means that whichever driver gets the keychain—"

"Knows he's the one who is supposed to the stop here in Rhyolite and pick up something extra. Most days, no one's around Rhyolite to even notice. Then they—"

"Load up the guns—"

"And bring them in through the Silver Swan when they deliver the lettuce. Which is how—"

"Gus and Warren found them!" If she was feeling so inclined, Rosie would have slapped her forehead. "They set up the salad buffets. On Mondays. And each of them must have found the guns by accident. Chances are, Gus found the keychain, too, and knew it was significant. From what I've heard about him, he wouldn't have been above trying a little blackmail."

"And got himself a bullet in the back of his head for his troubles." Mack nodded grimly. "OK, so we've got that worked out. Which means the only thing we need to find out—"

"Is who put the guns here in the first place and who's picking them up on the other end. No-brainer. It's got to be Carpathian. And all we have to do is prove it." Rosie braced her hand against the door of the truck, ready to haul herself inside. "I'll stay with the guns. You can follow."

"No way." He stopped her, one hand on her arm. "I'm not going to take the chance of getting separated. Not with you in there by yourself. You need backup."

Rosie darted a glance at the mineshaft, half expecting to see the man with the flashlight already on his way back up to the surface. She glanced down to where Mack's hand was on her shoulder. "I need to get moving, that's what I need. So if you'll just back off, Special Agent MacDougal, we can get this show on the road."

"Not a chance." Mack tightened his grip. "We go to-gether. And we don't go in the back of this truck. Too risky. My bike isn't far from here."

"We don't have time. And besides, I don't want to. I've spent a hell of a long time on this case and now that I'm fi-nally getting somewhere, I'm not going to take the chance of losing my best lead yet. I'm sticking with the evidence. And with the guy doing the delivery."

"Then I'm sticking with you."

"That's ridiculous." She pulled out of his reach. "We both don't need to—"

The crunch of dry soil beneath the truck driver's boots put an end to the argument.

Mack hopped into the truck, and when he offered her a hand up, Rosie didn't refuse. No matter how much she was tempted. She'd worry about her pride another day. Just like she'd worry about how very unwise it was for a very smart woman to allow herself one pulse-pounding moment of hanging on to Mack.

She didn't have time for regrets or for wounded pride. Rosie braced her foot against the bumper and when Mack hoisted her into the truck, she took a quick look around.

In addition to the two crates of 9A-91s the man had already loaded, the truck was packed with what looked like legitimate cargo, a hundred or so four-foot-high cardboard barrels. If the air-conditioning unit blasting cold air into the truck meant anything, the barrels were filled with lettuce.

Mack grinned. "Now who's looking pretty smart for dressing like he was going to church?"

Rosie didn't honor the question with an answer. It didn't deserve one, and besides, they didn't have time. No sooner had they squeezed their way between two rows of lettuce barrels and into the corner of the truck farthest from the door when the truck driver returned.

Rosie dropped to her knees and ducked behind a barrel. Mack dove behind the barrel right beside her.

From where she was hidden, she couldn't see much but she could hear plenty well, and she heard the truck driver slide a couple more wooden crates into the truck. After that, the huge back doors creaked closed and the inside of the truck was thrown into darkness.

"Told you we didn't have time." Rosie hissed the words and was rewarded with a grunt from Mack.

The engine started up and the truck ground into gear, and when it made its first, jerky movements, she lost her footing and sat down hard against the truck floor. In the cramped space between lettuce barrels, there wasn't much room to move. Like her, she imagined Mack with his legs bent and his knees tucked up under his chin.

How he managed to find her hand in the dark, she wasn't

sure. Then again, the way she remembered all the things she was supposed to have already forgotten, finding body parts in the dark had never been one of his problems.

He gave her hand a squeeze. "You OK?" he whispered.

"Oh, bring that up again!" Rosie snatched her hand away. "Just because I happen to be smart enough to know that statistically, drivers who exceed the speed limit are more likely to be involved in fatal accidents, it doesn't automatically follow that I'm afraid of the dark."

He grumbled something under his breath that might have been a word. Or maybe it was just a rumble of irritation. "Put on the brakes! I didn't ask if you were afraid. I didn't mean to imply you were afraid and I'm not drawing battle lines. I just asked if you were OK."

If he wasn't being so reasonable about the whole thing, Rosie might have been tempted to point out that whether he meant it or not, the allegation was as plain as the nose on his face. Or at least as plain as it might have been if there was enough light to see his nose. Or even his face.

But he had been reasonable. And she had not. The truck bumped over the rough terrain and her teeth banged together. "I'm fine," she said. She used her shoulder to nudge apart the two closest barrels, making a little more room for herself. "I'm just a little keyed up and—"

"As cold as hell."

"Not at all." Rosie hoped her voice wasn't shivering as much as the rest of her. She tugged her jacket tighter around her and nestled farther between the barrels, and while they afforded some comfort, it wasn't much. The barrels were cold. The air blowing in from the overhead air-conditioning was cold. Rosie was cold, too, from the tips of her hiking boots to the top of her head. But as cold as it was in the truck, it would be an even colder day in hell when she admitted her discomfort to Mack. "After the heat outside," she told him, "it's actually pretty pleasant in here."

"Right." She couldn't see Mack's face, but something told

her she wouldn't have liked the look he tossed out with the word. She heard him move and pictured him trying to wiggle his way into a more comfortable sitting position, just like she was. The next thing she knew, she felt his hand on her arm. She was just about to ask what the hell he was doing when he draped his suit coat over her shoulders.

"Oh, no." She pushed the coat and Mack away. "You need it just as much as I do. And besides, with my luck, I'd arrive back in Las Vegas all toasty warm and you'd freeze to death and end up being the hero. I can just hear the news story now: *FBI Agent Sacrifices Life to Save Fellow Federal Agent.*"

Mack barked out a noise of disgust. "Would it bother you?" he asked.

"If you grabbed all the headlines? Hell, yes." Rosie sighed with annoyance. Now that her eyes were adjusting to what little light seeped into the truck from between the two back doors, she saw her own breath puff out in front of her in a little cloud.

"I didn't mean that. I meant if I froze to death. Would it bother you if I froze to death?"

She gave him a sidelong look. She could see Mack's profile in the silver of light. She could see the faint glow of his white shirt, the darker band of his tie. She could tell he was leaning back against the wall of the truck, his arms braced on the floor on either side of him. Somehow he'd managed to stretch out his legs between two of the barrels, and though it beat sitting with his chin up on his knees, it couldn't have been a whole lot more comfortable than the way she was sitting. Her legs were already cramping. Then again, she would have traded a whole muscular system of cramps for one chance of seeing his face. Then she might be able to tell if he was teasing.

"You're not going to freeze to death." There was a small strip of floor separating them. She pushed the jacket back at him. "If anybody's going to freeze to death and grab all the glory, it's going to be me."

"Have it your way." He didn't reach for the coat. "Since I'm not cold, either, and—"

The truck bucked and swayed over the bumpy terrain, interrupting whatever it was Mack was going to say. It was just as well. Something told Rosie she wasn't going to like it, anyway.

At her side, she heard Mack flip open his cell phone and in the faint green light that illuminated the keypad, she saw him glance her way. "You got the plate numbers, didn't you?" he asked.

He was baiting her. And she wasn't biting. She flipped open her phone, too.

And found out fast enough that while cell phones might be good for making calls from the tops of mountains and the bottoms of canyons and everywhere in between, they were not so good when it came to capturing a signal from the inside of an insulated truck. With a mumbled curse, she closed up her phone.

"Doesn't much matter that I got the plate number when I can't call anyone to tell them to watch for the truck." Rosie shoved her phone into her pocket. "Did you let anyone know you were coming out here?"

"Did you?"

"My family knows I'm here." They hit a pothole that felt as if it were as big as a moon crater, and Rosie's jaw snapped together. Her head banged against the nearest barrel. "At least they knew I was there," she grumbled. "When I don't show up for my car, they'll know something is wrong."

"By then it will be too late. We'll already be back in Vegas and, no doubt, there's going to be a welcoming committee waiting for those guns."

"Good." It was the first encouraging news she had heard in as long as she could remember. "They show up to welcome the truck and we arrest their butts. How's that sound?"

"Like the first thing we've agreed on since—"

They hit another pothole and Mack didn't have a chance to finish the thought. Then again, he really didn't have to. They'd only agreed on one thing. Ever. And that one thing was something Rosie didn't want to think about.

"Shit!" She grumbled the word, a commentary on the thoughts that raced through her head and the sensations that flashed through her body and the fact that she bumped her head again. She rubbed the back of it with one hand.

"If you'd brace your arms . . ."

Rosie mumbled her opinion of his advice. "Those folks over in Quantico sure must be smart. What else did they teach you that I don't know?"

She saw the quick, bright flash of his smile. "I know plenty of things that you don't know."

"Yeah. Like how to strip?"

Mack chuckled. "Stripping, huh? They way I remember it, you're not too bad at that yourself."

"The way I remember it, you're not supposed to remember that." The truck made a sharp turn and Rosie braced herself, one hand against the floor, the other against the nearest lettuce barrel. When they straightened out again, they were on a paved road. The ride smoothed out, the tires hummed beneath them, and she sighed with relief and tried to make herself a little more comfortable.

It wasn't until she did that she brought up the subject again. "How did they talk you into that in the first place?"

"Stripping? Or stripping with you? Because if you're talking about the stripping-with-you part—"

"I'm not."

"No one had to talk me into that. No one but you, of course. And you were plenty good at the talking-into part."

"I'm plenty good at lots of things you don't know about."

"I'll bet."

"I meant stripping. On stage. I know it's what you did before, but . . . weren't you embarrassed?"

She saw him lean his head against the nearest barrel. "It was part of the job. And it's not as bad as it looks. Not if you go in with the right attitude and all the wrong sorts of experience."

"It's a long way from the Studs Corral to the FBI."

"It's a long way from the Partridge Family to the ATF."

"Oh, come on, Mack!" Rosie could hardly believe her ears. "You're not serious, are you? You don't honestly think there's any similarity between—"

"Similarity? Hell, no." He glanced her way and, even through the dark, she saw his eyes glitter with emotion. "No similarity. None at all. I was running toward something. I'm pretty sure you were just running away."

It wasn't a fair assessment. Even if it was true.

Rosie chafed her hands over her arms and wished she had the nerve—or was it the common sense?—to grab for Mack's jacket. Since she was apparently lacking in both, she left it where it was and glared across the darkness that separated them.

There was no way she wanted to get into the kind of let-it-all-hang-out rap session her mother found so damned appealing. No way she was prepared to lay her life story on the line to this guy. Not when, thanks to him, she'd already risked her reputation, her career, and the game face she wore for the world, the one that was all about how strong and unshakable she was. The one Mack had practically demolished with a kiss and had come close to reducing to ashes in the heat of his lovemaking.

But there was only so much any woman could take. Especially when her motives were in question. Especially when she was being accused of backing down.

"You've seen them," she said, and she couldn't help herself, her voice was sharp with emotion and the urgency of explaining what for so long had been so crystal-clear to her. "Just think of what it was like growing up with them. Protest rallies. Marches. Love-ins, sit-ins, be-ins. All I ever wanted to be was ordinary. By the time I got to high school, I was ready for some serious mutiny." She blew into her hands, warming them.

"If I got a tattoo, they never would have batted an eye. If I got my nose pierced, they would have decided I was a trendsetter and gone right out and done the same thing. If I danced naked in the streets, they would have declared that it was a perfectly healthy form of self-expression. I did the only thing I could do to show what a free spirit I was. I became a card-carrying Republican."

He didn't answer for so long that Rosie thought he might have drifted off to sleep. Which made the fact that she had bared her soul to him not only ridiculous but also pretty pathetic. It wasn't until she heard him shift his position that she knew he'd been listening all along.

"Don't you think that was hypocritical?"

Rosie's spine stiffened. "Not at all. It was the kind of structure I'd been searching for and it was just what I needed. My parents weren't thrilled." Remembering how they'd tried their liberal bests to practice what they'd been preaching all their lives—that it took all kinds to make up the world, that no one was ever really one hundred percent right and no one was ever really one hundred percent wrong, and that everyone had the inalienable birthrights of free speech, noninterventionist opinions, and a healthy dose of self-esteem—she hauled in a long breath and let it out slowly.

"They're very sincere," she told Mack. "They're honestly caring. But they didn't understand. Then when I announced I wanted to work for the government . . . well . . . Anyway, they didn't think it would ever really happen. In my heart of hearts, I guess I didn't, either. One look at the Malone name on my application, one little background check, and we all knew there wasn't one chance in a million that the ATF would want me."

"I'm surprised they did."

"You and me both. I got the job because I'm very good at what I do." It went without saying, but she figured it didn't hurt to remind him. "And I honestly think somebody, somewhere, just really wanted to stick it to my folks." Rosie knew irony when she saw it, and as she had so many times when she stopped to think about it, she chuckled. "They've pretty much accepted me for what I am. Even if they don't like the framed picture of Ronald Reagan I keep in my living room. And you still haven't explained how a guy goes from the spotlight at the Studs Corral to working for the FBI."

It was as smooth a segue as she was ever likely to come up with, and the kind of thing that would have worked like a charm on just about any suspect she happened to be interrogating.

She should have known it wasn't going to work on Mack. Then again, she never really had much of a chance to find out.

Before he could respond, the truck made a sharp turn. It bucked and jerked and the ground beneath them changed from smooth highway to rough terrain.

"He's off the road." To keep from getting knocked around, Rosie propped a hand against the barrels on either side of her. "And not because he blew a tire. He hasn't stopped."

"That's for sure." She saw the flash of Mack's white shirt when he sat up, alert and on guard in spite of the fact that they were being banged around like pinballs. "It's like he's headed—"

"Right into the desert."

Rosie's own words settled down inside her like lead weights. As curious about the turn of events as she was worried, she sat as still as she was able. When the truck finally groaned to a stop and the air conditioner switched off, she rubbed the spot on her back that was sure to be black-and-blue from slamming against the nearest lettuce barrel, and breathed a sigh of relief.

The relief didn't last long.

No sooner had the truck stopped than they heard another sound. A single car approached over the dry ground. The vehicle pulled to a stop beside theirs and at the same time they heard the truck cab door open and close, they heard another door open.

Rosie might actually have been startled when someone rapped on the back door of the truck, if she wasn't busy hopping to her feet and reaching for her Sig.

"Special Agent Malone? How are you doing?"

Rosie wasn't at all surprised to hear Emery Carpathian's voice from the other side of the insulated door. Which didn't mean she was about to offer a wholesale answer. She kept her mouth shut and slid Mack a look. There was something damned comforting about finding him at her side, his legs braced, his level gaze on the truck door. And his Glock in his hands.

"Special Agent Malone!" Carpathian called to her again. "I know you're being coy and that's OK. Really. I know you're in there. I was watching the mine entrance when you went down. I made sure you had enough time to sneak around the other way and hop into the truck. I just want to make sure you understand the gravity of your situation. I wanted you to know that I know about your undercover assignment. About everything you've been up to at the Swan."

"How—"

One hand up as a warning, Mack stopped the question before Rosie ever had a chance to ask it. While he started off one way, he signaled her around to the other side of the truck. She knew exactly what he had in mind and she sidestepped her way through the maze of barrels.

"You're wondering how I know all this." Carpathian sounded a hell of a lot more jovial than Rosie was feeling. "That's as easy as can be. Angela told me, of course. She was working for me, you know, as well as for her government. All along, she reported to them that she didn't know a thing about the 9A-91s, but that wasn't exactly true. You see, she knew I had acquired the guns through a series of deals with some friends who are . . . well, let's just say I don't think you'd approve of them. Angela found that out early in her investigation. Much faster than you did, actually." He paused long enough for the subtle message to sink it, and as if he knew exactly when it sent Rosie's blood past the boiling point, he breezed right on.

"It didn't take much to persuade Angela to help. As progressive as her country tries to be, it's woefully behind when it comes to consumer goods. And Angela was an avaricious little bitch. She loved the clothes and the cars and the jewelry. If she wasn't quite so greedy and so careless, I might not have had to dispose of her. But she was. She missed killing your friend Neeta and she missed killing you. She did a good job with that stupid Warren, but by then, I was beyond needing her."

While Carpathian was talking, Rosie moved slowly, careful not to make a sound as she angled between the barrels. Directly across from her, she saw the faint blur of Mack's shirt as he mirrored her movements.

"We never would have suspected you if you hadn't been so insistent on following Neeta," Carpathian went on, and as he talked, something clattered against the back door of the truck.

"A chain." The word escaped Rosie along with a breath of apprehension. She had no doubt the chain had been strung through the handles on the doors to keep them from opening. And when she heard the click of a padlock, she knew Carpathian was making sure they never would.

"You wouldn't let it go, would you?" Carpathian asked, and as if he knew he'd never get one, he didn't wait for an answer. "Your friend Neeta probably doesn't know much of anything, but I couldn't take the chance. I had to try to get rid of her. When you started hanging around her, it meant I had to get rid of you, too."

Rosie could picture Carpathian, his skinny little mustache twitching. "As for how I knew you were in Rhyolite?" The rumble of his laughter didn't do a thing to relieve the tension that snaked through Rosie's shoulders or the cold that settled in her stomach.

"The same way I found out that you were working for our Uncle Sam. Your family called you. Remember? After they stumbled on the guns in the mine, they left a message for you. They know you're a good daughter, and lo and behold, in their message, they mentioned how they knew you were also a very good ATF agent."

"And you had my phone tapped, you son of a bitch." Rosie ground the words out from between clenched teeth.

"In case you're wondering, Special Agent, I haven't abandoned the rest of my little stash. There's someone back at the mine right now, loading up the rest of the rifles. I know you share my sincerest wish that while they're working, your family doesn't show up looking for those silly mice."

"Mine voles," Rosie grumbled. "They're mine voles. And if anything happens to one hair on the head of any one Malone, you no-good, rotten, son of a—"

"I hate to lose those few guns you've got in there with you but . . ." She'd seen Carpathian enough times to know the gesture that would go along with the statement. The elegant little lift of his shoulders. The raised eyebrows and the little sneer that touched his lips, indifferent and nonchalant about the whole thing. "Sometimes that's the price of business." As if he turned away, Carpathian's voice lost strength, then gained volume again when he turned back toward the truck.

"So, Special Agent Malone . . ." Carpathian sounded as jovial as she'd heard him sound on the nights when he raked in the cash from Mack's shows. "I hope you'll enjoy our desert heat. At least for a while. Oh, and if you're thinking of using the 9A-91s to shoot through the truck door . . ." Rosie heard the edge of sarcasm in his voice. "I'm not that stupid! There's no ammunition packed with the rifles. I've made sure of that. Just as I've made sure that you won't be found. Not for a very long time."

The engine of the car started up and a door slammed shut. A minute later, the last sounds of the car driving away faded and disappeared into the desert air. Absolute silence pressed against Rosie's ears, broken only by the faraway call of a bird and the whisper of her own rough breathing.

"We've got to get out of here." Rosie holstered her weapon and hurried over to the door. Even though she knew it was locked, she tried the handle that flipped to open the door from the inside, and when it didn't budge, she gave it a punch. She yanked it again. "If that son of a bitch"—another punch—"gets within a hundred feet of my family . . ." She stepped back and gave the door a boot that would have made her kickboxing instructor proud. "I'll personally get that no-good scumbag up against a wall and . . ." One more punch, one more kick, and when nothing worked, she screeched her annoyance. "If he touches them, I swear he will never see the light of day ever again. I'm going to take that rotten, no-good bastard and I'm going to make sure—"

"All right. It's all right, Rosie." She'd been so busy battering the door, she didn't even notice Mack come up behind her. Not until he grabbed her, pinning her arms and hauling her away from the door. Even when she tried to squirm out of his grip, he held on tight, and the more she fought, the tighter he held her.

"It's going to be all right." He propped his head on her shoulder and spoke close to her ear, his voice low and soothing. "Nothing's going to happen to them."

"It had better not." Rosie was not prone to panic, but this time, she couldn't help herself. They were talking about her family, and a barely controlled sob bubbled through her words. "I swear, if anything happens to them, that guy's going to need both his hands to find what's left of his ass."

She let go of her anger with one final, shuddering breath. "You can let go of me now." She slanted Mack a look. "I'm fine. I'm calm. I just needed to get it out of my system."

He released her, and she aimed a laser look at the truck door. "That son of a bitch thinks I'm going to die out here. Doesn't he realize there's enough water in this lettuce to keep me going for days?"

"Which might be exactly what he has in mind." Mack rolled up his sleeves and, for the first time, Rosie realized that now that the air conditioner was off, it was getting warm. A couple more hours and the inside of the truck would be as hot as a Mexican jumping bean on a Tijuana sidewalk. "I don't know about you," he told her, "but if I had my choice, I'd pick a nice, quick death over one that might drag out for days. No doubt that's exactly what Carpathian has in mind. He thinks you're in here all by yourself, and I'll bet he's got this truck parked somewhere where nobody's going to find it. Not for a very long time, anyway."

"Charming." Rosie slipped out of her jacket and wiped the band of sweat from her forehead. "When I said I wanted evidence against the scumbag, this wasn't exactly what I had in mind. So I'm supposed to end up as roasted Rosie."

"Nice image." A shiver of disgust snaked over Mack's shoulders at the same time a sour smile brightened an expression that was just this side of grim. "Before we worry about that, we've got to worry about getting out of here. Don't even bother," he added when he saw her reach for her phone. "I tried mine again when you were doing your Ali imitation on the door. Can't get a signal. Not in a truck that's as well insulated as this one."

"Great." Rosie sat down on the nearest lettuce barrel. "Then if we can't get someone in here to get us out—"

"We'll need to figure out how to get out by ourselves." Mack dropped down onto the barrel next to hers. "Any ideas?"

"We could try shooting the door."

"Wouldn't work. Not from this side. And besides, even if it did, Carpathian looped a chain through the outside handles."

"Then how about the floor?" Rosie stomped her foot against the floor of the truck. "Maybe there's a part we can pry up or punch through or—"

"Did you hear that?" One hand up for silence, Mack stopped her. "Did you hear that noise?"

She didn't. But on the outside chance that he wasn't already hallucinating from the heat and the air that was getting more oppressive by the minute, Rosie bent her head, listening.

"I don't hear—"

"There!" Mack stood. "It's quiet. Like a scratching. Doesn't sound like it's coming from the outside. It's more like—"

"There!" Rosie heard the noise and she sat up like a shot. "It's coming from in here," she said. "Sounds like something scratching against wood, and there isn't much wood in here except for—"

Together, they turned to peer in the direction of the four crates of Russian assault rifles.

He slipped her a look at the same time he reached for his weapon. "You thinking what I'm thinking?"

"Not if you're thinking your Glock's going to help." Cautiously Rosie moved toward the crates. "We need light," she grumbled. "You got your flashlight?"

He turned it on. Rosie switched hers on, too, and holding them close to the nearest crate, they opened the lid.

Twelve pairs of tiny eyes looked up at them. Twelve noses twitched. Twelve sets of whiskers quivered.

For the first time in as long as she could remember, Rosie wished her family was around. "Congratulations," she said, glancing up at the bewildered expression on Mack's face. "Looks like we're the proud parents of a family of mine voles."

20

"Maybe they aren't very bright." Rosie stared at the mine voles. The mine voles stared back. "You'd think they'd panic or something, you know? You'd think they'd be scared. Or go all to furry pieces or—"

Maybe mine voles weren't as dumb as she thought. No sooner were the words out of Rosie's mouth than the voles went all to furry pieces. Squeaking with alarm, they scampered up the inside of the box and down the outside. They hit the floor and scattered.

Rosie jumped back and squeaked, too, and she knew the second the sound of surprise was out of her mouth that she'd never hear the end of it from Mack. She controlled another squeal and the impulse to hide out on top of the nearest lettuce barrel to get away from the stampede of mine voles around her feet.

Some of the voles disappeared into the maze of barrels. A few more headed for the other rifle crates stacked nearby. A couple headed for the door, and when they found their way blocked, scuttled over to the side of the truck and started up the wall.

"Brave little critters." Mack stepped back and trained his

light on the voles. They shot up the side of the truck, their footing sure and strong against the coarse insulation.

"Brave maybe, but pretty dumb." Her heart thumping from the excitement, Rosie watched the voles, too. "Wait until they find out they can't actually go anyplace."

Except that the lead vole did. It got as far as the corner where the ceiling met both the back and side corner of the truck, and it disappeared.

"There's a way out." Rosie and Mack moved forward together, both their eyes on the place where they'd last seen the vole. "It got outside," Rosie said. "Did you see that? It isn't there. It got outside."

She saw Mack's smile flash through the darkness. "That means we can, too."

An hour later, Mack's shoulder muscles ached, his fingers were bloodied, and his face was covered with the fine, powdery dirt that floated down from the truck ceiling. He scraped one hand across his face and realized that the dirt combined with sweat had made a sort of gritty mush that coated his cheeks and forehead and caked his lips.

He didn't much care.

He glanced down to where Rosie was stationed at the bottom of the stack of lettuce barrels he was perched on. When she signaled him that she was ready to hold the barrels steady, he gave the truck ceiling another pounding with the butt of a 9A-91, hitting it at exactly the spot they'd seen the mine vole disappear through a little hole—one that was getting larger by the second.

"Almost big enough," he called down, and he gave the ceiling one final bash. The last of the weakened metal pushed away and a shaft of sunlight no bigger around than a softball streamed into the truck. "What do you think?" He looked down to where Rosie was looking up, her hair bright as flame in the sunbeam, her face grimy, her shirt so sweaty, it stuck to every delicious curve. "Think we've got enough?"

"I think we've got plenty. You think you can get close enough?"

"We're about to find out." When it came to trying to stack them one on top of the other, they'd found out fast enough that the cardboard barrels were plenty heavy. That didn't mean they were especially stable. Or easy to walk on. Mack inched closer to the opening he'd created and reached for his phone. "If I stretch . . ." He did just that. At the same time, he extended the antenna, stuck as much of it as he was able through the opening, and dialed the office.

Rosie finished the handful of lettuce she was munching and sighed. It had been exactly one hour and fifty minutes since Mack called the office, and though there was no sign of rescue yet, she knew it was coming. She also knew a host of federal agents (both FBI and ATF) had been dispatched to Rhyolite and a call they'd received a few minutes earlier assured her that the assault rifles were secured, the men who were loading them onto a truck were in custody, and the Malones were safe and as happy as only a tree-hugging clan could be that the mine voles were not only not extinct but procreating their little hearts out in the 9A-91 crates.

All good news, and she should have been jazzed. She should have been flush with contentment and the satisfaction that came from knowing that as soon as they were out of there, they were headed back to Las Vegas to make sure Emery Carpathian didn't see the light of day again. Except from the wrong side of prison walls.

She should have been thrilled about beating the bad guys at their own game and ecstatic that her investigation was finally coming to a successful end.

She should have been. She would have been. If there weren't still plenty of questions that needed to be answered, and plenty of reasons she wasn't sure how to proceed with her relationship with Mack. Or even if she should try.

As tempted as she was to follow her family's example and

let it all hang out, she knew enough about Mack to know it wouldn't work. On stage, he might be the ultimate fantasy. Deep down inside, there might still be some remnant of the ultimate bad boy. But he'd worked too long and too hard to get where he was.

And there was no way in hell he'd risk that.

It was too important to him.

And he was too important to her.

Instead, Rosie stretched and yawned. "I'm bored." She groaned the word and drummed her fingers against the lettuce barrel she was sitting on. "I'm hot. I'm cranky. I hate the thought of sitting here doing nothing while everyone else is in on wrapping things up. I would have loved to see the expressions on the faces of those scumbags when they headed down into the mine to get the assault rifles and found us there waiting for them."

"You and me both." Mack didn't look any happier—or any cooler—than Rosie felt. His tie was unknotted and hanging loose. His sleeves were rolled above his elbows. His hair was slick with sweat and pushed back from his face. He dumped what was left of his dinner into the giant plastic bag of lettuce they'd pulled out of one of the barrels. Being careful to avoid the voles that raced across the floor of the truck every now and then, he paced back and forth as much as he was able. "We should have been in on the arrest," he grumbled. "After all the hard work—"

"All the dancing—"

"All the grief I got about this assignment from all the other guys in the office . . ." Mack shook his head and his sigh rippled the blistering air. "It's not fair."

"Neither is being locked up in here." Rosie fanned her face with one hand. "You sure they said they'd wait to arrest Carpathian? Because if I'm not in on that, I swear I'm going to raise holy hell."

"They said they'd wait until we got back to Vegas."

"Las Vegas." She stretched and rubbed the small of her

back. "Did they say how long it would be until they get us out of here?"

"They can't get us out until they find us." Mack stopped his pacing midstride when a vole darted out from between two barrels. "They obviously haven't found us yet."

"Reminds me of the time we were in Brazil." The trip to South America she'd taken with her family when she was fourteen to study rain forest defoliation was one of the low points of her life, and she'd never remembered it fondly. Which didn't explain why Rosie found herself smiling. Maybe it had something to do with the worry that ate through her gut when she thought the Malones were in danger. And something more to do with the relief that swept through her when she found out they were all right.

"It rained," she said by way of explaining the entire, excruciating experience to Mack. "For days and days. And there we were in this little shack, with the Amazon rolling in the front door. Dan and Francine, four kids, a guide who didn't speak English and most of his extended family, including the livestock. It was not a pretty picture."

If Mack had been there, he wouldn't have laughed. "What did you do?" he asked. "To pass the time?"

"We planned strategy for a rain forest summit that never got off the ground because none of the delegates could get there because of the flooding. We sang every song Pete Seger ever wrote. We played Twenty Questions." She gave him a quick look, wondering if she was as transparent as she feared. "What do you say, Mack? You want to play Twenty Questions?"

He looked at her uncertainly.

"Oh, come on." Rosie sat up, determined to get some answers to all the questions that had been pigeonholed thanks to Emery Carpathian's untimely arrival. And all the even more important ones that had been playing through her head ever since Mack whipped out his Glock, pulled out his credentials, and added a new level of complication to a relationship that was already complicated enough. "Who knows how long we're going to be stuck here. We have to do something. Go ahead, you first."

He still didn't look convinced or sure of the rules. "You mean, like, what's your favorite color?"

"Yellow," Rosie answered and shot a question back at him. "What's your favorite food?"

"Steak. Rare." He caught on and fell into the rapid-fire rhythm. "What kind of music do you like?"

"Classical, but not that heavy Wagner stuff. Mellow contemporary, like Sinatra and Tony Bennett. What was your favorite subject in school?"

Mack made a face. "None. Not in high school. In college, psychology. What should I call you, Ellie or Rosie?"

"My family calls me Ellie. My coworkers know me as Eleanor. The Rosie was all part of the undercover thing. You know, so I couldn't be easily traced. What's your ideal vacation destination?"

"Home. With the phone off. Favorite flower?"

"Tulips. Why, are you planning on sending some?"

OK, so it wasn't exactly subtle. It did, however, work.

Mack stopped and turned back in Rosie's direction. "Frequently," he said, and he sounded so matter-of-fact about it, she couldn't help herself. Her heart skipped a beat. "Why have you been at my throat ever since you found out who I am?"

"I imagine for the same reason you've been at mine. Professional jealousy?"

"Does that count as a question?"

"Does that?"

"I'm thinking maybe it's more, because we're both too afraid to simply face the facts."

"Which are?"

He drew in a long breath and let it out slowly, steeling himself against the truth. "A long time ago, I learned that it wasn't smart to need anybody."

"Because needing people only led to being disappointed."

"Because needing people meant I was weak."

"You still believe that?"

"I did." He didn't look any happier to admit it than Rosie felt at hearing it. "But the more I think about it . . ." He took a tentative step nearer. "Hell, we make a pretty good team, don't we? I mean professionally. Personally."

Her hopes blossomed along with a smile. "Well, except for the being locked in a truck in the middle of nowhere part. As far as the personal part . . ."

"I need you, Rosie."

A *nice, conservative, hardworking special agent did not*—

"Oh, but she does," Rosie mumbled to herself, and when Mack gave her a baffled look, she smiled. "You're a hell of a guy, Mack. But before you commit yourself, I have a confession to make, too. You were right. When you said I was running away from my family. I've spent my life running away from family. And now all I want is to have one. I want you to be my family."

"I love you, Rosie."

"Which leaves only one question. Want to do it again?"

"Want to . . ." Rosie's words struck hard, robbing Mack of his voice and his senses. He didn't have to think about it twice. The truth burned through him, hotter than the temperature inside the truck. Back at the Eiffel Tower, he'd wanted her more than he'd wanted his next breath. At Neeta's trailer, he'd made love to her because he'd had no choice, no options. Now he wanted her because he loved her. She was his future, the family he'd always longed for, the anchor he knew would secure the rest of his life.

"Yes." Not certain she understood everything it meant, he gave her a last chance to reconsider. "You know it's going to change everything, don't you?"

"Counting on it." There was a shimmer of emotion in

Rosie's eyes that burned through Mack like fire. Because he couldn't keep his hands off her a second longer, he reached for Rosie and drew her nearer. He yanked her shirt out of the waistband of her khakis. Tugged it over her head. He kissed her neck and the smooth little hollow at the base of her throat. He kissed the silky skin that peeked out from the top of her bra and the shadowy place between her breasts.

Rosie undid the buttons on the front of Mack's shirt. She whipped off his tie. She pulled off his shirt. She brushed her palms over the sleeveless T-shirt he wore beneath his dress shirt, massaging his nipples until she heard his breath catch.

He wrapped his arms around her and when he pulled her down onto the big, mattresslike bag of lettuce, she glanced up at the hole they'd made in the roof and the evening light that seeped into the truck.

"One more question," Rosie said, her words catching over a gasp when Mack stripped off her bra and unbuttoned her khakis. "How much time do you think we have?"

He settled himself over her, smiling down into her eyes. "Not nearly enough," he said. "Not for everything I have in mind."

Epilogue

If Emery Carpathian noticed that Rosie had a lettuce leaf tangled in her hair when she arrested him, he didn't comment on it. Then again, when Mack and Rosie burst into his office—side by side—to make the collar, he was probably a little too surprised to notice much of anything.

Carpathian didn't put up a fight and it was just as well. Rosie was sweaty. She was tired. And although her commitment to her career was as strong as ever and her faith in the system was unwavering, what Mack had told her back in the hot truck in the middle of the desert had convinced her that there were a few things she'd rather be doing than dealing with a scumbag arms dealer. OK, one thing in particular. With one particular guy.

If it was up to Paul and Brian and the whole host of other federal agents swarming the Swan, cooler heads would have prevailed and Mack and Rosie would have spent the rest of the night filling out forms, filing reports, and getting debriefed.

Luckily for Rosie and Mack, cooler heads did not prevail. By the next morning, though they might not have been well rested, they were well showered and completely lettuce free, and they promised they'd be in the office to fill out forms, file reports, and get debriefed ASAP.

After one quick stop.

Rosie found the wedding chapel listed in the local phone book. It promised understated elegance, dignified ceremonies, and unpretentious decor. All of which sounded exactly like what she was looking for.

The Malones took the edge off the understated elegance. The chorus girls who met them at the door of the chapel dressed in sequins and feathers added a new dimension when it came to the dignified ceremony part. As for the unpretentious decor . . . even the unassuming whitewashed walls and the simple pews inside the chapel were no match for the federal agents in their somber suits and striped ties.

Brendan and Neeta were given a place of honor at the front of the chapel, right next to Sid and Gloria. True to their word when Rosie called them in Fresno the night before, the two old partiers were right on time, and thrilled to be witnesses. And if they didn't understand why there was a wedding now when they'd seen Rosie in her bridal gown and already celebrated on the bus, they didn't ask.

After all, it was Las Vegas.

The ceremony was quick. The wishes of the onlookers were sincere. The happiness of the bride and groom was so complete and so evident that there wasn't a dry eye in the house. Even the Enforcer had his Ray-Bans on before he stepped back out into the morning sunshine.

"So, what do you say?" Mack snaked an arm around Rosie's waist and kissed her, and the crowd applauded. "I hear as soon as we get those reports done, we've got the rest of the week off. We could head down to L.A. or up to Tahoe."

"Or we could hang out here." Rosie's smile was ear to ear. "I've got a great CD collection and I hear you give private strip shows."

"You hear wrong, niña," Though there was a rumble in Mack's voice, there was a sparkle in his eyes that told her he was intrigued. "Unless you're willing to reciprocate."

"Come on, Special Agent MacDougal." She tugged him toward his waiting Harley. "Let's get those reports out of the way."

About the Author

Connie Lane has worked as a journalist, editor, and creative writing teacher. In addition to romance/suspense/comedy, she writes historical romances as well as category romance. She has been nominated for the prestigious RITA award by Romance Writers of America and has received the KISS award from *Romantic Times* magazine as well as a nomination from *RT* for historical romance of the year in the Love & Laughter category. She lives in a suburb of Cleveland with her family. She can be contacted at: connielane@earthlink.net.